D0901634

THE NEIGHBORS

Modern Middle East Literatures in Translation Series

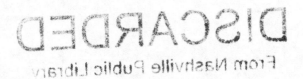

THE NEIGHBORS

AHMAD MAHMOUD

TRANSLATED BY
NASTARAN KHERAD

FOREWORD BY
M. R. GHANOONPARVAR

THE CENTER FOR MIDDLE EASTERN STUDIES
THE UNIVERSITY OF TEXAS AT AUSTIN

Cover art: *Exit Strategy*, © iStockphoto, Kevin Hill Illustration
Cover and text design: Kristi Shuey
Series Editor: Wendy E. Moore

Library of Congress Control Number: 2013941448
ISBN: 978-0-292-74905-4

Originally published in Persian as *Hamsayehha*, 1974.

The Center gratefully acknowledges financial support for the publication of *The Neighbors* from the Society of Iranian-American Women for Education.

In memory of my brother Mohammad,
who introduced me to literature and poetry.

TABLE of CONTENTS

FOREWORD

In the early twentieth century, Iran's southeastern province of Khuzestan became the site of the first direct clash between Western and Iranian cultures and ways of life. The reason, of course, was oil, discovered in abundance in that region, and the concession for which was granted to the British. By 1913, an oil refinery, which eventually became the largest in the world, was built in the small port city of Abadan. In time, the city became the residence of a relatively large number of British nationals, who lived in the affluent section in comfortable Western-style homes, and poor migrant Iranian laborers from other parts of Iran, who lived either in crowded, small oil company housing or in shantytowns. Hence, the clash was not only cultural but also economic, and increasingly political. This situation also extended to other cities and towns of the province where the Anglo-Persian Oil Company (APOC) had exploration and extraction projects. The son of an oil industry laborer, Ahmad Mahmoud (1931–2002) was born and raised in the provincial capital of Ahvaz, where he also worked in a variety of menial jobs during his youth. By the late 1940s and early 1950s, when Iranian prime minister Mohammad Mosaddeq spearheaded efforts to nationalize Iranian oil, Mahmoud, like many young people of his generation, had become involved in socialist-inspired politics, which generally meant the expression of discontent regarding the regime of the shah (considered by the majority to be a puppet of the West) and, concurrently, opposition to Western exploitation of and influence in Iran. The result of the nationalization of the Iranian oil industry in 1951 was the overthrow of Mosaddeq's popular government through a British-instigated coup d'état funded and executed by the CIA. The reinstatement of the shah's government and a police state following the brief moment of hope for democracy that Mosaddeq's government had instilled in the majority of Iranians was the cause of disappointment and despair for old and young alike, in particular, Mahmoud's generation.

The Neighbors [*Hamsayehha*], Mahmoud's first novel, is a product of and reflects not only the social and political events during those turbulent years when Mahmoud was growing up, from a naïve boy into a young man with dreams of social, political, and economic progress for his country (inspired by young, educated socialist activists), but also the lives of poor working-class families. Although Mahmoud had previously published several collections of short stories, the publication of *The Neighbors* in 1974 established him as an important writer, mainly because of his realistic depiction of life and historical events in mid-twentieth-century Iran. *The Neighbors* is largely an autobiographical novel. The life and experiences of the protagonist, Khaled, at least based on what is known about the author's background, reflect and seem to be a recollection of Mahmoud's own. As he stated in interviews in later years, this novel is about the period in his life when he was "entrapped in the game of politics." In fact, after completing his high school education, Mahmoud, similar to many ambitious young men whose families could not afford to send their children to a university, was admitted to a military college; and like his protagonist, he, along with many other military officers, was imprisoned in the wake of the 1953 coup d'état for leftist, socialist activities. The success of *The Neighbors* was not only due to its depiction of historical events that were of great interest to many readers, but also to the author's realistic portrayal of many working-class characters and their lives. In contrast to the often highly enigmatic, symbolic, and sometimes surrealistic fiction written by the best-known writers in the late 1960s and 1970s, Mahmoud's fictional replication of the tenants of a rental house in which several families live in one or two small rooms each—their interactions, relationships, and quarrels—struck a familiar chord with and was welcomed by Iranian readers. Although writing stories about the underprivileged has been quite common, even rather dominant, in the work of Iranian writers since the early decades of the twentieth century, Mahmoud, in contrast to those who romanticize the poor and present them as noble and stoic victims of the upper classes, presents us with a more realistic portrayal of the underclass, in which we find both good and evil characters, as well as some in between. Among numerous colorful characters in the novel, a most interesting figure is Bolur, an abused wife who is at the same time a seductress and source of sexual awakening for the teenage protagonist. The realistic portrayal of this character in particular has been a source of intrigue for both fans and detractors of Mahmoud's work since its publication. Although sexual scenes were not infrequent in classical and modern Persian literature, Mahmoud's depiction of the relationship between an older married woman and a young boy was rather unusual and, as some critics have pointed out, quite daring, even in the 1970s, when Iranians were exposed to an increasing representation of sexual scenes in various visual and written forms.

As in much of his work, Mahmoud is an unpretentious writer in terms of the use of the "literary" language in Persian. He writes in a simple prose and masterfully records the speech idiosyncrasies, individual linguistic patterns, and dialects of his characters. The difference between his use of the Persian language of the ordinary people and the efforts made by many other writers who were not members of lower social classes is that when he replicates the speech of ordinary people, Mahmoud seems to do it comfortably, almost effortlessly. The particular dialect of Khuzestan province that Mahmoud uses in his work is a mixture of the various dialects of the migrants and natives of the province that has evolved into a distinct version of colloquial Persian generally recognized by native speakers of Persian. Because of the presence of the British and later other foreigners in the area, as well as the indigenous speakers of Arabic, Khuzestani Persian also contains lexical borrowings, especially from English, that are not found in the speech of native speakers of Persian from other parts of Iran. The Persian reader's full comprehension of the dialect used in the novel sometimes requires the assistance of a native speaker from Khuzestan. In the same vein, the rendition of the dialogues found throughout *The Neighbors* is a daunting task for any translator. As the translator of *The Neighbors*, Nastaran Kherad, who spent part of her childhood before the Islamic Revolution in the region, has the advantage of not only knowing the local idioms, but also being closely familiar with the people and places that we find in Mahmoud's novel.

M. R. Ghanoonparvar

TRANSLATOR'S ACKNOWLEDGMENTS

The realization of this work of translation would not have been possible without the ongoing support of Professor M. R. Ghanoonparvar, who first encouraged me to translate *Hamsayehha*. I owe him an intellectual debt for trusting my abilities, kindling my ideas, and for reading, editing, and offering his insights on the text whenever needed. I am enormously grateful to Ahmad Aminpour, who offered his time so generously in honing the first draft of this manuscript. I will forever cherish our laughter and heated discussions in finding the right words and phrases to maintain the integrity of this work in English and to honor Ahmad Mahmoud as he ought to be. My special thanks are reserved for Wendy Moore, for editing this manuscript with patience and diligence and for pointing out the rough spots and refining this work so beautifully and effectively. Finally, I must thank Ariana Haddad for her passionate affection for Persian literature and Iranian culture, and for her contribution in editing the first draft of this manuscript with care and love.

Nastaran Kherad

THE NEIGHBORS

Once again Bolur Khanom's wailing resonates in the sprawling courtyard. Aman Aqa is at it again, beating her with his leather belt. The sun is not up yet. I jump out of my bedroll and quickly head out of our room. Mother has just put the kettle on the kerosene burner. It is twilight and cold.

Bolur Khanom's cries fill the courtyard. She's moaning, and cursing Aman Aqa's relatives, dead or alive—all of them. Suddenly, the door to her room flies open and she's thrown out. A few of the neighbors, their arms folded across their chests, looking anxious, come and stand in front of their rooms. Bolur Khanom's body is on display. I'm sure she's not wearing any underwear. One time I was in the pigeon coop—she didn't know I was there—and I heard her tell the other women, "The elastic of the underwear leaves a mark on my waistline. Besides, this way is better. You're always ready for it."

Aman Aqa darts out of the room and starts beating Bolur Khanom. I walk around the small moss-covered pool in the middle of the courtyard. I stand next to the pigeon coop and watch Bolur Khanom cursing and writhing under the lashes. Her thighs are already bruised.

A few days ago, while I was sitting on the stairs leading up to the rooftop, making a kite, Bolur Khanom came up and sat on a step above me; she then gathered her skirt and pulled it up. There were bruises all over her fleshy thighs. I asked her, "Bolur Khanom, why does Aman Aqa beat you so much?"

"'Cause he's a bastard," she said, laughing.

"'Bastard'? What's that mean?" I asked.

"You're too young to understand these sorts of things," she said.

Then she pulled up her skirt even higher, and I let go of my kite, staring at her fleshy thighs, which were pressed against each other. Here and there, all along her thighs, I could see patches of bruises as wide as Aman Aqa's leather belt.

"What are you looking at?" she asked.

"At the bruises," I said.

She burst out laughing.

"Does it hurt?" I asked.

"Not anymore."

"Not even a little bit?"

"Touch it and see for yourself," she said.

My heart began to pound. My throat grew dry. My hand was trembling like you wouldn't believe. When I slid my hand over the belt marks, my entire body suddenly grew hot. I pulled my hand back.

"Don't be afraid! It doesn't hurt," said Bolur Khanom, pulling her skirt even higher. "Look here!" she said, "Aman Aqa has no mercy whatsoever."

I ran my hand over her thigh again. She laid her hand on mine and pressed it. My knees were shaking. My mouth began to water. She slid my hand further up. Such smooth skin. Just like marble. Smooth and firm. Her thighs were pressed tight against each other. I don't think she was wearing any underwear.

"See? It doesn't hurt at all," she said. "There are bruise marks on my belly too," she added.

"Can I see them?" I asked.

"Not now," she said, smiling. "Maybe next time."

I heard Mother's wooden clogs clicking. She was coming toward the stairs. Instantly, Bolur Khanom got to her feet, letting her skirt fall, and hurried up the stairs. Mother stopped at the foot of the staircase. She saw that Bolur Khanom was climbing up the stairs and I was working on my kite. She didn't say a word. Just shook her head and walked away.

Bolur Khanom is cursing. Aman Aqa is beating her. The blows come down mostly on her back, waist, and buttocks, not on her belly. The neighbors are still standing in a row in front of their rooms, saying nothing.

Mother rushes out of our room. "Some Muslims you are," she growls. "Somebody stop this merciless Shemr! Aman Aqa! Shame on you! Enough already!"

As if waiting for this, Aman Aqa lets go of Bolur Khanom, twists the belt around his hand, and goes back to his room. He shuts the door behind him without saying a word.

Mother reaches for Bolur Khanom's bare arm and helps her to her feet. "It serves you right!" she tells her.

Bolur Khanom whimpers. She trembles in her muslin undergarment like a newborn baby bird. Her breasts heave up and down. Bolur Khanom wears a bra. I saw it once when she was hanging her laundry on the clothesline.

"What's this, Bolur Khanom?"

"A bra."

"What's a bra?"

With that, she unbuttoned her blouse all the way and showed me. "Put your hand here!" she had said.

No sooner had I reached out a hand to touch her breast than I heard the click-clack of Mother's clogs on the stairs again. Bolur Khanom buttoned up her blouse and went about rearranging her laundry on the clothesline, and told me to go fly my pigeons, the ones running around the edge of the rooftop, cooing.

Still sobbing, Bolur Khanom wraps Mother's chador around herself and sits in a corner of our room. Mother fixes her a cup of hot water with sugar. Father is praying in his own room. A rough grayish threadbare curtain divides the two rooms, separating Father's room from ours. I think the window coverings in Bolur Khanom's room are silk. They are blue. Smooth and translucent. The walls of Bolur Khanom's room are white. She has covered the mantelpieces in it with blue silk edged with white tulle. There is a large picture frame on the wall. Within it are pictures of Aman Aqa, Bolur Khanom, and a few other images, all arranged together.

"Whose picture is that, Bolur Khanom?"

"That's my sister's . . . do you want her to be your wife?"

I feel that I have turned red up to my ears. "No, I don't want that."

"Do you want to be my husband?"

I look at her. Her eyes sparkle. A smile has made laugh lines appear under her chubby cheeks. "Why don't you say something?" she asks.

I gather up my courage, and in a rasping voice, answer her. "What would I want to do with an old woman?"

She bursts into laughter.

Bolur Khanom is thirty-one years old.

"I was twenty-one when I got married," she had told Mother.

She said this last year.

Right after Ja'far hanged himself and his room was left vacant, Aman Aqa came and rented it. He whitewashed it at his own expense and moved in. It was then that Bolur Khanom said this to Mother.

"And I've been married nine years to this sick bastard."

"Who's this, Bolur Khanom?"

She smooths the creases beneath her breasts. "She is my other sister . . . Her husband is a land owner; he's got fruit orchards, does farming too." Then she looks at me and asks, "She's pretty, isn't she? Her hair is naturally curly."

Bolur Khanom's wavy locks are peeking out from under Mother's prayer chador. Her eyes are red from crying. No longer whimpering, she sips the warm water and sugar, and wraps the chador more tightly around herself. Mother bundles up the bedding and piles it up on the blanket chest. My sister is still asleep. Her head has fallen off the pillow and her mouth is half open. Bolur Khanom always says, "I'm so tempted to pour a hot spoonful of soup into Jamileh's mouth when she sleeps this way."

Father finishes his prayers and calls out to me.

"Khaled!"

"Yes, Baba?"

"Have you said your prayers yet?"

"I'll say them right away, Baba."

Father squats down next to the charcoal brazier and rolls himself a cigarette. Mother pours him tea and then begins to mend the lining of his vest, which has come undone from the top.

It's Friday.

If Father would leave the house, I could fly my pigeons and experience such bliss watching them. If Aman Aqa left, Bolur Khanom would go back to her room, and perhaps she'd call me up to show me the bruises on her belly.

The kids are making such a racket in the courtyard. It's amazing how they get up even earlier on Friday mornings than on other days. Mohammad the Mechanic's son, Omid, goes to school. He's in the second grade. I went to school up to the fourth grade. After I took the last test and passed it, Father said, "No more school!"

"But I still want to go to school, Baba."

"It's enough," he said.

"But I wanna get my high school diploma."

"A real man is one that, when you pat him on the back, dust rises in the air," he said to me.

Hajj Sheikh Ali lounges on a cushion. "Oussa Haddad! Khaled goes to school?"

"Yes, Aqa, he does."

Hajj Sheikh Ali sips the aromatic sweet beverage and asks, "What grade is he in?"

"As a matter of fact, Aqa, he's in the fourth grade."

"Can he recite the Hamd Surah prayers without a mistake?"

"Of course, Aqa. He even recites the Ayatolkorsi prayers without making a single mistake."

Hajj Sheikh Ali gulps his drink. "In that case, that's enough!"

"You mean he shouldn't be going to school no more?"

"Oussa Haddad, a real man is one that, when you pat him on the back, dust rises in the air. Just like yourself, a God-fearing believer."

Father shifts in his place and asks again, "You mean to say . . ."

"Yes, Oussa Haddad, too much schooling makes people unruly."

The kids are making a racket in the courtyard.

Some days Hasani, the son of Rahim the Donkey Keeper, goes along with his father to the brickkilns to take the donkeys to the brickmakers' pit and back again to the brickkilns, so that Mash Rahim can squat down for a bit under the brickmakers' sunshade, smoke a pipe, and drink a cup of tea.

The sun has already spread its rays in the courtyard. The odor of Khaj Tofiq's opium smoke wafts through the air. Amu Bandar comes out, sits himself down in the sunny spot in front of his room, and starts patching up his woolen sweater.

Amu Bandar's cart and long-handled broom are next to the wall of the pigeon coop.

Rahim the Donkey Keeper fills up the manger with straw for the donkeys and then looks up at the bulge in the sunshade's ceiling.

Sanam opens the door to her room. Huffing and puffing, she brings out the large pot of boiled turnips and places it on the four-wheeled cart, yelling, "Karam, get moving!"

"I'm coming, Naneh."

Sanam's weak and sickly son heads out of their room. He puts the kerosene Primus burner under the turnip pot and pushes the cart out of the house.

Father is still squatting down next to the charcoal brazier. It looks like he has no intention of leaving the house. On Fridays, my father goes to visit the clerics. First, he pays his respects to Sheikh Ali, from whom he sometimes seeks advice on religious matters, asking him questions about the rules on daily prayers, unintended transgressions, and prohibited acts. He consults with Hajj Seyyed Ali about reciting and interpreting the Koran, but in the presence of Hajj Seyyed Mohammad, the discussion usually revolves around the history of Islam, the rightful claim of Shi'ism, and the fallacy of Sunnism. But, today, it looks like he has no intention of leaving the house.

"Bolur . . ." It's Aman Aqa's voice. "I left you some money on the mantel top."

"To hell with your money," grumbles Bolur Khanom.

Aman Aqa gets on his green English bike and heads out for the teahouse. Aman Aqa's teahouse is located right at the intersection with the road leading to the harbor. Every now and then, Omid, Mohammad the Mechanic's son, Ebrahim and Hasani, the sons of Rahim the Donkey Keeper, and I all go together to Aman Aqa's teahouse so we can listen to the gramophone. It's a long way but it's worth it.

"Hey, Spider! Give them kids four watered-down teas!"

We sit at the table and the teahouse errand boy serves us tea. Our eyes are fixed on the large green horn of the gramophone. Spider lifts up its needle and plays a record. We drink tea as we listen to the singing. Sometimes we play dominoes too. Just for fun. For our health. Ebrahim likes to bet, but Omid and I never agree to that. "We're not gamblers," we say.

"So, what's the point in banging the dominoes around on the table for nothing?"

Once Ebrahim and Omid made a bet of a kiss. Ebrahim won and kissed Omid.

"All right, kids, you had your tea, and you gave a listen to the songs— now go home!"

Finally, Father stands up, walks away from the charcoal brazier, takes his jacket from Mother, wraps his keffiyeh around his head, and leaves the house.

Bolur Khanom leaves too. My eyes follow her. She still has Mother's prayer chador tightly wrapped around her waist. Her buttocks sway gently. She walks into her room and shuts the door.

When Aman Aqa was beating her, I didn't notice the belt hitting her stomach.

I open the door to the coop, walk inside, and shoo the pigeons out. The male white-tail looks mournful. Perched on a nail, he sulks. His red eyes look lifeless. Last week, a hawk caught his mate in the air. Since then, the white-tail refuses to eat.

I head out of the pigeon coop. I like the pleasant touch of the sun's rays warming me, forcing the damp chill of the room out of my body. I cherish the sun as I throw the pigeons their millet. The sky is the bluest blue. Hajar is hanging her sickly child's ragged diapers on the clothesline. It's about fourteen months since her husband left for Kuwait.

Rahim the Donkey Keeper smokes his pipe as he sits next to Amu Bandar. "If I don't change that straw mat covering the sun shelter," he says, "I don't think it'll withstand the next rain."

But winter's almost over.

Rahim the Donkey Keeper hands the pipe to Amu Bandar and calls out to Hasani.

"What is it, Baba?" Hasani comes out of their room.

"Come on and groom the donkeys!"

Rahim the Donkey Keeper's wife has been sick for a year. Now, she's completely crippled and housebound. Hasani looks after her. He and Ebrahim are twins.

Bolur Khanom comes out of her room. She's leaving for the bazaar, to buy groceries for lunch. Bolur Khanom is barren. They say her oven is flameless. She's been married ten years now. They say that Aman Aqa's to blame. Rumor has it that he's caught gonorrhea twice and syphilis too. Obviously, someone who has had all of these odd diseases wouldn't be able to father a child.

I feed the pigeons some more, then shoo them away. They flutter their wings a bit, but come and land on the edge of the rooftop again. I roll up a wet rag into a ball and hurl it at their feet; it makes them jump and fly away in flock, then soar.

Sitting beside the small pool, Hajar washes her sickly child's bottom. I bet the water is cold, 'cause the baby's sudden holler fills the entire courtyard.

I climb up onto the rooftop and whistle for the pigeons. I hear Hasani calling out for Rahim the Donkey Keeper: "Baba, hurry up! Mother's passing out."

Ever since Ja'far the Brickmaker hanged himself, Rahim the Donkey Keeper's wife has gotten worse.

~

The chill is gone. It's getting warmer each day. Sleeping indoors is no longer bearable. As evening creeps in, the neighbors sweep the fronts of their rooms, sprinkle the ground with water, and then unroll a carpet to sit on.

Khaj Tofiq piles up lumps upon lumps of charcoal, sprinkles some kerosene on them, lights a match, and sets fire to them. Then he squats patiently on his heels next to the fire and fans the charcoals.

By now, everyone has figured out that Afaq, Khaj Tofiq's wife, smuggles fabric and that Banu, her sallow daughter, is addicted to opium. Banu is more than twenty-five years old. Her skin is so yellow that you would think she had mixed water and turmeric and rubbed it all over her body. Her breasts are like a pair of sagging eggplants, hanging long and wrinkled on her chest. On hot summer days, when everyone is taking a nap, Banu gets stark naked and goes into the pool. "Khaled," she tells me, "you too should take off your clothes and come into the pool!"

I get naked and climb in the pool. The water is refreshing. The muck on the bottom feels cool. We play together. Hugging each other, we go under the water and stay there, tight in each other's arms, as long as we can hold our breath. Then we come up, take another breath, and go under the water again.

"Banu! I'm tired. I can't go on."

"Just one more time . . . that's all, one more time."

And then we do this again and again, till we're out of breath.

Bolur Khanom does not spread a rug on the ground. She owns a double bed. Together, she and Aman Aqa sit on the bed and eat their supper. Then, they set up the mosquito netting, and sleep right under it.

My father was out of a job all winter. Even now that the weather is warmer, he is still out of work. Every morning he goes to his blacksmith shop, and then returns home empty-handed. These days, the blacksmith business is really slow.

"Nowadays even the shovel handles are imported from abroad," my father laments, "not to mention the hobnails and pickaxes; from dawn to dusk, all I do is sit next to a cold furnace."

Father sits thinking and smoking well into the night. I'd say we've bought thirty-five pouches of tobacco on credit from Mehdi the Grocer.

I sit next to my sister in front of our room, licking the bottom of the pot of boiled egg stew. Aunt Ra'na barges in, beating her chest, her headscarf slipping around her neck, her hair disheveled. Her eyes are red and puffy from crying. Aunt Ra'na's husband is a laborer, her son is a boatman, and her daughter has been twice married and divorced and now lives with them.

Moaning dramatically, Aunt Ra'na sits down and wipes her nose with the end of her headscarf. "What am I supposed to do now, Sister? What misery! I have such bad luck. I'm so unfortunate. My world has come to an end."

My sister and I are still licking the empty pot of stew.

Mother frowns. "What's wrong, Sister?"

"What's the worst that could happen, Sister? My son, my precious son. May God's mercy be upon you, Son, now that you're at the mercy of the unjust."

As he chain-smokes, Father keeps his gaze on Aunt Ra'na, not saying a word. Father is not very fond of Aunt Ra'na, nor does he care for her husband or her son, Gholam. Aunt Ra'na beats her chest again and continues to moan and curse.

Since Bolur Khanom became our neighbor, Aunt Ra'na's son, Gholam, has visited us more often. "Khaled, can you take a message to Bolur Khanom?"

"What business of mine is it to take a message to her?"

"Well, cousins should be there for each other."

Aunt Ra'na finally begins to speak. This morning, Gholam was caught on the riverbank and taken to the military draft office. When the news reached Aunt Ra'na, she tied her chador around her waist and set off for the office, where she was not allowed in. So, she stood right there in front of the office, screaming and slapping her head and chest. A sergeant barked at her, then shoved her out and told her in a self-important manner, "Woman, it's not just that son of yours. Every young man must do his military service. He's got an entire life to live for himself, now let him live two years for the government. What's all this moping and screaming for?"

And now Aunt Ra'na has come to see if the orderly of His Excellency the Captain (Afaq sometimes takes smuggled satin fabrics to the captain's wife) could use his influence.

"Sister, can Afaq help us? Can the captain's orderly save my son, if he would agree to be of assistance?"

Mother tries to calm Aunt Ra'na down. The neighbors have gathered around us. The scent of Khaj Tofiq's opium smoke wafts through the sprawling courtyard. Sitting at a charcoal brazier, he smokes his opium at his leisure. Afaq hasn't come home yet. Banu is squatting down next to her father. Sticking her nipple into her sickly child's mouth, Hajar stands over Aunt Ra'na's head. Sanam also joins us, sitting next to Mother. Mother sets a cup of tea before Hajar. Hasani, Ebrahim, and Omid all lean against the kitchen wall and gawk at Aunt Ra'na.

Afaq comes in through the courtyard door. She goes into her room, unties the fabrics tied to her waist, and lets her chador fall from her head. She then comes out and sits by Khaj Tofiq. "Has Sheikh Sho'ayb come yet?" she asks.

I heard him sending word this afternoon that he wouldn't come. He'd said that the inspectors had become suspicious, so they'd blocked the way.

"May God curse them," Afaq says.

Aunt Ra'na asks Mother to go talk to Afaq. Sanam says that His Excellency the Captain has managed to get draft exemptions for a few people so far. She has witnessed this herself, she claims. "But then," she adds, "it will cost you money."

In the meantime, Aman Aqa arrives home on his bike. By the time he goes to his room to change and wash his face with water from an earthen jug, Bolur Khanom has spread the supper cloth on the porch bed and set Aman Aqa's special plate down upon it. On the plate, there are usually a few pickled shallots, green onions and sometimes a couple of radishes, a few slices of tomato, or a few leaves of mint and tarragon and other kinds of herbs and vegetables.

Sanam believes that Aman Aqa must have peculiar cravings to want to eat these strange things every night.

"Bolur Khanom! Is it true what Sanam says, that Aman Aqa has peculiar cravings?"

Bolur Khanom bursts out laughing.

Rahim the Donkey Keeper insists that Aman Aqa won't be able to get any sleep unless he drinks that poisonous arrack.

"Bolur Khanom! Is that true that Aman Aqa must drink arrack so he can go to sleep?"

Again, Bolur Khanom bursts into laughter.

If so, Mr. Captain must drink arrack too because I've seen similar things on his table whenever I've gone with Afaq to his house.

"Is there any way he can help Gholam?" Mother asks Afaq.

"Mr. Captain? Hah!" Afaq moves her hand and puckers her lips as if to indicate Mr. Captain is a nobody.

Afaq's hair is pitch black. It falls down over her shoulders. Her eyes are so black you'd think she dyes them with charcoal every day.

"Afaq Khanom! Why does Mr. Captain keep that monkey?"

"He can't father a child, Son. So, instead, he keeps a monkey."

The monkey is the size of a kitten. They have put a chain around his neck, and the captain's wife holds his leash in her hand. She's short, the captain's wife. Her hair is golden. Her ass is so big that it swings like a pendulum when she walks. Her hips sway from side to side.

The captain comes out of a room. His polished boots shine and he has twisted his mustache upward. It curves up like a scorpion's tail. His hat comes down to his eyebrows. The upper part of his uniform pants bulges. The captain is skinny, tall, and bony.

"Can you bring me a few yards of fine fabric, Afaq?"

Afaq nods her head. The captain's voice is husky: "I'm going on leave. I want to take some gifts to my dear mother and my dear aunts."

"So he cannot help us out!" Mother cries.

"He's such a swindler . . . I have yet to find anyone quite like him. So far, the son of a bitch has not paid for more than ten yards of fabric . . . and I don't dare complain about it."

Aunt Ra'na starts to whimper again.

At noon, Father closes down his blacksmith shop and spends the afternoon at home. "If I'm to sit idly doing nothing, I'd rather stay in my own house," he says.

In the afternoons, whenever I feel like it, I go to Aman Aqa's teahouse and listen to music on the gramophone. Or, if I feel like it, I go along with Ebrahim and Hasani to play dominoes and drink tea. The weather has grown quite hot. So, if I want, I can also go swimming in Charkhab Quarter.

"Aren't we going to Charkhab, Ebram?"

"Let's go!"

By the time we walk through the hot, dry sand and reach the moist sand at the edge of the Karun River, the soles of our feet are very burned. We like the pungent smell of fish coming from the water. Hot and humid vapor rises from the surface of the Karun. The river is calm. It floods in the spring and threatens the houses near its banks. We pass under the White Bridge.

"Ebram! I wish we had brought lines and hooks to fish."

"Tomorrow."

The surface of the Karun River looks like tarnished silver. It reflects the sun's rays.

"Look at that, Khaled."

An elephant-gray fish soars from the surface, bows in the air, and dives back into the water headfirst.

We hop over the rocks along the river's edge. With a stick, Ebrahim digs at the slime at the foot of the rocks. Long red worms wriggle over each other in the slime. "These worms are perfect for bait."

Charkhab is packed with people. It looks like everyone in town has left their houses to come here. The waves foam and crash noisily against the bedrock. It's gotten really hot. Now the golden dates are fully ripe. If we feel like it, we could go to the date groves and wolf down a stomach full of crisp unripe dates and succulent ripe dates. If the gardener is not watching, we could even steal loads of cucumbers. We could steal melons and watermelons too.

"Look, Ebram! The lotus fruits are even larger than jujubes."

Ebrahim climbs up the lotus tree, just like a monkey. He hangs from a branch and shakes it. The ground turns red as the fruits fall, each the size of a large jujube. We cram our pockets, and then run off along the stream up to the water pump. We swim in the pool under the large pump's spout, holding on to the pipe and pulling ourselves up. The Karun's cool water gushes out of the pipe, hitting our heads and faces. We put our clothes back on and set off again.

It's hot and suffocating inside the pomegranate orchard. The pomegranates are not edible yet. Feeling heavy from eating so many lotus fruits, we lie down alongside the stream. The cool sand feels good on our backs and necks. The tangled leaves of the mulberry trees block the sunlight.

The weather has grown awfully hot. In this heat, Father closes all the doors, sits in his room, and reads the prayer book *Qasemi's Secrets*. If you follow all the instructions in this book, you can become invisible. You can make a cloak of red leather and become invisible whenever you put it on. If you've got the guts and heart, and follow all of the instructions in this book, you can even conquer and tame the jinn.

Mirza Nasrollah the Dentist gave my father this book. Father says Mirza Nasrollah has knowledge of the great secret name of God. Mirza practices medicine too. Whenever my sister and I get sick and have an upset stomach, he prescribes herbal medicines and home remedies.

"Mother, I can't take this much herbal extract."

"Close your eyes, my son, and drink it all at once. Then wash it down with a sugar cube!"

I gulp down every last drop of the concoction in the copper bowl. I am burning with fever. The drink turns my stomach and I bring it all up. Mirza Nasrollah keeps writing prescriptions.

Khaj Tofiq is skeptical of the book.

"I saw a dervish with my own eyes," Father tells him, "a ring in his ear, his hands on his chest, standing right in front of Mirza Nasrollah's shop."

Patiently, Khaj Tofiq melts a tiny bit of opium in the pipe bowl.

"Mirza Nasrollah rejected the dervish," Father carries on, "but when we went together to his house at noon, I saw the same dervish standing in front of it, his hands still on his chest."

Khaj Tofiq puffs on his opium pipe. The hot charcoal turns from bright red to a smooth ruby velvet.

"At last Mirza Nasrollah gave the dervish some instructions and sent him away," Father says.

Father has made four steel knives. On the blade of each knife, he has carved some sort of motif that I can't make out. I'm sure he got the idea for the patterns from *Qasemi's Secrets*.

As he unrolls his prayer rug in his room, he attaches each of the four corners of it to the ground with one of the knives, and then recites prayers on it. There's no doubt Mirza Nasrollah has given him some spells meant to turn his business around. Mirza Nasrollah's workshop is the size of a chicken coop. His tools consist of a couple of files, one small and one large, and an iron clip. The entire ceiling is covered with spider webs. His clients are mostly Arabs who come from villages close by—for instance, from Zuyeh, Zargan, Daghaghaleh—and occasionally from places a bit farther away, like Chanibeh or even Susa.

"As long as I make two sets of teeth every month, life goes on," he says.

Father says God is the Provider. He hasn't given up hope. He is thinking of a new line of work now that business has disappeared. We're in debt up to our necks. In Charkhab, when I took off my clothes to swim, somebody stole my shirt. So Mother unstitched one of Father's old shirts and fitted it for me. I have grown into it. I look carefully at the shirts on all the kids my size, especially those that are white and striped like mine was. Somehow, I have a feeling that I'll find my shirt.

"God is the Provider," Father insists.

"God is the Provider," Mirza Nasrollah says.

Father also says, "No living soul's mouth will be left without food."

Father and Khaj Tofiq are talking about *Qasemi's Secrets*. Aman Aqa is just sitting there listening. Mohammad the Mechanic is there too. It's been about half an hour since he got back from work. His nails are always black underneath.

Father tells them, "If a person's heart is pure and he tries to follow the instructions in *Qasemi's Secrets*, then he can conquer the world."

Mohammad the Mechanic does not believe any of this. He doesn't pray. As far as Father's concerned, even one smile at Mohammad the Mechanic obliges one to do penance.

"Can we take a look at this book?" Khaj Tofiq asks.

"Mirza Nasrollah believes that I shouldn't show it to anyone," Father replies. Then he explains, "I did it once. I showed it to Hajj Sheikh Ali. Soon after, Mirza Nasrollah turned up and reminded me that he asked me not to show the book to anyone."

Aman Aqa believes in the book. Mohammad the Mechanic refuses to believe. Khaj Tofiq is adamant about getting to the bottom of things. "What're you saying? Should we try it once more?" he insists.

Father refuses. Aman Aqa talks about a dervish whom he saw become invisible right in front of his eyes.

"Even though Aman Aqa drinks," Father says, "as long as he has faith . . . eventually he will be redeemed and resurrected."

Mohammad the Mechanic, on the other hand, doesn't believe any of it. "There's nothing in this world other than what we see," he says. And he persists, "It's because of believing in this sort of nonsense that we're so miserable. We have to always work like donkeys and let others reap the profits. That's why we are always put down and have become a bunch of hungry slaves . . ."

He doesn't mince his words. He just ignores everyone and rambles on endlessly. Father isn't very friendly with him. He even walks past him in such a way so as to avoid having to answer his greetings.

Amu Bandar heads out of his room, sits beside the pool, and prepares to make his ablutions before prayers. Amu Bandar's daughter is a widow. Her husband was a truck driver. He got into an accident and died instantly. Amu Bandar works all year round to save some money to send to his daughter and her children so they can buy new clothes for Nowruz. Amu Bandar's wife has long since passed away.

"Amu Bandar, come and have a cup of tea," Khaj Tofiq calls to him.

All year long, be it summer or winter, Amu Bandar wears a frayed French military tunic, an old pair of military pants, and a pair of brownish boots that he patches up himself.

"Amu Bandar! Why don't you buy yourself some clothes?"

"My daughter's orphans come first, my son."

Nowruz has passed but Amu Bandar has not yet sent his daughter any money or clothes.

"Amu Bandar! Where have you been till this time of night?"

"I was at the police station, my son."

"Police station?"

"People have forgotten God, my son . . . Now how am I supposed to buy this year's Eid presents?"

"What's happened, Amu Bandar?"

"The sergeant major told me, 'Go away, Uncle!' I said, 'Where should I go?' I argued that I too work for the government. 'I work for the municipality. I am a sweeper. If you don't help me out, who else will?' The sergeant major said, 'The precinct chief is not here yet.' He said, 'Go on, and come back later.' I said I'd sit and wait for the precinct chief to come. A bow-tied young man came and told me, 'You're wasting your time, Uncle. They team up with the thieves.' I asked how it was that they could be thieves themselves? The sergeant major didn't let me go in the police station. I waited for the precinct chief. All of a sudden, I saw him rush out of the station, get in a car, and leave. Before I got the chance to tell him that I had been robbed of my money, the car belched smoke and drove away."

"Your money was stolen, Amu Bandar?"

"Yes, my son, in the produce market."

"How was it stolen from you?"

"After a lifetime, I got a craving to eat some sheep's kidney. I thought I'd buy some, bring it home, and grill it on skewers. I took some money from inside the lining of my hat to give to the kidney seller. When I put the hat back on, it was taken off my head just like in a sudden gust . . . two hundred and twenty-five tomans, my son . . . You think the sigh of the orphans will not bring torment on these thieves?"

Amu Bandar's daughter lives in Shahr-e Kurd.

"You want me to pour you more tea, Amu Bandar?"

"God bless you, Khaj Tofiq . . . just a cup is enough."

Amu Bandar gets up and goes to pray in front of his room. After spreading out the supper cloth, Bolur Khanom sets up Aman Aqa's special plate on it.

Father says, "This world is a prison for believers. Amu Bandar is sure to go to heaven. But, alas, that Mohammad the Mechanic doesn't give much thought to this sort of talk."

"We have been promised so many things that we're bursting with promises," says Mohammad the Mechanic. "The deeper we sink into misery, the more we are referred to the afterlife."

Hajj Sheikh Ali brings blessings to our house. He brings good luck for Father's business, though these days we can't afford to invite him. Back when we could, we would invite him, along with his son-in-law, his children, and his brother's children; it was like our Eid feast. We would eat a great deal of food.

"Hajj Sheikh Ali! What rules should one follow when one is uncertain about how much of the daily prayers he has completed?"

We unroll a rug for them in Father's room. We borrow extra cushions from the neighbors. Father's room is illuminated by the presence of Hajj Sheikh Ali. I kiss Hajj Sheikh Ali's hand. It's like a sheep's fat tail. Soft and white. Just like Bolur Khanom's hands. Hajj Sheikh Ali delivers a sermon on the merits of feeding and being in the company of the ulema. His son-in-law talks about the bounties of Paradise. His brother discusses the rewards for praising the Prophet and his family, then religious taxes to help the poor, and then the portion allotted to the imam.

Mohammad the Mechanic's place will be at the bottom of the inferno.

"What's the good of working hard to earn money and then squandering it on a bunch of potbellies?" he says.

Khaj Tofiq, busily clamping another bit of opium, talks through his nose: "Since the dawn of history the ulema have been the blessing of the earth, and anyone who dares oppose 'em will be doomed!"

Mohammad the Mechanic bursts out laughing.

Aman Aqa rises to his feet. Khaj Tofiq melts the opium in the pipe bowl as he blows at the pipe. Father is silent. Apparently, he believes it'd be better not to say more. Sometimes, Mohammad the Mechanic's words and laughter are a real turn off.

Aunt Ra'na's son pays us a visit—in his military uniform. It suits him well. Mother kisses his forehead. We set up a stool for him next to the pool; he sits on it with his legs crossed. Since I last saw Aunt Ra'na's son, Gholam, a month ago, he's grown a mustache. He has twisted his upward just like Mr. Captain's. It seems like he has greased it too. It glistens. Gholam positions himself in such a way that he has a good view of Bolur Khanom's room. She's inside. Mother sends me to Esfandiar the Iceman to buy a *qeran*'s (penny) worth of ice. She fixes Cousin a cool glass of sherbet made with rose water. We borrow the rose water from Bolur Khanom. The upper part of Cousin's pants bulges out. He has fastened his puttees so tight it's like they're glued to his legs.

Wrapped up in her chador, Bolur Khanom walks coquettishly past Cousin toward Mohammad the Mechanic's wife. Cousin greets her. Mother lays out a rug beside the pool, sits on the rug, and lights the three-burner kerosene heater to make tea. The sun has pulled itself up into the belly of the sky. It's over the edge of the rooftop. The air is humid, but not sultry, just humid. Cousin unbuttons his uniform's shirt. His chest is as hairy as a bear's. Bolur Khanom comes out of Mohammad the Mechanic's room. Cousin's head turns and follows her around the yard. Mother invites her over to sit. Clasping his hands behind his head, Cousin pushes out his chest. His shoulders are very wide.

"Gholam! Military service too tough?" Bolur Khanom says as she sits down.

Mother offers her sherbet.

Aunt Ra'na's son talks about his military service. "The commander sticks his finger under everyone's puttees; if they're loose, you're done for. The commander will pat the rump of a horse, and if it's a bit dusty, you'll have to deal with the Angel of Death . . ."

It's Thursday night. Bolur Khanom has plucked her black eyebrows. She has applied *sormeh* to them and has dabbed rouge on her wide cheeks. A strand of wavy hair hangs over her forehead.

Cousin gazes into Bolur Khanom's eyes as he talks. "They tie four empty copper bowls to one wrist and four to the other one. Four to this ankle and four to that one, and then they order you to get on your knees and go around the barracks ten times . . . It's real tough . . ."

Bolur Khanom shifts her large buttocks and asks, "Gholam! Have you ever been lashed?"

"Who would do such a thing to me?" Cousin answers boastfully.

"You mean they're afraid of you?"

Omid, Hasani, and Ebrahim come and sit on the edge of the pool. I go and stand beside Cousin; I know it makes them jealous. Cousin's arms are well defined in his military uniform. He swaggers, puffs out his chest, and moves his eyes and brows around as he talks. Just like Mr. Captain, to whose wife Afaq sells smuggled satin fabrics.

"Even the commander doesn't dare to mess with me, let alone the sergeant major . . . I am not some villager—"

Bolur Khanom interrupts him. "Mr. Gholam! Why do you play so much with your eyes and brows when you talk?" she says with a guffaw.

Aunt Ra'na's son blushes down to his neck. (Bolur Khanom is annoying me. What's up with her? I wonder.) Cousin doesn't talk anymore. He doesn't even drink his tea. As soon as Bolur Khanom leaves, Mother goes inside and comes back with a one-toman bill that she puts in Cousin's tunic pocket. Mother always saves some money in her bundle of clothes for such occasions. Cousin doesn't talk anymore. He buttons up his shirt, covering his hairy chest. He looks really angry. His forehead, cheeks, and entire neck are sweaty. He gets up to say good-bye. Mother insists that he stay for lunch.

"What are we having, Mother?"

"Plain bread, Son."

"Mr. Gholam! Come and see us again. Tell us more stories about military service," sneers Bolur Khanom.

Aunt Ra'na's son is beside himself with rage. He doesn't even stay for lunch. Rahim the Donkey Keeper returns with his donkeys. His donkeys have this bad habit: they won't come in through the broken-down door unless they rub their bodies against it first. Aunt Ra'na's son walks out of the door and doesn't even look back.

There was not a single bruise on Bolur Khanom's belly. She lied. I saw it myself. Bruise or no bruise, she'll show me her belly regardless.

Father has now closed down his shop entirely, and has started on his forty-day worship retreat in his room. He has made a set of prayer beads by stringing together a thousand beads.

The weather is so annoying. In the morning, when we wake up, the bedrolls are all soaked and sticky from the humidity; it's as though they have been peed on.

The sky is like a pot of curdled milk through which streaks of blood have run here and there. Like there's a lid on the town, a lid made of metal. The sun beats down mercilessly; it's getting closer to the earth, day by day. Each day grows longer and hotter than the day before.

As the debts pile up, so do Father's prayers.

"Mashti Mehdi! Give me another pack of tobacco and add it to our bill."

Mehdi the Grocer hesitates. He takes care of a new customer. Then tends to the next customer. And when there's nothing else for him to do, he goes to the back of the store and busies himself moving the basket of onions. Then, he brings out the nightingale's cage and hangs it from the awning. After emptying the nightingale's water cup, he refills it with fresh water. Then pours some millet for the bird at his leisure. And when he sees me still waiting, he takes a pack of tobacco off the shelf and hands it to me. I look at him. His brows are knitted. A line has formed on either side of his lips, and his face is completely blank.

Bolur Khanom showed me her belly on the stairs. There were no bruises from the belt. She was wearing a slip made of black tulle. The whiteness of her thighs still makes my heart pound. Aman Aqa is away on a trip.

"He's gone to Susa. He might go to Amarah too. Gone to bring back smuggled tea."

If Father has managed to conquer the jinn by now, he definitely knows about what Bolur Khanom has said to me.

"Can I touch it, Bolur Khanom?"

"Not now."

"I didn't see it all that well, Bolur Khanom."

"If you'd like, you can sneak into my room late tonight and I'll show it to you."

I am infatuated with Bolur Khanom. I lied when I said I didn't see her belly well. I even saw the tiny black mole below her navel.

The sunlight is almost over the edge of the rooftop. Perching on the parapet, a couple of wood pigeons coo. The henna-colored pigeon that was missing for a while has shown up again. It's a long time until midnight. Besides, who knows if Father will ever leave his prayer rug to go to sleep, or if Khaj Tofiq might wake up? He's such a light sleeper, waking up even if an ant sneezes. Not to mention Banu; I'd be surprised if she doesn't suspect something already. Lately, as soon as I manage to talk to Bolur Khanom, Banu shows up out of the blue. She laughs in a bizarre way, making peculiar gestures.

"Khaled, go and get some bread from Habib the Baker!" Mother gives me the notched stick.

"Mother, send Jamileh. I can't go."

But my sister won't give in to me.

Habib the Baker has just lit the mantel lamp.

"I've told you a hundred times not to come here around lunchtime or suppertime," I recall Habib the Baker telling me a few days earlier.

I sit near the sidewalk opposite Habib's bakery. Dough pans are arranged next to one another outside of it. The rice pudding seller keeps stirring the hot contents of his pot with a spatula. Khalifeh, the baker's assistant, has taken off his apron and slung it over his shoulder. He's squatting next to the pot of simmering rice pudding, all the while biting off pieces of the bread he has rolled up. He's a friend of my father's. When he notices me standing in front of the bakery, waiting for bread, he tries to hide himself. "I need to make a living too," he says. "I have to pay the workers . . . and buy wheat . . ."

So I sit on the gravel walkway and wait for the evening to grow darker and the supper rush to end. Habib the Baker's mantel lamp illuminates the alleyway. A group of donkeys trots past me. A soft dust fills the alleyway. At sunset the donkey owners take their donkeys to the Karun to water them. Every now and then I go with Ebrahim to take his father's donkeys to the banks of the river. We kids whistle for them so they'll come and drink. We rinse our faces, and then jump on the donkeys and poke them into a speedy gallop. I haven't mounted a donkey since the day that sharp spur snapped in the animal's leather covering. I didn't dare mention to Rahim the Donkey Keeper that I had turned a sewing needle into a spur to make the donkey I was riding gallop faster than Ebrahim's.

"Ebram! What if the needle broke through the donkey's cover?"

"Donkeys are not like humans . . . they won't feel pain from these sorts of things."

Ebrahim talks nonsense. How could it not hurt? What's the difference between the flesh of a donkey and that of a man?

I see Mother approaching.

"Why are you sitting here, Khaled?"

"I'm waiting for the supper rush to die down."

She takes the notched stick from me and walks to the bakery. I watch from afar as Habib the Baker bends, reaches under the bread counter, takes out whatever cold, burned, or doughy loaves of bread he has, and hands them to Mother. Obviously, he's discomforted, yet he just frowns and doesn't say a word. What if I had gone? I wonder.

It has grown darker. Again, the odor of Khaj Tofiq's opium drifts through the yard. Banu is sitting beside him. The faint glow of the lantern light silhouettes Khaj Tofiq's bony face. Rahim the Donkey Keeper reaches a hand under his wife's arm and helps her onto the mattress laid in front of their room. Her eyes are so sunken that you'd think they were just two dark holes in her face. Her lips are always chapped and dry. There are gray strands in her hair. Her elbows look like knots tied on thick ropes. She's been bedridden with an illness for a year now.

"My entire back is chafed, Sister," she moans. It sounds as if her voice comes from the bottom of a well.

"Naneh Khaled, do you have any fennel?"

"Fennel? What for?" Mother asks.

Hasani sucks up his snot, wipes his nose with his sleeve, and says, "My mother has a stomachache. She's got so much worse since sunset, when she heard that Ja'far the Brickmaker has hanged himself."

Mother becomes disturbed. "But why did anyone have to tell her that? The helpless woman lies there in the corner of her room, completely unaware of what's going on around her."

She finds some ground fennel among the odds and ends behind the mirror. Naneh Hasani is just a handful of bones. Only shriveled and dried out skin sticks to her bones. The ends of her hair are soaked in sweat. There is so much clutter on the mantel above her head: a bowl for herbal tonics, ground roasted coffee beans, jujubes, old vinegar, and Indian cubeb.

"Sister! May it not happen to you! I've been feeling cramps in my belly since sunset."

Rahim the Donkey Keeper's wife doesn't really talk; instead she moans and groans. "Sister! It aches below my belly. I feel like a woman after labor whose womb has been possessed by the jinn."

Mash Rahim stuffs his pipe and takes a deep drag. As he lets out the smoke, it seems to me that the ashes have been dumped in a well and now they're bouncing back up.

Rahim picks up the brush and goes to groom his donkeys.

Bolur Khanom sets up the mosquito netting.

"Bolur Khanom! I thought you'd sleep inside your room tonight?"

"Ssshhh . . . don't say that to anyone."

"I won't. But where will you be sleeping tonight?"

"Outside, under the mosquito netting. I'll go inside my room after you come."

Mother has spread out the supper cloth. There is dried pennyroyal, vinegar, onions, and salt.

We grind the pennyroyal between the palms of our hands and sprinkle it on the bread. We add some salt and vinegar and make a morsel of it with onions.

"It's better to eat light at night so you can sleep well," Father usually says. "If you eat heavy stuff, you'll have nightmares."

Mother calls Father. He comes out, whispering prayers.

Sheikh Sho'ayb barges into the yard riding a horse. We never close the house doors. Even at night we leave one side open. Sheikh Sho'ayb ties the horse to the post holding up the donkeys' sunshade, and as he goes to sit next to Khaj Tofiq, he mumbles something to Afaq.

I guess they're talking about smuggling again.

"Afaq! A *teshaleh*." A small boat slides into the second tributary of the river, where the current waters the palm groves.

Sometimes at night we kids hit the palm groves and play hide-and-seek. We jump across the tributaries that aren't too wide and run down to the riverbank.

"Come at ten thirty!"

I am hiding in the shelter of a boat, straining my ears to make out the shuffle of the boys' footsteps. Suddenly, I hear a commotion. I hear footsteps. It's not the sound of the boys' feet. It's not from the kids. The words slither through the humid darkness and reach my ears. I recognize Afaq's voice, which mixes with the whooshing sound of the pointy palm fronds. I shift in my hiding place in the boat and pull myself up. I lie down on the damp sand, prop up my forearms, and cup my chin in my hands. My eyes pierce the darkness of the night. I can see shadows in motion along the third branch that channels off the river. The river has risen. You can ride a *teshaleh* from the wide tributaries up to the heart of the palm groves. I get up and walk. The sand muffles the sound of my footsteps. I pause and rest my cheek against the rough bark of a palm tree. This way, I can hear the voices better, and I can see Afaq taking rolls of fabric from the *teshaleh* and hurling them to the ground. Her body is shapely in her black voile dress. Her hair falls over her shoulders. Her hips sway as she walks.

"It's a hundred and thirty yards," Sheikh Sho'ayb whispers in Afaq's ear.

After preparing the opium pipe, Khaj Tofiq hands it to Sheikh Sho'ayb and says in a drawl, "This bastard, Nur Mohammad, has become such an irritating nuisance . . . loitering around our house like a hungry jackal."

"Why should it bother you at all—when you bum around at home all day long?" Afaq cuts him short. "Nur Mohammad scares the shit out of *me* and makes me shiver to my bones . . . As long as you have your opium going, why should anything bother you, I'd like to know?"

Khaj Tofiq pushes out his lips in a pout. Hanging his head, he picks up the tongs and fiddles with the burning embers. Sheikh Sho'ayb smokes the lump of opium in one long drag and then drinks his tea. After that he gets up, grabs the horse's reins, and heads for the doors to the house. Following him, Afaq wraps herself in her chador and leaves the house. Mother gathers the supper cloth. Bolur Khanom is lying under the mosquito netting. Amu Bandar empties his pipe, blows out his kerosene lamp, and lies down in front of his room. Karam has not come home yet. During the winter, he comes home early. Once his pot is empty of cooked turnips, he pushes his cart home. On summer nights, his work doesn't come to an end so soon. On those nights, he sells cooked green beans, sprinkled with lime juice, in front of Tuba's bar. Lately, he has been bringing along a lantern too.

"How's business, Karam?"

"Not bad, Aman Aqa. God willing, it'll bring me six or seven tomans at the end of the day."

"That's all?"

"Well, I have to bribe that sly night watchman too. That costs me a couple of tomans or so."

The crotch of Karam Ali's black pants is hanging so loose and low that it looks like a sheep's fat tail swaying as he walks. His mouth is so big that he is always betting he can shove a saucer inside it, and of course, he always wins.

Banu unwraps a bedroll for Khaj Tofiq. Rahim the Donkey Keeper waters his donkeys, and lies down at a distance from Naneh Hasani. Hajar's child starts howling. What I really want to do is to go and stuff cotton balls into the mouth of Hajar's forever-crying baby.

Bolur Khanom keeps tossing and turning under the mosquito netting. I hear the creaking of her bed. She is doing that so she will stay awake until everyone goes to sleep.

I lie down. The sky is filled with stars. Amazingly bright. Father doesn't go to his room but sleeps right in front of its threshold. Khaj Tofiq's light goes out. Karam Ali hasn't come home yet. It will be quite a while before the arrack drinkers are done with their drinking binge. Aman Aqa will be back tomorrow, so if I don't make it to Bolur Khanom's room tonight, it'll be ages before he makes another trip.

Here comes the sound of Karam's cart.

"Bolur Khanom! Should I wake you up if you are asleep?"

"I'll be up on my own."

Most likely Karam Ali has eaten out. He takes the ewer and goes into the outhouse. It takes him forever. He does this every night. Sometimes I happen to go to the outhouse right after he has left; I can smell soap. No one washes their hands in the outhouse. I have no idea what he does in there, but it's as if he doesn't ever want to leave. Who knows? Maybe he falls asleep in there. With that long muzzle of his, and those eyes slanted and deep set like the cleft of a bird's foot. Move it, you!

Karam finally leaves the outhouse. His pace slows as he walks by Bolur Khanom's mosquito netting. Sanam's room is opposite Bolur Khanom's, right in the corner of the courtyard. Karam walks to the porch in front of their room and finally lies the hell down. Sanam is long asleep.

The courtyard is now completely quiet. Even Hajar's sickly baby has finally shut up. Father too has begun a faint snoring.

To get to Bolur Khanom's room, I'll have to first pass by the kitchen, and then walk past Mohammad the Mechanic's room and Amu Bandar's. I'll have to be careful not to trip over Amu Bandar's ewer. Once I reach the donkeys' sunshade, I can walk under it. Then there's the outhouse, next are the house doors, after that the pigeon coop, and finally Bolur Khanom's room. I wish I could just go straight through the middle of the courtyard, but I can't.

Khaj Tofiq sits up, picks up a clay bowl, and gulps down some water. He lights a cigarette, and lies back down while smoking. With each drag Khaj Tofiq takes, the cigarette lights up like a glowworm.

I hear the creaking of Bolur Khanom's bed. I lift my head up from the pillow and peek out. She must be awake, turning over on her side. Khaj Tofiq puts out his cigarette.

I hear the roar of the local train arriving from the harbor. It's eleven o'clock.

Bolur Khanom's breath is hot. It burns my neck and cheeks. Her body is on fire. Her belly is hard and firm, like rising bread dough. My hand glides over her hips. Incredibly soft. She has taken off her short muslin undergarment. The moonlight penetrates the room through the window. We're in darkness. In each other's arms. She presses against me so hard that I can feel my bones ache. My heart is beating like that of a timid sparrow.

"Why are you pressing me so hard, Bolur Khanom?"

"Ssshhh!"

I hush. My breath mingles with hers. Both of us are soaked in sweat. Her wavy hair has fallen on the pillow. Her cheeks smell of sweet briar roses. Her lips taste of bittersweet unripe dates. Acrid. Her plump body squirms like a snake. She sucks on my lips so hard that they throb. Her hips move up and down. I am breathless. The moonlight has crept further inside. Soon it will reach our legs. Bolur Khanom's grip loosens, and she lets go of my waist, as if she has passed out. She breathes softly.

A few of Father's friends from the bazaar have come to see him. They assumed he's been ill and that's why he hasn't opened his smithy.

"Oussa Haddad, may God bless you!"

"May He bless you as well, Hajj Nayeb."

"God Forbid—"

Father interrupts Hajj Nayeb. "No, thank God, I am well."

Hajj Nayeb's thick, bushy mustache quivers. "So, why have you closed down the shop?"

"Business is slow," Father says indifferently. "I just closed down for a few days."

Hajj Nayeb talks about everything. Mirza Sadeq and Mashhadi Iman nod their approval at his words. Father just listens. Mother appears flustered. "Khaled, run quick and buy some ice from the corner store!"

Mother is embarrassed to borrow rose water from Bolur Khanom. Taking the ceramic bowl for yogurt, she puts on her chador and goes to Mehdi the Grocer to get some lemon juice instead. "How many times should one feel embarrassed in one day, melting like a piece of ice on the ground?"

When I return from getting the ice, I notice that Father looks upset. Hajj Nayeb rolls a cigarette made with Father's tobacco and then blows its smoke into the air.

Mother offers them lemonade. "Pardon me! It's nothing fancy."

They drink their lemonade, get to their feet, say good-bye, and leave. Father's manner is cold as he sees them off. Once they're gone, Father comes and sits back down. He mumbles to himself as he rolls a cigarette, "No sign of humanity or piety left anymore. Instead of extending a helping hand to a body in trouble so he can stand up, they push him even further down."

"Why are you so upset?" Mother asks.

I have never heard Father use such a dismal tone; it touches my heart.

"Supposedly they're just paying me a visit, but in fact their intention is to snatch the blacksmith shop out of my hands."

Mother thinks that Father should reopen his business, but he says he won't do such a thing until he has finished his vowed forty days of prayers.

He stubs out the cigarette, makes his ablutions, and goes to his room. It is two hours into the afternoon. The yard is saturated in sun. It's like it has never seen a shadow and never will. It's so hot that it feels like the door of an inferno has been left ajar. Banu is taking a nap at the base of the staircase leading to the roof. Next to the clay water cistern, she has rolled out a mat and is lying on it, covering her body with a moist cloth. The base of the staircase is always shady, with a cool breeze that comes from the rooftop and fills that particular corner, keeping it cool.

Ebrahim and I have decided to keep an eye on Gholam Ali Khan.

"Khaled! Gholam Ali Khan has sent his wife and children away to Hamedan."

Gholam Ali Khan lives on the second floor of a house behind Habib the Baker's shop. He works in the police station, but I don't know why he always wears civilian clothing. He must trim his mustache using a straight ruler because it grows as thick as the tail of a large rat above his upper lip. He shaves his face so often that it's left blotches of crimson here and there. Nothing about him is as gripping as his green eyes. Not even his stiff gait, which makes him look like he has swallowed a stick. Not even his Adam's apple, which sticks out prominently on his long neck. Not even his wide ears. Gholam Ali Khan's eyes are as green as raisins.

"Khaled! There's a droshky coming again in the afternoon."

Today, Ebrahim and I have decided to pester Gholam Ali Khan. So right after Father retreats to his room and begins his prayers, Ebrahim and I head out into the alleyway. As I pass by the stairs, Banu lifts the hem of the cloth off her face and looks at me. Today, her gaze has been sort of strange. It tears my heart apart. She has never looked at me this way. If she has discovered that I went to Bolur Khanom's room, I am done for.

I steal my eyes away from hers, and, together with Ebrahim, head out into the alleyway. I leave, but I can't forget the suspicious look in her eyes. If Father finds out . . . What if Aman Aqa finds out!

The workers at Habib the Baker's shop are on their midday break. As always, his shoulders covered with a loincloth, Khalifeh is kneeling and mincing meat. We go into the old ruins across from Gholam Ali Khan's house and get to work. We collect smooth pebbles, just right for our slingshots, and poke the piled-up trash with a stick. We know that the droshky driver has crammed cotton balls inside the little bells around the horses' necks to stifle their sound; we know too that the sound of the wheels and the hooves gets muffled in the soft dirt covering the street. There isn't a soul in the alleyways. It's so hot that not even a stray dog would want to come out of its hole.

"Khaled, what do you say we make a ball out of some rags, pour some gasoline on it, and when the *Lady* shows up, set fire to it and hurl it at her?"

I'm ready for anything. But I still like to ask why, so I do.

Ebrahim narrows his eyes and says, "Why? . . . Because it's a sin. Because . . . adultery is a sin."

Ebrahim is older than me. He goes to mosque often and listens to the sermons; he understands these sorts of things better than me. "Adultery?" I ask.

"Yes . . . adultery."

Banu's scrutiny troubles me. Maybe we should forget about Gholam Ali Khan and mind our own business . . . Most likely, Bolur Khanom knows that adultery is a sin . . . but I'm not married like Gholam Ali Khan . . . am I? But what about Bolur Khanom? . . . She has a husband . . . The droshky appears.

"Ebram! Let's get all the guys together at sunset so we can boo the lady as soon as she comes out to leave."

The droshky comes and stops right in front of Gholam Ali Khan's house. The droshky driver is the same guy as before, but the woman is shorter and chubbier than the one we saw last summer. Gholam Ali Khan must have been waiting behind the door. The moment the droshky comes to a halt, he opens the door; the woman gets out and walks up the stairs to the house. The door is shut and the droshky takes off. It's so sudden that we're both taken aback. My eyes are still following the droshky when I hear glass breaking. I see Ebrahim running away, putting the slingshot around his neck. I barely have time to run when I see that Gholam Ali Khan has opened up the window, one of whose glass panes is shattered, and is cursing my mother and sister. What I really want to do is to stop and talk back, but I didn't break the window, so why should I wait around and be blamed for it?

The worst of the heat is gone. The sun has grown pale. It's hiding behind the edge of the rooftop. Omid, Ebrahim, Hasani, and I pick up our slingshots and head out into the alleyways. Our pockets are stuffed with perfect-sized gravel. I have to get even with Gholam Ali Khan and all the cussing and the name-calling he did for no reason. We ask Khaleq and Chinuq to join us. Chinuq's entire face is a nose and a mouth. You can barely see his eyes and forehead. We stop in the ruins across from Gholam Ali Khan's house to map out our ambush on his mistress when she leaves the house, so we can shower her with gravel. We're not even in position when all of a sudden Gholam Ali Khan, as quick as a comet, dashes out of his house. Before I even have a chance to run away, he grabs my neck and slaps me so hard across the face that I see stars.

"Why are you slapping me, Gholam Ali Khan?"

"You son of a dancing whore! *You* dare to break *my* window?" And he begins kicking me. The boys have already disappeared. I can't escape. I hold on to Gholam Ali Khan's legs. He grabs me by the waist, lifts me up, and hurls me to the ground like a ball. He beats me as if he were pulverizing some sort of grain, and he is swearing at me nonstop. He is cursing everyone related to me, dead or alive. Habib the Baker comes to my rescue and frees me from Gholam Ali Khan's grip. In such situations, Mother won't come out of the house at all. Father also stays in the house. I know a good beating is in store for me. Bolur Khanom comes and takes me home, all bloody. My nose, lips, mouth, and chin are all dripping with blood, but I haven't cried, not even a single tear.

I sit down at the edge of the pool to wash the blood off my face. The boys gather around me. Mother stands beside the pool and looks at me. Jamileh is glued to her. Mother does not say a word. I look at her; she looks as if she's ready to cry. I burst out crying: "Mother, I swear to God, it wasn't my fault at all. I didn't do anything wrong."

"Then who broke Gholam Ali Khan's window?"

"I don't know, Mother . . . I don't know who did it."

Ebrahim interrupts, "No one knows who broke his window. He just blamed it on Khaled for no particular reason."

I look at Ebrahim; he looks down.

"We were just in the abandoned building, playing around, minding our own business," adds Chinuq, "when out of the blue he came and started beating Khaled."

Chinuq's eyes are not visible at all, as though his face were just a mouth that talked.

I keep waiting for Father to come out and give me a good beating, but he's caught up in reciting his prayers.

The pale yellow sunlight is not quite gone from the edge of the rooftop when Gholam Ali Khan shows up in the company of a police officer with a warrant. Looks like he won't let me off the hook that easy. At least not until he teaches us a lesson so that the droshky can come and go without anyone causing trouble. Mother's face turns pale. The neighbors gather around and my sister begins sobbing.

"Gholam Ali Khan, forgive him, he's sorry."

"Gholam Ali Khan, greatness is a gentleman's trait."

"Gholam Ali Khan, I promise Khaled won't slip up like this ever again."

I didn't see it coming. I never would have imagined Gholam Ali Khan, a grown man, calling the police on a small boy.

The police officer takes hold of my wrist and leads me away. Tears trickle down Mother's cheeks. Father breaks away from his praying and stands motionless in the doorway, his eyes fixed on me. Bolur Khanom sends Ebrahim to fetch Aman Aqa. He darts out the door. Khaj Tofiq follows us to the end of the alleyway. Mehdi the Grocer mediates. Habib the Baker begs, but Gholam Ali Khan won't budge, not even a bit.

In the hallway at the police station, a short, bald sergeant with a henna-colored mustache and an unbuttoned uniform jacket asks Gholam Ali Khan, "Is that *him?*"

"Yes . . . the son of a bitch himself."

The police officer lets go of my hand.

The sergeant says, "Come forward!"

"I swear to God that I didn't . . . ," but the words are muffled in my throat, and I see stars again. With the sergeant's blow, I am flung to the side. My head hits the wall. Everything grows dark. I know that Father has never in his life set foot in a police station, and I'm sure he won't set his foot in one now either. As I try to lean against the wall, it occurs to me that Cousin Gholam serves in the army.

One of the sergeants reaches a hand under my arm and shoves me into the police station's courtyard. It also occurs to me that it'd be better if someone would get my cousin to come here instead of Aman Aqa.

Gholam Ali Khan goes into an office. A guard brings him a cup of tea. My head feels heavy on my shoulders. Pain shoots through my sides and my nose is swollen. One of my teeth feels loose.

I lower myself and lean against the stone wall of the station's courtyard. My back aches. I feel nauseous and my heart is heavy with pain. If only there were someone I could talk to and open up my heart to, perhaps then I'd feel better.

I think I hear someone calling me. "Aqa!"

Someone is indeed calling me. His voice is very low, so I prick up my ears.

"Sir, I am talking to you."

I turn around. I can see a pair of eyes through a round hole in the door to my right.

"Come forward . . . come and sit here!"

I wonder what he wants from me. I hesitate. Again, it's the same man's voice, "Please, come over here!"

I get up and walk to the door, which is only three steps away.

"Sit down and lean against the column next to the door."

I sit down and lean against the column next to the door, wrapping my arms around my knees. The man's voice comes from behind the door. It sounds like he has put his mouth to the crack between the door and the doorjamb.

"Listen to me, Aqa . . . you just listen . . . and don't ask a thing!"

I prick up my ears, now rather curious, and put aside my own misery.

"Listen, sir, I know you'll get out of here . . . sure you will . . . and when you're out, go to Mojahed Bookstore and tell the bookstore owner that Pendar has been arrested . . . Do you follow? . . . Pendar . . . The bookstore is on Pahlavi Street. Shafaq is a tall guy, with a big mustache . . . his eyes . . ."

Suddenly, one of the guards shouts into the yard, "Hey, boy, move over to that side!"

I get up and move toward the pool. My head is full of thoughts, and names like "Shafaq" and "Pendar." Was he about to say what color his eyes were? ". . . Tall guy, with a big mustache." It's a gloomy sunset, as if all the sadness in the world has been placed on my heart. God only knows how my mother feels right now. I can imagine her, sitting as she always sits, shedding tears quietly without uttering a word, and of course, Father is berating her. "You spoiled that boy," he'd blame her, "you, you always cover up his wrongdoings. See how far he has gone? Taken to the police station."

Mother just keeps crying.

Aman Aqa arrives on his bike. I regain a bit of hope, and with the back of my hand wipe the tears off my face. Aman Aqa props his bike against the wall, gives me a quick look, and without saying a word goes inside the office where Gholam Ali Khan and the sergeant are sitting. I guess Aman Aqa and Gholam Ali Khan are sort of friends. My arms still wrapped around my knees, I stay put next to the wall. If I could, I would chew Gholam Ali Khan's ears like I would a sheep's.

Keeping my eyes on the door, I imagine Shafaq as a tall man. Pahlavi Street is not that far from our house. I must have passed by Mojahed Bookstore a hundred times. I think I must have even bought books and notebooks from there. Yet I cannot remember seeing anyone there matching Shafaq's description. I wish he could have told me the color of Shafaq's eyes. I wish the guard hadn't noticed and I could have listened to all of the man's words.

It has grown dark now. Aman Aqa calls me. I get up and go inside the office. On my behalf, Aman Aqa has promised that I will never again show up around that house, and if I ever do, they can take me straight to jail. Gholam Ali Khan shoots a look my way. His eyes are as green as raisins. He has knotted his tie so tightly that it is the size of a thumbnail. He has shaved his face so meticulously that his cheeks are patchy with redness.

The sergeant stands up, grabs my earlobe, squeezes it, and says, "Always remember the promise that you've made here!"

I gather up a bit of courage and say, "All right! I'll keep that in mind, but you should also know that I didn't break the window."

Gholam Ali Khan's green eyes stay fixed on my face.

My mother has been waiting for me in front of the house. Jamileh's eyes are puffy from crying. Mother kisses me on the forehead. In a way, I am relieved; I know that Father will stop his beatings and yelling. Side by side, Aman Aqa and I enter the house. Father is sitting cross-legged and smoking. Hasani, Ebrahim, and Omid come and stand beside the pool and look at me. Chinuq, Khaleq, and a couple of other boys from the neighborhood are also there. Father's face is so cheerless that it pains me to see him like this. I think to myself that this must be the first time that I have really noticed the gray hair at his temples, and I think that this must be the first time that I have noticed how hollow his eyes have become, how his jawbones poke out, and how his forehead has become all wrinkled.

I stand kind of at a distance from my father, looking down. I feel like crying. I hear his voice, "Come and sit!"

Mother is still busy thanking Aman Aqa. "May God grant you all His blessings! May you have prosperity in life! Had you not intervened, who knows what would have happened to our son?"

"I said, come and sit!" I hear Father say again. His voice sounds heavy and dismal.

I feel guilty. I would rather have him beat me to death. The way he talks to me, I just want to die of shame. If only he would hit me, even one slap across the face, I would feel better.

I sit down. It's completely dark now. The pigeons on the edge of the roof have already fluffed their feathers and stopped their cooing. I feel dizzy. Suddenly, I remember Pendar, then Shafaq. I'm sure Pendar needs Shafaq's help. He needs Shafaq to send someone to the police station to bail him out . . . *Shafaq is a tall guy; he has a thick mustache, his eyes* . . . I wish the guard hadn't noticed and I could have listened to all of his words. I wish I knew why they'd put Pendar in jail. I wish the guard had left me alone, so I could ask the guy and find out the whole story.

"All right, boys, let's get going now," I hear Mother's voice.

The boys take off. The odor of Khaj Tofiq's opium has filled the entire courtyard. Rahim the Donkey Keeper returns home with his donkeys. Amu Bandar returned home earlier. He's making his ablutions. All he does is get up in the morning, go and rummage around the backstreets of the wealthy part of town, pick up the garbage, throw it in the dumpster behind Habib the Baker's store, come back at noon, eat his lunch, say his prayers, and then repeat the same thing in the afternoon.

"Why did you decide to break the window of someone else's house?" Father asks.

"It's over now, whatever it was," Mother answers instead.

"I didn't break it."

Mother touches my swollen nose. "God damn him. Look what he has done to my son."

"Woman, you think we can stand up to the government's people?"

With my arms wrapped around my knees, I watch Mohammad the Mechanic's wife spread out a rug in front of their room. Mohammad the Mechanic's wife has eyes like a deer's. The color of her face is exactly like that of the moon. Mohammad the Mechanic's wife says very little and minds her own business; it's like her presence is hardly felt in the house, if at all.

There's Banu staring at me from afar again. She's sitting right in front of their kerosene lamp, looking straight at me. Khaj Tofiq, having placed his pipe next to the brazier, and high on opium, slowly closes his eyelids and dozes off. You can find him in the same state when he's craving it too. The only difference is that when he needs his opium, his nose becomes runny. God forbid if he's high and someone happens to be sitting next to him at his brazier, and he's got the urge to talk, and God forbid if Mohammad the Mechanic is that someone. The two of them get really fired up. "What are you talking about, man? The world's always been the way you see it now . . . God's doing is not without purpose . . . a master should be a master and a slave should be a slave . . . otherwise life doesn't go on. If everyone in this world were a master, who would be a laborer then? Who would do a porter's job? Who would make bread for the rest of us to eat?"

But Mohammad the Mechanic knows how to deal with Khaj Tofiq. He gets tough with him. If it comes down to it, Mohammad the Mechanic can really put him in his place. "Of course you must say that. It's just brazier talk . . . When a man burns up a good one or two *mesqals* of opium every day, he must think and talk like that too . . ." Mohammad the Mechanic does not mince his words at all. "Thank God that you have someone like Afaq Khanom, whose hard work pays for your supply of opium so that you can sit and easily spin yarns like this."

I try to look away from Banu's piercing gaze. Father rolls a cigarette. What large hands he has! It occurs to me that this is the first time I've noticed Father's large, calloused hands.

Father smokes his cigarette, stands up, and disappears into his room. Bolur Khanom puts her chador on and comes toward me. *Go to Mojahed Bookstore . . . tell Shafaq that Pendar has been arrested. Do you follow?* Pendar's penetrating voice resonates in my ears.

"Khaled, I thought you were a boy with some sense; what came over you?" Bolur Khanom is standing above me. Mother has lit the Primus burner. I think we're having boiled egg stew for dinner again. I look up at Bolur Khanom. "Why did you disturb Gholam Ali Khan?"

Disturb? Gholam Ali Khan must have said something and Aman Aqa must have retold that something to Bolur Khanom.

"I didn't disturb anyone."

She bends down and sets a cup of sherbet in front of me.

"Drink it, Khaled. It's got catkin extract. It'll do you good, after getting scared to death like that."

Aman Aqa is sitting at the edge of the pool. Rolling up his sleeves to his elbows, he washes his face. I'm too embarrassed to look at him. I think if I am to take a beating from anyone, it should be from Aman Aqa, not Gholam Ali Khan. *Shafaq is a tall guy . . . tall . . . tall . . .* It is Pendar's voice, and I only got to see his eyes. I feel apprehensive. I pick up the glass of sherbet. Bolur Khanom leaves. Banu's piercing gaze follows her. I see Omid standing in front of their room. Hasani and Ebrahim are sitting next to their mother, worried that they'll find her dead one of these days. Sanam has already created a cloud of smoke. Lowering her head, she blows into the flames beneath a pot. All around the courtyard and at each corner there are hanging propane lamps and lanterns, spreading their faint light on the ground and the adobe walls . . . *He has a thick mustache too . . .* Naneh Hasani moans. Smoke gets into Sanam's throat, making her cough . . . *He has a thick mustache too, he has a thick mustache too . . .* The thought of Pendar will not leave me alone. I am nervous. Mother goes back to our room. The Primus is roaring. I hand the glass of sherbet to Jamileh, get up, and dart out of the house as quick as an arrow.

Even though some of Hokumati Street has been paved with asphalt recently, most of it is still cobblestone. All the streetlights are on. It is so much different from our street, where it is always dusty, and after each rain we get mud up to our knees. I have never seen all of the lights on at once.

I run nonstop, without pausing for a breath. I pass by the governor's massive stone office building. A tall, broad-shouldered guard keeps watch. I don't even want to look at him. Not too long ago, I used to come here and look around at the row of trees inside the yard enclosed by the huge fence of the governor's building.

"Khaled, let's go."

"Wait a minute. Let's take a look inside the governor's building. It's like heaven, it's fantastic. Look how beautiful those trees are!"

There's a row of willows, short mimosa bushes, tall palm trees, and colorful flowers.

"Come on, Khaled, let's get out of here!"

"Ebram, don't you want to be this guard?"

But now I don't even want to look beyond the gate. I don't even want to look at the guard. I run up to Mojahed Bookstore. A few customers are standing in front of the building. Inside it is well lit. In the back of the store, on a chair, a man with a swarthy complexion sits. He's reading a book and smoking. He has a thick mustache. From the way he's sitting, I can't tell if he's tall or short. A skinny boy helps the customers. I guess he's my age. At most, he's a year or so older than me. I mean, if you really want to take it further, he can't be more than sixteen years old. What about Shafaq? I shift from one foot to another in front of the store. I get shoved by a couple of passersby whom I ignore. I am anxious . . . *Mojahed Bookstore on Pahlavi Street . . . Shafaq is a tall guy . . . he has a thick mustache too . . .* Suddenly, he appears from the back of the store. It must be him. Tall, with a thick mustache covering his lips, high, bony cheeks, large black eyes. Brown-skinned too. He's one of those people who'll capture your heart at first glance. In his hand, he holds a book the size of his palm, its title printed in red. He hands it to the man with the swarthy complexion who's sitting on the chair, smoking. The man takes the book from him and hides it in the fold of a newspaper lying there on the bookshelf next to him.

I throw caution to the wind and slide into the store through the crowd of customers. The young, pale-skinned salesperson blocks my way, saying, "Wait outside if you need books."

"I don't need books."

"Then what?"

"I need to see Mr. Shafaq."

Shafaq's large eyes quickly turn in their sockets and stay fixed on me. The same goes for the man with the swarthy complexion. He closes his book and stubs out his cigarette. Both are obviously alarmed. I am taken aback too. They keep looking at me. The three of us are silent. It seems as if the customers have also noticed. The salesperson too has paused to look. I wonder what it is I have said wrong that has shocked everyone and made them so quiet. Shafaq's voice ends the stunned silence. His voice is husky and pleasant. "Help the customers, Peyman!"

The pale-skinned, skinny boy turns to the customers.

"Come closer!" And he motions to me.

I think I have already taken a liking to him, as if in these few silent moments we have talked a thousand times. I already respect Shafaq. Calm and dignified, I step toward him. He grabs my arm. I quiver for a moment. I walk with him up to the door that separates the bookstore from its storage room.

"You said you need to see who?" he asks quietly.

I hold my head up but am unable to look into his eyes. "Mr. Shafaq."

He looks straight into my eyes. "All right! That's me. I am Shafaq."

My voice trembles: "I know it's you."

He looks surprised. "You know?"

I answer hastily: "Yes, I know."

"How do you know . . . You don't know me, do you?"

The words become knotted in my throat. My mouth feels dry. "Mr. Pendar described you to me."

Again he looks at me like he did when I first came in, the moment I said hastily, "I need to see Mr. Shafaq." The same baffled look is on the face of the swarthy man sitting in the chair. Once again, I feel perplexed. All I want now is to turn away from their stares, head out of the store, and run away. Shafaq has taken hold of my arm. His startled voice fills my ears: "Pendar?" It sounds as if it's coming from miles away, yet it brings tranquility with it.

"Pendar?"

"Yes, Mr. Pendar."

"Where did you see him?"

"At the police station."

I can see his face turning pale. His lips, stiff and tight, press together. He turns toward the man with the swarthy complexion. The man lights up another cigarette and offers one to Shafaq. Again, there is silence. I no longer want to run away. I feel like I am helping him, but I can't yet figure out what's going on. So, I say, "I think Pendar needs your help."

The swarthy man takes a deep drag of his cigarette and says, "What does this Pendar person look like?"

"I didn't get to see him," I answer with ease.

"You didn't see him?"

"No, not exactly. Just saw his eyes. Through that round hole. I mean, the round hole in the door at the police station."

"What did he say to you?" Shafaq asks.

"He asked me to come and tell you that he's been arrested. He said that Shafaq is a tall man with a thick mustache . . . I'm sure he needs your help. You should do something so he can get out of there."

"Why were you there?" asks the man with the swarthy complexion, in a quiet and gentle manner.

I tell them the whole story.

Shafaq gently touches my nose. "It's swollen badly."

The other man closes his book and gets up from his chair. "All right," he says.

Shafaq puts his hand on my shoulder. "Thanks very much. We'll do something for him. Don't you worry!"

I move to walk out of the bookstore. Shafaq grabs my hand. "You didn't say your name."

"Khaled."

"Where do you live?"

"Off of Hokumati Street . . . where the cobblestones end."

"Stop by sometime, whenever you can. I'd be happy to see you." He squeezes my hand in his large hand as he says this.

Summer is taking its last breaths. Dust is everywhere. There are storms every day, diffusing plenty of dust into the air. My father has finished reciting his prayers but business is still the same. Every morning he goes to his smithy, but the most he can do is sell a few hobnails. If he's lucky, he might get a couple of axes to sharpen. Father is still adamant that one can do wonders with the help of *Qasemi's Secrets*. He never gives in to Mohammad the Mechanic. He says, "All the instructions in this book have been put to the test. If you think the book's not effective, it's because our own doings are no longer according to faith. Not our clothes, not our food, nothing."

"Whatever you say, good man!" says Mohammad the Mechanic. "You've forgotten all about work. You sit at home, praying and waiting for a miracle to happen?"

Father frowns and turns his face away from him. Mohammad the Mechanic won't budge. "No, really . . . you sat in your room for forty days, and prayed for what? What finally came out of it?"

Father gets mad. His voice is trembling. "Just one look into your face is enough to make one's forty days of prayers, no, even forty years of prayers, go to waste."

Summer is taking its last breaths. At sunset, the dust settles down and the sky turns red.

At night, we still sit in the courtyard, and we still sleep out there too. Squatting over the drain next to the pool, Hajar waits for her child to pee. The child is howling. It's not long past sunset. It has just gotten dark. The wood pigeons, perched on the edge of the roof, have fluffed their feathers. The night before last, I caught the henna-colored pigeon, clipped its feathers short, and I threw it into the pigeon coop. The specially trained male is following her around. I guess they will mate. Khaj Tofiq, crouching on his heels next to the pool, fans the charcoals in his brazier. Afaq prepares lamb stew. Its scent wafts through the yard. Banu sweeps in front of their room so she can spread out a carpet for the evening.

"Hey, it's not going all that bad with Bolur Khanom, right?"

I blush to my ears. "What do you mean by that?"

Banu mentions Bolur Khanom whenever she gets a chance. For sure she suspects something. I no longer get naked and go into the pool to hold her, so she gives me these glaring looks. Lately, she's taken a different tone with me.

"Why not? It's obvious that Bolur Khanom pleasures you with that big ass of hers."

Bolur Khanom is in the kitchen. I think she's planning to fix kebab patties for dinner. Mother is thinking about making boiled egg stew again. Hajar turns her fleshy buttocks around, walks into her room, puts down the child, and hands him a piece of bread. She then brings out the coarse kilim rug, shakes it, and spreads it out in front of her room. With the propane lamp beside him, my father sits on his knees, bending over *Qasemi's Secrets*. He no longer reads it; he just turns its pages, smoking constantly. Rahim the Donkey Keeper is grooming his donkeys; they let out a *firt firt* sound of joy. The singing of the crickets has filled the yard. Thank God Hajar's child's howling has stopped. Naneh Hasani, on the other hand, lies over there in front of their room, moaning. One cannot make out anything from her mumbled words. Sometimes she becomes delirious. Amu Bandar has just lit his lantern and set it in front of his room. He heads out of the house; perhaps he's going to buy some rice pudding.

I shut the pigeon coop's door and go sit next to Father. There's a pile of cigarette butts in a corner next to the Turkish rug. Someone walks in through the house doors. I recognize him once he comes into the light of Amu Bandar's lantern. It's Naser Davani—with his wide chin, dipped forehead, and bent and humped nose. He carries a heavy wooden chest on his shoulder. Hajar is flabbergasted. She carries her sickly child out of the room, sits him down on the kilim, walks quickly toward Naser Davani, and takes the chest off his shoulder. "Why, welcome home . . . why didn't you send word that you were coming?"

Picking up his sickly child from the kilim, Naser Davani kisses him and presses him to his chest. His face has become tawny, dark as melted copper. His cheeks are sunken. It seems like he has lost weight. The child clutches his father's amber-colored hair. Hajar is overwhelmed. She turns around in a frenzy, tidies up the frizzy curls that are falling over her shoulders, disappears into her room, brings out the Primus, puts it down, and lights it up. "You could've told me you were coming! At least I could've made you dinner."

"I'm not hungry. I ate two skewers of ground lamb kebab at Dar-Khoin Teahouse."

Naser Davani sets his baby down. The baby begins crying at once; Hajar caresses him. The neighbors gather around Naser Davani.

"May your eyes be bright, Hajar."

"May your eyes be bright too, Sister."

Hajar walks up to the pool, fills the kettle from the tap, and puts it on the Primus.

"Welcome back, Oussa Naser."

"Thank you, Amu Bandar."

Amu Bandar sits at the drain around the pool, making his ablutions. As always, the odor of Khaj Tofiq's opium wafts through the entire yard.

"Welcome home, Oussa Naser."

"Thank you, Khaj Tofiq."

Hajar is pumping the Primus.

"Good for you, Hajar."

"Much appreciated, Bolur Khanom."

There are patches of dried sweat visible in the crotch of Naser Davani's flannel pants.

Looking up from *Qasemi's Secrets*, Father asks Naser Davani, "How did you get home, Oussa Naser?"

"We came on a boat up to Gasbeh," answers Naser Davani as he takes off his pants. "Then, we walked up to Khosrowabad, and from there, we took a car."

Father lights a cigarette and gets up from beside the propane lamp. He puts on his heavy *giveh* shoes, and with dawdling steps walks toward Naser Davani. "Any dangers?"

"No, thank God."

Father's shoulders are stooped. "I hear a boat was sunk a few days ago. Is that true?"

"I heard that too."

My father, taking a deep drag of his cigarette, asks again, "They say there were about two hundred people on it. Is that true?"

Naser Davani gives short answers. He doesn't seem to be in the mood for talking. He looks tired. He folds his flannel pants and lays them on the kilim, walks up to the pool, sits at the edge of it, rolls his sleeves up to his elbows, and rinses off his hands and face.

Father comes back, sits beside the lamp, and stubs out his cigarette on the ground.

As she waits for the water in the kettle to start boiling, Hajar goes into her room. Naser Davani too goes into the room, and comes back with a towel, wiping off his hands and face before flinging it around his neck.

Mother sets a cup of tea in front of Father. He is deep in thought and doesn't even notice the tea. His fingers are fidgeting with the pages of *Qasemi's Secrets*. Jamileh bites off a piece of the lavash she has rolled up for herself. To wash it down, she sips some sweat tea after each bite. Her eyes are already looking sleepy. Mother is busy making stew. Hajar heads out of her room, wearing a pistachio-colored cotton summer dress with tiny lavender flowers. A dress I've never seen her wear before. Naser Davani sits in front of their room with his sickly child on his lap, talking to him. Hajar is still overwhelmed by the whole thing. Using the tips of her fingers, she keeps smoothing the fabric creases beneath her breasts. Naser Davani's gaze follows Hajar's big buttocks, which are tightly shaped in her new dress and sway as she walks.

"Oussa Naser!" It is Father's voice again. "How's business in Kuwait? . . . I mean . . . for blacksmiths."

"It's not all that bad. But I have to say, it's very hot. I mean, the weather."

The cup of tea in front of Father has grown cold.

"You mean it's even hotter than here?" Father asks.

"Here? . . . Here is heaven. Delightful heaven."

Summer is taking its last breaths. Around sunset, the heat goes down a notch or two. The wind coming from the north lessens the sultry air and humidity. The gentle breeze blowing over the Karun brings cool air with it. Khaj Tofiq looks subdued; he's puffing on his opium pipe. Rahim the Donkey Keeper is sitting next to his wife. Bolur Khanom is busy arranging Aman Aqa's special snack plate. Banu is dozing off. Amu Bandar has begun his evening prayers. Sanam is sitting in front of her room, sewing; Karam Ali's pants always get ripped at the knees. "I don't know how," Sanam mumbles, "but that rascal's knees sure have teeth in 'em."

Afaq reclines against kilim-covered cushions and smokes a cigarette. I have never seen her smoke before. As she awkwardly blows out the smoke, she complains to Khaj Tofiq. "You've become entirely housebound."

Khaj Tofiq heats up his pipe. Without looking up, he keeps on rolling the soft bits of a piece of opium into a tiny ball.

"At least you used to leave the house and wrap up a couple of deals or so in the market, earning a few tomans here and there . . ."

Khaj Tofiq scratches his nose.

". . . As if I have a man who takes care of me," Afaq says sarcastically.

Khaj Tofiq lights a cigarette, ignoring Afaq's words.

Naser Davani suddenly moves his child off his lap, gets up, and disappears into his room.

My father has not yet touched his cup of tea.

"The tea's gone ice cold," Mother tells him.

Father pulls *Qasemi's Secrets* closer, bends over it, and turns the pages. He pauses over several pages in particular for a few seconds, glances over them, and then goes on. Naser Davani, holding a transistor radio, comes out of the room. He sits down and plays with it. Suddenly, someone starts singing:

Your scorpion-like lock of hair is in position with the moon
Such is our fate as long as the moon stays for a brief moment in
the House of Scorpio

Father lifts up his head from *Qasemi's Secrets*, turns his gaze to Oussa Naser, closes the book, puts it aside, and leans against the wall.

Father's hand is searching for his pack of cigarettes.

∾

"Pendar is truly grateful to you," Shafaq says. "Even so, he is still in trouble."

"In trouble?"

"He's been taken to prison."

What I really want to know is why, but he keeps dodging the issue. I don't make out much from what he's telling me. "Well, they found newspapers in his pockets; I mean, what I'm trying to say is . . . they didn't just arrest him for no reason."

"But what's wrong with having a newspaper?"

"Exactly, but . . . ," he starts to explain.

He looks me in the eye as he talks. I like the sound of his voice. He speaks in a clear and dignified manner that would render anyone spellbound, even if he were to speak gibberish.

"Can you read?" he asks.

"I went to school up to the fourth grade."

"Why did you stop?"

I tell him why.

"What does your father do for a living?"

I tell him what he does.

He puts his hand on my shoulder. "Drop by anytime you feel like reading. I've got interesting fiction books."

All the shelves inside Shafaq's bookstore are stuffed with books, and that's just the front; he has plenty more of them in the back of the store.

Shafaq sells newspapers too. I noticed that the last time I went to see him. Yet it seems that the sort of newspapers he sells are rather different from other kinds; and it also occurs to me that he doesn't sell them to just anyone who comes to the store.

"Has the new edition of *The Nahjolbalagheh* arrived yet?" someone asks, and Peyman, bending down and reaching under the table, retrieves a bunch of old shredded papers piled up on each other, pulls out a newspaper from within, folds it, and hands it to the customer. Even the color and print of these newspapers are different from all the others I have seen.

Maybe I'll go and see Shafaq again tomorrow, and maybe I'll borrow some storybooks too.

I go and feed my pigeons. It's been a week since I last let them out to fly. This morning, when Father was getting ready to go to his shop, I feigned a stomachache so that I wouldn't have to go with him. I get bored there in the shop, and I have to put up with Father's impatience and ill-mannered way of doing things. It's impossible to talk to him. Wearing his leather apron, his sleeves all rolled up to his elbows, he sits in the doorway of his shop and smokes the day away. "If I could only change my profession, things might get better," he keeps saying.

He has consulted with Mirza Nasrollah: "All day long, I sit in a shop empty of customers and let out sighs of sorrow; do you suggest I consider a new line of business, perhaps?"

He has sought Hajj Sheikh Ali's advice too. "Bad luck; my horoscope reading didn't predict a good outcome either. I'm afraid I might lose this shop, and everything else too."

Ebrahim comes and sits beside me. The henna-colored pigeon mated with the specially trained male. The white-tail's chicks are all grown up. I may let them fly next week. Ebrahim mumbles something before he talks about the pigeons. Then he starts to mumble again. It seems like he wants to say something, but he's hesitant. Finally he throws caution to the wind. "Look, Khaled. I want to tell you something."

I'm not paying much attention to him. The black male, fanning his tail open, circles around his mate and coos. He sweeps his tail on the ground and fluffs the feathers on his neck.

"But you have to promise that it will stay only between the two of us."

I look at him.

He talks about Banu. ". . . We stayed so long under the water, till we lost our breath."

His eyes sparkle. His mouth begins to water. I remember Banu's words: "Hey, not bad, you and Bolur Khanom are really cozy now, aren't you?" She said this as she blocked my way to the staircase. When she talks, her yellow teeth make me want to vomit.

"Hey, the other day, on the roof, I saw what the two of you were up to."

Now I get it. For sure Banu doesn't know a thing. Bolur Khanom and I didn't do anything on the roof that would have made Banu suspicious. Last week, when I was flying my pigeons, she came and stood next to me, and we just talked. "Khaled! Aman Aqa's not coming home tonight."

"So!"

"I'll wait for you at midnight."

That's all we said.

Banu is just bluffing. Had she ever seen us, even once, she would have been outraged, exposing us without thinking twice. She can't imagine, not even in her dreams, that I have set foot in Bolur Khanom's room, let alone made out with her more than ten times already.

"I know everything."

Banu's pale face makes me anxious.

"What are you trying to say, Banu?"

"If you come into the pool with me this afternoon, I'll let it be."

She makes me sick, this Banu. The bones of her hips stick out like the bones of a dying mule's rump. Her thighs are fleshless and dry, her sagging breasts are like those of a cat that has just fed its kittens, hanging from her chest.

"What if I don't?"

"Then I'll tell everyone that you and Bolur Khanom . . ."

I get pissed. I look her straight in the eye. I feel the veins in my neck swelling up. "You'd say me and Bolur Khanom what?"

"I mean . . . that day on the roof . . ."

I take a step toward her. "Is talking to Bolur Khanom a sin?" I say this with such force she takes a step back. I don't budge. She didn't see this coming.

Ebrahim's mouth is watering. "We've been doing it every day. Well, not every day . . . I mean, whenever there's a chance . . . but, Khaled, don't you ever tell this to anyone."

I roll a moistened piece of cloth into a ball and hurl it at the feet of the pigeons. It makes them fly over and settle down on the parapet of the roof. I climb up the stairs. Ebrahim comes along. Once on the roof, he again insists that I not tell anyone about what's going on between him and Banu. I face him. "Look, Ebram," and I tap his chest with my finger, "I don't care to hear any of this . . . besides, if you're so afraid, why do you tell me these things in the first place?"

He steps back and plays dumb. "If you want, I can tell Banu that you also—"

I interrupt him quickly, "No, Ebram, I don't want that."

I walk toward the pigeons.

He follows me. "But you don't know how good it feels."

I ignore him. The sound of my whistling scares the pigeons away. They fly off, circle around the house a few times, and then little by little soar higher.

The sky is blue. It's very clear. Full of sunshine. No sign of dust is to be seen anywhere. Not even a cloud. The sun is gentle too. My gaze soars with the pigeons.

Ebrahim calls me, "Khaled, look!"

I look down. Wearing a small headscarf, Bolur Khanom sweeps the porch in front of her room. The way she moves, you can see her slip, the same black tulle slip. Blood rushes to my face.

"Wasn't it you, Ebram, who used to say that adultery is a sin?"

Ebrahim smiles. His broken, twisted teeth show. "Come on, man . . . it's all a bunch of baloney," he says.

He stares at Bolur Khanom's white, fleshy thighs. The crotch of his black pants bulges. He squeezes his thigh. I grab his arm. "Ebram, shame on you." My voice sounds muffled and coarse.

"You're so dumb . . . isn't it such a waste not to peek at those white thighs?"

I can't stand it anymore. I grab his collar and push him away from the edge of the roof.

He gets upset. "Why're you doing this, Khaled?"

"Go ahead and look, and I'll tell everyone what's going on between you and Banu."

"But we're friends, aren't we?" he says remorsefully.

"All right, we're friends . . . but I don't like you to stare at Bolur Khanom with those wicked eyes of yours."

He steps back, smiles, and in a low voice says, "So it's true what Banu says, that something's going on between you and Bolur Khanom! Huh?"

I dart toward him, grab his collar again, and glare into his eyes. "Banu is a filthy liar."

"Ooh . . . oh . . . oh . . ."

"And you. If you play that shit with me again, I'll kick your ass."

Ebrahim is older than me, but there's no way he can beat me up. His arms are as thin as a water pipe stick. His neck is so thin that it makes me wonder how it can hold up that big head of his with all that hair on it. The crotch of Ebrahim's black pants always hangs so low and loose that the elastic cords holding them up dangle around as he walks.

Omid comes up the stairs, panting, "Khaled, Gholam Ali Khan is moving out."

Ever since that day Aman Aqa promised on my behalf that I would not show up around Gholam Ali Khan's house again, whenever I have to pass by the abandoned building, I take a different path, so to avoid being around his house. Not that I'm scared of Gholam Ali Khan, no. I do it out of respect for Aman Aqa, who gave his word of honor on my behalf. I don't know why, but each day I feel more ashamed of myself around Aman Aqa. There are times now when I can't even bring myself to look him in the face. I don't even go to his teahouse anymore to listen to the gramophone. Aman Aqa loves me like a son. Since he can't father any children, he buys me things now and then. "Come over here, Son . . . A peddler came to the teahouse today . . . I bought you these red socks . . . They're nice, aren't they?"

I'm so ashamed of myself.

"Come, Khaled, and see if these *giveh* shoes fit you."

I look down and take the shoes.

The red socks are still in the blanket chest in the back closet. I have kept them to wear on Nowruz.

"Now everything's all right, huh?" Ebrahim is flattering me.

"What do you mean by 'now everything's all right'?"

"I mean, now that Gholam Ali Khan is moving out of the neighborhood."

I put my hand on his shoulder, and in a scolding tone, say to him for the first time, "But, Ebram, it was you who broke the window, don't you remember?"

Ebrahim drops his head down and doesn't say a word.

~

Naser Davani is talking to Father. He's not annoyed like he was the night he
returned from Kuwait; he's even a bit of a chatterer this evening. "When
you get there," he tells my father, "first thing you gotta do is go to the
teahouse on the bank of the river Shat. I mean behind the fish market . . .
You know where it is? . . . Never mind, even if you don't know, ask anyone
and they'll show it to you. It's as famous as the Hindus' sacred cow . . . All
kinds of dealers and smugglers hang around the teahouse. That's all they
do; it's their business, finding passengers. For the boat fare, they'll charge
you three hundred tomans, and another hundred for their commission.
That is, if it hasn't gone up since last year . . . but you know what, Oussa
Haddad, one should be sharp and clever. Quick and careful too. You never
know, they might take you to an island in the middle of the sea and leave
you there, to the mercy of God. And of course, you don't see it coming.
They tell you if you walk for ten minutes in the direction of kiblah, you'll
reach Kuwait. And how would you know that? And you walk, and walk,
and walk till you drop to your knees, and it's then that you realize that
you've been hoodwinked. You realize that they have stranded you in a
place where there's no water, no people, and no help . . . They've done it
a hundred times. Do you remember Hamid, the one-armed lad? Do you
remember what the newspapers said about what happened to him?"

Naser Davani crosses one leg over the other. He swirls a teaspoon in
his cup of tea and then twists the pipe's soft reed around the water pipe's
base, calling out to the teahouse manager, "Morshed, tell your boys to get
me another water pipe."

The sound of dominoes hitting the table fills Morshed's tiny
teahouse. The sun is creeping closer, leaving only the sidewalk in the
shade. My father sits on one of the teahouse's benches. I sit next to him.
The voices are jumbled up.

"I am sure you have found a job, isn't that so?"

"Yeah, but it's out of town . . . a few miles away."

"What are they building?"

"I guess a police station."

The teahouse manager pulls the sunshade open. The shade extends
to the curb along the street. Naser Davani carries on, "Once the number
of boat passengers reaches full capacity, then you set off at night in a

truck for Gasbeh. From there, you need to go on foot, at least for a good two hours . . . on foot all the way up to the end of the estuary. Then, God willing, and if there's no bullying guard around, you'll board the boat. The sails are hoisted, and they set sail . . . but, Oussa Haddad, God forbid if the gendarmes show up. One should act real fast so as not to fall into their hands, because the dealers never take any responsibility. They abandon you in that vast estuary to the mercy of God, and they themselves take off. They know of so many hideouts, while we can never find our way into one . . ."

Morshed sets the water pipe in front of Naser Davani. He takes a deep drag, scratches the hump on his nose, and continues with his chatting. "God Forbid, the gendarmes might even shoot at you."

As he rolls a cigarette, my father's lips are closed just like melted lead. His attention is completely focused on Naser Davani and his words.

". . . And that's when you'll hear bang, bang, whiz, whiz. They hunt people down like ducks. Now bring a donkey, as they say, and load up trouble. Just imagine, you are gunned down, blood is gushing out your body like water out of a spout, and you're in that endless estuary, in complete darkness; and you're like a blind man, and you have no idea where to run to . . ."

Naser Davani pauses for a breath, then continues, "You know what, Oussa Haddad, that's the bad part of it. All the trouble is in crossing the border. Other than that, once you get to Kuwait, you can be sure that there's always plenty of work . . . any kind of work."

The tall young man standing next to me, wearing a keffiyeh on his head, and the middle-aged man beside him make a wager on the next car they see driving by.

"For what?"

"For two small cups of tea."

"All right. Got it."

"Vauxhall?"

"Which one?"

"The third one."

The third car that passes in front of the teahouse is an Opel. The tall young man raises his voice, "Morshed, two small teas on Baba Khan's bill."

Now Naser Davani is bragging: "When I got there, I had a job not even halfway into the day. One must be sharp and quick. Mr. Sahib liked me. You know why? Because I know the Farangis' tongue. I picked it up when I was in the air force. I'm talking about the twentieth of Shahrivar, the last month of summer . . ."

He takes another drag from the water pipe and plays with the smoke. "As soon as I got there, I went to the Ahmadi District. I told Sahib, '*I mason*,' in English, letting him know I am a bricklayer. He smiled, slapped me on the nape of my neck, and had them hire me. All of 'em are like that. When they like someone, they slap him on the neck. Soon I learned how to butter them up."

He picks up the top of the water pipe and blows on it, shifting the half-lit charcoals. "Twenty-five rupees a day." He looks at my father.

"Go for it," says Baba Khan.

"For what?" the tall young man asks.

"For a water pipe," says Baba Khan this time.

"Name it," the tall young man says.

"A passenger sedan."

"What number?"

"The seventh."

Naser Davani still looks at Father. "Each rupee is equal to eighteen rials."

An elderly, hunchbacked man is sitting on the other side of Naser Davani. Facing him is a small-framed man. They're playing matches with one another.

"Morshed!"

Morshed is sullen. "Spit it out."

"Give me two large teas on Yadolla Rumzi's bill."

Morshed's tone is anything but gentle as he asks, "How many will that make?"

Yadolla Rumzi sneers. He forces a smile and says, "That'll make it twenty-two cups of tea plus three water pipes."

Morshed scratches his bald head and grunts, "How many did you say?"

Yadolla Rumzi is not sure. "Twenty-two."

"Twenty-four," Morshed corrects him.

"No, by your life, it's twenty-two," retorts Yadolla Rumzi.

Morshed slaps Yadolla Rumzi's hump and curses him. "By your own fucking life . . . as if the bastard had breast-fed me!"

Yadolla Rumzi tosses the matchbox onto the table and shuts up. The voices are jumbled. The clicks of the dominoes and the clings of the cups and saucers are all mixed up. The rotten smell of the curbside sewage suddenly sweeps through the air. A herd of sheep passing by the teahouse has stirred the slime. Naser Davani rambles on. His talk stinks of bragging. "Two months passed, and I told Sahib, '*I good mason*.' I told him, '*Twenty-five very kam . . . tirty rupee hast lazem*.' He really liked what I said to him. You don't get what I told him? I told him I'm a master and an expert at what I'm doing. My work is worth more than twenty-five rupees. You should ask your man to give me thirty rupees . . ."

My father doesn't seem to be listening to what Naser Davani is saying. Deep in thought, he reclines further on the bench. His hand searches in the large pocket of his jacket and brings out the West End watch wrapped in a handkerchief. It's been more than two years since he bought that watch. He's been taking care of it as if he were caring for his own eyes; never allows even a bit of dust to sit on it.

I can't believe what a windbag Naser Davani has turned out to be. All my father asked him was, "Oussa Naser, how could one get to Kuwait?"

He won't drop it. He takes drag after drag from that water pipe, babbling away. He has even burned out the tobacco of his second water pipe. He scratches the hump on his nose and goes on, "You know what Sahib did after I told him *tirty rupee hast lazem*? . . . He laughed again and had his men increase my wages."

He takes something that looks like a notebook out of his jacket pocket. The notebook has a lead stamp seal. "Praise God, the day before yesterday I bought a piece of land, around a hundred square meters. Now I want to take out a small loan from the bank and raise a four-wall, build a house, you know, to free myself from renting places here and there. It wouldn't cost me much . . . I mean, building the walls . . . You know, Oussa Haddad, one should be mindful of his own life and work."

My father is still deep in thought. I doubt he even realizes I'm sitting next to him. "Morshed, a cup of tea," he says. Then he shifts a bit and looks at me. "Morshed, make it two."

Naser Davani twists the soft pipe reed around the base of the water pipe and rises to his feet. Before he leaves, he stands in front of Father and says, "Well, Oussa Haddad, if you want, I can tell you more tonight about what you should do once you're in Kuwait." With that, he takes off.

Gholam the Drowsy walks in. His lower lip sags. His hair looks like an old piece of white felt. Dark, bulging veins run down his long neck. By the time he tosses a bit of *shireh*, opium residue, in his mouth and washes it down with a few gulps of tea, my father has taken out his watch a few more times, looked at it, and wrapped it again in his handkerchief.

Gholam the Drowsy sips his cup of tea, savoring the opium in his mouth.

Father tucks his right leg underneath him and faces Gholam, asking, "Gholam, do you have any West End watches?"

Gholam's clammy eyelashes part. "Black face or white?" he asks through his nose.

"Black face."

Gholam barely has any energy to talk. "Have 'em," he says as he comes and sits where Naser Davani was sitting a minute ago. He rolls up the loose-fitting sleeve of his shirt and takes off a black-faced West End watch from among the various watches he has on his wrist. Its face has turned brown with age. Gholam hands it to Father. "It works perfectly."

I'm certain that Father wants to sell his watch. My stomach churns. My father's faint voice pushes through the past and comes to me. His voice, accompanied by the familiar happiness that brings joy to his eyes, lands on my ears. "Khaled," he tells me, "go on and get that watch in my pocket."

I take the watch out of the handkerchief and give it to Father.

"Bring me some cotton balls."

From behind the mirror, I retrieve the bag of cotton balls and put it in front of him.

"Do we have any white petrol?"

Father's poignant tone pulls me out of my memories. "But . . . this . . . this is . . ."

I look at my father. His face has turned pale. As he measures up the worth of Gholam the Drowsy's watch, Father's gaze stays fixed on its aged surface. My eyes wander to Gholam's sagging lips. I hear Father's low voice, "But . . . this one is old, Gholam."

Gholam becomes annoyed. He forces his words out. "Good man! What difference does it make, for a West End watch, new or old, lasts forever?"

Father looks at the back of the watch; its plate is worn. "Well, then, how much?"

Gholam squats on the teahouse bench. "Hey, look, are you seriously considering it or you just want to fool around?"

I have never seen Father mess with anyone. He only speaks when it is necessary, and only asks for something when he is really in need of it. He presses his lips together. His Adam's apple moves up and down. He swallows his saliva and keeps quiet.

Gholam's drowsy voice is like a titmouse's chirping. "Morshed, get me a cup of strong tea with sugar cubes."

"You didn't answer, Gholam," my father says. He sounds dejected.

Gholam sniffs his runny nose. "For you, and only for you—because I really like you—a hundred and fifty tomans."

Father gazes at Gholam's smudged, protruding cheekbones.

Gholam shifts in his seat. "I knew you were not serious."

"For the same model," Father says, "and if it were like new, how much would you pay to buy it?" His voice has a tremor in it.

Gholam's clammy eyelashes hardly move. "It seems you're well-off."

"I have no intention of joking around," says Father.

"Hey, man, seems like your stomach is full, and you're really in the mood to amuse yourself," Gholam says, as he slowly drags his feet, gets down off the bench, and takes the cup of tea from Morshed.

"To be honest, Gholam, I want to sell my watch. Here it is," Father finally says.

I look at Father's eyes; so lifeless. I think this is the first time I've seen such agony in my father's eyes. Perhaps this is the first time I've realized how much Father really loves his watch.

Gholam sips his tea. "Well, if it's the same model, seventy tomans, and that's only because I'm fond of you."

Father is astonished. His face is completely white. His hand, which is holding out the watch to Gholam, drops. His words turn into a mumble in his throat. "A bit of fairness would be a good practice too, you know? Good man, what you're offering is even less than half the price!"

Gholam is not in a good mood. He sneezes, and sniffs his runny nose. He is not in the mood for talking at all. The opium hasn't taken effect yet. His eyelids are almost shut. His nose is clogged. "Brother, I need to eat and smoke my opium too. It's not like I'm a Farangi, or own a watch factory. And it's not like I'm selling a watch every day."

Father's fingers are fidgeting. He unties the knot of the handkerchief from the steel band of the watch, and weighs it for a few moments. Then he hands it to Gholam. Father's hand is shaking. I have never seen his hands tremble. Can a hand that hammers iron soft get a shaking palsy like that?

"Look, Gholam! Look at it carefully! It's perfect. And I have taken care of it as if it were my very own eyes. It doesn't move slow or fast, not even a second off in the entire twenty-four hours of a day."

Gholam eyes the watch. "It's not all like what you say."

"I even guarantee it for a year," Father assures him.

Gholam puts the watch on the table. "Same price." His voice has new life. The opium has begun to work its way through his body. "Brother, what do I even need another watch for? I've got so many of them already . . ."

Gholam shows his wrist, which is covered with more than ten different models of watches. "Even if I manage to sell these, it'd be a real feat."

He moves to walk away.

Father grabs his hand. "If you pay me a hundred, it'd be a deal."

"Same price."

"Is that the best price you can do?"

"Now that you're such a nice man, I'll pay you eighty tomans, and no more bargaining."

The deal goes through.

Father brings out his suitcase and props it in front of his room. He puts his wrapped bundle of bedding and clothes on top of it. He bends and kisses me on the forehead and cheeks. I feel the roughness of his calloused hands on my cheeks. He hugs Jamileh, kisses her cheeks, and caresses her soft hair. With Jamileh still in his arms, he says to Mother, "Take good care of the children!"

Then he faces me. "Till I come back from Kuwait, go and work for Aman Aqa. He has given his word to pay you too. All you need to do is help him with his chores."

He kisses Jamileh's cheeks again, smells her hair, and puts her down. He said his farewells to the neighbors the night before. Squatting down on the threshold of his room, Amu Bandar makes his ablutions. The sun has not come up yet. There is still a gray darkness. The weather is sort of chilly. The donkeys are making noise under the sunshade. The roar of an oil train pulling into the station comes from a distance. Its sound rises and falls. Father lifts up the suitcase from the ground. At the house doors, he puts down the suitcase and his bundle and kisses Amu Bandar good-bye.

"God protect you, Oussa Haddad."

Father lifts up his suitcase and bundle again and heads out of the house. Mother reminds him to write us a line as soon as he arrives. I walk him to the end of the alleyway. He kisses my cheek again. I look at his eyes. They've welled up with tears. I hear Habib the Baker wishing him luck.

2

"Khaled, go to the butchers' market and buy a piece of sheep's stomach."

Mother makes such a delicious tripe soup that you would want to eat your fingers with it too.

It is Friday morning. The sun is up. I have arranged with Aman Aqa to take Fridays off. He's not against it. He lets me come to the teahouse whenever I feel like it, and if I don't, that's all right by him too.

Along with Ebrahim, I hit the alleyways and backstreets. This is the shortcut we use whenever we want to get to the butchers' market faster, though we'd rather take the longer way, so we can pass through the town's main square. There are always tons of exciting things to see. For instance, the con artists who play a sleight-of-hand game with cards. Now I know what tricks they have up their sleeves. They distract villagers coming to town and swindle them out of their money. "The blank card for me, the card with the black mark for you; if you spot it, you win. One toman against five tomans."

Reza Kermanshahi quickly spreads the cards on the ground and Ahmad the Tarantula coaxes the villagers into playing. In the blink of an eye, their pockets are empty, and Reza Kermanshahi and Ahmad the Tarantula are nowhere to be found.

Then there are those who play tricks on people using a belt. No matter how clever you are, you can't ever find the way the belt is folded. You are always tricked. The pencil you think you have placed in the fold of the belt somehow gets lost. The storytellers with their large canvas portrait shows are especially amusing to see. Mokhtar takes complete vengeance on the murderers of Karbala. You know, an eye for an eye, serving justice!

By the time we reach the square, the sun has already spread everywhere. It's such a treat for my eyes; they take such pleasure in the color of sunshine.

Jalil Kuwaiti has caught a fish again. I don't think you can find a fish as big as this one in the whole entire world. I mean, where can you find a fish whose tail and head still drag on the ground after it has been mounted on a mule?

Jalil Kuwaiti puts one shoulder under the fish's tail and pushes hard. The fish topples down headfirst off the back of the mule. A large butcher knife in hand, Jalil gets to work cutting the animal. No one can beat him when it comes to catching a *narbach*. That's a large fish, sometimes even up to fifty kilos. No one is as persistent as he is; if he decides to, he can wait on the bank of the Karun for a week for the right moment to catch the fish he's looking for. And what's even more fascinating is to see him pulling a *narbach* out of the water. You should play around with it for a while and keep loosening the line till the fish really tires out.

Jalil Kuwaiti has yet to cut the fish open when the square becomes strangely crowded. From all five streets leading to the square, all kinds of different people begin to converge together.

"What's going on, Ebram?"

Ebrahim is squeaking like a gopher. "How should I know what's going on?"

In the blink of an eye, the square is crammed with people from different walks of life: old, young, in work clothes, in clean ones, in grease-smudged overalls; and among them, there are several women and girls without hijabs.

I am astonished to see so many people all at once, filling up the square. Quickly, I move back and climb on the wide, barrel-shaped veranda of a house that has not yet been demolished so that a shop can be built in its place.

Ebrahim too pulls himself up and stands beside me. Both of us look on, our mouths agape. There is a hubbub of voices. The crowd gets denser as more people continue to pour into the square from all directions. Suddenly, a broad-shouldered young man of medium height climbs onto the shoulders of a few others and begins to speak. For a second, I catch sight of Shafaq making for the middle of the square through the crowd. But I lose sight of him, and no matter how hard I try, stretching my neck, I can't spot him again. I have never seen such a large crowd anywhere, except for maybe occasionally on the mourning days of Tasu'a and Ashura, but even then it's not this crowded. It looks as if the young man is about to sing mourning elegies, but I know that today is not a holy day, nor a commemoration of any of the Imams' martyrdoms or deaths. If it were, the first thing my mother would have done this morning is dress herself in black, which she did not do today.

I hear the broad-shouldered young man's voice. But I can't make out what he's saying. Every now and then, the crowd shouts, "That's right!" Suddenly, I see the air filled with tons of colorful papers, stacks of papers, each the size of the palm of my hand. I want to jump off the veranda and pick up a couple of them, but in such a crowd it's out of the question. A bit further away from the veranda, another stack of papers is scattered into the air. And then another stack. Is it Peyman who's scattering the papers? I call out to him, but he doesn't hear me.

"Do you know him?" Ebrahim asks.

"Yeah, man . . . he works in a bookstore."

Peyman disappears into the crowd. The young man of medium height is still talking. Then, suddenly, he jumps off the shoulders of the people carrying him.

The way everyone converged in the square was amazing, but boy, even more astonishing is the way they disappear all at once! Before I can even figure out who they are and what they have gathered around for, they disappear from the square. Then I notice a group of policemen, wielding clubs in their hands, running up Kalantari Street toward the square.

I don't hesitate. Before the policemen reach the square, I jump off the veranda, run to the middle of the square, and pick up a few papers—and good thing I do that, because as soon as they enter the square, they hurry to pick up all the papers lying on the street, and snatch the rest out of the hands of whoever is still holding on to them. My curiosity has gotten the best of me. I can't wait to find out what's going on. I fold the papers and hide them under my shirt, and together with Ebrahim walk in the direction of Jalil Kuwaiti, who is just about to cut the fish open. After grinding a knife with a sharpener, he pokes the tip of it into the belly of the fish.

A policeman walks by, glaring at us. I am so frightened, worried that he might have seen me hide the papers under my shirt.

The policemen collect all the papers and disperse, running down the streets.

It dawns on me that I have to go and buy tripe. I know if I don't hurry I'll miss it, because tripe is so delicious that it sells out really quickly, faster than the sheep's heart, kidneys, liver, and tender meat.

"Come on, let's go, Ebram!"

So we run on.

We are almost out of breath by the time we get home. I give the tripe to Mother. I'm still anxious to figure out what those people were up to. I can't wait to find out what it is written on the papers that caused the policemen to snatch them out of people's hands.

I go into Father's room and draw the curtain, covering the opening. Ebrahim and Jamileh sit opposite me. The writing on all the papers is the same. I can't make any sense of it. Eventually I am able to spell out a word and read it, but I can't understand what it means. For instance, I can't figure out what kind of a beast this "bloodthirsty exploiter" is that feeds only on blood and has an appetite that is insatiable. I am sure there must be a reason for calling this exploiter "bloodthirsty." There's got to be a reason.

Ebrahim says, "There must be something going on that made people talk."

I manage to grasp a few things about this beast. For instance, I'm beginning to comprehend that it also sucks oil sometimes instead of blood; that clues me in as to why on some of the papers, instead of "bloodthirsty," it's also described as "oil-thirsty."

"It's better to suck oil than blood," Ebrahim says, blinking his ever-clammy eyelashes.

He believes that if this beast indeed craves human blood, it must be really horrifying. I dart a glance at him. He has such a sallow complexion, as if he's rubbed a paste of water and turmeric onto his face and neck.

"No, Ebram, it's not just that, there must be other things that we don't understand," I say.

Ebrahim asks me to read it once more. I struggle to read it again. Ebrahim's head weighs down his thin neck. His eyes are watery. Ebrahim and I wonder about the words I misread. We have never heard such things. My sister keeps very quiet, looking at us, listening with such wonder to what we say. Ebrahim gets excited. "I got it! I know what's going on."

Amazed, I look at him. "You figured it out?"

"Yep."

"Then tell me how."

He mumbles something but fails to say even a single clear word. He hasn't figured out anything. He just thinks he has. I am about to rip up the papers and throw them away when my sister says, "No, Dadash Khaled, don't rip them up. Make me a kite out of them."

That's an idea. I can make two good kites with them and then run them up into the belly of the sky.

I get up and ransack the odds and ends behind the mirror in search of glue. I find some. Grabbing Mother's scissors, I sit down to make my sister a kite.

At night I usually get a ride home on the back of Aman Aqa's Riley bike. Sometimes I go home on foot before Aman Aqa takes off. If this were a few years back, I'd grab ahold of a moving carriage or car, and ride home in the back of it. But now I feel embarrassed to do that.

For lunch, Aman Aqa ordered us kebab. He wrapped up my share of kebab in a piece of bread and gave it to me before sitting down with Mashti Iceman and Jan Mohammad to eat. I ate half of my greasy bread wrap and saved the other half for Jamileh.

Today I walked home.

"Jamileh, come here! I have brought you kebab."

I take the bread-wrapped kebab out of the piece of newspaper. It has gone cold and grease has congealed on it. The weather is growing colder. Mother looks at me, suspicious. I tell her how I got the kebab.

Jamileh and I warm up the kebab on the kerosene burner and then go into Father's room and sit there to eat.

Mother is busy; she has piles of clothes all around her as she sorts through our warm clothes so she can mend them. It's halfway into autumn. Jamileh will be nine years old at the end of this winter. I pull the dividing curtain aside, allowing the light of the kerosene lamp to reach Father's room. When Father was here, he used the propane lamp in his room so that he could read the prayer books *Anvar*, *Johari*, or *Qasemi's Secrets*, for instance. We would light the kerosene lantern. With him gone now, one lamp is enough for all of us. We sit down on Father's special rug and cover our legs with a blanket. Jamileh takes a morsel of the kebab wrap. She offers a piece to me too. "Eat, Dadash!"

"No, Jamileh. That's your share. I ate mine for lunch."

"Well, I ate lamb stew with rice and chickpeas for lunch too."

My eyes become wide with surprise. "*Chelo khoresh?*"

For the past twenty days, ever since Father had to leave for Kuwait because business had grown stagnant, we haven't had anything other than boiled egg stew or *kachi*, a sweet paste made of flour, sugar, and vegetable oil, or sometimes maybe sheep tripe. Usually for breakfast we have plain bread and tea.

"Where did you eat *chelo khoresh*, Jamileh?"

Jamileh puts the tip of her finger on her nose.

"Shhh, Dadash Khaled . . . Mother will hear us."

I don't exactly understand what she says. "But why shouldn't Mother hear that you had *chelo khoresh* today?"

Jamileh's voice is so low I can barely hear her, "She was there too. She saw it."

"So why does Mother—"

"She asked me not to tell you," she interrupts me quickly.

"But, Jamileh, where did you have *chelo khoresh*? Why do you have to keep it from me?"

"At the house of the chief of the barracks," says Jamileh, swallowing her bite.

I gaze at her. She looks rather guilty. Mother has asked her not to mention anything. But Jamileh's tiny heart is not capable of keeping secrets from me.

"This morning, right after you left with Aman Aqa for the teahouse, me and Mother went to the house of the chief . . . on Timsar Street."

"Why did you go there, Jamileh?"

"We went there so Mother could wash their bedsheets."

My mouth is agape. I can see Mother through the narrow gap of the curtain dividing the two rooms. I look at her. Sitting beside the oil lamp, she stitches something. A lock of hair has fallen over her cheek. I can still see a trace of youth in her face, but her cheeks look flaccid. The light from the oil lamp casts her profile in shadow. Her bottom lip is drawn. There's a slight furrow in her brow. Her eyes are barely visible, hollowed out and shadowed.

I hear her singing soothingly,

> *If I knew that my fate would be like this,*
> *I would've drunk poison instead of my mother's milk.*

It's not the first time I've heard her sing this heartfelt folk song. But it's the first time that her singing has sounded so heart wrenching. On the fifth day after Father left for Kuwait, Mother put her precious copper pot under her chador, went to the coppersmiths' market, and sold it. For a few days we could afford to drink tea with caramelized candy and eat boiled egg stew and *kachi*.

The water in the kettle is boiling. I watch Mother pour it into the teapot. She loves tea more than anything else. She can't go a day without it. "It makes your tiredness go away," she always says, or, "It opens your eyes."

She lowers the flame of the kerosene three-burner heater and sets the teapot on it.

"Say, Jamileh, how long did you stay there?"

"Till sundown, Dadash Khaled. You wouldn't believe how many bedsheets were there," she says, stretching her arms open as far as she can, "tons of them."

Mother brings the cup of tea to her lips. Under the yellow light of the oil lamp, her hands look awfully white. They look wrinkled and swollen.

"And then at lunchtime they gave you *chelo khoresh*, huh, Jamileh?"

"Their servant gave it to us . . . but Mother didn't eat it. She lied and said that she's fasting. She said she'd taken a vow to fast on Mondays."

I move to drag myself out from under the blanket.

Jamileh grabs my wrist. "Where're you going, Dadash Khaled?"

"Nowhere in particular."

"Don't you tell Mother that I told you." She has stopped chewing the morsel of food in her mouth. "Please, you mustn't tell her . . . she'll punish me." My sister is begging me with her eyes.

I sit back down. "I won't. But tell me what you were doing there?"

"Nothing, Dadash Khaled. I just sat next to Mother and watched her. I sat there so long that my legs started to hurt . . . but you know what, Dadash?"

"What?"

"When the chief's wife came to see how Mother was doing washing the bedsheets, she took a look at me, then she went and came back with a red dress. It was a bit too big for me, but she gave it to Mother and said, 'Put this on your daughter!'"

"She took it?"

"No, Dadash."

"What happened then?"

"Mother just smiled and said, 'I appreciate it, madam,' but then lied and told her, 'but I've taken a vow not to have my daughter dress in red till she's ten years old.'"

"Then what?"

"The chief of the barracks' wife frowned, picked up the dress, and left without saying a word."

Jamileh has finished eating the bread and kebab. Her eyelids are already heavy with sleep. Her voice too sounds sleepy.

"But, Dadash Khaled, don't you tell Mother that I told you about all this, all right?"

Jamileh slides into her bedroll and lies down. Soon her breathing becomes a soft snore. With my wrist still in her hand, her fingers begin to go limp. I pull the blanket up to her chin, get up, and go sit next to the three-burner heater.

"Do you want some tea?" Mother asks.

"I do, Mother."

She pours me a cup. I look at her as I take the cup from her hand. For a few seconds, our eyes stay fixed on each other. Mother lowers her head. "What is it, Khaled?"

"Where were you today, Mother?" my voice trembles.

Mother's hands stop mending. With her head still lowered, she says, "Jamileh told you?"

"Who took you there?"

"I myself asked around to find a job."

"Well, but who found it for you?"

"What difference does it make?"

"I just want to know."

Mother's hands start moving again. "Gholam, Aunt Ra'na's son."

I am beside myself with rage. "Aunt Ra'na's son!"

"I didn't do anything wrong, dear," Mother's voice softens. "It's not like I begged for money. Besides, there's no shame in working. Until your father sends us some money, we have to somehow make ends meet."

I put down the cup of tea, feeling all choked up. "You should've waited a few more days for Aman Aqa to pay me . . . I would've given you all of it."

Mother's eyes light up. She puts my winter jacket down, takes my hand, and draws me to her.

I lay my head on her chest. She kisses me on the forehead. Her heartbeat fills my ears. Two teardrops fall down on my cheeks, one after the other. I take Mother's hand and bring it to my cheek. Her hand is wrinkled from having spent too much time in water. The scent of soap on her hands is pleasant.

Aman Aqa's teahouse is located at the harbor intersection.

All kinds of people hang out at Aman Aqa's teahouse. For instance, you can always find workers from the pumping station there whenever they want to sneak away from work. Travelers waiting on the road drink a few cups of tea before getting a ride. Before taking the mountainous, winding road running to the north, or taking the tiring and breathtaking road leading to the harbor, diesel and petroleum oil-tanker drivers pull the brakes and drink a half cup of tea or so while standing. Sometimes they come inside and sit for a few minutes. Sometimes some of the drivers eat their breakfast there in the teahouse, or smoke a water pipe before they set off. In just one month, I have seen so many different kinds of people that it is enough for the rest of my life.

In the teahouse, Aman Aqa is completely approachable and amusing. It's like comparing apples and oranges. He's nothing like the man he is at home, especially when he lashes Bolur Khanom with his leather belt.

"Spider, take two teas to that table."

"Right away, Aman Aqa."

When Spider is high on his opium, he does everything around the teahouse all by himself.

"Aman Aqa, where's that water pipe I ordered?"

"Khaled, sonny, get a water pipe ready quickly."

"Right away, Aman Aqa, right away."

In the teahouse, Aman Aqa's tiny eyes are always bright with contentment. His thin, drawn lips are always parted in a smile. During this past month, not even once have I seen him get angry with anyone.

He has taught me lots of things, Aman Aqa. For instance, he has taught me how to hold the sugar cone hammer, and how to break the sugar cone into perfect cubes. "Look, Khaled, you should hold it like this, and, bam, with just one soft knock; otherwise, it'll all break into tiny pieces and powder."

All of Aman Aqa's sugar cubes are the perfect size.

I have also learned how to carry five cups in one hand, and I have learned how to prepare a water pipe. I have also learned how to play fast and slow rhythms by tapping the bottom of a glass cup softly against the center of a saucer.

Aman Aqa's teahouse is large and quadrangular. It has an awning in front to stave off the summer heat. There are three rooms in the back of the teahouse. One is used as storage. Spider sleeps in the second. And the third one is kept empty just in case, once in a while, Aman Aqa wishes to have some private gatherings with friends, to drink arrack or maybe smoke opium. This room's floor is covered by two ten-foot-square Lori tribal rugs. There's also a bed with linen. Once, Spider let out that sometimes, after all the customers have left at the end of the night, Aman Aqa sends for Mahin Jiju to come and spend the night with him in that room. There's a painting of a half-naked woman hanging on the wall too.

It seems that today is one of those days where Jan Mohammad has decided to cut his work short. His yellow hard hat under his arm, he enters the teahouse. He takes special care of his mustache. He always carries a small mirror and a pair of scissors with him. The first thing he does when he sits is take out that mirror and look at his mustache. If needed, he brings out his scissors too.

"Jan Mohammad must trim his mustache ten times a day."

"He must be feeding it with fertilizer for it to grow wild like that."

Jan Mohammad starts to lash out at that, but calms down the moment he sees Aman Aqa bursting with laughter.

Jan Mohammad's work clothes are a bit too baggy and loose. They're supposed to be a dark blue, but having been smudged with so much grease and oil, they have turned black. Today, there's a white tag on his chest, as wide and long as two fingers. He didn't have that on yesterday. There is something written on it too. He sits on a bench in the teahouse, folds his right leg under his bottom, and takes the mirror out of his pocket. Spider serves him tea. I walk past him and greet him. The tag reads: "The Oil Industry Must Be Nationalized." I remember the papers with which I made Jamileh a kite. Aman Aqa leaves the counter and walks toward Jan Mohammad so that he can tease him again. They're close friends. Sometimes they eat their lunch together. If they have bazaar-bought kebab for lunch, they even retreat into the third room and drink arrack with it. Yet I don't understand why, with all the friendship between them, Aman Aqa still enjoys teasing Jan Mohammad. "I see that you too have stuck a tag on your chest."

Jan Mohammad twists the end of his mustache. "Why not?"

"You surely cannot play with the lion's tail with such words," Aman Aqa says, gently slapping Jan Mohammad's shoulder.

"The lion's old now, man. His mane is falling out," Jan Mohammad says in a matter-of-fact tone.

I don't know what this *lion* thing is they're talking about. I don't understand how a lion could have anything at all to do with a white tag.

Aman Aqa sits down beside Jan Mohammad and says, "But an elephant is worth a hundred tomans, dead or alive."

I can't make any sense out of what they're saying. Jan Mohammad uses words like the ones written on those papers, the scattered papers I picked up at the square on that crowded day; those with which I made my sister a kite that flew so lightly in the air. Jan Mohammad's large teeth show as his thick lips part. His voice is hoarse. It's neither high- nor low-pitched, and he speaks in a monotonous tone. "The time when they could plunder us is over. The lion should fling his tail over his shoulder and hit the road. Now there are possessions and their lawful owners. Everything is well accounted for. People are their own bosses."

The way he talks, it's obvious that he believes in what he says, and clearly he'd stand up for it. I can tell because the veins running up and down his neck swell up and turn blue when he talks.

Aman Aqa is in the mood to tease him. "What're you talking about, my good man? We still can't even make a hole in the butt of a needle."

Jan Mohammad gets real mad. If it weren't for the sake of their friendship, I'm sure Jan Mohammad would strangle Aman Aqa with his large hands.

Letting out a loud guffaw, Aman Aqa gets up and goes to sit behind the counter.

Jan Mohammad sips his tea, fiddles with his mustache a bit, puts the mirror back in his pocket, and takes the water pipe from my hands.

"Khaled, don't you listen to what Aman Aqa says. He's completely on the wrong track."

"Nevertheless," sneers Aman Aqa, "we're still struggling to make a hole in the butt of a needle."

A green oil tanker stops in front of the teahouse. The driver comes in. "Aman Aqa, bring me a water pipe!"

Oddly enough, there's a tag on the driver's chest too. I doubt that Jan Mohammad and the driver know one another, because they exchange just a glance and a smile. The driver goes and sits somewhere on the other side of the teahouse. I fix his water pipe while Spider serves him tea.

The driver's helper hasn't come inside the teahouse yet. He's checking out the tanker. Maybe he's applying grease or something, or filling up the radiator with water. Now I can tell these sorts of things apart. I'd like to know what the driver's helper is up to. I mean, I want to know if he also has a tag on his chest. "Aman Aqa, should I take a cup of tea to the driver's helper too?"

Aman Aqa is in a jolly mood. "Take it, my son."

I take the cup of tea from Spider and head out of the teahouse. The oil tanker is parked under the awning. I take a look at the driver's helper. "The Oil Industry Must Be Nationalized." I ought to ask him. I ought to find out what that means. If a driver's helper is wearing a tag, why shouldn't I wear one? Why shouldn't Ebrahim, Hasani, and Omid wear one? Why shouldn't Khaleq, Chinuq, and all the other boys in the neighborhood wear one?

"Hey, man, what's that you're wearing on your chest?" I ask the driver's helper.

He looks at me with his heavy-lidded eyes. They are red and puffy, as if he hasn't gotten any sleep in a while.

"Can you read?" His voice sounds sleepy too.

"Of course I can."

"Then read it."

"I read it . . . but what does it mean?"

The driver's helper wipes his hands with a rag and says, "Well, it's clear. It means the oil industry must be nationalized."

I ask him again what that means.

Taking the cup of tea from my hand, he tosses the sugar cubes into his mouth, and with a swollen cheek, says, "Well, it means that the British should pack up and beat it."

I understand now. So, the British are what Jan Mohammad meant when he referred to the *lion*.

"The British?" I ask with curiosity.

"Yes, the British."

Bit by bit, I begin to get the picture. Aman Aqa calls out to me.

"What happens after the British beat it?"

The driver's helper hands me the empty cup and reaches down under the oil tanker.

"Then? . . . Well it's obvious. Then the oil will be ours."

Aman Aqa calls me again. If he had left me alone, I would have asked the man why the British should beat it. I'd ask him what the hell the British are doing in our country in first place, and what do the British have to do with our oil. If he let me, I'd ask him a lot of things, whatever I could think of. But Aman Aqa keeps calling me.

"I'm coming, Aman Aqa."

I walk into the teahouse.

"Come and fix a water pipe."

There is always a bowl of soaked tobacco ready. I mean, every morning when I get to the teahouse on the back of Aman Aqa's bike, the first thing I'm supposed to do is fill the bowl with tobacco and top it off with some lukewarm water. The bowl of soaked tobacco barely lasts until noon, and then I do the same thing in the afternoons.

The weather has grown cold. Today we have lamb stew for lunch. Its scent is drifting throughout the teahouse. Bolur Khanom must have learned from Aman Aqa, for her lamb stew is just as aromatic and delicious as that served in the teahouse.

I stuff the top of the water pipe with tobacco. "Whose order is this one, Aman Aqa?"

"Bring it over here," I hear Jan Mohammad say.

I shouldn't have asked at all. Jan Mohammad always smokes two water pipes, one after the other. I put it in front of him and make for the door of the teahouse, so I can talk to the driver's helper. But before I can get out, the driver's helper comes in, along with two other people. They seem to be travelers. Both of them carry a bundle. The driver's helper talks to them. There is more than enough room for four people on the front seat of an oil tanker. I serve them all tea. From what they say, I gather that they're leaving for Kuwait.

It's been more than a month since my father left. He has yet to contact us. A week after he left, Fulad brought us news of his safe arrival.

I can see the sky through the teahouse's window. Cumulus clouds are piling up. The pregnant autumn clouds over the Gulf usually bring storms, and in the blink of an eye, a flash flood is racing, collapsing all the straw huts north of Pumping Station No. 3. The weather has turned real cold today. It's got the chill of winter in it. It makes a person want to huddle up near the gas flames of the oil refinery, which look like dragons snaking out of the earth, roaring. When the north wind blows, you can hear the roar of the flames even in the teahouse. In sunshine, their color fades, but when it's cloudy, like today, they take on a beautiful orange color. They take on an even more beautiful color at night.

Sneaking out of work, their hands stuffed into the pockets of their work clothes and their bodies hunched over, two of the pumping station workers walk into the teahouse. Jan Mohammad examines his mustache carefully in the mirror once more, puts his yellow hard hat on, and heads out of the teahouse.

A letter comes from Father. It's been exactly forty-eight days since he left for Kuwait. Since my father's been gone, the nights have become strangely solemn. I can still smell the scent of his body in his room. When I lie down on the rug, the smell of his tobacco fills my nose. It's been forty-eight days that we've had to feel his absence. When we gather around, I feel like I hear him praying, as though he were still in his own room, praying on his prayer rug.

Father's letter has arrived. He writes: ". . . Praise to God, today is my ninth day at my new job . . ." It has taken a week for the letter to arrive. In that case, it's sixteen days since Father started to work. Mother's eyes are sparkling with tears. It's cold. We sit around the brazier. ". . . I miss you all. The traveling will only be short-lived . . ." The scent of freshly brewed tea is delightful. The room is warm from the heat of the brazier, the three-burner heater, and the oil lamp.

Mother pours tea. On cold autumn and winter nights, whenever he was in a good mood, Father would usually tell us about his life. He would talk about a time when he had to leave the house at dawn to go harvest the crops on the farm. He would tell us about when he was orphaned as a small boy and faced becoming the breadwinner of the family; and even later when he became an apprentice at a blacksmith's. He would also tell us about some of his other memories and how he had spent his hard life. ". . . I am well paid. Twenty rupees a day . . . ," the letter continues.

Mother counts it. "Each rupee is worth eighteen rials." She looks happy. She doesn't laugh, but she's happy. I can see this in her eyes, and I can tell from her lips, which are not puckered.

We've had our dinner. Jamileh's eyes are fixed on my lips. ". . . Don't you be worried. My place is safe and I'm comfortable . . ." Mother sighs. "Never forget to pray. Never. As soon as I get paid, I'll send you money so you can pay some of the debts." Jamileh's eyes are heavy with sleep. Naser Davani's radio is playing at full blast. That's what we always get for a few days whenever he changes the batteries.

Bolur Khanom comes to our room. She's holding a box of Japanese watermelon seeds in her hand. "He's gone out drinking again," she says, sitting beside me.

Since I have started working at Aman Aqa's teahouse, I feel like I don't want to touch Bolur Khanom anymore. Aman Aqa is constantly before my eyes. "Hurry up, Son, take a water pipe to that table." Aman Aqa's tiny eyes are filled with joy. "Hurry up, Son, get the empty cups."

I have a feeling that Mother is suspicious. She no longer welcomes Bolur Khanom as warmly. Jamileh fetches a plate. Bolur Khanom pours the seeds on it. She sits herself next to me in such a way that her knee touches mine. I think tonight is one of those nights where as soon as Aman Aqa sets foot in the house, he'll start beating Bolur Khanom with his leather belt. That's what's sure to happen whenever he goes out drinking. Even if it is the dead of night, he has to beat her up.

The seeds are tasty; salty and seasoned with dried oregano too. Only Aman Aqa knows where to buy such good seeds. Mother pours tea for Bolur Khanom. All of a sudden, we hear Ebrahim's scream, jumbled with the noise coming from the radio. Naser Davani must have turned it off, since the noises die out quickly, leaving only Ebrahim's sharp, metallic shrill. And now even Hasani's crying. Mother gets to her knees and heads for the courtyard, and I follow after her. Hearing the crying, the neighbors have also all come out of their rooms.

Mother gets a hold of Hasani's arm. "What's happened, Hasani? What's wrong?"

Hasani is nearly choking. "My mother," he cries, ". . . my mother died."

The yellow light of the kerosene lantern has left Rahim the Donkey Keeper's room partly dark and partly lit. Rahim moves about frantically, utterly at a loss. Banging the crowns of their heads with their fists, both Hasani and Ebrahim walk into the room. At the sight of his mother, Hasani throws himself over her dead body. Quickly, Sanam helps him to his feet and takes him out of the room, then comes back and takes Ebrahim out.

Rahim the Donkey Keeper takes his pipe out from under his sash and gropes for his bag of tobacco. Then, he puts the pipe back under his sash. Mohammad the Mechanic's wife blocks Omid from coming into the room where Rahim the Donkey Keeper's wife lies stretched out. The covers under her body have become all rumpled. Her arms are stretched lifeless beside her and her skin is yellowish. The veins running through her arms are dark green and her hair is disheveled, with so many gray strands in it.

Rahim the Donkey Keeper takes the sash off from around his waist. His pipe falls to the ground. He unwraps the sash and covers his wife's dead body with it. Noticing me standing in the corner of the room, Mother comes toward me. Taking my hand, she leads me out of the room. "Go and stay with Jamileh."

In Rahim the Donkey Keeper's room, all kinds of smells are mixed together—dampness, herbal remedies, body odor, burnt food, even the smell of urine.

I leave the room. It's cold. The air is chilly. It is so sneaky that it even finds its way through your clothes and stings your skin. Khaj Tofiq, Naser Davani, Karam Ali, and Amu Bandar are all standing around together. Afaq has taken Hasani and Ebrahim to her room. Banu stands right at the door. Khaj Tofiq has bundled himself up in a woolen robe. Amu Bandar too has pulled up the collar of his worn military jacket, which comes down to his ankles. His small head is almost lost in his collar. Holding her anemic child to her chest, Hajar stands in front of Mohammad the Mechanic's room, shivering with cold. She's talking to Mohammad the Mechanic's wife. I can't hear them, but from where they stand and the way the light shines on them, I can see their faces and that their lips are moving. The lanterns have brightened the ground in front of each of the tenants' rooms. It is a dark night; cold too. We can hear a cargo train coming from the harbor. It must be eleven. Mohammad the Mechanic comes in through the house doors, walks around the courtyard pool, and moves closer. When he has to work the night shift, he returns home late at night. It takes him a good hour to get to town from Well No. 5. As he comes closer, I notice the white tag on his chest. Jan Mohammad's voice echoes in my ears: "Those times are over when they could plunder us." He twists his mustache. "Now everything is accounted for. No more hunger and unemployment. Now, we're our own masters."

It is only Bolur Khanom who has not come out yet. She's still right there with Jamileh, sitting by the brazier. "For the love of God, don't talk about the dead," she always says. "It makes my hair stand up."

Whenever I'm in the mood and feel like teasing her, I talk about the dead. That big woman begs me like a child, "Fine, then just let me kiss your lips." She smacks my chest gently. "You're turning into a bad boy, Khaled," she says with a grin.

I'm amazed to see a person her age so terrified of the dead.

"Go back to our room, Khaled!" says my mother again, looking out of Rahim the Donkey Keeper's room.

"I'm going, Mother."

"Go inside, dear . . . you'll catch a cold."

The only noise you can hear now is the sounds the donkeys are making. The yard has fallen silent. Bewildered and panicked, Rahim the Donkey Keeper heads out of his room. "It's all over . . . it's all over. Somebody, please go after the undertaker," he laments.

"*La elahah ellallah*," Khaj Tofiq begins to recite in Arabic.

"There's no god but God!" Amu Bandar repeats. Then he adds, "There's no undertaker till tomorrow morning."

"There's no god but God," Khaj Tofiq repeats to himself.

"Why isn't there one?" Mohammad the Mechanic wonders.

"The municipality is closed now," Amu Bandar explains.

"Won't the body decay before morning?" Karam Ali asks.

Ebrahim's and Hasani's sobs are heard again as they head out of Khaj Tofiq's room. Rahim the Donkey Keeper can't stay in one place. Smacking his thighs, he says, "So what the hell are we supposed to do?"

"There's no god but God," Khaj Tofiq says.

From over the edge of the roof, a cold wind sweeps through the yard. Amu Bandar creeps further into his jacket. Karam Ali walks toward his room. Khaj Tofiq's nose has started to run. It's pitch dark around the outhouse and the pigeon coop. A host of people led by a mullah passes by the house. A short, stocky man holding a lantern walks ahead of them. The light seeps in, brightening the yard for a few seconds. A black cat is crouching on the pigeon coop. I'm about to go and scare the cat away when Mother grabs my hand and pushes me toward our room. "I said, go inside!"

Bolur Khanom leans against the wall and pulls the brazier closer to her, then she reaches to take Jamileh in her arms. There's barely any color in her face and she looks just like the plaster on the wall. As I sit next to the brazier, my ears are filled with Father reciting prayers. "God is dignified, and Praise be to Him, and there's no god but God . . ."

If I didn't feel so sad and depressed, I would definitely tease Bolur Khanom.

"Khaled, come closer, come and sit near me." Bolur Khanom's voice sounds as if it is coming from the bottom of a well. "Sit beside me, Khaled. My body is frozen."

I hold her hand. It feels like ice. I sit closer to her.

"Your body is so warm, Khaled."

I feel warm. My heart beats fast.

We buried Naneh Hasani's body. Both Ebrahim and Hasani are completely out of it. Their voices are hoarse, their eyes red. My mother kept them at home and did not let them go to the graveyard.

It was before noon when the municipality's beat-up hearse came and carried Naneh Hasani away. I remember that the van first belonged to the slaughterhouse. There are four rows of hooks attached to its high ceiling from which the sheep's corpses used to be hung and taken to the butchers. After typhus decimated the people of our town, the vehicle was given to the city so they could collect the corpses from the streets and alleys and speed them away to the graveyard. Ever since, a bit more than five years, this very van has been our town's only hearse.

"Come on, hurry up. Throw it in here."

Everyone knows the hearse driver. On the mourning nights of the month of Moharram, he sings elegies at Bushehris' Mosque. He stands on a stool, and soon he is surrounded by groups of men slapping their chests as part of the mourning ritual. Habib the Black's voice is so heartrending that it could split a rock open. "Oh, you youngster, Akbar," he sings in commemoration of Imam Hossein's son murdered at the Battle of Karbala.

"Oh, Leila's offspring!"

"Alas! After you, the wronged!"

"Oh, shame on this worthless world!"

"Hurry up," berated Habib the Black, "I have three other bodies to run to the graveyard before noon; that is, if there are not more of them by now."

The hearse driver has a swarthy complexion. He is short. His cheeks are round and full. He has two gold-covered teeth too.

When the neighbors were about to take the body out the doors of the house, Habib the Black's lips began to quiver. I think he was reciting the prayers for the dead.

The hearse took off, and so did everyone else, setting off for the graveyard. Mother wanted me to go to the teahouse, but I didn't. I got together with the men and went to the graveyard instead.

We buried Naneh Hasani next to the grave of Ja'far the Brickmaker; right there behind the brick Four-Arched Candle House, with its crumbling ceiling under which you could always find a few half-burned candles. Naneh Hasani's grave is no more than fifteen paces away from the pit that collects the runoff from the place where they wash the dead bodies. The water is even blacker than ink.

Khaj Tofiq stood before us, and we all lined up behind him, reciting the prayers for the dead. Rahim the Donkey Keeper closed the lid of the coffin. After filling up the grave with earth, we left a marker so that Rahim the Donkey Keeper could haul over some two hundred bricks to the graveyard, once he could afford it, and then Naser Davani would finish the grave pro bono.

At the moment, Rahim the Donkey Keeper is thinking about the provisions for the funeral ceremony. Mehdi the Grocer closed his store and came along to the graveyard. "I'll provide cigarettes for the funeral service," he says. "It's not like it will be a whole lot."

Habib the Baker is here too.

As we're about to leave the graveyard, a corpse is carried in by a group of wailing mourners. A young woman following the corpse has scratched her face so badly and plucked so much of her hair out that she looks more like a wild animal than a human being.

It's cold. I have wrapped my jacket around myself, but the cold still somehow finds its way through to my body. My back feels frozen. Hunching over, Rahim the Donkey Keeper walks on ahead of everyone. Khaj Tofiq is barely visible in his too-loose trousers and jacket. The women didn't accompany us to the graveyard.

"Taking part in funeral services and visiting the ill are forbidden to women."

"What else is forbidden to women?" Father asks Hajj Sheikh Ali.

Hajj Sheikh Ali, reclining onto the back cushion, says, "Leadership, judging, and consulting are also forbidden to women . . ."

Father repeats after Hajj Sheikh Ali, "Kissing the Hajar stone, running between Safa and Marveh while on Hajj, and entering the Kaaba are also among the things forbidden to women."

Despite all this, Sanam would not give up, and accompanied us men to the graveyard; but now, all worn-out, she's trudging behind us.

I noticed whenever I went somewhere with Father and Mother, Mother always kept herself behind us. I never saw her even walk shoulder to shoulder with us. "Why are you lagging behind, Mother?"

"Women should always walk behind men, my son."

"But, Mother, I think I have heard it should be the other way round."

Mother looks me in the eye. "No, my dear, we're very different from them."

I don't drop it, insisting on finding out what exactly is the matter. "How are we different, Mother?"

"It's a sin." Mother gives it to me straight.

"A sin?" I don't let her off the hook that easily.

Mother loses her patience. "It's not a sin . . . but, what can I say . . . it's part of our traditions."

I don't understand what my mother means by any of this. It doesn't make any sense to me.

Somebody calls my name. I turn around. It's Shafaq. I stop. He reaches me and puts his hand on my shoulder. "Where have you been, young man?"

Nobody has ever called me a "young man." Not Mother, not even Father.

Get a water pipe over here, boy.

Right away, sir.

You're still too young to understand these sorts of things.

But I'm fifteen years old, Baker Habib. I'm not a kid no more . . .

Hey, kid, I'm talking to you.

Are you talking to me, Khaj Tofiq?

Come over here, boy.

I'm coming, Oussa Naser.

I feel I have suddenly become a grown up. I have been feeling like this, little by little, ever since that day I met Shafaq for the first time.

"Where have you been, young man?"

"I've been around."

"Then why haven't you stopped by to see me?"

It's been twenty days since I last went to see him.

"Well . . . as I told you . . . it's because I go to Aman Aqa's teahouse . . . I work there."

"Where are you coming back from now?"

I tell him the story.

"You said whose wife is dead?"

I point at Rahim the Donkey Keeper, who's quite far ahead of us now.

"The one clasping his hands behind his head?"

We start to walk together. I feel the warmth of his hand on my shoulder.

"Can you come and see me today, around sunset?"

"Yes, I can."

"Don't forget," he says as he begins to walk away. "Be sure you come."

The others are way ahead. I run until I catch up with them. Everybody's mumbling the prayers for the dead under their breath. The street is grayish. Clouds have covered the entire sky. Along the street, on the flat walls made of adobe, there is something written in blue and red. It looks like what was written on the flyers at the rally. I try to keep the words in my mind so that later I can ask someone what they mean. I know what "united" means, but I still can't make out "bloodthirsty exploiter." These words have left their mark in my memory. Words like "united," "autonomy," "plunderers," and other words that are all unclear to me. There's this one word that I can't even pronounce, something like *imprelis* or *impralist*. It's a tough word. My tongue twists when I want to say it. A herd of sheep comes running our way. We walk through them. An old, gaunt ewe leads the herd. It sounds like she has caught a cold. Snot is running from her nose. Even though we have walked past the sheep, the stench of their fleece and dung is still in the air. To top it off is the lingering stench of the curbside slime along the street.

At the sight of us back in the courtyard, Hasani and Ebrahim head out of our room, wailing and clasping Rahim the Donkey Keeper's legs. He has closed his eyes. His Adam's apple shifts along his long throat. Taking his boys' hands, he walks them into Khaj Tofiq's room, where they all sit beside the brazier. While Rahim the Donkey Keeper stuffs his pipe, Banu serves them tea, and Khaj Tofiq gets his opium pipe ready. Huddled up like two shivering, inexperienced young birds, both Hasani and Ebrahim continue sobbing. Ebrahim's large head looks wobbly on his neck. Rahim the Donkey Keeper doesn't say a word. Afaq, who went out early in the morning, hasn't returned yet. This morning, Sheikh Sho'ayb came and got her.

"You didn't go to the teahouse, Khaled?" Mother asks.

"No, Mother, I didn't."

"Khaled, you have changed a lot these days," my mother says, frowning. "You don't listen to your mother at all."

She holds my hand and takes me to our room.

Bolur Khanom and Jamileh are still beside the brazier. Bolur Khanom's face has turned the color of amber.

"Did you go to the graveyard?"

"I even went inside the mortuary."

"Don't say another word, Khaled . . . not another word," says Bolur Khanom, terrified.

Actually, they wouldn't let me in, but somehow I slipped inside.

"I saw how they washed the body."

I feel a strong urge to tease Bolur Khanom. Her mouth is wide open. She covers it with her hand. Her eyes are ready to pop out.

"I even saw how they laid her down on her right side in the coffin."

As she sits down before the Primus and prepares to light it, Mother berates, "Shut up, Khaled."

I keep quiet. Poor Jamileh begins crying for no particular reason. Mother calms her down. My lips press hard against each other. My gaze is fixed on Mother.

"Why should you say these things?" she says in a softer tone. "Can't you see Bolur Khanom's frightened?"

I sit beside the brazier. The last thing I wanted was for my mother to talk to me in such a tone in front of Bolur Khanom. I look at her. You can see only the whites of her eyes, as if she has no pupils. Her lips tremble as though she is having an epileptic seizure. And her face is as pale as a piece of white cotton fabric. I call Mother. She leaves the Primus and rushes to take Bolur Khanom's hand. "Are you all right, Bolur Khanom?"

Bolur Khanom blabbers. Incoherent words come out her mouth. Suddenly, she starts to hiccup.

"May God not forgive you, Khaled. Look what you've done to this poor woman."

I am so surprised at Bolur Khanom, a grown woman, and at her age! What's a dead body to be so frightened of like this? What would she have done had she seen Ja'far the Brickmaker?

"Father, why did Ja'far the Brickmaker kill himself?"

"Well, how long can a man stand hunger, joblessness, and humiliation?"

Ja'far the Brickmaker's face had turned dark blue. His mouth was hanging open. His tongue, swollen, was locked between his teeth.

"You mean one should do such a thing to oneself because of hunger or not having a job?"

"Well, Ja'far did."

The rope had tightened on his Adam's apple. Hanging like that from the ceiling, he seemed even taller.

"But Ja'far shouldn't have done that." That's what Mohammad the Mechanic said that day. "Or at least, he should've killed the brickkilns' owner, who made him so miserable, then killed himself."

Bolur Khanom's feeling better. Little by little, the color returns to her face. Now, her face is more of a straw color rather than white, though her lips are still trembling. The water in the kettle is boiling. Mother fixes Bolur Khanom a drink of sugary hot water. Her hand trembles as she looks at me.

"Bolur Khanom, I didn't know you would get this scared."

She doesn't talk. Beads of sweat are forming on her forehead. Sipping the sweetened hot water, she leans against the wall and closes her eyes.

Around sunset, the sun shows itself a bit, and then disappears again. I wrap my father's milk-and-honey-colored woolen sash around my neck. "I'll be back soon, Mother."

I pass by Gholam Ali Khan's house. The curtain hanging behind the window has changed. Khaleq and Chinuq are coming my way. Khaleq is carrying a half-full sugar sack on his back.

"What's that, Khaleq?"

"Potatoes."

Khaleq is driving Mehdi the Grocer mad. God forbid if he turns his back, in a moment Khaleq has pocketed something: two eggs here, a few potatoes or onions there, a handful of raisins, or whatever . . . it doesn't matter to Khaleq. Nobody can beat Khaleq in stealing a chicken either. He goes to the butcher's shop, picks up a fresh sheep's intestines, and goes to Prison Square, where lots of chickens are always running around. Sometimes he goes behind the huts by the riverbank and sometimes he goes to the dumpsters on the outskirts of town. There he sits beside mounds of garbage, hurls a long piece of intestine a good three or four meters, crouches in a corner, and waits for a chicken or a rooster to come and pick at the intestine. Once the bird has swallowed a good foot or two of the intestine, he then takes a deep breath and blows through it. He blows and blows until the intestine bulges inside the chicken's throat and chokes it. Fluttering its wings won't help the poor bird either, because before it can struggle free of the intestine, Khaleq has pounced on it like a cat, clutched its neck, and carried it off.

"Where did you get all these potatoes from, Khaleq?"

"Well it's obvious, I bought them from the vegetable market, as I always do."

Since Chinuq's mouth is so big, it looks like his entire face is laughing. Even though Khaleq is the younger brother, Chinuq looks up to him.

It was on a Sunday that their father died, and it was on the following Sunday that their mother also died of typhus. Neither of them shed a tear. People said they were traumatized. They used to live in the same room in which Mohammad the Mechanic and his family now live. The next day their uncle came, picked up their odds and ends, and took them both to his own house. For a few months they worked as apprentices in their uncle's carpentry shop, but then they both hit the streets and went out on their own. If it weren't for Khaleq, Chinuq would have starved for sure.

Khaleq is driving Mehdi the Grocer mad. "If I see you pass by my store ever again, I'll break your legs."

Chinuq mocks him. Mehdi the Grocer goes ballistic. He darts out of the store and chases him away. Before he realizes it, Khaleq has pocketed a few eggs.

"You only bought potatoes, Khaleq?" I know that he hasn't bought them. I just ask. He also knows that I know.

"No, I got a fish too for tonight's dinner."

They pay twenty-five tomans for rent each month. They stay in Hajj Bandari's house, which is bigger than the house we live in.

It's crowded in front of Mojahed Bookstore. Most of the people are there for newspapers. From behind a crowd of customers, I wave my hand at Shafaq. He waves back and motions for me to enter. "Come in, Khaled."

I weave through the crowd of customers into the bookstore.

"Salaam."

"Salaam, come and sit."

I sit down on a stool in the back of the store.

"Would you like some tea?"

This is the last thing I expect. Nobody has ever asked me if I would like to have tea. Whenever I went to the teahouse with my father, he would order me tea without asking me if I wanted it or not. When we went to Mirza Nasrollah's workplace, he would only ask Father if he wanted tea, not me.

"Oussa Haddad, do you care for some tea?"

"Yes."

And then Father would ask for some for me too.

"Oussa Haddad, would you care for some tea?"

"No, not right now."

And in that case he wouldn't ask for any tea for me either.

"Would you like tea?"

I blush. "Yes." I feel like my ears are burning.

"Peyman, go and order three cups of tea for us."

"Three?"

Shafaq looks at his watch. "A friend will join us in a second."

Peyman walks out. Shafaq helps the customers.

"Has the new edition of *The Nahjolbalagheh* arrived yet?"

I've heard this very question from a few other customers, and seen them get a newspaper instead of *The Nahjolbalagheh*. I have seen *The Nahjolbalagheh*, and especially liked Imam Ali's letter addressing Malek-e Ashtar, which Father read to me a few times. I am sure that *The Nahjolbalagheh* is the book of Imam Ali's teachings and has nothing to do with these newspapers, which have something in red written on top of the first page.

Peyman brings the tea himself. No sooner does he set the cups of tea down on the bookshelf than a thin young man walks in and shakes hands with Shafaq. Shafaq introduces us to each other. I am beginning to pay more attention to their names. Pendar, Peyman, Shafaq, and Bidar, the new man I just met.

He doesn't have a mustache. Clearly, his beard and mustache are only just beginning to grow. He can't be over twenty. He looks a little familiar to me. I have a feeling that I have seen him somewhere.

Bidar sits down. All three of us begin sipping our tea.

"I think you two can become good friends."

Shafaq always smiles when he talks. I mean, a kind of smile that makes his speech even more pleasant. I think of *The Nahjolbalagheh* again. I'd like to ask Shafaq. I'd like to ask about *The Nahjolbalagheh*, and the newspapers too. I'd like to ask him why Pendar was imprisoned. I'd like to ask him the meaning of the words written on the adobe walls, as well as those on the flyers. The same flyers I used to make my sister a kite that soared so lightly in the sky.

Bidar knows that I work at Aman Aqa's teahouse, and he knows that Aman Aqa's teahouse is located at the harbor intersection. He also knows that the harbor intersection is close to Pumping Station No. 3. It seems like Shafaq has told Bidar everything he knows about me.

"Can you read newspapers?"

I don't tell them I can't. "Yes, I can."

Shafaq pulls out a newspaper hidden among a bundle of other papers, folds it, and hands it to me. "Put it in your pocket! You should read this one at home."

I'd like to ask why, so I do. "You mean, I can't take it out of my pocket on the street?"

"Bidar will explain it to you."

I look at Bidar. He has striking hazel eyes. His skin is white, as if there is no blood under it at all. His ears are small, and his smile is faint and rather forced. When he was sitting on the stool, he looked taller, but now, as we head out of Mojahed Bookstore, I realize that we're the same height. It is his torso that is longer.

Bidar keeps me company up until we reach the doors to my house.

I have already taken a liking to him.

I have become real good friends with Spider. He's been working at Aman Aqa's teahouse for five years. Spider has no family. "It's only me and my shadow," he tells me.

Truth or lie, it wouldn't matter to me. He is a nice fellow, that Spider. Short and thin. He's addicted to *shireh* too. When he is high, he reminisces. If he's telling the truth, he must have it tough all right. Whereas everyone has to serve two years mandatory military service, he had to serve for eight years. He ran away from his mandatory service more than thirty times, only to get caught and drafted over and over again. Once, he opened fire on the commander of the squadron with a machine gun in the hopes of shredding him to pieces, but the soldiers rushed and snatched the machine gun out of his hands just in time. He had to do six months in jail for that. His nose is so large that it is the first thing on his face that grabs your attention; then you realize that on each side of the protruding hump on his nose there are also two eyes, and under the tip of that nose—the size of a potato—there's also a mouth.

"Khaled, I am like your father. I want the best for you."

"Thanks, Spider . . . thanks a lot."

Spider scratches the hump on his nose. "You know what's in that bag?"

"No, Spider, I don't," I lie.

"Then you haven't done a wise thing . . . maybe there's opium in it."

"I know for sure that it's not opium."

He doesn't insist. I have hidden the box of newspapers under Spider's folded blanket in the storage room. I wish he hadn't found out. "Spider, don't tell Aman Aqa."

Spider is high. When he has taken his *shireh*, he scratches the tip of his large nose so much that it turns red. He speaks through his nose. "Why do I have to tell him anything . . . If I say anything, it's for your own good . . . You're still too young to know people's real intentions."

Spider is high. Whenever he is this way, he gossips about the customers: "You see that fellow? He is one of those guys who would cut his mother's tits for a penny . . . You see that one, the one sitting over there, smoking a water pipe? He's a child molester. Before he became a diesel driver, he used to repair bikes."

Spider knows so much about everyone that you would think he has the birth certificates of all who patron the teahouse.

"Now, Jan Mohammad is a nice man. He's got a heart as clear as a mirror. Don't pay any attention to his temper . . . he's got a solid foundation."

The closer it gets to eleven, the faster my heart beats. Bidar has instructed that no one should find out. It was when I was trying to hide it that Spider noticed. "What's that, Khaled?"

"Nothing."

"What do you mean, 'nothing' . . . there must be something?"

"It's what you see."

"Why are you hiding it then?"

"Someone's supposed to come and pick it up at eleven."

He looks at me. He takes the box from my hand, looks it up and down, then gives it back to me. "Put it in my blanket," he says.

The sky is dark. If it rains, he might not show up. The roar of the gas flames reaches the teahouse from afar. Aman Aqa is behind the counter, with the brazier before him. Spider is high. He alone attends to everyone, but there aren't even that many customers. At the most, there are twenty of them.

Bidar said *he* is short. He said that his right hand is bandaged with a poultice, from his wrist to his palm. Has a blond mustache too. His hair is short. The back of his head is flat. "He will come in exactly at eleven," Bidar said.

I feel sick to my stomach. I've never felt so uneasy before. I feel like I have a fever.

"What's in the box, Bidar?"

"Just newspapers."

"Like those Shafaq sells?"

"Not much different."

Spider talks about people when he is high. "You're still too young . . . you should always keep both of your eyes open. You see how miserable I have become? . . . It's all what people did to me . . . Do you see that fellow sitting cross-legged, sipping his tea? Do you see his prayer beads? You see how fair, simple, and honest he looks? If I told you he had played a trick—pocketed a hundred thousand tomans, and sent someone else to jail for it—would you believe me?"

The roar of the gas flames is completely muffled now by the sound of a thunderstorm. The smells of rain and winter drift through the teahouse. Any minute, the rain will fall.

"What time is it, Spider?"

He glances at his watch, which looks rather like a patched-up rag on his wrist. "It is still a quarter till eleven." Then he looks at me. His eyes now have a hint of color. His voice is scratchy. "But, Khaled, open up your eyes real good . . . you see what kind of misery life and people have brought me?"

It's started to rain. Such large raindrops!

Bidar's words are like Jan Mohammad's. "All we ask is why the hungry should get hungrier, and the rich richer?"

Father believes that God is the Provider. "This is all God's will. When you are born, your destiny is already written on your forehead."

The rain has turned into a downpour. If it goes on like this, there will be a flood. I look through the window. The rain is pounding the asphalt. It's like smoke is rising from the ground.

"Spider, how much time is left?"

"You're too jittery!"

"How long?"

"Ten minutes."

I wish I hadn't agreed to it. What if it continues to rain like this? Bidar's voice echoes in my ears: "He'll come. He'll certainly come. Even if stones were to pour down from the sky, he would come."

I go and stand next to the door of the teahouse. I look at the sky, which is turning dark. Spider passes by me. "You got yourself into trouble."

Spider's words are something else. Nothing like anyone else's. His are very strange.

"One day you may open your eyes and see that you're in trouble, and you won't be able to do anything about it. Too late."

"If God doesn't will it, not even a leaf will fall from the trees." Father's words are like Hajj Sheikh Ali's.

Mohammad the Mechanic's words are like Bidar's: "Everything can be changed. Everything."

A large oil tanker is pulling up to the teahouse. It has come from the direction of town. It's green. Its windshield wipers swish back and forth speedily. Water has pooled on the street. The oil tanker heads toward the teahouse for a break, pulling over to the sunshade. The driver gets out of the tanker's cabin. He is short and fat. There's a white tag on his chest. His head and cheeks are covered by a black woolen hat. His driver's helper steps out after him. The helper's right hand is bandaged. My breath feels trapped in my chest. I stare at his blond mustache. The driver's helper smiles as he comes toward me. What I really want is to run away. I can feel my heartbeat in my temples. Streaks of pain shoot through the back of my head. I mustn't waste time. I am to say the first sentence. If I don't say it right away, and he walks past me, it'll be impossible to convince myself to go and talk to him. Once he's even with me, I hear a voice escaping my throat. It sounds nothing like my own voice. It sounds like Bidar is speaking instead of me. "Do you intend to drive up to the harbor?"

He pauses. It is *him*. He smiles. His warm voice pleases my ears. "Nonstop to the harbor."

The words are jammed at the back of my throat, choking me. I swallow my saliva. My voice is raspy. "Don't you get tired?"

"It's better this way."

"What if there's a traveler on the way?" This time I speak with a bit more ease.

"We'll give him a ride."

The driver's helper puts his big hand on my shoulder and squeezes it gently. Then he walks away and sits at a distance, with the driver. Swiftly, I go toward the samovar. I take a cup of tea from Spider, turn around quickly, and put it in front of the driver's helper.

"Leave it in the tanker! I'll go and hide it right away."

We both smile.

The white-tail pigeons have gone missing. It's time for them to lay their eggs. For sure this is Ebrahim's doing. He's completely out of control. These days he doesn't mind Rahim the Donkey Keeper's words at all. It doesn't matter how hard Rahim the Donkey Keeper tries to get his son to go along with him to the brickkilns, it's useless. He comes up with some kind of excuse to get out of it. He'll feign a stomachache, a toothache, or a headache. If none of this works, he'll stand in Rahim the Donkey Keeper's face and tell him, "I can't go today. Hasani's going with you. Why do you need me to come too?"

Unlike Ebrahim, Hasani is submissive. He drops his head, mounts Charmeh, and rides him to the brickkiln. His father mounts Dizeh.

Aman Aqa has killed two partridges, so he asks me to take them to Bolur Khanom. I ride home on Aman Aqa's bike. Its seat is too high for me, so I sit on the frame to ride better.

It's almost noon. There's such a hullabaloo going on in the house that it's a sight to see. Last night Afaq didn't come home. Now, this didn't alarm Khaj Tofiq, since there have been other nights when Afaq hasn't come home, especially when she had to go and fetch the smuggled goods. Sometimes she goes by boat, and sometimes on horseback.

All the neighbors have gathered in the courtyard, even those from two alleys down and two alleys over. The inspectors caught Afaq with five rolls of satin at Sheikh's Garden. She was captured during the night coming from Sheikh Sho'ayb's house. They held her through the night and now they have brought her along to search her house. Banu is trembling like a frostbitten little chick. Hunching over, she stands beside the pool. I think perhaps she's a bit overdue on her opium. Afaq does not budge at all. Standing tall, both of her hands at her sides, she pretends she has no clue what's going on. Her ebony black hair has fallen over her shoulders. She has wrapped her chador tightly around her waist. The inspectors have poked everything with their iron prods: even the floor of Khaj Tofiq's room, their bundled bedding materials, Rahim the Donkey Keeper's straw rick, as well as Sanam's gunnysacks of dung.

Ebrahim sits on the pigeon coop, his knees drawn up to his chest. His watery eyes twitch rapidly in their sockets. Omid is at school. Hasani is at the brickkiln.

Bolur Khanom stands on the threshold of her room. I weave through the crowd toward her and prop the bike against the pigeon coop. "Bolur

Khanom, Aman Aqa sent these partridges and asked that you clean them and marinate them in lime juice for tonight's dinner."

She takes the partridges, her hand trembling. She has turned white. "Why do you look so pale, Bolur Khanom?"

Her face is exactly like it was the day I told her about the corpses. Her lips quiver. "It's nothing."

I know she is lying. There must be something wrong to have caused her to look so petrified. The color of Bolur Khanom's face doesn't turn white just like that. Her body doesn't tremble for no reason.

"Bolur Khanom, do me a favor and keep this bundle in your room till tomorrow . . . for my sake."

Bolur Khanom frowns. "I'll take it this time, Afaq Khanom, but keep in mind that if Aman Aqa finds out, he'll raise hell."

There must be something going on. I peek into Bolur Khanom's room. I can't see anything in particular. No wonder Afaq looks so sure of herself and stands right there, her arms resting at her sides. For sure, the smuggled fabrics are in Bolur Khanom's room. I am about to walk into her room when she grabs my arm. "Don't go in, Khaled!"

Her lips have turned white.

"Is there something in there?"

"Hush."

"Well if you're that scared, I'll go into the alleyway and you open the window, drop them, and I'll take 'em to Habib's bakery till the inspectors are gone."

Bolur Khanom's throat seems to be dry. Her voice sounds choked when she talks. "No, Khaled . . . that can't be done."

"Well at least don't lose it. If the inspectors take a good look at you, they'll be able to figure out the entire thing. You should see yourself in the mirror."

The inspectors have ransacked Khaj Tofiq's entire room, but they haven't found a thing yet. They are going to tear down the high wall up to the ventilation outlet over the door. With his crossed eyes, Nur Mohammad stares at the wall. "No, man . . . the plaster is old. Don't you see? It was walled up long ago."

Finally, they pick up their iron prods and start to leave. Since that day the municipality sent people to cut down the palm trees behind our house and fill in the narrow creeks, Afaq has had a hard time doing her job. She has lost her hideout. "May God disgrace them," she said that day. "Now we have no hideout no more."

Since they cut down the trees, this is the seventh time Afaq has been caught. For five of those arrests, she paid a fine and they let her go. Once, she was jailed for eleven days, during which time Khaj Tofiq succumbed to such misery from not having his opium.

Without Afaq, both Banu and Khaj Tofiq would give up the ghost within just a few days.

"Get moving!"

Afaq unties her chador from around her waist and throws it on her head. "Tofiq," she faces her husband and says, "have someone come and bail me out. Go on and see Sheikh Sho'ayb."

Khaj Tofiq's large nose has started to run. The inspectors barging in unexpectedly must have ended his opium-smoking session too early. The weather is cold. It stings you. Khaj Tofiq takes the Yazdi handkerchief out of the pocket of his loose pants and blows his nose into it.

The inspectors push Afaq forward and set out, leaving the house. The neighbors follow them. Bolur Khanom takes a deep breath, and a tinge of color returns to her face. Mother calls me. She wants to know why I'm home early, so I tell her why. Ebrahim jumps down from the pigeon coop. I get in his face. "Ebram, the white-tail pigeons—"

"They're lost, aren't they?" he interrupts, not letting me finish.

Now I have no doubt that he's the culprit, and I say, "Well, in that case, you know where they are?"

"How should I know?" he throws up his arms.

He then steps aside and starts to walk away. I grab his arm. His big head wobbles on his spindly neck. He sticks his hands into his jacket pockets. The jacket is too large for him. It comes down to his knees. His eyes are watery. His hair is just like a dirty old piece of black felt.

"Look, Ebram . . . I don't want to fly pigeons anymore . . . I'd even be thankful if you could sell them for me."

Ebrahim turns, excited. A few lines appear around his mouth. "Well, if I sell them for a good price, what's in it for me?"

"Two rials for each toman."

"That's a deal."

So we agree on selling the pigeons. They're no longer any use to me. I spend most of my time at the teahouse, so I don't have time to fly them. Besides, even if I had enough time, what's the use in keeping pigeons? Ebrahim's grin shows off his yellow teeth.

"I'll sell 'em all by tonight . . . going to take 'em to Jasem, right away." I have always wanted my pigeons to be like Jasem's. Especially that dark pair—those two that, when they really want to, soar high in the sky, doing somersaults and putting on such a show.

"But, Ebram, may the holy Saint Abbas be our witness." Ebrahim nods his big head. "Saint Abbas between us."

He darts off toward their room, comes back with a gunnysack, and before I know it, he has gone to the pigeon coop. I suddenly feel depressed. I change my mind. I don't want to sell my pigeons. I want to head out of the house, but my feet are rooted to the ground. So I squat down in front of the chicken coop. The male Abyssinian pigeon is in Ebrahim's grip. He is the blackest of blacks. He's like a crow. His eyes are red. I can feel that he's looking right at me. It's a sad look. His beak is as big as a grain of Karuni wheat. What a show he puts on in the sky! And what a swagger: he fluffs out his chest feathers, opens his tail like a fan, circles and coos around his mate. He's even better than Jasem's pigeons.

Ebrahim throws the male Abyssinian inside the sack. The poor bird flutters at first, then settles. His coo is broken in his throat. The sound is so sad. I feel like crying. I get up, lean against the bike, and call Ebrahim.

"What is it, Khaled?" Ebrahim's voice sounds like a titmouse's.

"Come out here and I'll tell you."

"Come out?"

"Yeah."

"Changed your mind?" he says as he comes out of the pigeon coop.

"Look, Ebram." I put my hand on his shoulder. "I've changed my mind. Leave them for now."

Ebrahim seems downcast.

"But look, Ebram, you have my word, which means we're partners now. For now, you feed 'em till we sell 'em, then we share the money— half you and half me."

Ebrahim cheers up. "Swear to Saint Abbas?"

"I swear to Saint Abbas."

We shake hands. I take the male Abyssinian out of the sack and free him. The poor bird flies off before even touching the ground. The flutter of its wings drives all my sadness away. The male Abyssinian begins to soar and do somersaults. At least now I can be sure that Ebrahim won't steal my pigeons.

It's been more than a week since Aman Aqa bought a new radio, one that's smaller than an icebox. It's a GEC radio. It shines so—you wouldn't believe it. He wipes it off a few times a day. It's a deep brown, and sometimes even a cherry color in some places. Bolur Khanom has sewn a strip of tulle to the hem of a piece of blue silk fabric so as to cover the radio with it. It doesn't match the color of the radio at all.

A lot has changed since the day Aman Aqa brought the radio to the teahouse. The gramophone is no longer wanted. We moved the bulky box of the gramophone and its even heavier green trumpet to Aman Aqa's private room, the one that shares a wall with the storage room. Now the oil refinery workers come to the teahouse even more often than before, so they can listen to the news on the radio. Sometimes, after the news is over, they gather around and discuss what they've just heard. There's fire in Jan Mohammad's voice. He talks with such fervor, much more so than the others. Bit by bit, I am beginning to fathom what he's saying. For instance, now I know what "exploiter" means, and that it doesn't mean what Ebrahim and I thought it meant. Now, I even laugh at Ebrahim when he says, "It's better that he drink oil rather than human's blood."

Bidar has explained to me the meanings of all the words I had meant to ask Shafaq about.

"Say, Bidar, what do those words written on those papers mean?"

He patiently explains them all to me.

"All right, what about those written on the walls?"

He explains again.

His words are strange. I mean, not all that strange . . . it's just that I still don't understand their meanings. I have to concentrate real hard to understand what he says, even though he explains some of the things two or three times.

"The Majlis—parliament—has demanded that the prime minister explain why the British should take away half of the oil revenues as taxes and surcharges. The prime minister has responded: 'Well, that's their fair share; they're entitled to it.' And then he'd added: 'Think of it as the one-fifth, the religious tax, that we're supposed to give to the poor.'"

"But I thought only the progeny of the Prophet were entitled to a portion of the religious tax. Besides, aren't the British nonbelievers and non-Muslims?" I ask Bidar.

Bidar smiles and starts to explain. From what he tells me, I gather that the prime minister is a conniving man and collaborates with the British.

"Say, Bidar, who is this prime minister, anyway, who dares to impose all this without anyone standing up to him?"

He explains, trying hard to clarify things and make me understand.

Finally, I figure out what Jan Mohammad is talking about. Now I even discuss these sorts of things with him whenever there's a chance, saying stuff like, "Jan Mohammad, I hear that the British want to help us."

Jan Mohammad's eyes open up. He gazes at me and says, "The British?" and then quickly turns the conversation around. "Who told you these sorts 'a things?" He can't believe I could be talking about such things. "Come closer!"

I take a step toward him.

"Remember this! Them British don't even go visit their own fathers' graves unless they have an ax to grind."

Bidar is a teacher. He is not as young as I thought he was. He's been a teacher for two years now. He's already done his mandatory military service too—as a reservist officer, of course. He is more than twenty-four, even though he hardly looks it. Twenty is the oldest I would have guessed. I know the way to the school he teaches at. I know where his house is too. He teaches both third and fourth grades. They have crammed at least seventy children in each class.

"Look, Khaled, according to the school policies and procedures, there should be no more than thirty pupils in each classroom."

Once, I went to see him at school. Together we went to his class. The children were squeezed together like dates in a box. A few were sitting in the windowsill. Some were squatting on the floor, and on each bench, instead of three children, there were six. None of them were wearing clothes any better than what Ebrahim and Hasani wear.

"I know for sure that some of these kids don't eat anything for breakfast before they come to school, or at the most, some have a stale piece of bread and sweetened tea. Of course, I mean the ones whose families are even capable of providing this."

Bidar reaches for my arm, and we head out of the classroom. "Khaled, come see me tonight. I need you to do something for me."

I am thinking about when I myself used to go to school.

"Did you hear what I said?"

"What time?"

"At eight."

The sun is still there, hovering in the sky, when I walk out of the teahouse. By the time I get home, the sun has already set.

I eat my dinner and then get up.

"Where are you going, Khaled?" Mother asks.

"I'll be back soon."

Sitting beside the kerosene heater, as always, Mother is doing her mending and sewing. There's no end to this needling thing of hers. Jamileh drinks sweetened tea with her bread. Mother looks concerned. It's not often that I go out of the house at this hour of the night. She looks at me, drops her gaze, and keeps on with her needling.

The weather is cold. The cold air stings my cheeks. Bidar is waiting for me at Chellab's liver kebab place. Inside, there are four men sitting at a table and eating liver with onion and pickled pepper.

"Come in, Khaled," says Bidar, swallowing the morsel of food in his mouth.

I walk in and sit next to him. The place is so tiny that there is barely enough room for six people. It's such a clean place, you wouldn't believe it. The trays, plates, and glasses all sparkle. There's only one bench, two chairs, and two small tables. There's also another small table underneath a brazier full of hot coals. The warmth of the fire offers such a delightful feeling. Chellab is a small-framed man. His mustache comes down around the sides of his mouth. He has a penetrating gaze. His eyes burn you like two balls of fire. I have seen him before. He has earned himself quite a reputation as a fighter. He's very quick and has a lion's heart.

"Do you want to eat some liver?" asks Bidar.

"No, I just had my dinner."

The bench is covered with a kilim that almost touches the floor. My gaze drops under the table, where there are a few cans of paint and paintbrushes. Bidar notices my gaze. "What are you looking at?"

I point to the cans of paint.

He smiles. "This place is the *guys'* hangout. They keep the cans and paintbrushes here to use them in the middle of the night."

Everything makes sense now.

"Surprised?"

I shake my head. I don't know whether I am surprised or not. It just strikes me that Chellab has a peculiar personality. So I ask him, "In that case, these fellows here eating liver kebab are the ones who're supposed to write the slogans on the walls, right?"

"No."

It's not a convincing no. I haven't guessed wrong. I look again. They're eating with such gusto. I can tell they're the deep and mysterious sort.

Bidar finishes his dinner and stands up. "Let's go!"

"Where?" I ask.

"Not that far," he answers. "Around here."

We head out of Chellab's liver kebab place. It's cold outside. Inside was warm from the burning fire in the brazier. Bidar carries a brown briefcase that is obviously weighing him down. A little ways from Chellab's place, he stops. We stand in the corner of a wall. It is dark and no one is in the streets.

"I think I can trust you now." Bidar's words stroke my ears.

His words please me. I feel like he's counting on me, just like he would a man. I don't respond.

"Can you help us tonight?" Bidar asks.

I can feel my heart hammering. My temples too. I feel a sudden burning sensation in my entire body. "What should I do?"

He is silent for a few seconds, and then very quietly says, "I want to give you a hundred flyers that you need to slip inside the houses along Hokumati Street, from the beginning of the street up to where the asphalt ends."

My throat and my mouth are completely dry now. I can barely talk.

"But, Khaled, no one must see what you're up to."

There's not a living soul to be seen in the entire street. Here and there, the streetlights are off, leaving most of the street in darkness. The cold, biting wind chills you to the bone. Since I met Bidar, over this past month, I have seen less and less of Shafaq. In a way, it's been kind of intentional, as I've gone less frequently to see him. I'm beginning to realize that what Shafaq and his friends are up to smells of danger.

"Why are you quiet?" Bidar asks.

"Well . . . what are these things that nobody is supposed to see me with?"

"They're related to petroleum," he says quietly.

Without thinking much about what he has just said, I say, "All right, but why shouldn't anyone know about them?"

He makes me understand that the government doesn't like these flyers, and if the police were to catch me with them, they'd put me in jail. I can imagine that Pendar too must have done such things, and that's why he was arrested.

"So what do you say?" Bidar asks.

I don't want to say no. I feel like I want to help him, even if it is only because of my grudge against Gholam Ali Khan. Or that dwarf sergeant who slapped me so hard across the face in the hall of the police station that my head hit the wall. Besides, now that they trust me like this, it's not a man's way to walk away.

"All right, Bidar, give them to me."

He takes a stack of papers out of the briefcase and hands it to me. "Hide them!"

I put the stack of flyers against my stomach, under my belt, and button up my jacket.

"Do you know what time to start?"

"When?"

"At exactly nine you must slip the first flyer inside the first house on Hokumati Street."

"Why not now?"

"Because the other guys also start at nine. You are all set to start at once and quickly finish it at the same time."

"The others are also on Hokumati Street?"

"All over the streets of the town. There is only one other person on Hokumati Street, but he'll start from where the asphalt ends."

I ask him to tell me why we should all start at once.

"Because, if you start earlier, they might see you, and ambush the others who start after you. But when you all start at once and finish simultaneously, their chances of getting their hands on any one of you are much smaller."

We shake each other's hands warmly.

"Good luck!"

And we part ways.

Suddenly, my entire body begins to tremble and my teeth won't stop clicking against each other, as if I've caught a fever. One minute I feel very hot, and the next I feel icy cold. My nose starts to run. I walk along a half-lit street and come to Morshed's teahouse. It's not far from the intersection at Hokumati Street, but for sure it is more than a ten-minute walk to reach the top of the street, where I am supposed to start. I go inside the teahouse. Naser Davani is there, smoking a water pipe. The click-clack of the domino tiles can be heard. A few fellows sit in the teahouse playing.

Naser Davani calls me. "Where have you been?"

"I'm coming back from Aman Aqa's teahouse." Then I ask him what time it is.

He looks at his watch. "Twenty minutes to nine."

I walk out of the teahouse. By the time I reach Hokumati Street, I can feel my temperature rising, burning, then falling, and I grow icy cold. All the way to the top of the street, it goes hot, cold, hot, cold. Once there, I stop and look down the street, all the way to the end, as far as my eyes can see. The entire street is well lit. There's not even a single lightbulb that is burned out. Hunching over, a tall man walks past me. I ask him the time. Reluctantly, he pulls his hand out of his coat pocket and looks at his watch. "Nine," he says.

"Nine sharp?"

"Two minutes till."

The tall man walks away. I should start in a couple of minutes. My hand slides under my jacket and then down under my shirt, reaching for the flyers. I look at the first house. The door is ajar. The overhead light is on. I pull out one of the flyers and fold it. The tall man has gained a distance of a hundred feet. I start to walk. My body is shivering. I look around, slip the flyer into the doorframe, and pass on quickly.

It's over. The job is done. Easy and effortless. Now and then, I heard footsteps. That's all. A few times, I had to stop for the passersby to gain a little distance, and then I would resume my task. I run back home quickly. There are a few flyers on the doorstep of our house. It dawns on me that I should grab one before I go to my room so I can read it; I bend down and pick one up. Aman Aqa has come home from work. Things have changed a lot in his teahouse since the day he replaced the gramophone with the brand new radio. There are many more customers now, particularly more oil refinery workers, who show up out of the blue exactly when the news is being broadcast.

Mother is still sitting there sewing. I sit before the kerosene lamp and read the flyer.

～

Sanam caught Banu and Ebrahim red-handed in Rahim the Donkey Keeper's straw shack. She rushed into the straw shack, grabbed Banu's panties, which were lying beside her, and dashed out into the courtyard. She then proceeded to hold up Banu's flowing, dirty red panties like a banner and wave them, all the while ululating and announcing to everyone that Ebrahim had become a groom.

Just how many days or weeks she had been spying on them God only knows.

Ebrahim, realizing that he was in over his head, darted out of the straw shack like a comet and beat it. Banu covered her calloused knees with her skirt and squatted down in the straw shack. Khaj Tofiq panicked. Like an angry wolf, Afaq attacked Sanam and snatched Banu's panties out of her hand. Then she rushed into the straw shack, clutched Banu's hair, dragged her off to their room, and whacked her with a pair of tongs until she dropped.

Banu is absolutely silent. She doesn't even cry; nor does she say a word to show that she is regretful.

Ebrahim doesn't come home at night. He's staying with Khaleq and Chinuq.

Afaq and Sanam are now like soft butter and a knife, like a bull seeing a red rag. Afaq heaps every cussword she can think of on Sanam. "The slut's forgotten that when she was young, she would come out from under the legs of this fucker or that fucker every day."

Sanam has realized what a terrible mistake she has made. She has realized that she cannot stand up to Afaq. What trouble she has caused for herself by provoking Afaq with her accusation God only knows.

Sanam has given in, but it is Afaq who won't let go. Whenever possible, whether the moment is right or not, she attacks Sanam with some nasty curses. "The skirt-over-her-head whore slept and slept with so many boaters that her useless husband died from the shame of it. Now the bitch is disgracing my daughter."

And no matter how often Sanam turns a deaf ear to her, she won't let up.

Ebrahim is out of control, ready to do anything. At night, he stays over with Khaleq and Chinuq, and during the day, he goes off with them to mug people. The way things are going, I have a feeling that he'll be dealing with the police station one of these days.

Rahim the Donkey Keeper is thinking of remarrying. "If there's no one to watch over Hasani and Ebram," he reasons, "they'll turn out rotten."

If you ask me, Ebrahim has already turned rotten.

". . . Besides," Rahim the Donkey Keeper says, "during the winter, one would like to come home and find a warm room, a brazier, a fire, and a kettle of hot water. He'd like to have a few cups of tea . . . Besides, I can't do mending or patching, and I can wash no dishes."

The women are whispering:

"Oh my God, Naneh Hasani's shroud has not dried yet."

"Oh Lord, there's still the smell of poor Naneh Hasani in his room."

Rahim the Donkey Keeper goes after Ebrahim and catches him over at Khaleq and Chinuq's. He pins him down, ropes his arms and legs, hauls him home, hangs him from a nail on the wall just like a goatskin water bag, and beats his bottom with a pomegranate stick. Once he's whipped him real good, he leaves him hanging from the nail until dawn. But does Ebrahim pay any mind to this?

Again, same old same old.

Once he's released and off the nail, Ebrahim runs away, finds Khaleq and Chinuq, and, again, same old same old—he starts prowling the streets like before.

"Uncle, give me a pack of Gorgan cigarettes."

He takes the pack of cigarettes from the shopkeeper, opens it calmly, lights one, and then drops his head and walks away.

The shopkeeper raises his voice and says, "Hey, boy, you didn't pay for the cigarettes!"

Ebrahim turns around and sticks out his tongue at him. The shopkeeper swears and chases after him. Khaleq lifts the cash drawer. Ebrahim drops the pack and runs away.

Ebrahim is totally on the wrong track.

The woman Rahim the Donkey Keeper has found is a widow of forty-five.

The neighbor women have already gone through her entire pedigree. She is tall. She is a hairdresser. She threads faces.

"Oh my God, she is such a slut, I don't know how she came Mash Rahim's way."

"Sister, it's not just that. They say she is a matchmaker too."

"She has ten lovers too."

"They say she was a respectable housewife once."

Rahim the Donkey Keeper has bought a new pair of *giveh* cotton shoes and a used jacket from a secondhand store.

Father has written: ". . . There is money to be made in Kuwait, but with humiliation . . . You must presume that the Arabs are the servants of the Farangis, and you are the servant of the Arabs. They talk to you in such a way, and beat you with palm branches as if you aren't a human being . . ." I read the letter, fold it, and give it to Mother. She doesn't say anything. She just stares at the amber-colored coals in the brazier. The room is warm. The smell of freshly brewed tea wafts through it.

"I think Amu Bandar has come back from the mosque," Mother says.

I get up and wrap the milk-and-honey-colored sash around my neck. I put on my jacket and head out of the room.

Amu Bandar has stuffed all the crevices of his room with rags. We have stuffed the cracks in our windows and doors with cotton, and Mohammad the Mechanic has sealed his with cement, paper, and tar.

Amu Bandar's room is the size of a grave. The good thing is that it gets warm quickly in the winter.

Amu Bandar is squatting next to the charcoal brazier. His hat is beside him. He has covered his shoulders with a blanket and has turned up the hem of his pants over his legs so that he can patch and mend them. I say hello as I enter. He lifts up his head and says, "Greetings to you, Son."

I sit facing him. The ceiling, the door, and the walls of his room have turned black from the soot and smoke of burnt dung.

"Do you want tea?"

"No, Amu Bandar, thanks."

He puts his pants down and pours himself a cup of tea. Stirring it, he says, "What news from your father?"

I tell him.

"Praise be to God! He is all right, then."

"Thank God," I say. "Just half an hour ago, Lotfi the Plaster Maker was here. He's come back from Kuwait."

"Well?"

"He brought us the letter from Father."

"When you write him," he says, "please send him my regards too."

"I will," I say. "Amu Bandar, he sent the money he borrowed from you too."

He gulps his tea, looks down, pulls the pants across his legs, and says, "I'm not really in a hurry for it . . . If your family needs it, you can have it till he comes back."

"We really appreciate that, Amu Bandar . . . but he sent a bit of money for our everyday expenses too."

He refills his cup of tea. This time he sips it drop by drop.

"You know what . . . I don't need money right now . . . I can live on a loaf of bread and a cup of tea."

On the wall behind him, over the mantelpiece, there is a portrait of Imam Ali. I tell him, "But, Amu Bandar, your daughter's children—"

He looks at me and interrupts me. "It's a long time before Eid's night."

Amu Bandar has grown thinner. Older too. These past few months, I haven't really gotten a chance to see him much, or to take a good look at his face. His neck sticks out from the collar of his worn-out military tunic. It looks so very dry, as if it's the neck of a living chicken whose feathers have been plucked off.

I put the money on the pillow he is resting one of his arms on. One hundred twenty tomans. Father also borrowed money from Mirza

Nasrollah. He sold his watch too. And my mother had to sell the bronze samovar. Five days after he left for Kuwait, we had to sell the large copper pot too. The portrait of Imam Ali is faded. It has blended in with the faded color of the adobe wall. Amu Bandar puts his patched-up pants down, stuffs his pipe, takes a drag, and looks at me. He talks through the puffs of smoke coming out of his mouth. "Alas, the ways of this world . . ."

The sky bursts. A dark mass of clouds has been hovering over the town since sunset.

"To hell with these times! Winter is back and Oussa Haddad is still away in a foreign land."

I am solemn. Amu Bandar runs his hand over the pillow, picks up the money, and puts it inside the lining of his hat. He takes another drag of his pipe, looks at me again, and says, "But, my son, just make sure to ask me if you need money. Don't be shy and stand on ceremony."

I bend over the brazier. The wind sweeps into the room through the cracks in the door. I look at Amu Bandar. He always colors his gray beard with henna and trims his mustache. He doesn't allow his beard to grow more than a fist's length, according to faith. The color of Amu Bandar's eyes is tarnished. He says, "You know what, Khaled, the one thing a man leaves behind in this world is just a memory, good or bad. Everyone must lay their head down on the tombstone. Nobody takes more than a shroud with them."

"Amu Bandar, we'll never forget your—"

He interrupts me. "My son, if we, the wretched, don't help each other, who will do that, then?"

Amu Bandar's words send a shiver through my heart. It sounds like Bidar incarnated in Amu Bandar's body; as if Amu Bandar were speaking with Bidar's idiom. "You know what, Khaled . . . we ourselves should care about one another . . ."

Bidar's anemic face always begins to redden as he says things like: "We should be united. We won't be able to make it if left alone. We'll be shattered and destroyed. We should be welded to each other like iron, like steel . . ."

Amu Bandar says, "We should back each other up. We should keep each other from falling."

My heart trembles. "Thanks, Amu Bandar . . . For the time being, we don't need any money, but if we need it, we'll certainly ask you."

He pours himself more tea. He pours a cup for me too. I can't turn down his offer. The tea is very hot. There is a strong fire going in the charcoal brazier. The tea tastes like henna water. Now Amu Bandar is really in the mood to talk. He's surely got lots on his mind; it's as if all along he's been waiting for someone to sit down and listen to his words as he pours himself out—all his pent-up feelings—real good. Mostly he talks about his daughter. He talks about his grandchildren and says that it's only for their sake that he continues to go on living. "It's all for them that I'm working so hard, collecting people's garbage every day from dawn to dusk, just for a few tomans."

He says his time is already over; he's lived his life. He has sifted his share of flour, so to speak, and has hung his sifter up. Suddenly he feels desperate to be with his grandchildren. "You don't know, Khaled, how much I miss them. How I want to be able to take a few days off and go see them. Alas, Khaled, when you work for the municipality, you can't have a life of your own . . ."

Amu Bandar's voice is coarse. It's sleepy. It's tired. "I slaved my life away in the service of the government . . . all for what? . . . Have I wasted my youth only to come to this? . . . You think the government cares about poor people? . . . You think they appreciate your efforts? May spit be on this world."

Amu Bandar's chest is heavy with sorrow. From what he says, I gather that his idealized view of the government is broken.

There was a time that his eyes would light up when he talked of the government. He would look straight into your eyes and speak with such confidence and dignity: "Well, no matter what, I too work for the government. Not everyone can get government work, either."

But since the day he was robbed of his money in the butchers' market and he went to the police station, where they didn't give a shit about what he said, his notion of the government has completely changed.

His deep drags at the pipe have saturated the tiny room with smoke. The wind shakes the double doors open. I get up.

"Don't bother yourself. I'll close them myself," he says.

"No, Amu Bandar, I'm leaving anyway." So, I leave the room.

The courtyard is quiet. The sky is dark. The donkeys are making noise under the sun shelter. I enter our room and squat down at the brazier, next to where Mother sits, humming a song as usual, while her hands are busy sewing. It's never-ending, her sewing. Just like the saddle on the donkey of Dajjal, the Impostor. It's torn on all sides, and despite all of Mother's mending, the seams keep coming apart. Jamileh is doing her evening prayers. All at once, the doors fall open. The canvas curtain is pushed to the side and through it steps in Aunt Ra'na's son. "Salaam, dearest Aunt."

Mother greets him back.

Gholam fetches the stool from the corner of the room, sets it down beside the brazier, and sits on it. He turns his face to me and greets me. He rubs his hands against each other. "It is so cold," he says.

I don't want to talk to him at all.

He unbuttons his military jacket. Mother pours him a cup of tea. He picks it up, lobs two sugar cubes into his mouth, and, through a full mouth, says, "Dear Aunt, are you going to Mr. Colonel's house tomorrow?"

Feeling provoked, I totally lose control. I get in his face and ask him, "If washing people's clothes and bedsheets is such a good thing to do, why doesn't Aunt Ra'na do it herself?"

Gholam's eyes are round. His hand, holding the cup, freezes at his mouth. Mother glares at me. "Khaled, I told you already that I myself asked Gholam to find me some work."

Gholam's eyes are still wide open. His hand slides down. His voice sounds like that of an adolescent whose voice has just changed. "Since when have you become the head of the household?"

What I really want is to just get up, give him a good whack in the chin, and say, "For your information, let me tell you that you guessed right. Know this too, that my father has sent us money, and I've got my wages too, so you better know that I don't want you to send my mother to do other people's laundry . . . Is that understood?"

Aunt Ra'na's son's voice loses its strength. "All right, Khaled, calm down. Nobody's forcing her."

I know my face has turned all red. I move away, lean against the wall, hug my knees, and place my chin on top of my kneecaps. I don't want to look into Cousin Gholam's narrow eyes.

He lobs two more sugar cubes into his mouth and gulps down the cup of tea at once.

Mother asks if he has eaten dinner.

He cheers up again. "I have . . . I was at Mr. Colonel's house . . ."

I heard from Aunt Ra'na that Gholam was going to dust Mr. Colonel's Persian rugs.

"They were having *fesenjan* stew."

I am so mad at Gholam. I would tear him to pieces if I could. I wish Bolur Khanom would show up so she could put him in his place. I'd be happy if he would just get up and get the hell out of here. I just can't stand seeing his disgusting face.

He shifts his position on the stool and starts talking nonsense. "How would I know that Uncle Haddad has sent you money?"

Mother tells him that he should not take my words so seriously. Gholam's tone has turned gentle now.

"Well that's clear . . . It's obvious that when one is not in need, one wouldn't need to serve others."

Jamileh has finished her praying. Now, she's dozing off. Mother strokes her soft hair. "Get up, my daughter, and go to bed."

Jamileh goes to lie down in her bedroll. Aunt Ra'na's son changes the subject. "Every day, they make you spend more money. It doesn't even occur to them to wonder where these poor villagers are supposed to get that kind of money . . . The city fellows are doing a tad better. For instance, if I don't have money, the relatives do, thanks be to God. I tell myself there is dear Aunt, Uncle Haddad . . . or a friend or an acquaintance."

Mother keeps on with her sewing. She's quiet, no longer humming. Her face, in the glare of the kerosene lamp, appears rather like a silhouette. Her lower lip hangs loose.

Aunt Ra'na's son leans forward and pours tea for himself. If I could, I would take the cup from him and kick his ass out the door.

As he sips his tea, he thickens his voice and mocks Mr. Sergeant's voice: "Gholam, why are your boots dirty?"

His tone becomes obsequious: "Sir, I have run out of polish, sir."

It's Mr. Sergeant's guttural voice again: "You have? Your fine is to get two cans of polish and polish all the troops' boots."

He takes on a sycophantic tone: "But, Mr. Sergeant, I don't have that kind of money. I'd be thankful if I could afford to borrow a little money to get myself a can of polish."

"And your fine for your back talk is to get a broom on your own and sweep the sleeping quarters for three days, three times a day." Now,

Gholam is begging. His small eyes grow narrower, and lines appear around his mouth. "Have mercy, sir. I beg you, sir, have mercy on me. I have no one to ask for help. Where would I get all this money from?"

He dumps all the tea in his mouth at once and gulps it down. "Well, dearest Aunt. That's military service, all right. There are to be no 'whys' and no 'I can'ts.' Take a breather and you're locked up. Dare talk back, you get extensions. Stand up for your rights, you're thrown in jail."

I have never despised Gholam so much. The more he talks, the more my entire body cringes with disgust; it's as though he's chewing on me.

Gholam gets to his feet.

"Where are you going?" Mother asks.

"I just came by to say salaam," he says.

He shifts from foot to foot, and says, "So, dear Aunt, thanks be to God that Uncle Haddad has sent you money."

Mother gets up, goes to her bundle, undoes it, and comes back with a folded note, tucking it in the pocket of Gholam's jacket.

"Dear Aunt, your generosity makes me feel embarrassed."

Mother sits down. "Don't even mention it," she says.

I know that it's not less than ten tomans. Nobody knows Mother better than I do. Her hands seem to belong to a moneyed woman.

Every time the door opens, a lashing wind storms into the teahouse. I don't remember ever seeing the door of the teahouse open and close as much as it has today. The eleventh oil tanker has just pulled over. Today is much different from the other days. The drivers have no intention at all of leaving the teahouse. Feeling cozy and relaxed, they sip their tea, smoke their water pipes or cigarettes.

There are eleven drivers and eleven drivers' helpers altogether.

The first driver, after parking his monstrous oil tanker under the shade, came in and immediately asked us to turn up the radio's volume. "Aman Aqa, why is that croaker of yours so out of breath?"

"At your service, sir. Right away. Spider, turn the volume up!"

All the drivers and their helpers have a white tag on their chests: "The Oil Industry Must Be Nationalized." I think the sound of the radio must reach as far as Pumping Station No. 3. Jan Mohammad shows up, a big smile parting his lips. "Greetings, everyone," he says. He waves his hand at Aman Aqa and sits down, and as always, the first thing he does is look his mustache up and down in a mirror.

Losing no time, I go and hand him the twisting hose of the water pipe. "How are you, Khaled?"

"I'm well, thanks." I pause. "It seems like there's something going on today," I say, looking in the direction of the drivers and their helpers, whose noises are mixed with those of the radio.

He looks at me and says, "It's still a while before the news broadcast."

He doesn't say enough for me to figure out what's going on. He looks pleased. His eyes are bright with a smile. Raising his voice, he says, "Aman Aqa, what's the time according to your watch?"

"Nine thirty-five."

He sets his watch.

Once again, the teahouse door opens. A few workers from Pumping Station No. 3 come in together. I am sure they have sneaked away from work, as usual. All of them have a white tag on their chest. Now everybody in town wears a white tag on their chest. I mean, at least eight out of ten people.

It's warm inside the teahouse. The Farangi heater is ablaze. Spider adds more logs to it. The door opens every second, each time ushering in a group of workers in blue overalls. I don't even know many of them. A handful of them I am seeing for the first time. Little by little, all the chairs and benches are taken. I'm sure that if Spider weren't high, Aman Aqa wouldn't be able to handle all these customers. I've gotten all the water pipes ready and taken them over to their tables, but before I know it, it's time to go and prepare another bowl of soaked tobacco.

Jan Mohammad didn't give me a proper answer. As I gather up the empty cups, I walk along with Spider, who's serving tea to everyone. "Spider, do you know what's going on today?" I ask.

Without turning his face to me, he says, "I don't know, but there must be something going on."

I hear another oil tanker pull the brakes in front of the teahouse. The driver's helper is the same fellow I gave the box of newspapers to to take to the harbor.

I take a cup of tea from Spider and go to him. Greeting him, I set the cup of tea in front of him.

He shakes hands with me. "How are you, comrade?"

"Good," I say. "What's going on today?"

"How can you not know what's going on?"

I am embarrassed. I feel like I have committed a sin. His tone makes it clear I should know what is going on. How could I not know?

"Haven't you gotten together with the other comrades?" the driver's helper asks.

It's been two days since I've seen Bidar, so I say, ". . . Two days . . ."

"Didn't you listen to the news last night?" he asks.

I tell him that we don't have a radio at home.

"Then listen. Today, at ten o'clock, the prime minister is supposed to talk on the radio."

Now I know why Jan Mohammad reset his watch, and why all the drivers and refinery workers have swarmed into the teahouse.

Aman Aqa calls me: "Khaled, fix a water pipe."

There is a jumble of voices. The radio plays a song. Aman Aqa doesn't get a chance to wash the empty glasses. Spider swiftly weaves back and forth between the tables. He carries more than ten glasses in his hands at a time. The teahouse is filled with water pipe and cigarette smoke. It has started raining. I look out through the south-side window. From a distance, I can see smoke rising into the air, right there in front of the checkpoint at the harbor intersection. I see water streaming down the street. What a downpour! I look through the east-side window. The heavy, thick strings of rain are fighting the gas flames. The flames writhe and thrash about like a wounded dragon. They drop, then swiftly twist around the strings of rain like ivy vines and sharply shoot up.

The song is over. Abruptly, everyone falls silent, as though they have just stopped breathing. Now, the voice of a man, fierce and strong, rises from the radio, shaking the teahouse. I think it's the prime minister, but no, it's not him. After the gruff voice of the news announcer, the prime minister begins to talk. His voice sounds too stiff. Just like Mr. Captain's. The same captain Afaq takes the smuggled satin to.

I have heard that the prime minister is a military man and that he's a stubborn man who doesn't give a damn about anyone's opinion.

Everyone is listening carefully, so carefully, so as not to miss a word. The prime minister's words do not sound promising. They don't appeal to the workers. Now I understand these sorts of things better. Even if you were dumb, you could read it on their displeased faces. The prime minister's speech is over.

"Fat chance."

Next on the radio is a program about the art of puppetry.

"Was that the important speech?"

The program's host explains, "Staging a successful puppet show depends on the craft and skill of the hands wielding the puppets."

It's nonsense. No one is listening anymore. There's a clamor of voices. They are discussing and evaluating the prime minister's speech. Their lips are pursed. The prime minister believes we are not capable of making a ewer, and even if we were to make one, water would leak out of it. He says that if we nationalize the oil industry, we will be destroyed, that expelling the British is a mistake. Of course, these are not his exact words, but something along these lines. For instance, we don't have petroleum engineers. Our economy rests on oil. If they boycott our oil and decide not to buy it anymore, we'll go bankrupt. Things of this sort.

The drivers get to their feet and head out of the teahouse. They look exhausted as they walk out, as though they have been toiling to move a mountain out of the way.

The rain hasn't stopped yet. It whips the earth. There will be a flood any moment.

The oil tankers shake into motion, one after another.

The workers are still here, sitting and talking. Their words are jumbled up. "He is the servant of the British," I hear.

"He's taken an oath to protect their profits."

"As long as he is in charge, the British have no worries."

I am sure the oil company workers understand these things better. I mean, they are dealing with the British firsthand. Yet the prime minister is not a person of little importance. It's not like he was appointed based on the size of his belly, or because he has pretty eyes. Besides, he's not just talking when he says we will end up walking the streets bare-bottomed, miserable, and hungry if we are given the oil industry to run on our own. I am sure he must know something we don't know. The prime minister is not someone to fiddle with. He is not like Karam Ali, who bet he could stuff a saucer inside his mouth, but instead had it shatter in his mouth, ripping up his tongue and all. Poor, wretched boy lost his profession because of betting. Now if it was summer, he wouldn't need to shout. He would just push his cart with the pot of hot beans on top of it up to Tuba, the arrack seller's pub. Time is not on his side, because it's winter and he has to sell turnips, and that means shouting to grab the attention of his customers.

It's been two days since Karam Ali's wide mouth was shut. The split in his muzzle has been filled with rags. Sanam is planning to set up an oven next to the donkeys' sun shelter and bake homemade bread. "I can't afford to wait until Karam Ali's mouth opens again," she says. "I've got to do something before we starve to death."

"I have recommended you," says Bidar.

"But I don't have good handwriting, nor can I write fast, Bidar!" I say.

He puts his hand on my shoulder and looks at me kindly. "They will do the writing. You just keep them company."

"They? How many of them are there?"

"Three."

We are to write on the wall of the dam on the west bank of the Karun. The dam is soft and even, and is more than a hundred meters long. It extends all the way from under the traffic police post, situated at the beginning of the dam, up to the house of the barracks' commander, which is adjacent to the post office.

"If you write this slogan in nice handwriting, tomorrow morning there will be such an uproar. The railway company employees who pass over the bridge will all gather around the railing to look at it. That alone will look like a protest."

The paint will turn black the moment the sun rises and casts light upon it. Cleaning it off won't be such an easy job, either.

I meet the others. They look very familiar. I must have seen all three of them more than a hundred times. All it really takes is one day of pacing up and down Pahlavi Street, and you'll get to see all the people of the town.

"I am Iman."

He is short and swarthy, well built, with eyebrows that meet, curly hair, and black eyes. He must be an athlete to have such a prominent chest and full arms, which stand out from his sides.

"Azad."

Too tall and thin, with a pointed chin. His skin is pale, his eyes are the color of agate, his hair is amber-colored, and he takes long strides as he walks.

"Hemmat."

He has a sharp gaze and can't stand still, squirming constantly. He's medium height. His forehead extends up to the middle of his head. His nose looks like a ball of rice that has been smashed on his face. Hemmat's mouth is wide.

We get a taxi. The night is young. The sky is cloudy. It's a bit hot. It looks like it might rain. We pass under the tall arches of the White Bridge. A few people are walking alone on the bridge. A tall policeman talks to a middle-aged policeman in front of the traffic police post. The taxi turns around the triangular lawn at the entrance to the bridge and comes to a stop opposite the post office building, where we get out. Light shines from the bulbs inside the house of the barracks' commander and cuts through the dense branches of the trees. A red light on the tall wireless mast flashes on and off. The weather is warm, but I'm shivering. My teeth won't stop chattering. I lock my jaws so that the other guys will not hear it.

At this time of night—and in the winter at *that*—if they see us, aren't they going to ask what the hell we're doing along the bank of the river?

They have thought of that too. It's not their first time doing this. They have done it so many times that to them it is as easy as drinking a glass of water.

"Those who drink arrack have such bizarre cravings. Sometimes they take their liquor and go to the slope of a mountain, sit right there in the snow and drink."

They have brought with them half a bottle of raisin arrack, two glasses, and two pieces of pickled cucumber. We pass behind the short wall of the barracks' commander's house. We then walk around the newly built post office and slide down the steep slope onto the riverbank.

The river is choppy. The Karun has risen from the recent heavy rains. It's thunderous and stormy. It has taken on the color of a sapphire in the darkness of the night.

We climb over the large and small boulders until we're under the first arch of the White Bridge. I carry the can of paint. Azad, his long legs striding ahead of us, has the brush.

The wind is howling through the arches and columns of the bridge. It sounds like the humming of thousands of people huddled up together. The Karun's east bank, with its small bright lights, seems to be miles away. The sound of the waves is mesmerizing, inflicting fear on one's entire body. My teeth have not yet ceased chattering. I have kept my jaws locked together so long that they are beginning to hurt.

Iman leans against the smooth surface of the bridge's first inner column. It's very dark under the bridge. Iman stands in the dark, searching for better-lit spots. Hemmat takes up his position behind the water level tower. If it continues to rain like it has, the entire tower will be under the water. Above us is the small kiosk for the traffic police. The sound of passing cars honking their horns fuses with the roar of the river. We check out the area, and then Azad begins. He rolls up his jacket sleeves and dips the brush into the paint. The brush is wider than the width of four fingers. The paint is not visible at all. The white surface of the dam on the west bank of the Karun is wet for only a second under the brush before the wind dries it. All at once, the sound of a policeman's whistle startles us. Azad stops writing. I look up and see a policeman running quickly toward the triangular lawn. Azad darts a glance at me, shrugs his shoulders, and carries on with his writing. His amber-colored hair looks brown in the dark. For a second, a thunderbolt, followed by a rumble, illuminates every surface. The clouds split apart and moonlight pours down. Now our shadows stretch long before our feet. I look at Iman, who pulls himself into the shadow of the bridge. We all step into the shadow and wait there for the moon to disappear behind the clouds. Hemmat whistles a familiar tune. We gaze at the water level tower. Hemmat's shadow has moved away from the tower's shadow. We hide the can of paint and the brush behind a large boulder, covering them with large and small stones, and sit a few feet away on a large cliff protruding out of the sand along one of the Karun's basins.

I see Hemmat coming our way. Following him at a distance is a policeman from the kiosk. Iman strides toward us, jumps over a few rocks, and then sits down beside us. Azad shakes the bottle of arrack and taps its bottom with the palm of his hand, causing the cork to loosen up. He dribbles some of the liquor onto the damp sands. The strong smell of alcohol fills our noses. The policeman reaches us. He is short and stout; his mustache covers his entire mouth. "What y'all doing here?" he asks.

Azad holds out to him a glass brimming with arrack. "Please, enjoy yourself, Sergeant."

The policeman steps forward, standing over us. His hand rests firmly on his weapon's holster, fastened around his waist.

"Drink it up, sir," drawls Iman.

Iman stretches his words and stammers in such a way that you'd think he had drunk an entire bottle of raisin arrack all by himself.

The policeman toughens up, and in a scratchy voice, says, "You couldn't find anywhere else for drinking your goddamn arrack but the riverbank, in this cold?"

"'A place is joyful when the heart feels joyful,'" Iman recites in a drunken voice.

The policeman refuses to take the glass of arrack. Azad gets to his feet and insists some more.

"Hurry up and beat it, you all," warns the policeman.

Leaning back on a rock, Iman pleads, "To your health, Sergeant; there's just a few ounces left . . . and as soon as we finish it, we'll up and go . . . We're at your service, sir."

The surface of the Karun, under the moonlight, has taken on the color of red sand. The waves crash against the bridge's columns, which tear the water in all directions, and then continue rolling along boisterously. Florescent bulbs illuminate the interior of the police station and the kiosk.

"Get moving, then!"

"Don't reject my hand, Sergeant. Drink this glass up," Azad insists.

The policeman has a change of heart now. "I shouldn't drink while on duty," he says hesitantly.

Now it is Azad's long and pointy chin that moves. "Come on, man, take it . . . Whose business is it anyway? To your health!"

The policeman takes the shot of arrack. "To your health!" he says just before downing it all in one gulp. He wipes the tip of his mustache with the back of his hand.

Azad takes the empty glass from his hand and refills it. "One more shot, Sergeant!"

The policeman steps back. "One was enough . . . Now, hurry up. If you weren't nice guys—"

"Praise to all men with a grain of graciousness," Iman interrupts him.

The policeman lights a cigarette and walks away. The moon has crept under a cloud. We can see the policeman's silhouette move up the steep hill that leads to the post office. We don't lose any time. Azad strides toward the wall and quickly begins to write. Any slight sound startles us. The bright light of the bulbs inside the commander's house has spread all the way to the edge of the dam. We're almost done. There's only a twelve-letter word left to write. The way Azad is writing it, its "E" stretches as long as a foot. Right after we write "S-T-E'-M-A," the policeman appears again. He must suspect something to keep coming and going like this. He comes out from behind the post office. Azad is writing the letter "R." In the time it will take for him to reach the dam, climb down, and pass the water level tower, we will be able to write "G-A-R-A-N," the remaining five letters of *este'margaran* (colonizers). At the pace Azad writes, it's done in the blink of an eye.

The policeman walks down the slope of the riverbank. Finished. The writing is done, but I tremble all over. We leave the can of paint and the brush behind a rock and take off.

Azad begins to sing:

> *The night, cloudy, and the moon, streaked,*
> *The fine wine of Khollar in the chalice, waiting.*

Iman steps out from under the bridge. (Our sign was, as soon as we heard Azad singing a tune we would know that the job was finished.) At any moment the policeman will reach us. Azad, holding the arrack bottle by its neck, stumbles toward him. Hemmat walks away from the safety of the water level tower and begins unbuttoning his fly.

"You're still here?" The policeman's voice sounds muffled.

"We're leaving, Sergeant."

The policeman quickens his pace to match ours. "Where's the other one?"

"He's gone to shit," says Hemmat.

The policeman looks at the bottle of arrack. "You finished that arrack?"

"No, sir, we still have some."

"Give me a shot."

Azad pours him a shot. The policeman sends it down his throat, and, his voice choppy, says, "You don't eat anything with it?"

"We got pickled cucumber, if you'd like, sir."

The wrinkles on the policeman's face are now looking more defined. I feel such joy, as if I've been given all the goods in the entire world. I would never have thought of fooling a policeman.

"Give me a cigarette."

It is Iman, who had supposedly gone to shit.

We walk up the slope. The policeman parts ways with us and walks toward the post office. We pass by the barracks' commander's house. The commander's car arrives and stops in front of the house. As he steps out of the car, the commander looks at us for a second, and then stiffly walks toward the door of the house.

The soldier guarding the door clicks his boots.

Hasani has found himself a sunny corner in the yard. He has taken off his shirt and wrapped himself in a blanket so that he can search through the shirt's seams. Mother washes Hasani's clothes whenever possible. I have no idea how there's always lice in them.

Folding his arms around a bundle of clothes, Rahim the Donkey Keeper comes out of his room and sets off for the public baths. "Hasani, sweep the floor before I come back from the baths."

"Sure, Baba."

Mash Rahim takes off. Hasani's eyes follow him. He gets up, folds the blanket, puts his shirt back on, and goes into their room. There are patches of crusted sweat and dirt on his black pants.

Ebrahim has turned into a complete wanderer. He doesn't even set foot in this house anymore. Like an ass, he stands erect, face-to-face with Rahim the Donkey Keeper, and says whatever cusswords he wants to. He follows Khaleq's and Chinuq's asses around. Last time I saw him, he didn't seem to be doing all that bad. He was wearing new clothes, some of those Kuwaiti trousers and a black woolen turtleneck sweater with long sleeves. There was even some color to his skin, and his cheeks looked sort of pink. "How're you doing, Ebram?" I asked him.

"Thank God, not bad."

He had a Gorgan cigarette at the corner of his lips and a benzene lighter in his hand. Like one those *jahels* or smugglers, or a pirate, he had shoved a handkerchief in the back pocket of his pants, its edges hanging out.

Ebrahim follows Khaleq's and Chinuq's asses around, stealing.

"Dear Uncle, don't take your eyes off this bike."

A middle-aged man with salt-and-pepper hair and a hand-wide beard darts a glance at Ebrahim. "What will happen if I leave it there like that?"

In a matter-of-fact, blunt tone, Ebrahim says, "It'd be taken."

Surprised, the middle-aged man pushes up his camel wool hat from his forehead and asks, "They'll lift it?"

Ebrahim lights a cigarette and says, "Yeah, they'll lift it . . . Not much of a surprise, is it?"

The man stands up straight, with his arms akimbo, and asks, "How will they lift it?"

"Like this."

And he puts the cigarette between his lips, takes the bike off the edge of the pavement, and shows the middle-aged man, standing there motionless, how they might lift his bike.

"What'd you think you're doing?"

Ebrahim lets the cigarette drop from between his lips and says, "Just wait a second and I'll show you how they'll lift it." And then, his foot on the pedal, he hops along with the bike a few steps, jumps on its seat, and quickly rides away, winding through the crowd.

The man raises his voice. "Hey, where are you going?" he calls after Ebrahim. But his voice gets smothered in the cacophony of the crowded marketplace. "Hey, boy, where are you taking my bike?" he shouts this time.

Ebrahim has already disappeared among the people, four-wheeled carts, and trucks.

The middle-aged man takes off his hat and runs after him.

Hasani's cheekbones protrude. There's barely any life in his eyes. His arms and legs are as thin as a water pipe's hose.

"Hasani, feed the animals some hay!"

Hasani turns his head and says, "Sure, Baba."

"Hasani, hurry up and groom the animals!"

"Sure, Baba."

"Hasani, you must get up early in the morning and take the animals to the brickkiln; I have something to take care of. I'll come later."

"Sure, Baba."

"Hasani, shake and dust the blankets and air them out in the sun!"

Ebrahim's eyes have come alive. Now, there's a bit of flesh to his face, giving some thickness to his once bony neck and cheeks. I hear he goes to the Zurkhaneh gym too. Not to mention his visits to the *jahels'* teahouse. He deals with Asad the Pawnbroker too. "What do I do with this, Asad Aqa?"

"What did you do with the other ones?"

"Do you want me to take it to the stockroom?"

"Once you finish, come and get your money."

"How much will you give me for it?"

"Like always."

"But, Asad Aqa, this one is a three-rifle Raleigh, and it runs perfectly."

Asad the Pawnbroker looks the bike up and down, hardens his voice, and says, "That's it. I won't pay even a *papasi* more than fifty for it."

Ebrahim haggles. "Seventy."

Asad Aqa's voice becomes gruff. "Take it to the stockroom and shut up, asshole. Yeah, right, like he paid sweat-earned money for it!"

Rahim the Donkey Keeper returns from the baths. There's still a pale yellow sun visible. By the time the sunlight slips below the roof's edge, Rahim the Donkey Keeper has shaved, trimmed his mustache, put on the jacket he bought from the secondhand market, and slipped on his new *giveh* shoes. He throws a loincloth over his shoulder and heads out of his room. "Hasani, eat your dinner and go to sleep before I come back."

It has grown dark. Hasani stands on the threshold of their room. He seems unsure of what to do. My mother calls him. Hasani tilts his neck to the side, and then comes and sits next to the brazier. Clearly, the cold has permeated his entire body. He's shivering. Mother pours him tea. He drinks it while it's still very hot. Mother asks him, "Where did your baba go?"

In a muffled voice, he answers, "I think he went to bring his wife home."

Hasani's eyes are moist. He drinks a second cup of tea. His hand, still holding the cup, is shaking. His large head wobbles on his thin neck. Mother gives us each a plate of food. The cooked lentils are hot, hot. She has made them so spicy that beads of sweat gather on your forehead. Hasani no longer shivers. He eats his dinner, then moves back, leans against the wall, hugs his knees, and stares at his feet. He's despondent. Not in the mood to talk at all. Mother tells him he can sleep in our room if he likes. "I'll spread bedrolls for both you and Khaled in the other room."

"I wouldn't mind it, but I'm afraid my baba would get mad at me."

Mother says, "He won't do that; I won't let him."

Hasani's face is long and pointy, his forehead narrow—the distance from his hair down to his eyebrows is not more than a knuckle joint. Mother pours Hasani tea again. Then she puts a bowl of salted almonds in front of us. While we eat the salted almonds, Mother spreads the bed linen for us in Father's room. It's still not far into the night when we lie down. I don't feel sleepy at all. Hasani is restless. He keeps tossing and turning. One minute he folds his legs and presses them against his stomach, the next he lies flat on his back, then face down. I hear him moan faintly. I ask him why he's so restless. He says, "It's nothing."

Mother is still sitting next to the brazier, doing nothing at all. Just sitting. She's gotten into the habit, during the winter, of sitting next to the brazier, hugging her knees, till midnight. If she has sewing and needlework, she keeps herself busy this way; otherwise, she keeps drinking tea till midnight. She entertains herself with drinking tea and flipping the charcoals, that's it.

Hasani stretches his legs and turns over. I'm guessing he's suffering from something, and that's why he is so restless. I ask him again, "Are you in pain or something?"

"No."

"Then why do you keep tossing and turning?"

"It's nothing, I just am."

I know he is lying. I mean, if you're feeling all right, you would just sleep.

"But, Hasani . . . it seems like you're in pain."

He turns his head and looks at me.

"You're in pain, aren't you?"

"I'm afraid, Khaled . . . I'm afraid."

"Afraid? What're you afraid of, Hasani?"

He whispers, "Please, Khaled, talk quietly!"

His voice sounds like a tiny mouse's, as if he is squeaking.

"Got it. Now, Hasani, tell me!"

Hasani mumbles, "I don't want anyone to know."

I promise him that I will keep his words and pain to myself.

"You know, Khaled . . ."

But he changes his mind and does not say whatever he was about to say. Instead, he rolls his body over and folds his legs into his stomach, still agitated. I move closer to him. "Tell me . . . I promised you I would not tell anyone about it. Tell me. Maybe I can help."

He turns over again and looks at me. His lips are trembling. "Remember you promised."

"All right. I promise you, like a man would."

"You know, Khaled . . . I can't . . . It burns . . . I can't piss . . . It aches . . . I feel like I'm on fire."

I can't make anything out of what Hasani tells me. I pull myself up, lean on my right elbow, and crane my neck. I can see Mother through the doorway, still sitting next to the brazier, dozing off. I can hear Jamileh snoring quietly. The glow of the lamp has left Mother's face half lit and half shadowed. I'm sure Mother won't hear us. I reach for Hasani's arm and squeeze it. "What did you say, Hasani? I don't get it . . . How come you can't piss?"

"You don't know how painful it is . . . it burns." His speech is muffled and confused. "You can't imagine, Khaled . . . it burns. I can't even piss, not until the pus comes out . . . It burns so much that I'd rather die."

I'm still trying to make sense of what he's said. Hasani's eyes are sunken. His eyelashes are moist. He pulls himself up and sets the pillow against the wall. His long face moves as he mumbles. Apparently, Chinuq took him to Abbareh, where he met Gongeh. Chinuq himself paid Gongeh's prostitution fee for Hasani. I have heard about Abbareh from Ebrahim. Gongeh has managed to fix up a hut for herself along the big creek that irrigates the farmlands south of town. Gongeh is a young mute woman. At first, she worked for Javaher the Crippled. Then she split from Javaher, and moved further out, past the huddled gypsy tents. There she put together some sort of a hut for herself, so that she could work on her own. I heard all this from Ebrahim. "You don't know how good it feels, Khaled." Ebrahim swallows his saliva as he tells me this with such enthusiasm. "Her fee is only five rials. Imagine that, only five rials! And you know what? When she used to work with Javaher the Crippled, you could've even fucked her for a bit of opium worth only two rials. I must've stolen opium from Khaj Tofiq ten times and gone to her."

Ebrahim told me that Javaher is an addict, that she uses so much opium that her water pipe is always ready in her hand, and that she always sits in front of her door so that she can hunt customers for her whores.

"Last time I went to Gongeh," Ebrahim said, "on my way I pocketed a mousetrap from the gypsies and sold it for one toman."

I have seen the gypsies. A few times, whenever we went to the field, we passed by their tents. Their men sit in front of their tents and work all day long. They make reels for wells, sieves, small metal baskets, wooden pans, mousetraps, and, God knows, a thousand other odd gizmos. Their women rove around town from sunup to sunset, calling out, "We sell kebab skewers, we have charcoal bellows, we read your palms, we tell your fortunes . . ."

Hasani is writhing around. I wish this pain would leave him alone so that he could finally get some sleep. I tap his shoulder gently and say, "Why don't you go and pee, then?"

He moans, "But you don't know how painful it is."

It has been around twenty days since he went to Gongeh.

"Is Chinuq sick like you?" I ask.

His voice sounds as though it is tinged with tears. As if he's got the hiccups, he says, "No . . . nothing is wrong with him."

I insist that he go to the outhouse and relieve himself.

He finally gives in, pushes the blanket away, and heads out. Mother is stirring a cup of tea. The gleam of the lamplight, creeping through the doorway, has reached as far as our bedrolls. Hasani comes back, weeping.

"Now what, Hasani?"

He says that he's finally relieved. "But you can't imagine how painful it was, Khaled."

He lies down, covers his head with the blanket, and stays still, like a rock. But I can't fall asleep. I'm still thinking about what could have happened to Hasani.

It's around midnight when Mash Rahim comes home. Mother gets up and peeks out into the courtyard through the crack between the windows. Hasani is snoring quietly. I get up and stand behind Mother. I can see Rahim the Donkey Keeper. All the doors in the courtyard are now ajar, and in front of all of them, there is a streak of light on the ground.

There is a tall woman with Rahim the Donkey Keeper. The woman is a good head taller than him. She has wrapped herself tightly in her chador. Her hips sway as she walks. Rahim the Donkey Keeper goes into his room with the woman. The streaks of light in front of the rooms disappear.

What a tall woman Rezvan is. Even taller than Afaq. Bolur Khanom doesn't even come to her shoulders. When she talks, all the other women fall silent. They gaze at her mouth and listen. A tinge of incredulity and distrust colors their faces.

"What was I supposed to do, Sister?" says Rezvan. "People say so much nonsense behind a widow's back . . ."

Rezvan's eyes exude confidence. Her speech is gentle and agreeable. ". . . He kept badgering me about his two motherless kids . . . My heart is not made out of stone . . . I felt bad for his kids; otherwise, he's too old . . . To be honest, I'm too old too."

Rezvan has given all the neighbors candies, sweets, and mixed nuts and raisins. Rahim the Donkey Keeper went to the public baths early in the morning, then came back, ate his breakfast, and took off for the market to buy some foodstuffs for lunch.

Rezvan has rubbed rouge on her cheeks. The women of the neighborhood are whispering among themselves. "She is such a whore she will have Mash Rahim wrapped around her little finger."

Some of the neighbor women have come to have a closer look at Rezvan. Holding their babies against their chests, they talk to Sanam.

Rezvan is moving things around. "Come, good boy . . . take the other end of this kilim and let's air it out in the sun."

Hasani bends over. Rezvan puts the folded, damp kilim on his back. Hasani is dead tired and out of breath by the time he takes the kilim up the stairs to the roof and spreads it open.

Rezvan is sorting things out in her room. She is wearing a scarf so as to keep the dust off her pitch-black hair. She picks up Naneh Hasani's odds and ends and wrinkled and crumpled clothes, and piles them under the donkeys' sun shelter. She pours some kerosene on them and sets them on fire. Then she sits beside the courtyard pool and patiently washes years of dirt off the Primus burner and the kerosene lamp. Rahim the Donkey Keeper's room looks clean and fresh. The scent of aloeswood wafts through the room. Hasani has not come back down yet. He is lying on the kilim in the sun. Afaq comes out of her room. She sees that some of the neighbor women have gathered around Sanam, whispering gossip. Afaq starts grumbling. She is still mad at Sanam. Whenever she gets a chance she gives Sanam a taste of her nasty swearwords. Afaq walks by the women. They fall silent. Afaq glares at Sanam and grumbles, "The pot is calling the kettle black?"

Sanam bites her lip and turns around. Afaq heads out of the house.

I bend down to close the door of the pigeon coop. I hear Bolur Khanom's voice saying, "Aman Aqa is planning to go on a trip."

I stand up. Bolur Khanom has walked past the pigeon coop. Rezvan is standing in her doorway looking around the yard.

I don't feel like working. I hunker down on a bench in the corner of the teahouse, hugging my knees. This morning, as soon as I got to the teahouse, I started the bowl of tobacco soaking and then sat down. I tried to entertain myself with listening to the songs on the radio, but it didn't work. I can't stop thinking about Hasani. I know that early this morning he headed out to the brickkilns without even drinking his cup of tea.

For the second day in a row Mash Rahim hasn't gone to the brickkilns. Yesterday was Friday, so Hasani didn't go either. The way it's going, Rahim the Donkey Keeper will sleep the day away in the arms of Rezvan tomorrow too. What pain Hasani must be experiencing in this cold. He himself said that *it* is gonorrhea. Perhaps Aman Aqa might know better what to do.

"Aman Aqa has caught gonorrhea a couple of times and even once had a bubo. That's why he's sterile."

"Of course, dear, with someone who's caught all sorts of diseases, it's obvious that he won't be able to make a baby."

I look at Aman Aqa. He is reclining behind the counter, smoking a water pipe. There's a cup of weak tea in front of him. A few out-of-town customers sit here and there, eating breakfast: bread, cheese, and sweetened tea. From the look of their bundles and bedroll covers, you can tell that they're on their way to Kuwait. These days, whenever you talk to anyone, you'll find that all they want is to scrape together some travel money so that they can set off for Kuwait.

"Man, I'm rotting to death here! How long can a person stomach a life without any work?"

Most of the men in our neighborhood have gone to Kuwait. Alavan the Blacksmith, Hasan the Carpenter, Zayer Yaqub, Abol the Patcher, Naser the Kerosene Seller, and even Rajab Mofangi, who can barely keep his own ass clean.

Spider stands beside the samovar, pouring himself a cup of tea. He has tossed a bit of *shireh* in his mouth, savoring it under his tongue. Once he's high and in a good mood, I might ask him if he can come up with some sort of remedy for Hasani's pain. I definitely must ask him. Spider knows a lot about these sorts of things. "I have seen enough of this world," he always says. "I have swallowed so many snakes that I have turned into a dragon."

Spider takes the handkerchief off his shoulder and blows his nose. It occurs to me that it'd be better if I asked Aman Aqa. I mean, at least he knows Hasani better than Spider does, and he might even feel pity for him.

The sun is up in the sky. For sure, Hasani must be writhing in pain and dying each second as he takes the donkeys, with their loads of raw bricks, from the brickmakers' field to the brickkilns.

I get up from the bench. I simply cannot stop thinking about Hasani and his watery eyes, his trembling lips, and his big head wobbling on his thin neck. I can't get him out of my head. This morning I saw him coming out of the outhouse weeping. His long muzzle was trembling, as if he had had a seizure.

I pass among the chairs and tables and walk up to the samovar counter. I hold my hands over the hot coals in the brazier and look at Spider. He looks at me and says through his nose, "What's the matter, Khaled?"

The words are on the tip of my tongue but don't escape my lips. Obviously, Spider is not in the mood; otherwise, he would have pestered me until I told him what was on my chest. The *shireh* has not worked its effects on him yet.

I am even more impatient. I don't think I will feel at ease until I do something to help Hasani.

"You can't imagine, Khaled, the kind of pain I am going through."

A huge oil tanker passes by the window, pulls over, and stops under the sunshade. The customers crane their necks to see better.

"I die a thousand times before I pee."

I try to walk in the direction of Aman Aqa, intending to bring it up somehow. My heart feels heavy. I think of Shafaq's words: "Khaled, remember that if the poor don't help each other, they will be ruined."

Shafaq's expression doesn't leave any room for doubt.

"You should always remember that their pain is your pain too."

I wish Hasani's pain was from anything but gonorrhea. I wish he had broken an arm, or his neck. At least you wouldn't be embarrassed talking about it. You could tell everyone. You could ask for anyone's help. But gonorrhea . . .

"One should have a battle with oneself . . . One should first change and improve oneself, then demand changes for a better society."

No, I wouldn't ever open my mouth before Shafaq and tell him about a thing like that.

Aman Aqa has put aside the water pipe. He calls out to me, "Khaled."

I walk up to him.

"You don't seem quite yourself today!"

"No, Aman Aqa, it's nothing."

"Then go and have some tea. You will feel refreshed."

The words are on the tip of my tongue. "Aman Aqa . . ." I am about to tell him that Hasani has caught gonorrhea, but the words are stuck in my throat.

"What is it, Son? What is it you want to say?"

I mumble.

"Tell me! Don't be shy!"

"No, Aman Aqa, I'm not being shy."

Suddenly I feel I would be much more comfortable talking about it with Shafaq. It's not like I myself have caught the disease. I am only helping Hasani. That's not something to be embarrassed of.

Aman Aqa's tiny eyes are fixed on mine. "Why don't you talk?"

So I tell him that I just need to leave for an hour.

"You're going home?" he asks.

"No."

"That's not something to be shy about, my son . . . just go."

I take a deep breath and pull up the collar of my jacket. The passengers are haggling with the driver's helper. I get going. I hear Aman Aqa's voice: "But, Khaled, you're not at all yourself today!"

Spider is now wound up.

I reassure Aman Aqa that I'm all right, and head out of the teahouse. The cold is lacerating my ears. I proceed along the asphalt road toward town. By now, most of the drivers know me. Any one of them passing by will give me a ride. It's a long way from the harbor intersection to town. If I walk all the way in this cold, I will freeze. So I wait at the head of the road. The weather has turned cloudy. The sun is so pale, as if it has lost all its light. I notice that there are six gas flare stacks. When I first started working at Aman Aqa's teahouse, there were only three of them. Then they added another one. There were five of them on Friday night, and now there is a sixth one sprouting from the ground.

"That's all the wealth of the nation smoking up into the air."

"I don't get it, Bidar. How is that the wealth of the nation?"

He explains that these natural gases can be used in so many different ways, rather than being wasted like this.

My eyes follow the twists and turns of the dancing flames until I'm jolted by the sound of a truck stopping before me. "Hop in, Khaled."

I know both the driver and his helper. I sit next to the helper, feeling cozy. It's warm in the truck cabin. The driver is passionate as he talks about oil and how the British plunder it. These days, that's what everyone talks about.

". . . The only way out is to nationalize it . . ."

Even the schoolchildren say the same thing. Even the bazaar merchants say the same thing.

". . . They're gone, those times when we needed a guardian . . . Now, we are mature and capable. We should throw all the British into the sea."

The driver's mustache covers his lips. He lays his bulky torso upon the wheel and says, "You think we're crippled? Or you think our own educated youth can't replace the Farangi staff? Or is the ripe fruit good only for the animal to enjoy?"[1]

---

1. This proverb is usually directed at those who have the best things in life bestowed upon them but do not possess the refinement to appreciate them.

I think the driver's helper is in the mood to tease him. These days, if you want to piss someone off, just tell them that we are not capable of managing the oil industry. That's enough to make their eyes pop out and have them start on a long ramble about how and why we can run it.

I get off the truck near the town.

"Good-bye."

"May God be with you!"

The truck heads toward the slope of a hill east of town. I sink my hands inside my pockets and begin to walk.

"Hey, Khaled, you've grown so tall! You don't look like a sixteen-year-old at all."

I have noticed it myself too. Suddenly, I have grown tall, and there's a line of black hair above my upper lip.

I pass through a couple of alleyways and backstreets. I turn in to a twenty-four-meter-wide street. I hunch down from the cold. I have tucked my head inside the collar of my short jacket.

The thought of Hasani won't leave me alone. I have decided to go and tell Shafaq everything, without any hesitation, whatever happens. It's not like I can tell these things to Rahim the Donkey Keeper. If he were ever to find out, Hasani would be done for. He would take his anger with Ebrahim out on poor Hasani. Yet, again, I feel I cannot take another step.

"Public Hospital."

It occurs to me suddenly. I'm filled with joy. Why didn't I think of it sooner? I'm certain that this hospital is for treating diseases just like this one. For treating afflicted people like Hasani, like Spider, and even myself, and many others of this town.

I walk across the street and go inside the hospital.

The sun has come out from behind the clouds and regained some of its intensity.

A large building with a gabled roof sits in the middle of the vast grounds of the hospital. Iron railings separate the brick building from the hospital itself. The railings were once white. Now, with age, they have become a dirty gray. There must be more than a hundred people leaning against the railings under the sun. They have clothed themselves with whatever they had on hand. A middle-aged man with a swollen stomach moans. His black beard is flecked with white. His pale skin is spotted like the peel of a rotten banana. Next to him sits a young woman. She is hugging her knees and rocking back and forth. On the ground before her lies an old man. Only his head is visible above his covering. His cheeks and the area under his eyes are so puffy that it looks as though his skin will burst at any minute. The old man's eyes are closed. His mouth is half open. Saliva dribbles from the corner of his mouth. A little boy with burns all the way from his toes up to his knees sobs. Like a piece of rotten meat, he has fallen into the lap of the young woman.

I turn my head and walk swiftly toward the entrance of the brick building. People are standing in two lines that go all the way to the end of the railings. A tall man in a dark blue woolen sweater stops me, asking, "Where are you going, boy?"

"I have a patient with me."

"That's all right; go on and stand in the waiting line."

The shiny rim of his hat gleams in the sunshine as he talks and moves his head.

I look at the end of the line, jumbled along the railing. The tall man says again, "In the line! You need to get a number!" And with his hand he points to the edge of the hospital's grounds.

People go get a number, stand in line or squat down in front of the iron railing, then carry their sick on their backs inside through the back door of the building, and there, in front of the examination room, they wait for their turn to be seen.

An old man carrying a young man on his back goes toward the examination room. I walk along with the old man and ask him, "Is he your son?"

He looks at me but doesn't say anything. The young man is very thin and small, yet the old man is panting.

"What's his illness?"

He looks angry. "I don't know, some sort of a disease without a cure."

The young man's bare legs dangle like pendulums with every step that the old man takes.

Behind the building, voices are muddled together. All kinds of voices: begging, moaning, yelling, even cursing and swearing.

"They have kept me waiting for ten days, and now they're telling me that they don't have vacant beds."

"Then what am I supposed to do? What should I do with this child in my arms? I can't just watch him die . . ."

"In that case, why don't you just close the damn place down?"

"May God humiliate you! I hope you too watch your children die before your eyes."

"Take pity on me . . . I am dying."

No one responds to them; it's as if no one hears them.

I walk into the building since no one's there to stop me. The end of the line for the examination room reaches outside the building. In the shady area everyone is shivering. I can hear their teeth chattering. In the hallway, all kinds of smells from different medications blend in the air. The plaster on the walls is flaked in patches. Mold has made the plaster bloated at the base of the walls.

If I want to see the doctor, I need to have a number. And if I want to get a number, I have to stand in line until noon. If I wait in the line, I need to have two tomans to pay for the number. And even if I get a number, I need to go and stand in the line in front of the examination room . . . but then there's no use in that, because Hasani is not with me.

I stand in the hallway feeling useless. The cold has found its way into my body. I can hardly breathe with the smell of medicine and decay. I walk toward the end of the hallway. A man in white comes my way. I gather my courage and yell, "Aqa!"

The man in white stops.

"I have a question."

He starts walking. "If you're sick, wait in the line," he says.

"But I'm not sick."

He stops again and looks at me.

"I'm not the patient."

"Then what do you want to say?"

I feel embarrassed. My whole face turns red. The words are stuck in my throat.

"So why don't you talk?"

"I don't want anybody to hear us, Aqa!" And I shoot a look at the people lined up in front of the examination room.

The man in white walks on. I follow him. The end of the hallway is empty of people. The man stops, looks around, and says, "There's no one here . . . Talk!"

I mumble at first, then I quickly tell him the entire thing without a pause.

The man is calm. He just smiles. He does not look surprised by what I've just told him, as if he has already heard this from more than a hundred people. I look down. I hear his voice: "You got money?"

I stay quiet.

Again it's his voice: "They won't do anything for you here."

"It's not for me . . . as I said," I tell him.

"It doesn't matter."

I lift my head up and look into his eyes, which are moist and narrow.

"If you got money, bring him to me around sunset, and I'll tell you what to do."

Then he gives me the address. I realize that he is not a doctor. God only knows how many times I must have passed by his house. "Injections and Bandages," the sign reads.

"I'll see you at sunset."

His teeth have turned yellow from too much smoking. His lips are chapped. I head out of the hospital. The only thing I can think of to come up with some money is to sell my pigeons.

Karam's mouth is covered in bandages.

"The sort of things that you do . . . All I can say is that nothing you do is like what normal people would do. I want to know who in their right mind would bet on shoving a saucer into his mouth?" says Sanam.

Khaj Tofiq has taken Karam to Mirza Nasrollah. If Afaq ever finds out, she'll skin Khaj Tofiq's head and put on a show for everyone to see.

Mirza Nasrollah has prescribed an herbal remedy.

"Khaj Tofiq and his wicked plans," Sanam says, "not even in his dreams could he play out his scam, dumping that opium-addict daughter of his on my son. All Banu is good for is getting laid by that Ebram, in Rahim the Donkey Keeper's straw shed."

"I took Karam Ali to Mirza Nasrollah," Khaj Tofiq says to the neighbors, "only for the sake of God . . . and God forbid, if Afaq finds out, she will make such a show . . . You can't even imagine."

Afaq is still not on good terms with Sanam.

Karam's mouth is still held shut with bandages. He dies and comes back to life each time he tries to make himself understood or asks for something.

It's been about a week or so since Sanam propped up a minuscule oven next to Mash Rahim's donkeys' sun shelter. She gets up at dawn to knead dough. She starts up the oven and bakes forty-something loaves of bread by noon. She gives them to Karam in bunches so he can deliver them around the neighborhood.

Since the day Sanam first lit up her oven, Mother has been buying her daily bread from her. "It's cheaper this way," she says, "and I don't need to go through the trouble of haggling with the baker; besides, it doesn't have any junk in it like the baker's bread."

When Father sent home some money, we were able to pay off our debt to Habib the Baker. We're waiting for Father to send us more money so we can pay off our debt to Mehdi the Grocer too. At the beginning of each month, no matter what, Father sends us some money.

Her chador tied around her waist, Sanam is already baking bread. The yard is full of sunshine. The heat from the oven is particularly pleasing. Sanam's loaves of bread are like cookies. They taste like the boiled yolk of an egg.

"Sister, I'm not in it to pocket people's money. I buy two *mans* of Karuni wheat, and don't mix anything else with it. I don't expect much. I'm thankful to God as long as I can manage a life with a couple of loaves left for me and Karam."

Habib the Baker comes in through the door. He has soaked his baking sleeve, and now, squeezing the water out, is about to put it on his arm. "Well, well, well . . . Sanam Khanom. I see that now you're my competitor! Is that so?"

Sanam pastes the dough to the arc of the oven, sits by the fire, and, in an impatient tone, says, "You call this competition, Baker Habib? All I'm doing is kneading two *mans* of flour into dough and baking a few loaves for the neighbors and myself. How's this going to mess with your business, which, thanks to the Almighty, allows you to sell thirty, forty *mans* of bread every day?"

Habib the Baker, putting on his baking sleeve, steps forward. His eyelashes are burnt. His cheeks are bony and brown. "And I am sure you have a permit, isn't that right?"

Sanam peels the bread off the oven, tosses it on the straw mat, and, without looking at Habib the Baker, says, "Permit? . . . What do I need a permit for, Baker Habib?"

Habib the Baker's voice gains force. "You think this town has no rules and regulations?"

Sanam sprinkles flour on the mound of dough and says, "It's not like I have a workplace that I'd need a permit for!"

Karam Ali heads out of their room. Habib the Baker says, "It doesn't make any difference, Sanam Khanom. When you're baking bread to sell it, you need to have a permit too."

Sanam stretches the dough on the board and says, "May God bring good your way, Baker Habib. Just let me be!"

Karam looks at Habib the Baker. If that big mouth of his weren't filled with bandages, he might be doing the talking instead of his mother.

Sanam pastes the stretched dough onto the arc of the oven, and then, with a pair of tongs, piles palm fronds on each other. The dried fronds catch fire. Flames blaze out of the oven. Habib the Baker steps closer and peeks in. "What a pity . . . How well this oven has turned out . . . What a nice curve and shape . . ."

Sanam moans, "For the love of God, man, let me do my work."

Habib the Baker stands up straight, with his arms akimbo, and in a gravelly voice says, "Your work, hah?" Looking into Sanam's pallid eyes, he goes on, "Tomorrow, when an inspector from the city comes here and tumbles down your oven with an ax, you'll see for yourself what it means to work without a permit."

The veins in Sanam's neck swell. "What business is it of the city *ispector* to dare come and touch my oven?"

Karam starts to grumble. He can't speak. He just shakes his head, chin, and hands, and shifts from one foot to the other.

Khaj Tofiq puts on his woolen robe and heads out of his room. "What's going on, Baker Habib?"

"It's nothing," answers Habib the Baker.

"He's come here, with those long legs of his," says Sanam, "threatening me that tomorrow the *ispector* will come and tumble down my oven."

Khaj Tofiq sides with Sanam. The rumors going around—that Khaj Tofiq has plans for Karam Ali—may not be rumors at all.

"He's got some plans, dumping Banu on Karam."

"Afaq won't let that happen."

"How naïve you are; it's all Afaq's doing . . . She's the planner—Khaj Tofiq only carries out the plans."

Khaj Tofiq squabbles with Habib the Baker.

Rezvan too comes out of her room. She has reddened her cheeks with rouge and has penciled her eyelids with black *sormeh*.

There are rumors about Rezvan too.

"Who knows where she spends her days?"

"The other day, a young man with a bushy mustache walked her up to Habib the Baker's shop."

"Good for Mash Rahim," someone sneers.

"He should wear his hat slanting sideways," says another.[2]

Karam gazes at Rezvan. Rezvan smiles at Habib the Baker. Habib smiles back and asks how she is doing. Rezvan plays with her chador, pushing it back and forth on her head, and coquettishly says, "Thank God, I'm fine."

The front of Rezvan's chador is open down to her feet. Her tight dress hugs her shapely body. Karam's eyes are fixed on Rezvan's bosom, which is even more voluptuous than Bolur Khanom's. Habib the Baker's gaze is locked with Rezvan's. There's a strand of curly hair hanging on Rezvan's forehead.

The women in the neighborhood talk behind Rahim the Donkey Keeper's back.

"Old age and a cuckold!"

"Don't say that, Sister . . . If the poor old man finds out, he'll die of grief."

"What're you saying, Sister? If a woman goes loose, the first one to find out is her own husband."

"How odd! You think he'll be able to see her from the trenches of the brickkilns?"

Rezvan walks out of the house. Karam's gaze follows her buttocks to the door.

Khaj Tofiq reaches for Habib the Baker's hand. "God won't be pleased if you stand in the way of an old woman trying to make ends meet."

Habib the Baker darts a look at Sanam. "And I'd like to know if God would be pleased if an old woman stood in the way of my twelve-member family's daily bread?"

---

2. A derogatory saying used to refer to a man whose wife cheats on him with his knowledge.

Habib the Baker has eleven children, all from one mother. Nine girls and two boys. The oldest one is thirteen, the youngest six months. Not to mention that one of his daughters died and his wife is pregnant again.

"God is the provider," my father always says. He also says, "An open mouth won't be forsaken without sustenance."

"He who gives teeth, provides food too," says Mirza Nasrollah.

Habib the Baker does not give in. In a gruff voice, he says, "Either she will quit this business of hers or I will come back, along with an inspector, first thing tomorrow morning."

Sanam loses her patience. "Go on and bring whatever *ispector* you want and eat whatever shit you like."

Habib the Baker gets mad. "You ugly baboon, why don't I eat you, who's even worse than shit."

Karam Ali rushes to attack Habib. Khaj Tofiq stops him. Habib the Baker curses and leaves the house. Karam stands there grumbling. Words rumble in his throat but fail to come out.

Standing in their doorway, Banu calls out to Khaj Tofiq.

Khaj Tofiq tells Sanam, "Don't you worry! He can't do a thing." Then he gets hold of Karam's hand and says, "Let's go, boy . . . let's go and have a cup of tea."

Khaj Tofiq's teapot is always beside the brazier.

Karam walks with Khaj Tofiq. Sanam's voice rises. "Karam, come and stack the bread!"

As soon as he finished his lunch, Aman Aqa set off for Susa to get some smuggled tea. He will even go up to Amarah if he has to.

So, I hopped on Aman Aqa's bike and rode home.

It's pitch dark now. The cold stings all the way to the bones.

Bolur Khanom looks around the yard and then comes to our room. Now I know that Mother knows about the whole thing but pretends not to.

Bolur Khanom greets Mother and sits beside the brazier. She has brought a bag of Japanese watermelon seeds. Bolur Khanom always keeps these kinds of snacks in her room. As soon as she makes herself comfortable, she says, "She's gone too far . . . that woman, making up her face and going out like that every chance she gets. Poor Mash Rahim, who works his life away at the brickkilns to make ends meet, and at the end losing face like that."

Mother shoots such a look at Bolur Khanom—it's even worse than a thousand cusswords. Bolur Khanom drops her eyes and falls silent. She offers Mother her roasted seeds. Mother pours her a cup of tea.

At sunset, when I came home and told her that Aman Aqa had gone to Susa, she said that she'd be waiting for me tonight. "Promise you'll come! If you don't show up, there will be no more of you and me."

I didn't say anything. I just smiled.

"I won't sleep till you come," she said.

I don't feel like I want to go to her room. I break into a sweat, thinking of Aman Aqa. If only Aman Aqa weren't so nice to me, I could at least convince myself that it was all right. Now, I can't even bring myself to go to Bolur Khanom. Aman Aqa's small eyes chastise me. "Khaled . . . you are like a son to me!"

If only he had scolded me, even once. I wish that he had yelled at me.

"Khaled, my son . . . do you want me to buy you this undershirt?"

He takes the undershirt from the street peddler's hands and gives it to me. "See if it fits you."

Aman Aqa's penetrating gaze through the narrow slits of his eyes sends a shiver through my entire body. "I think of you as my very own son, Khaled!"

Yet, the sweet scent rising from Bolur Khanom's body stirs a sort of restlessness in me. Her body's warmth is so gratifying that it makes me lose all my senses. It's not just her warmth, which makes me shake all over; it's the other feelings mixed with this warmth, which cannot even be described. It's beyond description the sort of feelings I get—like when I feel her firm belly against mine. Despite all this, the thought of Aman Aqa kills all the joy, taking away the warmth and leaving my body cold instead. There is trouble in my heart: *Aman Aqa . . . Aman Aqa . . . you and Aman Aqa . . . It's a good thing you have going on—why don't you just enjoy yourself?*

Bolur Khanom is telling a story to Jamileh. Her gaze is on me. Her eyes are full of lust. She moves closer and presses her knee against mine. I become aroused. I move back, lean against the wall, and cover my legs with the blanket. Bolur Khanom looks at me and smiles.

Mother is busy knitting me a warm sweater. With some of the money Father sent home, she bought a few skeins of wool yarn and started to knit. She has knitted its back and front already. Only the sleeves are left, which I'm sure will be finished in a couple of days. And once I pick up my new pair of trousers from the tailor, I'll be wearing a new set of clothes. The burgundy goes with black. I saw that color combination on one of the boys from uptown. Mother rummaged this shop and that until she found the burgundy yarn.

Mother puts down her knitting and asks Bolur Khanom, "Would you care to have some dinner?" But she has already eaten. She's never shy about her stomach. She takes good care of it. There is always the smell of delicious food coming out of her room.

Mother gets up to prepare dinner. "Khaled, spread out the supper cloth!" she yells, and leaves the room. We're having *dizi* tonight. Since Sanam set up her oven, this is our second time having an oven-made *dizi*.

Bolur Khanom tells another story to Jamileh. Using her eyes and brows, she reminds me not to forget to come to her room tonight. I am in such a mess. The more I think of Aman Aqa, the more I want to run away from Bolur Khanom. I tell myself that, once and for all, I should go to her tonight and tell her that it is over. Tell her that I am ashamed of what I'm doing to Aman Aqa. Tell her that I cannot sleep with her while the small, smiling eyes of Aman Aqa are tearing my heart.

Bolur Khanom keeps sending signals with her eyes and eyebrows. I lose patience and say, "All right, Bolur Khanom, all right, I got it."

Jamileh's sleepy eyes open. "What did you get, Dadash Khaled?"

I don't answer her. Jamileh doesn't insist. Bolur Khanom continues with the story. Mother comes back. We chop up the bread and put the pieces in the bowls and then pour the *dizi* over them. The scent of the oven-made stew is so appetizing that it makes your mouth water. The large chickpeas are puffed up, the dried lemon swollen and juicy, the mix of meat and sheep lard squashed flat. It's been five months since Father went to Kuwait, and this is the fourth time we've eaten such a scrumptious meal. In those first days, Mother hid the large copper pot under her chador and took it to the coppersmiths' market and sold it. We got by for a few days, but soon we were unable to afford to buy food again. Since Father began sending home money, we're doing better, little by little. Who knows? Maybe next time when we get the money, we will even be able to eat *baghaleh polo*, a dish of cooked fava beans and rice.

"Come and eat with us, Bolur Khanom."

"No thanks, you enjoy it!"

Jamileh moves toward the supper cloth. She eats her dinner, and then goes to sleep soon after. Mother clears off the supper cloth and returns to her knitting. Bolur Khanom talks to Mother. I get up and go to Father's room. Since the day Father went to Kuwait, I have been sleeping in his room. Bolur Khanom is talking. Her voice is low. I listen in. It seems like she is talking about Mahin Jiju. I think she has found out that Aman Aqa brings Mahin to his teahouse. ". . . I hear he takes a whore to the teahouse . . ."

I hear a cup of tea being stirred.

"I want to go to the teahouse one night and catch him red-handed."

"Don't do such a thing!" Mother says.

"I want to teach him a lesson so that he will never do these sorts of things ever again."

"If you hassle him," Mother responds, "he'll dare to do it with more audacity." To make her point, she talks about her older brother, who in time divorced his wife and brought home a whore instead.

"But what else is he after that he can't get from me?" says Bolur Khanom. "I prepare his special foods myself . . . I tend to him in the best way . . . and if I weren't good in bed, I'd say there would be . . ."

"If you provoke him," Mother reasons with her, "you'll make him worse. You should let him come to his senses on his own."

Bolur Khanom is adamant. "Shame on him! I don't even know how he can bring himself to eat with a spoon that everyone else has eaten with."

Again, I hear the sound of a cup of tea being stirred. My eyelids feel heavy. I hear Mother singing to herself:

> *Where is the grief caravan driver to carry my griefs away?*
> *I'll mount the caravan, roaming around the bazaar and alleys.*

Mother's singing seems to come from miles away.

I put on my short jacket. Quietly, I open the door and tiptoe out. All the doors are closed. The slits around the sides of all the doors are dark. I tiptoe past the kitchen and the donkeys' sun shelter. For a second, I pause next to the pigeon coop. It's really cold. The cold could crack the skin. I think the surface of the pool is frozen. I hear someone cough. I prick up my ears. It's coming from Khaj Tofiq's room. His sleep is so light that he even wakes up from the buzzing of a fly.

"The opium addicts are always asleep and awake."

"They are never fast asleep."

"Ah, that sort of asleep-and-awake state is so enjoyable, hard to describe."

The noise of the donkeys is mingled with the mumbled whispers of the night. In the distance, the wind is playing with the whistle of a train. The sound of the whistle rises and falls. It moves far away and bounces back again. If this is the whistle of the ammunition train that comes from the harbor, it must be one hour after midnight.

I creep past the pigeon coop toward the wall. It is only a few more steps to Bolur Khanom's room. The door to Sanam's room starts to move. Before it opens, I scurry into the outhouse. I stay there for a few moments. My heart is racing. The outhouse is pitch dark. Nothing can be seen. I hear the sound of footsteps. Then I see Karam Ali's thin silhouette standing on the threshold of the outhouse, holding a lantern. I cough. He drops the canvas curtain hanging in front of the outhouse and steps back.

"Who's in there?"

"It's me . . . I'm coming out."

He puts down the lantern. I step out of the outhouse. Cautiously, I walk toward the sun shelter. Karam is inside the outhouse. I'm indecisive. If I go back to our room, it will be very hard to get out again. So, I turn around and tiptoe quickly up to the door of Bolur Khanom's room. I look around. Karam Ali is still inside the outhouse. Whenever he goes to the outhouse, he'll stay there a good half an hour before he leaves. I snatch the door handle. The door is unlocked. I walk into the room. Bolur Khanom is awake.

"Is that you, Khaled?"

"Shhh!"

The room is amazingly warm. I tell her that Karam is inside the outhouse. A shaft of light from the streetlamp passes through the window glass and the gauzy curtain, which reaches down to the floor. I hang my short jacket on the hanger, pull myself up onto the bed, and lie down. The smell of Aman Aqa's body fills my nose. Bolur Khanom's arm circles around my neck. I push her hand back.

"What?"

"Wait till Karam goes back to their room."

It's a nonsense excuse. I shouldn't have come in the first place, but now that I have, avoidance does not make any sense. Bolur Khanom circles her arm around my neck again. I get hot. I pull her into my arms. My hand slides down onto her buttocks. She is not wearing any panties.

"It's better this way . . . you're always ready for it."

The scent of Bolur Khanom's body makes me dizzy. She unbuttons my shirt. I take off her sheer undergarment. Both of us are naked now and wrapped around each other like ivy plants. Bolur Khanom's breath is hot, as if she has a fever. It sets my cheeks and neck on fire. Her lips are hot and taste like fresh dates. Her body's warmth blends with mine. We roll over and over. She bites my lips. Her tongue wiggles inside my mouth. Her hands are locked on my waist. My belly is tight against her belly. We're panting. The bed is creaking. It moves back and forth. We go limp, and next to each other, we lie breathless. Aman Aqa's small eyes give me shivers.

"Khaled, you're like my son . . . You are my son."

My entire body turns cold.

When I step into our room, I hear Mother's voice. "Where were you, Khaled?"

She sits up on her bedroll. She chides me with her eyes.

"It's nothing, Mother; I just went out for a bit."

"Are you feeling bothered?"

I stand on the threshold between the two rooms. "What do you mean?"

Her voice too is chiding. "'Cause, you stayed out so long."

I don't say anything. Just drop my short jacket on the rug and lie down on my bedroll and swear that I will not touch Bolur Khanom ever again.

Now, even the schoolchildren have sewed tags to their uniforms that say, "The Oil Industry Must Be Nationalized." Bidar has said that I shouldn't wear one. "This sort of thing is an unnecessary display. There's no need for one to give himself away so unnecessarily."

I've thought a lot about what he said. I think I'm beginning to figure out a thing or two, but I'm still not completely clear about it.

I have found a buyer for the pigeons. I mean, Ebrahim and I went out and together we found him. Fourteen pigeons—and what playful ones! When I put them in a sack and handed them to Jasem, I felt a lump in my throat. I gave Ebrahim two tomans out of the seventy-two I got for them.

"You said fifty-fifty," he said.

"Yeah, but you were supposed to feed them too."

I have lost track of how long it's been since Ebrahim joined Khaleq and Chinuq and moved in with them.

"Well, then give me another five tomans."

"But you're doing good already."

I head out so I can go and buy Hasani's injections; I didn't say anything to Ebrahim. By the time I get back, Hasani should be home from the brickkilns. I should take him to Ali Aqa. We should somehow find a way around things so Mash Rahim does not find out anything. The needles and the medication cost thirty-two tomans.

"Ali Aqa, you think Hasani will be cured by these shots?"

He promises that the injections will get rid of the infection.

Mother wants to know how much I got for the pigeons. I lie to her. "I sold them for forty-two tomans. I gave two tomans to Ebrahim for finding the buyer."

I don't tell her about Hasani. What pain I went through in lying to her.

A few of the lightbulbs are out on Hokumati Street. This is the first time that I've seen this happen. Young people, standing in groups under the light poles, are busy talking. As I pass by, I catch some of their words.

"That's what's called historic determinism."

From the look of them, it's obvious that they are college kids.

"What 'historic determinism,' dear friend? They themselves are behind all this chaos."

I slow down.

"This policy is outdated. The time has passed when they could fool us by telling us that it's the British policy. Now, everyone is alert. Now, the world has changed."

One of them clears his throat and reads in a dignified voice, "From Indonesia to Andalusia, the banner of bloody vengeance is aflutter . . ."

I pass by them. I see another group standing a bit south of the Hokumati Building. Their voices are loud and mingled. The veins in their necks are bulging. Any minute now they could get into an argument.

In front of the large stone facade of the Hokumati Building, there are two guards on patrol instead of one, both armed. They used to only have batons. Now there are more newspaper sellers. They run around the streets and alleys calling out in search of customers. Some of them look to be anything but newspaper sellers. Bidar has assigned me to go to Azad's house tomorrow afternoon at five and help him fold newspapers, and then get a bundle of them and sell them at night on Timsar Street.

"He'll let you know what time you should start selling. Be there earlier to give the guys a hand . . . There are three thousand newspapers that need to be folded."

I walk past the Hokumati Building. At the intersection, I see another group. Their look makes it clear that they are high school boys.

"The exploiters and the colonialists always dig their graves with their own hands."

"You just go ahead and get hooked on these pompous words, but in the end, you'll see the world is just the way it always has been."

"Pompous words, you say? Man, history has proved that."

"All right, history has proved that, granted. But tell me, if the nationalization of oil in a country is inevitable according to history, does that have to just happen in the south?"

I slow down so I can hear what they say.

"You wouldn't have said that if you had a Marxist worldview."

The voices become louder.

"What do you mean by that? Why shouldn't the oil be nationalized in the north as well? What does that have to do with a Marxist worldview?"

They're school kids. Their talk and vocabulary are beyond me. I can't make out a thing. I walk on.

Morshed's teahouse is crammed with people. The volume of the radio has dropped. The customers have gathered around a young man. They sit so close to each other and so quietly you'd swear they aren't breathing. The young man is reading aloud from a newspaper. I stop and listen for a few moments.

". . . This is the cry of twenty million plundered people who have risen courageously to cut off the hands of a bunch of bandits. This is the righteous cry of twenty million honorable people who, for years and years, have carried the burden of colonialism on their wounded shoulders. This is the irreconcilable cry of the unwavering combatants that shudders . . ."

I must go and buy the injections. I speed up my pace. All the walls are scribbled in many different colors. In blue, purple, red, and black: "We want bread instead of cannon!" "Peace is victorious!" "Hands of plunderers and colonialists off our land!" Pahlavi Street is more crowded than ever. I walk up toward the pharmacy. I cut through words as I pass people by:

". . . Maybe economic sanctions . . ."

". . . Even the world, even . . ."

". . . You don't know what a precious piece it was . . ."

". . . Only through union and alliance . . ."

". . . I punched him in the mouth so that his teeth . . ."

". . . Being to this extent leftist is dangerous . . ."

". . . Everyone has turned into a ball of fire . . ."

". . . You think they stay quiet . . ."

Somebody steps on my foot. I spin around and glare in his face. "Watch your step, man!"

He smiles and hands me a leaflet. By the time I reach the pharmacy, I have three other leaflets.

It's crowded inside the pharmacy. The customers are waiting their turn in line. Some are sitting and reading newspapers. Some are gathered together and talking among themselves:

"Suppose we kicked the British out."

"An impossible hypothesis."

"Granted, but I just want to know on what vessels can we carry the oil to the other countries?"

A tall man, who is also stocky, says, "You're troubled by this?"

"You think this is a small problem?"

The tall man says, "Rest assured the Easterners will do anything to help in order to get the Westerners to leave our country—"

A middle-aged man interrupts him. "Hmm . . . out of the frying pan and into the fire."

"The fire?" says the stocky man. His eyes become narrower, and look surprised.

"Of course, good man. Colonialism is colonialism. It doesn't matter whether it's black or white."

The stocky man lights a cigarette. "You're way off track, Brother."

The middle-aged man, dressed in neatly pressed clothes and his hair slicked back carefully, says, "What difference does it make in your opinion?"

The stocky man takes a drag on his cigarette. "Once a government is capable of doing away with the exploitation of an individual by another individual, rest assured that it will be able to solve the problem of plunderers and colonialism, because colonialism has its root in the exploitation of individuals by individuals."

I get the injections and head out of the pharmacy. It's like all the people of the town have left their houses only to come out and gather on Pahlavi Street.

A small-framed young man weaves speedily through the crowd, handing out pamphlets. Following him, two others are snatching the pamphlets out of people's hands.

The front of Mojahed Bookstore is jam-packed with people. Maybe the new edition of *The Nahjolbalagheh* has just arrived. I wave a hand at Shafaq. He smiles and waves back.

I turn from Pahlavi Street in to Timsar Street. With his pants rolled up, holding a pail of water and using a ball of mesh wire, an elderly man curses as he scrubs the paint off his newly built walls. "Sons of bitches," he grumbles, "they think that they can kick the British out like this. Look how filthy they have made this wall. The plaster is not even dried yet."

Two young men, holding newspapers under their arms, mess with him. "Hey, Uncle, why don't you just guard it at night so no one dares to do this again?"

The man loses it and curses. "It's the doing of sissies like you . . . It's not like you have paid a mason's wages or paid a hundred tomans per thousand bricks."

The youths laugh out loud and tease him again.

A little further down, a few people are gathered in front of a bakery. A radio is at full blast. The radio host, with his gruff voice, puts on such a show.

From here, there's no more asphalt. Everywhere the ground is muddy from the rain over the past few days, which poured and beat down on the town and its vicinity.

I stride along the wall. I slip a few times. I reach Mehdi the Grocer's shop. A few people are standing in front of it. The radio host is tearing his throat as he shouts.

Hasani is standing in front of the house doors. His eyes are watery. His nose is runny. He's shivering with cold. He has wrapped himself in his father's old short jacket. I show him the needles. A smile appears on his chapped lips. He chirps, "Where did you get the money?"

I tell him how. He becomes sad. I tap him on the shoulder. "Not to worry! I can buy pigeons again. Let's get going. You should go to Ali Aqa and get your shots every day for a week."

Mash Rahim has gone to the mosque. Hasani pulls up the heels of his shoes, and we take off.

If you drop a needle in Aman Aqa's teahouse, rest assured it will not hit the floor. The place is crammed with people. Everyone expects to hear the most current news any minute. They sit in groups, talking and discussing. Their words are muddled together. It's warm inside the teahouse. The smoke from cigarettes and water pipes has thickened the air. From the east-side window, I can see gas flames rising and falling. It's cloudy. The flames are a striking orange color. Spider is in such ecstasy. He's on the go. I hear someone calling me.

"Khaled, one water pipe!"

I walk to where the bowl of soaked tobacco is. The singing coming from the radio cuts off abruptly. And at that, all the patrons fall silent too, as if no one is in the teahouse.

"Spider, stop making noise with those cups!"

The boisterous voice of the radio announcer bursts out. He calls people's attention to an important piece of news. These days everyone is thirsty for news.

"What's the recent news?"

"Have you heard what the prime minister said?"

"They say that the British have given a warning."

Breaths are held in lungs. Eyelashes are unmoving. Gazes are locked. The radio announcer's voice rises. All breathe out suddenly. The shouts are muddled. The prime minister has been shot.

"He said where?"

"At a funeral service."

"Didn't you hear . . . at Shah Mosque."

"Finally, they got him."

"Well, he was hardheaded."

"Khaled, we're holding a meeting on Tuesday at five o'clock."

"Where?"

Bidar gives the address. Everything is new to me. I have opened my eyes to a new world. Now, from the sorts of things I hear, I can grasp why the lives of the destitute worsen each day, and why people like my father have to pack up their bundles and go from one foreign country to another in search of work so that they can earn a petty sum of money. I head out of the meeting thinking about the things I have heard. There are things that I cannot make sense of. I try to keep them in mind so I can ask Bidar when I see him; or if I don't get to see him, I'll remind myself to ask him in the next meeting. But this town is so small that we run into each other a good two or three times a day.

"Khaled, come to Chellab's stand at eight thirty!" says Bidar.

I show up there at eight thirty. He hands me a bundle of pamphlets, and together we walk toward the neighborhood where I'm assigned to slip them inside the houses.

"Khaled, Friday morning, bring your lunch! We're going out for an excursion."

Friday morning I pick up my lunch bundle and take off. Sometimes we're more than a hundred and fifty people. Most of them ride their bikes. I get a ride on the front of one of the bikes. We head out of town. We usually ride up to one of the villages nearby, like Shekareh, Daghagheleh, or Zargan, and unpack our stuff on the grass. The shade of the trees is blissful. The smell of the grass is delightful. We play with hard-boiled eggs. I am the champ among sixty people. They applaud me. I am on cloud nine, elated and joyful. They lift me up on their shoulders. We sit together in groups and begin discussing things. I listen to what they say. I make new friends. I like what I hear, as if their words have been taken out of my mouth; the words that I have kept in my heart and have wanted to express for years but couldn't. I feel relieved. At noon, we gather around each other, set out whatever food we have, and share it with others. For only the little bit of omelet I have brought with me, I am offered ten different kinds of food in return, a bite from each dish. We drink tea. Afterwards, I head out with some of the older and more informed guys to the villages nearby, to the orchards and farms, and they begin talking to the villagers. I listen to what they say. They talk about the lands on which the villagers have to work their lives away for the landlords. They talk about the petty portion the farmer gets annually. They talk about the village children who don't have a school. They talk about proper hygiene, medicine, and the partitioning of the land. At sunset, we head off for town together. We arrive home at night. I feel happy and content. I let myself fall asleep as I think about all the things I have heard during the day.

"Khaled, come to Statue Square tomorrow at ten."

The cold has broken. Sometimes clouds gather in the sky, yet it won't rain. It is Esfand, the last month of winter, but the sun is hot. The wind no longer stings. The Karun River roars. The scent of spring is everywhere.

Statue Square is becoming crowded. From all the surrounding streets, groups of people converge onto the square. It's sunny. The more people swarm Statue Square, the faster the shopkeepers begin to pull their front shutters closed. By now they have figured out how to respond quickly to situations like this. If people swarm like this and a clash sparks in a corner of the square, it's likely windowpanes will be shattered.

Access to the White Bridge is blocked. The crowd has stopped traffic. People honk their horns all together. There is such a commotion in the square. I catch sight of Shafaq, who is elbowing his way through the crowd toward the entrance of the White Bridge. Following him is a heavily built, muscular laborer holding a loudspeaker in his hands. The sound coming from the loudspeaker rises. It is Shafaq speaking through the loudspeaker: "My friends, give way to the passing cars!"

A wave ripples through the crowd at the entrance of the bridge.

"My friends, don't give them any excuses!"

People disperse from the square. The traffic slowly moves from the entrance of the bridge toward Pahlavi Street. The sound of honking horns can still be heard here and there. Suddenly, slogan banners open up and rise over the crowd. South of the square, people give way for a big truck. The truck drives to the middle of the square. In it, there's a high table against which a microphone and its long stand are propped.

Unexpectedly, a middle-aged man of medium height hops onto the table. Two young men pull themselves up and stand on either side of him. The middle-aged man shouts slogans. Words fly from the wide mouth of the loudspeaker. The hubbub has dropped. The honking horns are no longer heard. Even the cars have stopped on the bridge and no longer move. The middle-aged man is wearing an azure shirt. His hair is soft. His long hair falls over his swarthy face as he shouts slogans and waves his hand.

There are all kinds of people in the square, all mixed together. Oil company workers in blue, railway workers with their muscular bodies and sunburnt faces, textile workers with their pale skin, high school kids, office staff, bazaar merchants, women, old and young people.

The middle-aged man speaks. The subject is oil and the colonialists.

"We demand that the hands of the plunderers be removed from our country's oil industry."

Thousands of voices rise up and shout:

"Yes!"

"We demand bread instead of cannon."

"Yes!"

I have pulled myself up onto the iron railing around the square. The colorful slogan banners wave about in the air. Hands turn into fists and rise over heads.

"Do not allow oil dealers to exploit our national wealth!"

"Yes!"

Out of the blue, there is the sound of shooting. The sound of a bullet being shot into the air is followed by a second shot and a third. The crowd wavers. The banners come down, and in the blink of an eye the sky is full of colorful pamphlets. I jump down from the railing. The crowd is rushing toward the streets. From the wide street to the north, a group of policemen, batons in hand, scurries down toward the square. The square begins to empty. I feel like I am trapped. Voices are muddled:

"They were shooting."

"They shot in the air."

"Run . . . this way!"

"They're coming."

"Here they are."

"Is anyone shot?"

"This way . . . run!"

Everyone is running. Some fall to the ground. Others help them to get up. I run with the crowd. At the edge of the sidewalk, I feel my ankle twist. I am thrown to the side. Two people grab my arms, help me to my feet, and then run on. The legs of my pants are muddy. I scurry away from the square and turn into the first alley. No one follows me. Everyone runs past the alley. I go to the end of the passageway. On the right there is a narrow blind alley. I pause. I'm hesitant. I want to turn back. A few people quickly run past the head of the alley. I hear people cursing. It sounds like people are being beaten up. I force myself to walk on. My right leg won't budge. Limping, I pull myself toward the last house, across from the dead-end alley. I hear footsteps. They sound forceful. Like the sound of a set of boots, with their soles made of nails, hitting against rock. I throw caution to the wind. I grab the doorknocker and bang it. The sound of footsteps looms not too far away. Someone opens the door. I hurl myself inside and shut the door behind me. The sound of the footsteps is getting closer. They lack a sense of urgency as they hit the ground and pause for a short while before starting again. I take a deep breath, lift my head up, and see a middle-aged woman standing over me looking flabbergasted. Her lips quiver. "Who are you?"

I fail to say anything. Then I mumble, "Madam, please let me stay here for a few moments."

The woman does not say anything. I sit on the bottom step of the staircase that leads to the roof. I am entirely soaked in sweat. My burgundy sweater is dusty. I shake out the legs of my pants. I hear the lively voice of a girl. "Who was that, Mama?"

Then the girl herself appears. A small boy is beside her. Both of them come and stand next to the middle-aged woman. The girl's black eyes are captivating. There's a sort of innocence and gentleness in them. Her soft hair has fallen over her shoulders. Her bangs are brushed carefully away from her eyebrows. She is of medium height. She whispers in her mother's ear. The girl's eyes now reveal her surprise; they have turned an olive color. Her eyes change color every second, yet the captivating black color conquers all the other shades, like a fractured black diamond. The small boy is quiet. Holding his hands behind his head, he stares right at me. His mother starts to speak, but so quietly that I can hardly hear her.

"Were you at the meeting?"

I wipe the sweat off my forehead and say, "No . . . I was just passing by."

I feel ashamed of the lie I've just told. I bite my lower lip.

"Then why did you run away?" she asks.

I don't want to answer her. I don't want to lie to her again, so I say, "I was afraid I might be arrested for no reason."

It is the girl who speaks now. "Please come inside the room until it clears up."

Her teeth are a bluish white. There is a sort of softness in her tone that gives me a tremor.

I can hardly talk. I have never talked to a girl who speaks so softly and melodiously.

"Hey, buddy, look how you've got it going with that Bolur Khanom!"

"Banu, if you keep saying these things to me, you'll see what I can do to you."

Banu's mouth opens up wide, to her ears, showing her big yellow teeth. "When I catch you red-handed, I'll show you what it means to be so bold like that."

She runs her long fingers through her frizzy hair and walks toward the water tap to make her ablutions.

I hear the soft voice of the girl again. ". . . But it's not polite of us to let you sit on the staircase like this."

I lift my head. "I appreciate the gesture . . . If you don't mind, I'll just sit down for a few minutes and then leave."

"In that case," says the woman, "please come and sit in the room for those few minutes."

I get up to my feet and have every intention of leaving, but my leg does not oblige. I sit down. "I think I have sprained my ankle," I say.

I roll up the leg of my pants and see that my ankle is swollen. The woman steps forward and looks at my foot. "It's badly swollen," she says.

I swallow my saliva. My gaze entwines with the girl's. I move a bit. The color of her eyes is that deep black again. Her eyelashes are long and curved. The color of her skin is that of moonlight. When she shifts from one foot to another, her breasts tremble softly, as if they are ready to burst out of her shirt. She steps closer. "Just try your best to make it into the room."

I can't say no to her. I get up. I press my hand against the wall and hop.

The room is warm. It's open and spacious, with colors that offer tranquility. The colors of the curtains, the wall color, and the colors of the Persian rugs . . . it all soothes my anxiety. The sofa is very soft and comfortable.

I start to feel the pain in my ankle again. At first the pain was tolerable, but now jolts of it shoot through my leg. The girl disappears and comes back with a cup of tea. The woman sits across from me. The girl sets the cup in front of me, and she herself sits on the arm of the sofa. The small boy stands next to her. I stir the cup of tea. I look at the girl out of the corner of my eye. Her pants hug the curves of her thighs.

I hear the woman's voice. "Bahram, go and see if the street has cleared up."

Bahram heads out of the room.

I cherish the cup of tea, sipping slowly.

The mother says, "But you can't walk with your ankle like that."

The girl says, "Give us your telephone number, so we can call your house and have someone come and get you."

I smile. The woman is quick to grasp things.

"Give us your home address," the girl says.

I feel embarrassed. The sprawling courtyard in ruins; the adobe walls; Sanam's oven; Rahim the Donkey Keeper's donkeys; Amu Bandar's decrepit, patched-up cart; the small, suffocating, run-down rooms; and the entire courtyard full of mud, up to the knees, from the last few days of rain.

I lie again. "I am just passing through."

The girl's face becomes forlorn. "So what are you going to do with your ankle like that?"

I put the palms of my hands on the sofa's arm and stand up, my right leg in the air.

"Why are you standing up?" the woman asks.

"I must leave now."

"But you can't even take a step," says the girl.

"Don't you know anyone in this town?" the mother asks.

I think of Shafaq. "I know someone who runs a bookstore."

Panting, Bahram comes in. His voice falters as he says, "Mama, I walked up to the square. Everything is cleared up . . . there are only a few officers in the square."

The woman strokes his soft hair. I can't stand on one foot anymore. I sit down again.

"Where is this bookstore?" asks the woman.

"On Pahlavi Street," I tell her. "Mojahed Bookstore."

Bahram says, "I know where that is, Mama."

"It's not far from here, my son," says the woman. "Go and ask him to come."

Bahram stands on the doorstep. "What's his name?"

"Shafaq."

The girl gets up from the arm of the sofa and goes to sit next to her mother. I'd like to look at her but I feel timid. Instead, I stare at the navy blue flowers of the rug. The swelling in my ankle grows by the minute, so does the ache. I untie my shoelace. The woman's voice sounds pleasing in my ears, "It'll swell even more. You'd be more comfortable if you'd take your shoe off."

The soles of my socks are patched up. I let the shoelace be and drag my foot.

"Take off your shoe . . . You'll feel better."

"No, madam, I can't take it off."

My voice is hoarse. I feel drops of sweat forming on my forehead. I lean back on the sofa, and lift up my head. Again, out of the corner of my eye, I look at the girl. She is looking back. My heart is pounding. This pounding is strange, yet sweet. At the beginning, when I looked at Bolur Khanom, my heart would race. But this is a lot different. My heart is about to leap out of my chest. My entire body is trembling. It is as if something in my heart has been unleashed.

"Would you care for some more tea?" It's the girl's voice again.

"No, Miss, thank you."

The woman keeps insisting that I take off my shoe. "Try to take off your shoe; you'll feel much better."

What I really want is to get up and run away. These goddamn socks—I never would have thought that they could cause such a headache. I am pissed at myself. I curse myself with whatever curse words I know. *You could spend thirty-two tomans on Hasani's gonorrhea, but you couldn't buy a pair of socks for yourself, huh? . . . Now suffer!* I bend down. I grab the sole and the tip of my shoe and try to wiggle it. It won't budge, as if my shoe is glued to my foot. I let it be, breathe in deeply, recline, and stare at the ceiling.

"It won't come off?"

"No, madam."

My foot is now completely swollen.

"If you had listened to me when I first . . ."

Bahram comes in. He is out of breath. His cheeks are red. Drops of sweat have formed on his forehead.

"He wasn't there, Mama. The bookstore was closed."

The woman looks at me.

I look down and say, "I'll walk somehow."

I put my hands on the arm of the sofa and raise myself up.

The woman says again, "I don't think you'll be able to walk on that foot."

"I know, but I have to get going somehow."

"Wait a little longer," says the girl, "maybe the bookstore will open up soon."

I look at the girl's eyes, which are again the color of black olives. A faint smile is on her lips. I breathe deeply, recline, and stare at the ceiling.

This is the second time that Bahram has gone to get Shafaq. "Mama, it's still closed."

It's around noontime. The sky is gray. The lamb-shaped clouds are entangled.

Once again, I put my hands on the sofa's arm and try to stand up on my left foot, just for a few seconds. I don't dare put down my right foot. My ankle almost fills out the bottom of my pants.

The black-eyed girl says, "How do you expect to walk on that foot?"

There is a sort of compassion in her voice that fills me with joy. My voice trembles: "I have to . . . I have to leave eventually."

I hop to the doorstep. Black-Eyed wants me to stay. "If you stay a little longer," she says, "the bookstore might open up."

"I think it should have opened by now."

This morning I saw Shafaq walking toward the bridge to open up the way for the passing cars, which were causing such a raucous all over town with their honking horns. Later I saw him elbowing his way through the crowd and going toward the big truck.

I look at the woman. She says, "It'll be hard for you to get anywhere on that foot."

"I'll go to the end of the street and get myself a taxi."

"But you don't know anyone in town," says the girl.

The look on the mother's face tells me that she has not believed my words. She asks Bahram to walk me to the street.

"Sure, Mama."

I head out of the room. Black-Eyed disappears and comes back quickly, throwing her coat over her shoulders. "I'll go with them, Mama."

I press a hand to the wall and take small hops. By the time I'm out the door, I already feel exhausted. I lower the tip of my right foot to the ground. A streak of pain shoots through my entire body, from the sole of my foot to the crown of my head. I hold up my foot, lean against the wall, and look at Black-Eyed. There's compassion in her eyes. I lower my gaze. The weather is sort of chilly. My spine feels stiff. I hop again.

"Bahram, help him walk," says Black-Eyed.

I smile at her. The smile she gives me in return overwhelms me with pride.

Bahram steps closer to me. I lay my hand on his shoulder and try hard to walk, but it's impossible. "Thanks, dear Bahram. It's better that I hop. I think I can reach the street better this way."

The street is completely deserted. I lean against the light post and look at Black-Eyed for a moment. I drop my gaze and say quietly, "Forgive me for the trouble I have caused you."

"It was no trouble at all."

I take pleasure in her words. I look at her. She smiles. Her eyes are the color of black olives again. I feel such ecstasy, the way she looks at me. She wants to say something. She opens her mouth but doesn't speak. I gather my courage. "Did you want to say something?"

She looks down. "Why didn't you want to give us your home address?"

I start to shake. So all this time she's known that I was lying. From the look on her mother's face, I could see that she knew I was lying, but not from the look on Black-Eyed's face, not at all. She must really be able to mask her feelings to be able to show complete indifference to my lying.

My voice trembles, "I told you that . . ."

Bahram stops a taxi. I prefer to leave it at that. I don't have anything to say anyway. I direct my gaze at the ditch along the street, realizing that I have to jump over it on one foot. I pretend that I have to focus all my attention on jumping over the ditch, and swallow the rest of my words. Bahram opens the door of the taxi. I get in, look at Black-Eyed, and smile. I shut the door.

"Good-bye."

Her tone is melodious. "Good-bye."

I nod to Bahram. The taxi takes off. I turn my head and look through the rear window. Bahram is waving his hand. There is such tumult in my heart. I can't stop thinking about Black-Eyed. It is as if we have known each other for years. Neither the look in her eyes nor her voice seemed unfamiliar.

The driver slams on the brakes. It's the end of the asphalt road. It is a long way to my house. I try to convince him to drive on, but he won't budge, not even an inch. "It's not worth it to go through all that mud, up to my fenders, for just a one-toman fare."

I get out. It feels as if my soul leaves my body as I try to jump over the ditch along the street. I struggle and get myself to the gabled house.

No matter what, I've got to get myself home. I feel utterly helpless. Even when I had two good feet, I would slip on the mud ten times between the end of the asphalt road and home—now I have only one good foot to rely on. The weather has really grown cold. I doubt that the month of Esfand has ever been this chilly. Pain shoots through my ankle up to my kneecap, to the point that it makes me want to pass out. If I touched the swelling around my ankle, I know I would scream from the pain. The lamb-shaped clouds are dense. God forbid it should start to rain; I'd be in big trouble. The rainfall in Esfand mostly comes in showers, causing floods.

A car stops. Hajj Sheikh Ali says good-bye to the driver and gets out of the car. Lifting up the hem of his robe, he crosses the ditch, waits on the paved sidewalk for the driver to drive past him, and walks in my direction.

"Salaam, Aqa."

Hajj Sheikh Ali stops. His turban is snow white. He looks at me. His henna-colored beard moves as he says, "Salaam to you."

I read it in his face that he is taken aback at not seeing me rise up to my feet before him. He is about to take off when I say to him, "Aqa, can you help me? I'm in trouble."

He looks at me over the clear lens of his glasses. "Is that you, Khaled?"

His tone of voice and the way he looks at me are demeaning. What I should have done was get up to my feet the moment I saw him, greet him politely, and kiss the back of his hand.

"Yes, Aqa, it is me."

He asks about my father.

"He sends letters," I tell him. "He sends his regards."

"I guess he'll return for Nowruz." Then he adds, "We miss him. God-fearing men and good believers like Oussa Haddad are hard to find these days. God willing, he'll return soon and we can come and pay him a visit."

Hajj Sheikh Ali's henna-colored woolen under-robe hardly hides his protruding stomach, which sticks out like a drum; you think that any minute it will rip apart his robe, his shawl, and his shirt.

"Oussa Haddad, I miss the delicious meals that Naneh Khaled makes."

Father brings Hajj Sheikh Ali's hand close to his lips and says, "Your wish is my command, Aqa! We will invite you soon."

Hajj Sheikh Ali reclines on the cushion, belches, and says, "Oussa Haddad, it seemed like the *fesenjan* stew didn't have an adequate amount of meat this time. Isn't that so?"

Father lowers his head, rolls his cigarette, and says, "My apologies, Hajj Aqa. What can I say? Business is very slow these days."

Hajj Sheikh Ali moves to leave.

"Aqa," I call out to him. "As I mentioned, I'm in trouble, Aqa."

He pauses, pushes his glasses up, and looks at me inquisitively. "Trouble?"

"Yes, Aqa. I have sprained my ankle. I can't move."

He stares at me for a few moments. The pupils of his eyes start to move fast. His henna-colored beard moves, and, as if he's offended by what I'm saying, he retorts, "Are you suggesting that I should put you on my back and carry you home?"

Despite all the pain I am in, I feel like laughing out loud, but I curb myself. "No, Aqa, I would never suggest such a disrespectful act."

"Then what?" he snaps

My voice falters as I say, "If it's not much trouble . . . can you please, on your way home, ask someone to come and get me?"

He takes off. "Who says I am walking in the direction of your house?"

Blood rushes to my temples. What I'd really like to do is yell and cuss him out with a few nasty curses.

"Oussa Haddad, Khaled is still going to school?"

"Yes, Aqa; as a matter of fact, he's in the fourth grade."

"Too much schooling makes one unruly and stray from the path of religion, Oussa Haddad."

I am about to faint from all the pain. My entire body is frozen. I am trembling all over. I open my mouth to say all the cusswords I know to that Hajj Sheikh Ali, but I have no strength left for yelling. It occurs to me that I should knock on the house door. I get up from the high step in front of the house. Holding on to the doorframe, I sound the knocker. The door opens quickly. A little boy wrapped in a threadbare blanket appears. "Who are you looking for?" His chin is narrow. The marks left from smallpox are all over his bony face. His thin neck is like a water pipe's hose.

"I need someone to help me walk home."

He sniffs. I think he has a cold. "Wait a minute," he says, "I'll go and get my uncle."

The little boy goes back inside the house. I lean against the arched awning, still holding up my right leg. A young man comes out. He has high cheekbones. His eyes are deep set. His mustache has grown down to his chin. He takes a look at my foot and asks, "When did you sprain your ankle?"

"This morning."

"Where?"

"At the square."

"You were at the meeting, weren't you?"

I look down.

"Wait here, Brother, so I can put on my boots."

He goes into the house and comes back quickly, putting on an old pair of military boots.

"Come, Brother, put your arm around my neck."

He gives me his shoulder, and I let the weight of my body fall on it. He asks my home address.

"It's not that far. It's near Habib the Baker's shop."

I limp along with him.

~

My shoe had to be torn open so I could get my foot out of it. Mother prepared boiling water and massaged my ankle gently in the hot water. She has beaten egg yolk and salt, and rubbed the paste onto my ankle and wrapped it with a felt cloth. The pain intensifies minute by minute. Obviously these sorts of home remedies are not useful. Someone sent for Mirza Nasrollah, but he has come down with an illness and is housebound. Bolur Khanom has one foot in her room and another in ours. I have sent Omid to let Shafaq know.

I lie down in Father's room, propping my leg on a pillow. I can no longer tolerate this pain. I feel nauseous. I can feel the throbbing of my ankle deep in my temples. Shafaq, along with Omid, comes in through the door.

He smiles tenderly. "What's happening, Khaled?"

I tell him the entire story. He listens and laughs gently. I know he's laughing like this so that I will not lose my nerve.

"It's not a big deal. Don't even worry about it. I'll see what I can do for you."

He lights a cigarette. Hasani comes in. He has been to get his gonorrhea injection. Shafaq gets up. "I'll go after a bonesetter," he says, and heads out of the room.

Hasani sits beside me. "There is a lot less pus now," he tells me. "It doesn't burn as much either."

I am not in the mood to listen to him. The pain shoots from my ankle through my knee so badly that I want to scream.

I can't eat. It doesn't matter how much Mother insists that I eat something. She has made me a rich dessert of flour, sugar, and saffron. I force myself to eat two spoonfuls of it, and then push the plate aside.

Rahim the Donkey Keeper calls to Hasani. He gets up and leaves.

Peyman brings me news from Shafaq. "Keep your ankle warm until tomorrow morning when the bonesetter comes and sees you."

My back feels stiff. I can hardly move. My ankle has grown to the size of a pumpkin. Bolur Khanom comes in. She has brought me a medicine dropper full of something. "Take this! It'll soothe your pain."

She squeezes thirty drops into a glass of water, and I gulp it down at once. Bolur Khanom leaves, taking the medicine dropper with her. I shift my back, prop my ankles up, and pull up my body. Mother places two pillows under my back and shoulders. It feels like the pain is subsiding. I can move my leg around a bit. Mother sits next to me. It must be a couple of hours into the night. I can't smell Khaj Tofiq's opium smoke. He must be done for the night. At noon, when the neighbors all poured into our room, I felt like passing out, but now I feel a bit calmer. My eyelids feel heavy. I see Mother's distressed face through my half-closed eyelashes. She hugs her knees and rests her chin on them—and all the while she seems to be getting farther and farther away. In a flash, the pain wakes me up again. Streaks of pain shoot from my ankle up through my hips. The pain is so intense that I want to bite the ground. "Mother!" I yell.

My mother jerks and her eyes open.

"Mother, I am dying."

Her voice is sleepy. "Bear with it, my son, it's almost morning."

I pull myself up further and lean against the wall. "Can you wake up Bolur Khanom? I wish she hadn't taken the medicine."

Mother is uncomfortable waking up Bolur Khanom in the middle of the night. I've got to tolerate the pain. What a long night! The light from the lantern reflects on the adobe walls. The shadows on the walls give the impression of thousands of living creatures intertwined with each other. Mother's eyelids close again. She has covered her shoulders with a blanket. The kerosene burner is next to her, a kettle of warm water upon it. Jamileh snores softly. A strand of hair has fallen out from under Mother's scarf onto her forehead. There are more gray hairs each day. She is turning completely gray.

I was thirteen when I got married. Two years later God granted me Khaled.

Mother is breathing loudly. She must have fallen asleep. I call to her. "Mother, why don't you go and sleep!"

She opens her eyes.

"Come on, Mother. Go and sleep."

"I feel more at ease being near you, dear," she says in a muffled voice.

I hear a door open. It must be Amu Bandar coming out of his room to get ready for the morning ablutions. Or maybe it is Rahim the Donkey Keeper on his way to the public baths.

Amu Bandar says his prayers right at the prayer call.

Since marrying Rezvan, Mash Rahim has started going to the public baths before dawn a few times a week. The burner is almost out of kerosene. Its wick is flickering. I can smell the stench of the burned wick. Mother gets up and blows it out. The light goes off. The cracks in the windowpanes are filled with the gray light of dawn.

"Mother, it's morning now. For the love of God, go on and get that dropper from Bolur Khanom."

I know it's useless. I know that Mother won't go, not until Aman Aqa leaves the house. Every morning Aman Aqa goes to the teahouse before sunup and eats his breakfast there.

Mother opens the window. The fresh morning air flows into the room. I hear the swishing sound of the mudguards on Aman Aqa's bike.

Mother looks out at the courtyard through the window. Wearing her chador, she walks out of the room and quickly returns with the dropper. Aman Aqa has left a message telling us to send for him if the bonesetter does not show up. I take the dropper and lean back. I clench my teeth from the pain. My head feels heavy. My eyelashes close. The pain is receding, bit by bit.

I wake up to the sound of Sanam's screaming. The courtyard is full of sunlight. Habib the Baker has plotted with the city inspector and now they have come to knock down Sanam's oven.

I hear the inspector speak in formal language. "This is not a lawless city, madam. The city has rules and regulations to abide by."

Mother looks out the window. She says that this inspector is the son of Hajj Ba'ak, the charcoal seller. I must have seen Hajj Ba'ak's son a thousand times. He is thin and of medium height. Smallpox scars cover his entire face. His long muzzle is like that of a jackal. He always pulls his hat down over his forehead to hide his baldness. The rim of his hat is wider than the collar of his jacket. Sometimes, at night, he goes to Tuba's saloon and drinks a few glasses of vodka. After he's done drinking, he tags along with some of his fellows to the opium house to smoke. I have heard stories of his drinking and smoking from Aman Aqa; and other things I have heard from Khaj Tofiq. Like that Hajj Ba'ak's oldest son has only finished the sixth grade. The now deceased Hajj Ba'ak was friends with the chief of police. He used to sort out for him the large fine Karachi charcoals, and sometimes even, they sat at a brazier and smoked opium together. It was the chief of police who recommended Hajj Ba'ak's oldest son to the mayor, and the mayor gave him a position at city hall. Hajj Ba'ak's son quickly got the hang of things at city hall, and lo and behold, he has become somebody there.

I hear Sanam's voice trembling with rage. "If you touch my oven, I'll kill myself."

Khaj Tofiq says, "This poor woman needs to earn a living too, don't you think?"

From the look of things, Habib the Baker has thought of everything; he has even brought with him a pickax. He retorts, "It has nothing to do with me. The inspector himself has ordered that the oven should be demolished."

"The inspector is no stranger; he's one of us," argues Khaj Tofiq.

"Official regulations do not distinguish strangers from friends," replies the inspector formally.

Khaj Tofiq tries to work things out. "The late Hajj Ba'ak had enough honor to—"

The inspector cuts Khaj Tofiq short. His voice is loud and authoritative. "This oven must be demolished!"

Sanam's screaming fills the house: "That easy, huh? You think I'm gonna let you tumble it down like that? If I had to, I would stop the mayor himself from doing it. I'll set myself on fire. I'll smash your face, and kick the mayor's ass too!"

Habib the Baker is taken aback. "Oh . . . oh . . . oh . . . you say this to the inspector's face?"

Sanam lets him have it. Her voice can be heard seven blocks away. "Get your asses out of here and hit the road!"

The inspector speaks in a measured manner. He is enraged, though. "Don't insult a government official. You don't want me to throw you in jail, do you?"

"Oh, oh, oh! Look who's talking. Now Hajj Ba'ak's son is a big man. That mother of yours got pregnant after being paid only four tomans for the night, and now you have come here, showing that ugly face of yours to me."

Suddenly, Habib the Baker screams. Mother reports that Karam Ali, with that bandaged mouth of his, has snatched the stone mortar and is beating the hell out of Habib the Baker. Sanam too has gotten the iron oven rod and is attacking the inspector. Habib the Baker and the inspector run away. I hear Sanam boasting, "He has brought me the *ispecter*!"

I know that Hajj Ba'ak's son won't let go of a matter like this that easy. I can predict that he'll come back with such a plan that it'll make both of their jaws drop to the floor.

Shafaq arrives, bringing with him a middle-aged man with a henna-colored beard. He asks, "How did you pass the night?"

"Very badly."

Mother goes to prepare boiled water. The bonesetter sits down. He unwraps the felt cloth from my ankle. He touches the swelling with a finger. Pain shoots up to my kneecap. The man asks me to move my foot. I can't. Bolur Khanom comes in. Mother says to her, "Bolur Khanom. Do me a favor and make some tea."

Jamileh fetches the stool and sets it beside my bedroll. Shafaq sits on it. The middle-aged man gingerly examines my foot. He doesn't think it's fractured. "It's just a sprain. Nothing to worry about," he says.

I feel relieved.

Mother brings the copper basin and places it in front of my foot. She fetches the kettle of boiled water. The middle-aged man puts my foot in the hot water and massages it, including my toes. My entire body aches. I want to cry. If only Shafaq and Bolur Khanom weren't here.

The man looks at my ankle as he talks to me. He asks how I happened to sprain it. In a hoarse voice, I tell him how. He takes hold of the sole of my foot and my toes with both his hands and gives them a swift jerk, taking me by surprise. Pain shoots up to my brain. "It's over," he says.

My joints are back in place. He mixes egg yolk, flour, salt, and oil, and rubs the paste onto my foot before wrapping it with the felt cloth.

"Don't remove it till it peels off by itself."

As Shafaq is about to leave, he takes two books, each the size of the palm of my hand, out of his jacket pocket and tucks them under my pillow. "Read these books so you don't get bored. I'll come to see you again."

The middle-aged man instructs Mother to keep my foot warm at all times, and then leaves with Shafaq. My foot throbs. The pain subsides. My eyelids are heavy. Sanam's screaming starts up again. Mother peeks through the widow and says that all the neighbors have come out of their rooms. Hajj Ba'ak's oldest son is back again, this time with a police officer. In his hand, Habib the Baker carries a pickax. Sanam has just lit the oven. Without bothering to ask what's going on, the policeman slaps Karam across the face so hard that his wounded mouth begins to bleed again. Frustrated, Sanam rips the collar of her dress open, hurls herself to the ground, and smears mud on her head. Standing to the side, his arms akimbo, Hajj Ba'ak's oldest son smiles victoriously. Khaj Tofiq wipes his runny nose with a handkerchief. Bringing down the pickax with all his might, Habib the Baker smashes Sanam's oven to pieces. The policeman stands right there, as still and unmoving as the Sekandar Dam, and no one dares to say a word.

All the neighbors have come to see me at least once, but it is Bolur Khanom who comes every day and spends a couple of hours sitting beside me.

Hasani too. On the way back from the brickkilns, he first goes to Ali Aqa to get his injections, then comes and sits beside me for half an hour or so. Apparently, he had his last shot tonight. From what he tells me, he's been cured.

I have read all the books given to me. Shafaq hasn't come again, but Bidar has come once. He took the books Shafaq left me and gave me a few others in return.

A letter has arrived from Father. He has sent some money too. Finally, we've managed to pay off all of our debts. Slowly but surely, we are getting by better than before.

Nowruz is a few days away.

I get out of the bedroll, and with the support of my cane, stand in front of the window. Shadows have stretched all the way up to the foot of the wall. Rezvan comes in through the house doors. She smiles at me and goes to Mash Rahim's room. Banu sweeps the front of her room. A stray cat jumps down from above the donkeys' sunshade into the courtyard and sneaks into the pigeon coop. He must be after a chick or a pigeon's egg. He rummages the corners of the pigeon coop, then comes out. All of a sudden, I hear Rezvan scream. She rushes out of the room, her hair uncovered, and begins cursing Rahim the Donkey Keeper's relatives, dead and alive.

Apparently, Mash Rahim has caught Rezvan in the butchers' market. God only knows who has told him about Rezvan's sly doings. And only He himself can know how many days Mash Rahim must've spied on her. The other women have worked out the entire thing. Mash Rahim saw Rezvan flirting with a beefy young man in the butchers' market. Next, he saw that Rezvan get into a taxi with the lad. Rahim the Donkey Keeper then went home to wait for her return. Rezvan, thinking that Mash Rahim was working at the brickkilns, ate out, and now that she's returned home, Rahim the Donkey Keeper, without bothering to ask any questions, has started beating the hell out of her with a stick.

Rezvan loses it completely and in retaliation curses Rahim the Donkey Keeper with all kinds of cusswords. All the neighbors have come out of their rooms. Some of the kids from other houses are already in the courtyard. Rahim the Donkey Keeper scares them away with the stick. "Bastards! A man can't even have some privacy in his own home!"

The children run away, but when they see Rahim the Donkey Keeper turn around, they come back inside again.

Afaq reaches a hand under Rezvan's arm and takes her to her own room. Rahim the Donkey Keeper grumbles and goes into his room. "It's not like I got married so that she could kill me bit by bit."

I can walk now with the aid of a cane. If I'm careful and do not put any pressure on it, my ankle won't hurt at all. I lie down in my bedroll. During these past few days that I have had to stay home, I've read a few books and thought a lot about Black-Eyed. Once I'm able to leave the house, I will somehow make sure our paths cross.

Why didn't you want to give your home address?

I can only imagine what she must be thinking. I will use thanking her as an excuse to go and see her.

I pull myself up and lean back against the pillow. Mother comes and refills the teapot with water and lights the lantern. I am almost done reading the last borrowed book. I hope that tomorrow Bidar will come again and bring me a few more. I am getting used to reading. As soon as I put down a book, I reach out for it after a few moments, as if I'm missing something. What an adventurous book this last one is. And how I enjoy reading it! This Pavel guy is such a character. He has lost his eyesight but still doesn't give up. What genius! Not everyone can live a life like Pavel's. Only those made out of steel could go through such a difficult life and still remain sane and intact.

Thank God, Rezvan has stopped her cursing for now. The tea is brewing. Mother brings the cups and saucers and sits herself down. She barely has time to sit down and pour herself a cup of tea before the door opens and Aunt Ra'na walks in, in the company of her daughter and her son, Gholam. Without much in the way of a greeting, Aunt Ra'na comes and kneels down next to me and kisses my cheeks, saying, "May I die for you . . . I wish your aunt's leg had been broken rather than yours . . . Look what's happened to my dear son!"

Leaving me alone, she turns to face Mother and begins talking nonstop. "Why didn't you tell me, Sister? Should I be the last to know that my son's leg is broken? Sister, I'm upset with you . . . You should've said something."

Mother cuts Aunt Ra'na short. She explains that she has been busy, that she had no one to send after her. Aunt Ra'na keeps complaining. Mother pours her tea. Aunt Ra'na's son fetches the stool from the corner of the room, places it beside my bedroll, and sits on it. I let my eyelids fall.

"How did you sprain your ankle?" Gholam asks.

The last thing I want is to answer Gholam. I just say, "Well . . . you know . . . it happened."

Aunt Ra'na's daughter holds Jamileh in her arms. She's sort of pretty. She has dabbed her cheeks with a bit of rouge. Her hair is shiny. She kisses Jamileh and asks me how I'm feeling.

"Not bad," I reply.

Gholam says, "You didn't say how you sprained your ankle."

"It just happened," I mumble.

"What's with the attitude?" he asks.

Aunt Ra'na takes off her head covering, and as she stirs her cup of tea, she begins instructing my mother in home remedies. "Sister, get the fresh skin of a sheep's tail and rub it on his foot!"

Two of Aunt Ra'na's front teeth are missing.

". . . With oil and salt . . ."

"My ankle has healed now, Aunt," I tell her. "It doesn't hurt anymore."

"Why didn't you send for me earlier?"

Not that we sent for her just now, either. Somehow, Nur the Brickmaker had heard about it from Hasani, and he had told it to Ashur the Boatman, who had told Aunt Ra'na's son.

Gholam asks about Father.

Mother says, "Praise to God, he is well. We even had a letter from him a few days ago."

"He must have sent money too."

"A little bit of money, yes."

Gholam looks at me and smiles in a way that drives me insane.

I think Aunt Ra'na's daughter has threaded her eyebrows. It seems like she is wearing a bra too. She has changed a lot, Aunt Ra'na's daughter.

Now Aunt Ra'na complains about her husband. "The lazy ass stays home all the time without lifting a finger. I even pay for his tobacco and pipe. How much can a woman do for a husband like that, Sister? The entire winter, he didn't go to work, not even for a day. Look at my hands! How long do I have to go on washing people's clothes? How long can I clean this one's house and that one's?"

Aunt Ra'na's hands are pale. Her hands and her fingers are puffed up, making them look old and wrinkled.

Aunt Ra'na's son lights a cigarette and plays with the smoke. This is the first time I've seen Gholam smoking. Mother looks at him. There is reproach in her eyes. Gholam sends the smoke out from between his lips and says, "I am in the service, Aunt . . . You can't help it. Besides, smoking is not a big deal."

Aunt Ra'na waves her hand and says, "Enough already! If mandatory service is all that bad, why did you have to go and sign up for the army? Your lazy ass wants to stay in the army to have free food and not have to work."

Gholam has decided to remain in the army. He is supposed to go for training so that he can become a third sergeant. The only problem is that he is illiterate. He has started to learn how to read. There are eighty-six other privates in his brigade who are illiterate and are being taught how to read and write in the barracks.

"I can be promoted to first sergeant," Gholam says. "My life will be good then."

I don't know why I hate Aunt Ra'na's son more each time I see him. I can't stand seeing him anymore. He twists his mustache as he listens to the noises coming from the courtyard. He's lost interest in Bolur Khanom since the day she made fun of him. But now, it looks like he's not so disinterested after all.

Hasani opens the door and comes in. He kneels next to me and says, "Khaled, it's the same person who came the other night."

It is Bidar. I get up and lean on the cane.

"Don't go out, Khaled!" says Aunt Ra'na. "It's not good for your foot. Whoever it is, ask him to come in. We're not strangers, are we?"

"No, Aunt Ra'na, I'll go to the door. I won't be long."

I ask Hasani to get the books out from under the pillow and hand them to me.

Gholam reaches to snatch the books from Hasani. "What are these books, Khaled?"

I take the books from Hasani. I don't answer Gholam, and walk out of the room with Hasani.

Bidar has brought me new books.

Still relying on my cane, I head out of the house. The day after tomorrow is Nowruz, the New Year. Father had written that, if possible, he would come home, but he didn't come. There's still time, though. Who knows? He might still make it so we can spend Nowruz Eve together.

It's been more than ten days since I last went to Aman Aqa's teahouse. I won't go there again until the holiday of Sizdehbedar. Even then, I'll play it by ear.

I toddle up to Mehdi the Grocer's shop. He's on good terms with me now that we don't owe him any money. He smiles as soon as he sees me. "How did you sprain your ankle?" By now I have it all memorized. I say the whole thing in a few words.

Mehdi the Grocer comes out from behind the counter. He brings a stool and places it in the entrance to his shop. "Sit down and let's have a chat."

I sit on the stool. The sunlight is pleasant. For no particular reason, my hand goes toward the book in the back pocket of my pants. I take it out. Two customers come in. I read a page or so while Mehdi the Grocer tends to them. I mark where I leave off. Even with my foot like this, I want to get up and go and see Black-Eyed. I can't stop thinking about her. My heart races whenever I think of her. For some reason, I become sad. Thinking about Black-Eyed is nothing like thinking about Bolur Khanom. Mehdi the Grocer brings another stool and places it next to mine. "Tell me, Khaled, how are things with you?"

"Good."

"What's the news?"

These days everyone wants to know about the current situation. They want to find out what's happening with all the commotion over petroleum. Mehdi the Grocer too wears a tag on his chest, which now looks soiled and greasy. "I mean the strike at the refinery," he says.

I tell him what I have heard from Bidar. "The refinery workers have stopped working. A few Englishmen got killed. The British closed down the refinery. They're packing up and getting ready to beat it. They have finally realized that their time of plundering is over. They have realized that everything has an owner, and there are rules and laws for running things. It's not some trivial thing to joke about. So far, they have pocketed three hundred pounds sterling a day, and no one has even made any inquiries."

Mehdi the Grocer's face lights up. "Three hundred pounds sterling a day?"

"Maybe even more."

"You know how much good we could do with that kind of money!"

"Without a doubt."

"You know what would be each person's share!"

Ebrahim shows up. "Hey, Khaled, how's it going?"

"Fine."

Mehdi the Grocer gets up to help a customer. Ebrahim sits in his place. "I heard you sprained your ankle."

"You see that it's sprained."

"I heard you were at the meeting."

I don't answer him. He lights a cigarette and inhales the smoke. He offers it to me. "You smoke?"

"No."

Ebrahim looks clean-cut in his new clothes. There's even some color in his cheeks. He has ditched Mash Rahim for good, and he knows what happened to Hasani. "That idiot," he puffs, "it's his own damn fault . . . clinging like a flea to Baba and not letting go. He should hang out with me, and I'll have him getting laid by a fine ass instead of going to Abbareh to sleep with Gongeh and getting gonorrhea."

He wants to pay me back the money I spent on Hasani, but I don't accept it. From the look of things, Ebrahim is not doing all that bad.

He digs his hand into his pants pocket and brings out a handful of small and large bills and shows them to me. "This here is *money* . . . Hasani will be doing himself a favor if he leaves Baba . . . and who can live with that whore of his, after all? And Baba thinks he's married a lady? Hah!"

He shoves the bills back into his pocket and tells me about the way he makes his money, and the way he spends it, buying all kinds of stuff. He says he is friends with Mahin Salaki now. I have heard a thing or two about Mahin Salaki in Aman Aqa's teahouse, like that she is gorgeous and dances at wedding parties and her going rate is fifty tomans. I think Ebrahim is embellishing the whole thing. Being a friend to Mahin Salaki costs a lot of money. I tell him this, and he bursts out laughing. "This is where you're completely wrong. A couple of cash robberies cover the cost of her for an entire week."

"Aren't you afraid of getting caught?" I ask.

"Cowards cannot live the good life," he says.

There is no use in talking to Ebrahim. He won't be convinced. Khaleq then shows up, and the two of them take off. I wonder how they have managed to avoid dealing with the police station and all so far. Who knows? Maybe they have found a way around it or some sort of a deal is going on. I remember Amu Bandar when his money was stolen from him in the butchers' market. *After a lifetime, I craved some sheep's kidney. I thought I'd buy some, bring it home, and skewer it on the hot coals. I took some money out of the lining of my hat to give to the kidney seller. I had barely put the hat back on when my money was snatched away from me as if in a sudden storm.*

Mehdi the Grocer prepares his water pipe and comes and sits next to me. He takes a drag and says, "He is such an ungrateful person."

"Who?"

"Ebram."

"Why?"

"Some time ago, he came with Khaleq and Chinuq to swindle me." He takes another drag and adds, "They said they had a large case of Sarneizeh tea for sale. They fooled me so that I almost paid them half as the deposit. The three of them were at me trying to pull the wool over my eyes."

Mehdi the Grocer is cross-eyed. The tag on his chest is a dirty gray.

"You were saying, Khaled . . ."

"Saying what?"

"The British."

All of a sudden, the workers at Habib the Baker's shop say the Salavat out loud. They have lit the evening oven.

I decide to start walking slowly toward Black-Eyed's house. By the time I get there school should be over. I will wander around near her house until she shows up. So, I get up and put the book in my pocket.

The ground is completely dry and no longer muddy. The sun is pleasantly warm. The sky is a clear blue. The town seems so quiet that it makes you want to doze off. All the walls along Hokumati Street are covered in scribbled slogans. The bold handwriting on the front wall of the Hokumati Building reads: *The hands of the plunderers must be removed from our national wealth!*

I wonder when they wrote this slogan, because the guard has failed to notice it.

Once, when we decided to write on the wall facing the police station, one of the truck drivers, a comrade, brought his truck and parked it in front of the police station. He put the hood up and pretended to work on the engine until we finished the job. The lights in front of the police station were on, but it was so late at night that not a soul passed by on the street.

When we finished the job, the truck drove away slowly and the two of us walked alongside it, making it our shield. A bit later, we hopped into the truck and the driver stepped on the gas pedal and sped away.

I imagine they must have played a similar trick while writing on the Hokumati Building.

From Hokumati Street I turn and go across Pahlavi Street. Someone calls my name. Azad is heading toward me. "I see you are walking again."

"Yes, as you can see I am."

Azad is happy to see me. "Where are you headed now?"

I want to tell him everything. I want to tell him how I have fallen for Black-Eyed. I want to open up to Azad, in the hope that he will help me. Maybe he could come up with better ways to start a friendship with Black-Eyed. After all, he is a few years older than me, and the way his social life is, I'm sure he has had more encounters with girls than me.

"You didn't say where you are going?"

As much as I want to, I don't dare open up to him. I'm afraid he might laugh at me or make fun of me. "Nowhere in particular," I say, "just walking. I got bored sitting at home."

"Let's go to the teahouse, then, and have a cup of tea."

So we go.

The customers hanging out at Shekufeh Teahouse are completely different from those who go to Morshed's or Aman Aqa's teahouses. These are mostly young, and college-educated at that. They sit together in groups and discuss things. They talk about petroleum and the refinery workers. Their voices are fused. The teahouse is surrounded by small rooms with French doors. There are more people sitting in these rooms. Each room opens up to another room. The ambience in the teahouse is pleasant and evokes good feelings. When you step into the teahouse it feels like you have entered into a different world.

I sit down. Azad introduces me to three people who are gathered together engrossed in conversation. I change my mind about going to see Black-Eyed. Their talk fascinates me. All I want to do now is sit and just listen; besides, I don't have an excuse to part ways with Azad.

They bring me tea. Across from me is a young man whose voice somehow sounds familiar. I feel like I have seen those eyes somewhere, maybe in a passing moment, or perhaps in a half-dark night. All I know is that I've seen those eyes. Those large, striking black eyes. And the way he talks! There's a distance, but a vague familiarity; a slippery and unsteady sort of connection, which I cannot grasp, yet it now connects me to this young man. He speaks with such passion. I bring my head close to Azad's ear and ask, "Who is this man?"

He whispers, "He was just released from prison."

"What's his name?"

"Pendar."

My mind thinks back. The sunset at the police station comes back to life before my eyes, and Gholam Ali Khan's thin mustache and small eyes that look like two raisins.

"Aqa . . . can you hear me?"

The sun has gone behind the parapet of the police station's roof. A sad feeling has clutched my heart. I feel like crying.

"Listen, Aqa . . . you just listen . . . and don't say anything."

An officer takes tea to Gholam Ali Khan. My teeth feel loose. My head is about to explode with pain.

"Tell Shafaq that Pendar has been arrested. Mojahed Bookstore is on Pahlavi Street."

I stir my tea and look at Pendar. He talks about the prison and the resistance he showed. He talks with such enthusiasm and eagerness that it brightens his striking eyes.

I've been pacing around near Black-Eyed's house for half an hour or so. Some of the shopkeepers in the neighborhood are beginning to notice me. I see their eyes following me until I disappear from their sight.

A small boy who looks very much like Bahram walks up the street. The color of his shirt, his height, and even his walk are not any different from Bahram's. I am overjoyed. Despite my injured foot, I move to walk in his direction. My heart races like that of a frightened little sparrow. Limping, I get myself to the alley to catch up with Bahram and talk to him. The small boy gets closer. It's not him. I am miserable, as if someone just poured a pail of ice-cold water over me.

The sky has grown dark. At the turn leading to the alley, a dusty streetlight comes on. I throw caution to the wind and walk into the alley right before the eyes of the grocer. The sound of the cane on the asphalt gives me away. Its clicks are like the blows of a hammer to my temples. I reach the corner of the second alley. The overhead light is not on. I get closer. I'm sure this is her house. How could I forget it? The very house I had frantically jumped into and shut the door behind me. Everything comes back to life in my mind.

"Were you at the meeting?"

"No . . . I was just passing by."

I have no doubt that this is the same house. The lights are not on. Random thoughts attack my mind. Is it possible they have gone on a trip for Nowruz? Is it possible they have gone to a party, and they will be back late?

I linger for a few more moments in front of the house, surveying the walls and the door. There's a light on in the window of the house opposite. The shadow of a man's head appears on the pink curtain and passes by. I turn around. I feel all the sorrows of the world filling my heart. I head out of the alley. The suspicious look from the grocer whose shop is right in front of the alley pierces my entire body like a pointed iron rod. What I really want to do is smack him on his head with my cane so hard that he'd pass out. Mehdi the Grocer is nothing like him. If as many as a hundred strangers passed him by in a day, he wouldn't give a damn. I should somehow get close to this particular grocer. It may work to my advantage.

I turn in the direction of Pahlavi Street, which is crowded at the moment. Tomorrow night is Nowruz's Eve. Those who can afford it are out doing their Nowruz's shopping. My ankle begins to hurt again and I feel tired. I should go to Mojahed Bookstore and rest a bit.

I come across a group of youths selling newspapers. Their hollers fill the street. No one stops them. Iman is with them. His voice is the deepest of all, but he is shorter than the others. Raising a bundle of newspapers over his head, he calls out to people. The picture printed on the front page annoys me. These sorts of newspapers publish in secret. I haven't gotten used to that picture yet. I cannot relate to it. All the guys are trying to grow a thick mustache so as to look like this man who's always on the front page. Once I got into an argument with Bidar over it. "I still don't understand why that picture should always be on the front page of our papers."

"When you realize the significance of universal unity, it'll all make sense to you," Bidar responds.

"How are the two related?"

"You'll see for yourself, little by little."

I doubt that I will ever understand.

Mojahed Bookstore is closed. One can never figure out when it's open and when it's closed. There's no sense of order or regularity to it; or if it has any, I'm not aware of it.

Shekufeh Teahouse is not that far away. With the help of my cane, I begin walking over there so I can rest a bit. The teahouse is more crowded than ever before. Some of the people are the same ones who were here this morning. Pendar is also here, and next to him is Hemmat, squirming in his seat. His sharp gaze seems restless. Noticing me, he waves his hand. "Come here, Khaled!"

He introduces me to Pendar. "Let me introduce you to a nice guy."

I shake Pendar's hand. "I know him," I say.

Pendar's striking gaze meets mine. "You know me? From where?"

I let him know how and from where.

He shakes my hand warmly. "You cannot imagine how happy I am. I always wondered if it'd ever be able to meet you."

He looks me over again. "You look different, though. I have to say, you seem like you've grown. Last time I saw you, you seemed much younger."

I agree. I have gotten tall all of the sudden, not to mention the dark hair growing above my upper lip.

"All right, then! Don't you want to sit down? What's happened to your foot?"

Hemmat explains.

He bursts out laughing. "One shouldn't be too hasty when running away."

"I wasn't that hasty."

"Oh yeah? Looks like you were in such a hurry you panicked and didn't watch your step. If you ask me, one should always remain calm and cool in situations like that. That way you know better what to do and how to do it."

Maybe he is right. Maybe I did panic and that's why I now have to deal with this damaged foot. I sit down. I have taken a liking to Pendar. This morning I was so impressed by his stories of prison and his resistance. I wish I were that brave and resilient. That day when Gholam Ali Khan dragged me to the police station, I felt so helpless and pathetic, as if the world had come to an end. I had lost all my self-confidence.

"When you're being interrogated, you should imagine that there's a dagger placed under your chin or under your tongue, and if you say 'yes,' the sharp tip will pierce you and if you say 'no,' you'll be safe."

I've been captivated by Pendar's stories since I heard them this morning. He talks in such a way that you can't help but listen. When he speaks, he's even more impressive than Shafaq.

"So, tell us what you've been up to these days."

I tell him what I'm doing, but I add, "I don't think I want to go work at the teahouse anymore, at least not for a while."

"Don't you think you should attend night school?"

"I hadn't even thought of it."

As I think on it now, it doesn't sound bad at all. If I could work at Aman Aqa's teahouse during the day and go to school at night, it might work out for me after all. I give it some thought, and then leave it for the moment and keep on listening to Pendar.

"By the way, you didn't say why you were there that day at the police station."

I tell him the entire story. He bursts out laughing. "I never really thought you'd give my message to Shafaq. But when they took me to my house and searched the entire place, and put their fingers on everything, I just knew."

They offer me a cup of tea and bring Pendar a water pipe. He smokes as he talks. I finally find out why he was arrested, and I get to learn about lots of things from what he says. I feel like he deliberately talks about these things to teach you about what to do and what not to do if you get arrested. The sorts of things he tells me remind me of Pavel, the character in the book I've just read. The one who went blind and wouldn't give up. People like Pavel and Pendar are hard to find. Could one possibly tolerate heavy handcuffs for ten hours and not say a word? I wonder what kind of a thing these bulky handcuffs are that force your shoulders and chest to stretch out and paralyze your wrists. From the way Pendar describes them, I cannot imagine tolerating them around my wrists for even one hour. I think of my ankle. It was just a sprain, but I was ready to bite the ground. I cursed the entire world. The only thing I don't like much about Pendar is his mustache. The same thick mustache, like the one on that man on the front page of the papers.

Azad strides in and flings himself right onto the bench. "What's new, everyone?"

News is plentiful.

～

The entire town is elated. Drivers have their lights on and keep honking their horns, making such a clamor. The sounds coming from the cars' radios are all jumbled up. The news announcer speaks with such passion: "Due to the people's demands, the parliament has passed the oil nationalization bill."

Their faces lit up with joy and smiles, people have gathered around a group of street performers who are dancing cheerfully. Some sweet-sellers have stuffed their large round trays with candies and sweets and are offering them to passersby. People hug and congratulate each other, even though they may be strangers. As everyone goes around celebrating, so does the latest news, prompting the question, "Have you heard the news?"

"What news?"

"The warship *Mauritius* anchored in Shatt al-Arab and aimed its cannons at the refinery."

"I heard the British paratroopers have landed in Cyprus."[3]

Faces are fiery red. "Over our dead bodies."

The veins on people's necks swell. "If we have to, we'll fight with teeth and claws." "We've had enough of it."

The thought of victory has made everyone impatient. People are ready for any kind of action. People's mouths froth from all the passionate shouting.

"Hah! Warship my ass. What do they take us for—a bunch a cowards?"

"They're just bluffing."

The news goes around that a committee has formed to demand that the government provide people with weapons to defend their victory.

"We'll fight shoulder to shoulder."

"We'll throw them all into the sea."

"Their time is over."

"They have to pick up their tails and beat it."

People have taken to the streets in groups.

In the middle of the square, with rags and wood, people have made an effigy of a British official and set it on fire. They have put a pair of shorts on the effigy, and instead of using leather for his crotch, they have dyed it black with oil. They have placed a wide-brimmed hat on his head. They have brought the large penis of a bull from the butcher's shop and stuck it between his lips instead of a cigar. The British official has a small dog that is being walked on a chain behind him. The dog too is made of rags, and its large drooping ears are dyed black. People gather around the effigy, cheering and laughing.

Children have made a poem for it:

> *Master, go home!*
> *Doggy, go home!*
> *Farangi is faithless,*
> *His donkey is saddleless.*

---

3. Cyprus was used as a headquarters by the British and Americans as they staged the 1953 coup d'état that removed Iranian prime minister Mohammad Mosaddeq from power.

Mehdi the Grocer has hired a band of entertainers and brought them to the neighborhood, and they're making such a racket. Everyone has come out of their houses to gather around the musicians. They have joined hands and are dancing to the music of the drums and the *sorna*.

Khalifeh and Mehdi the Grocer rush into the middle of the crowd and start a stick fight. Khalifeh places the stick on the back of his neck, wraps his arms around it, bends over at the waist, and dances around. Behind him, Mehdi the Grocer dances in sync with the rhythm of the music as he hollers. The *sorna* plays the stick dance tune. Khalifeh, who's been turning around in circles, stops suddenly and places the stick between his calves. Mehdi the Grocer twirls the stick around his head. The sounds of shouting and clapping are blended.

Nowruz has arrived.

Black-Eyed was away on a trip.

I must've gone to her neighborhood to see about her more than ten times before Sizdehbedar. Somehow, I finally managed to butter up the grocer across from the alley. I know how to handle him now. He is one of those ardent admirers of the prime minister. The day after Sizdehbedar I run into Black-Eyed. She is with Bahram. I cross paths with them so abruptly that I take them both by surprise.

"Ah . . . you . . ."

I greet them. The cane is no longer necessary, but I still hold on to it. I think Black-Eyed is happy to see me. Her eyes—those eyes that invite you to love and worship them—sparkle.

"How's your ankle?"

"Getting better."

I fall silent. I have so much to say to her, yet still I fall silent. I mean, I can't talk. The words claw my throat but don't come out. I struggle even to say a simple thank you. "I'm really grateful that you let me into your house the other day," I say, and then shift my gaze to Bahram, "and you too."

She laughs. When Black-Eyed laughs, you can feel the spring, its scent, and the blossoming of the flowers, the freshness of the leaves and the grass.

"Don't even mention it," she says.

"Just the fact that you let me in was already a lot." It is all I can say, so I leave.

Spring is here. The Karun is torrential, roaring and muddy, turning the color of café au lait. Its variable waves roll down, crashing against the houses along the banks. The waves bring sheep carcasses from villages near and far and leave them behind on the banks. The torrent has reached up so high that the large slogan we scribbled on the dam's concrete wall has disappeared. The water level tower is submerged. Your head spins just looking at the water from behind the railings of the White Bridge. At night, it is the roaring of the Karun that you can hear, even from far away, but in the daytime, there are other sounds that are growing louder by the day. Different groups of people, holding up banners, walk around the streets chanting aloud their slogans.

An assembly of delegates has been sent by the prime minister to get the British aboard their vessels and on their way home. What a warm send-off! The airport is crammed with people in the afternoon heat. There is no room at all. Colorful banners wave over the heads of the crowd, so many that a needle thrown in the air would not hit the ground. The colorful banners float in the air overhead. A few even managed to slip away from the crowd, drifting all the way up to the airplane's stairs, where the government delegates stand. All sorts of news circulates as the crowd intensifies and people grow excited.

"Have you heard the news?"

"No, what news?"

"They say that the workers have broken into the British officials' houses and have killed a few of them."

"They have set some of their cars on fire too."

"But the British won't budge that easy."

"To hell with them."

"You think they will just leave like that?"

"We'll throw them out."

"It's not like their fathers' blood has been spilled here."

"It's over now."

Nothing can stop them. In no time they close down the bazaar, offices shut down, and the public pours into the streets in groups.

"Let's go to the telegraph office!"

"What's going on there?"

"Some have gone on a hunger strike."

"What for?"

"So that those who were arrested recently get released."

It is the third day since seventeen workers began a hunger strike at the telegraph office. Many are expected to side with them. If their demands are not met by tomorrow, another group will join them.

"Have you read the bakers' union's manifesto?"

"What was written in it?"

"They are planning to go on strike too."

Sizdehbedar has come and gone, and I still haven't gone back to Aman Aqa's teahouse. I don't want to go there anymore.

"Khaled, your foot looks better now—why don't you come to the teahouse?"

"I might come one of these days, Aman Aqa . . . My foot still hurts a bit."

But it's not that. I have gone over everything and have figured things out. If I keep working at the teahouse, the best I can do is to become like Spider; if I get lucky, maybe I'll turn into someone like Aman Aqa. In just a few months, I'll be nineteen. I have grown a beard and a mustache, my legs are getting longer every day. No, working in the teahouse is not for me. I should start attending night school.

I am in Pendar's division now. We hold our weekly meetings on Friday afternoons. Sometimes, we change the time and the location. Including Pendar, there are four of us. I listen to the news and debates. I take newspapers and pamphlets to the meetings of the young textile workers and hand them out. They hold their meetings on Friday nights. The four of us are assigned to deal with all the workers under the age of twenty-three.

I put the papers against my stomach, tighten my belt, smooth the creases of my shirt, say good-bye to the guys, and head out of the house. The Karun, stormy and fuming, stretches out in front of me. Water has reached the foot of the narrow sidewalk that lies in front of the houses. This is the third Friday that we've held our meeting here in this house. It's grown dark. The lights of the White Bridge have just come on. I walk past the narrow sidewalk and turn into the log sellers' alley. Stacks of logs, damp and clammy, are piled up by the wall. The bitter smell of the freshly cut willow branches fills my nostrils. A few of the log sellers sit together around a fire with a kettle hung over it. The only light in the log sellers' alley is provided by the flames that blaze up and then die down. As I get closer, I can smell the scent of fire, the smell of smoked fish, and the bitter smell of willow branches, all mixed up together. A middle-aged man sitting close to the fire has cut open the bellies of mullet fish and is busy cleaning them.

I head out of the log sellers' alley and turn into the run-down street of the date sellers. The pungent smell of rotting dates wafts through the air. The pavement feels tacky. Date juice is all over the ground. I jump over the narrow ditch along the street and walk on the soft, dusty part of the sidewalk. Suddenly I freeze. Ali the Devil has come out from under a grimy streetlight across the street and is heading my way. The guys have given him this name.

"He's such a devil, he can read the words on the newspaper inside your pocket even through your shirt."

"He's got a sense of smell like a dog."

"His eyes are like a vulture's."

"He is devious, just like a fox."

Ali the Devil's eyes are blue. His eyebrows are arched and pointed. His blond mustache, as thick as yellow Shami fava beans, covers his upper lip, and his nose reminds you of a shark's muzzle sensing blood. He appears so suddenly, as if he'd always been there waiting for me.

He has been following me for some time now, but he hasn't been able to pin anything on me yet. He carries a pistol and always wears a jacket, be it summer or winter, and you can see the pistol bulging under his jacket.

Somewhere in the dark I turn around carefully and walk slowly toward the log sellers' alley. The sound of Ali the Devil's footsteps is barely audible on the soft, dusty ground. It sounds as if he's walking faster. Maybe he noticed me turning around. I'm afraid to even sneak a quick look, as if I can feel his cold pistol on the back of my neck.

Once in the log sellers' alley, I begin to run. The smell of the roasting mullet wafts through the air, mixed with the bitter smell of willow branches. The middle-aged man is still roasting the mullet over the fire. I pause for a moment at the stacked logs. In the safety of the wall, I run all the way to the bank of the Karun.

Pendar is about to leave the house. I push him back inside. "Ali the Devil is coming," I warn him. We go inside, walk up the staircase to the roof, and look out the window in the brick wall along the edge of the roof. Ali the Devil is heading out of the log sellers' alley. Standing at the edge of the narrow sidewalk along the wall, his arms akimbo, he looks around. He walks up and down for a while, lights a cigarette, takes a deep drag, and disappears into the log sellers' alley.

The weather has grown much hotter. Right before sunset, everyone sweeps the fronts of their rooms, sprinkles the dusty earth with water, spreads out a rug, and lights their lanterns.

Karam Ali has begun selling his cooked beans. Naser Davani has bought a hundred square meters of land in the vicinity of the stagnant marshland far off at the edge of the city. He's planning to build a four-wall on it so as to be free from renting, once and for all. "I'll borrow money from the bank," he says. "All I need to do is find a guarantor. Instead of rent, I'll pay off the mortgage in installments. I don't think that the interest will be all that much."

Bolur Khanom is upset with me. "Khaled, you're such a bad boy these days. Don't tell me that you're seeing someone else . . . Is that it?"

My ears are deaf to her words. I have taken a vow not to touch her ever again. The more I think of Black-Eyed, the more I run away from Bolur Khanom.

Rahim the Donkey Keeper and Rezvan quarrel every night. "Woman, you should be ashamed of yourself, the sorts of things you do at your age. It's shameful."

"Take it or leave it. You don't want me this way, so be it—just divorce me."

"Divorce you?" sneers Rahim the Donkey Keeper. "I'd kill you before doing that. Your hair should turn white like your teeth in your husband's house."

Bolur Khanom gets her beatings as usual. I'm beginning to think that Bolur Khanom herself is really to blame. She stirs things up, complaining so much, and that leaves Aman Aqa no choice but to beat the hell out of her with his belt.

Amu Bandar was sick for a few days. Mother looked after him. He feels better now, but he has turned his cart upside down right by the pigeon coop and doesn't leave the house.

The story about Karam Ali and Banu was not just passing gossip after all. Afaq and Khaj Tofiq have worked the matter out, and now Afaq does whatever she can to please Sanam. For her part, Banu treats Sanam like her future mother-in-law and does her chores. From the look of things, I think that one of these days Sanam will roll up her sleeves and go ask for Banu's hand in marriage for Karam.

I have quit the teahouse and have not been back at all. I have talked to Mother about going to night school once the summer is over and the schools are open again. Father has written that he wants to come home. "I am homesick. I miss you all. I am planning to come back sometime in the fall and see you. If the work situation has improved, I'll stay; if not, I'll have to go back to Kuwait again." Sitting in front of their room, Omid is doing his homework. His mother is preparing Shami kebab for dinner. I have never known anyone this quiet in my entire life. She minds her own business in such a way it is as if she's not in the house at all. Bolur Khanom spreads a rug on the wood-framed bed and waits for Aman Aqa to come home. The smell of Khaj Tofiq's opium wafts through the courtyard. As usual, Banu has taken her place next to the brazier, and is dozing off. Khaj Tofiq is immersed in his opium, warming his pipe and inhaling its smoke gently. If someone were to sit next to him at the brazier, he'd begin talking nonstop. He'd talk of his youth. About a time when opium was like saffron and its scent could be smelled seven blocks away. Or about the opium pipe bowls, engraved with Naseroddin Shah designs, he owned once and how they are difficult to find now. Once at the brazier, Khaj Tofiq can talk and talk until morning. But if left alone, he picks at the embers under the ashes, looking to find a smooth lump of hot charcoal to use to smoke his opium. Banu dozes off, and Afaq is not home yet.

I lie down in front of Father's room, reading a book under the lantern's light, which I have placed overhead, and wait for Bidar to show up. I am in charge of the young textile workers' library. Pendar has given me the books. There are more than a hundred. Each book circulates from one worker to the next until it eventually gets in the hands of all the workers. I'm in contact with only three of the other guys from our meetings. I know some of the workers only in passing, and others I don't know at all. Two days ago, two of them were fired from the factory, a few of them were beaten up, and two others were arrested. I wait for Bidar to arrive. We're supposed to come up with some sort of plan for them.

Instead of Bidar, Aunt Ra'na's son comes in. For sure, he's come to squeeze some money out of Mother. I tuck the book under the corner of the rug. These days, unconsciously, I get fidgety as soon as I run into someone in a military uniform. Instinctively, I shun anyone in a police uniform.

"Hello, Khaled."

"Hello."

"Salaam, dear Auntie."

"Salaam, Gholam."

Aunt Ra'na's son kisses Jamileh, goes into the room, brings the stool out, and sits on it. His gaze is on Bolur Khanom, sitting on her wood-framed bed on the other side of the courtyard.

Gholam extends his hand and brings the book out from under the rug. He must've seen it when I was hiding it. "What's that you're reading?"

I just ignore him.

At the garrison, Aunt Ra'na's son has sort of learned to spell out words. "You didn't say what you're reading?" he says again.

What I want to do is hit him in the head with both of my hands.

"Don't tell me! I'll read it myself."

He struggles to spell out the title. "Pu . . . r . . . p . . ."

I save him the effort. "*The Purpose of Literature.*"

He throws the book on the rug, puckers his lips, and says, "These books won't get you anywhere."

Mother pours him a cup of tea. He unbuttons his jacket, showing off his hairy chest. His body is as hairy as that of a bear.

"Dear Aunt, what news from Uncle Haddad?"

"Praise to God, he is doing well."

"He hasn't sent a letter?"

"Yes, he has."

"How about money?"

Mother shoots him a look. If Aunt Ra'na had looked at me like that, I would have died of embarrassment. That good-for-nothing doesn't have any dignity. It's as if the military's free food has turned him into a parasite.

Gholam's mustache glistens. The ends curve up like the tail of a scorpion. He talks about the sergeant-training classes. "They have asked me to buy three two-hundred-sheet notebooks, along with a couple of erasers, pencils, and rulers. The sergeant has asked me to get chalk for the blackboard too."

His eyes stay fixed on Bolur Khanom as he talks, his pupils moving fast. Mother asks him how it is that the sergeant has asked him to do all the shopping.

"No, dear Aunt. He asks others to buy things too."

I notice Bidar standing between the double doors of the entrance to the courtyard. I put on my good pants and head out the door. "Mother, I'll be back soon."

Gholam asks, "Where?"

"I have something to take care of."

I leave the house. Bidar is on a bike. I sit in front of him, and together we ride along Hokumati Street and head uptown.

We pass through a few alleys and backstreets before we get off the bike. He gives me the address. "I'll go in first. You come in a few minutes after me. Pay attention! Before you come in, first walk past the house door a few steps, then come back and enter the house. I'll leave the door ajar; you close it behind you."

Bidar leaves. I lean against the wall. It's dark. At the end of the alley, there is a grimy light overhead, hanging from a house. I hear footsteps. I walk slowly. A tall man is approaching. He walks past me, then under the grimy light, and disappears from sight. I walk back to the house. Bidar is waiting in the hallway. Together we walk down to the basement.

I only know Shafaq, Pendar, Bidar, and Azad, and not the other two. I have never met them before. Everyone refers to one of them as "Doctor." I cannot even imagine being in a meeting sitting next to someone who is a doctor. There are seven of us altogether. The Doctor has a goatee. He is of medium height. There's a certain charm in his hypnotic gaze. The air in the basement is warm and oppressive. The fan hanging from the ceiling makes a clicking noise. There is also a pitcher and a few glasses. The plaster on the walls is covered in moldy patches. Mold has formed at the base of the walls. The Doctor smokes his pipe.

Shafaq smokes his cigarette. As he talks, I'm surprised to hear that the Doctor knows me so well. The subject today is the young textile workers.

The man sitting next to the Doctor is short and skinny. His face is hairless and riddled with smallpox scars. His forehead has advanced to the middle of his head. His chin is pointed. His nose is small, out of proportion with the rest of his facial features, and he's got an involuntary twitch in the lower lid of his right eye that spasms every few seconds. Everyone calls him Nader. I guess he's around thirty-five years old. I have a strange feeling about him, as if I shouldn't trust him. In contrast, I liked the Doctor at first sight.

His eyes meet mine. "Tell us everything!" he says.

Lowering my gaze, I slowly recount all that has happened in the textile factory. "They used to give the workers a cup of milk every day at ten o'clock. But for no particular reason stopped doing so for a few days. The first two days, the workers just grumbled, but on the third day they began voicing their complaints to the point that the matter got out of hand and led to a fistfight with the foremen. Things then got even worse. The executive director called the police. The policemen cracked down on the workers, beat up a few, and arrested two of them. Later, they laid off seven of them."

"Well, what can we do now?" asks the Doctor, looking us each carefully in the eye.

Bidar says, "What does this matter have to do with the police, anyway?"

In a low voice, Nader says, "Well, this is the characteristic behavior of an employer, to stand in the way of the workers. Besides, history has proven that as the industrialization and development of factories increase, so do conflicts; on one hand, new types of problems emerge and on the other, a set of new disagreements between the employer and the employee comes into existence."

Nader's eyelid twitches, and his pointed chin moves as he talks. ". . . Nevertheless, it is the responsibility of the workers to be aware and to take advantage of the lessons of history so as to be able to stand up for their own rights. There's the issue of capital here and the issue of interest. And the foundation of any production plan is based upon higher revenues and an increase in output. Consequently, the last thing he wishes to do is to give in to the workers' demands . . ."

No, I can't trust him. But I envy him for the things he knows and I don't.

Nader turns his sharp gaze on me. "That being said, I think that the time is ripe to start up a strike in the factory, especially now that a single demand has caused all of them to protest."

"I believe so too," agrees Shafaq.

Pendar asks my opinion.

"Well, yes, . . . maybe that's possible," I say.

"Maybe?" says the Doctor.

"Are you doubtful?" Nader asks.

I shrug, and in a hesitant voice, say, "Not that I have doubts . . . no."

The Doctor says, "In my opinion, before we do anything, we need to determine whether or not the textile committee possesses a strong political leadership. We should be certain, also, that they're capable of mobilizing the workers."

I have difficulty understanding what they're saying and answering their questions.

Nader says, "That's what Khaled should find out."

I don't want to be the chink in somebody's armor or show any signs of weakness before the Doctor. In a subdued voice, I say, "Of course that's possible . . . the committee can certainly mobilize the workers."

"We should make the final decision tonight," the Doctor says, "and report the result to the *top*."

"We should plan on an organized strike," Pendar says. "An organized strike should paralyze the factory until the prisoners are released and the laid-off workers are reappointed."

Their words get jumbled up. I think about the people on "top," who get mentioned in every meeting, yet I have never been able to get to know them. It strikes me that Nader, or the Doctor, or even both of them, must be calling the people on "top" every night to report, consult, and get orders. I laugh at my silly thoughts.

I hear Shafaq say, "I suggest that we get other groups of workers ready to go on strike in support of them, if necessary."

"You mean the railway and oil workers as well?" Bidar asks.

"Not all together," answers Shafaq.

"I agree," Nader says. "If the strike drags on for a few days without a positive outcome, the railway and oil workers should also go on strike."

"We can even prepare the bakers' and the bazaar merchants' guilds for a strike as well," adds Azad.

Things turn serious. My attention goes to the Doctor's hands, and to the little spoon he scoops the half-burned tobacco out of his pipe with. He could be around forty years old. There are streaks of gray in his beard. Whenever he looks at me, I drop my head. It's hard for me to look him in the eye. I wish I could be in his position, able to be in contact with the people on "top." These "top" people are a mystery to me. Some vague and hazy images take shape in my mind. People without faces or people who have covered their faces and walk in fog and smoke, their voices full of intensity, their tones impressive, seeing everything, understanding things better, knowing more, and assessing things well . . . I hear a new word. "We should first give them an *ultimatum*."

"Of course! We should give them an ultimatum.

Ultimatum? Before I even get the chance to think about what it means, I hear Nader say, "We should give the employer a few days' grace period." I look at him. There's the twitch again. ". . . We'll give them time to reappoint the workers, as well as give them the usual cup of milk at ten o'clock."

Pendar turns to me. "Can you prepare the textile boys in two days?"

It's suffocating in the basement. Full of smoke. The dim light fixed onto the wall clashes with all the smoke.

As if to himself, Nader goes on, muttering irrelevant things. "How much does a textile worker earn to begin with, that he has to pay out of his own pocket for a cup of milk?"

Their arguments become incoherent, the kind of off-track rambling that has nothing to do with the issue, nor does it help resolve the problem whatsoever. The Doctor redirects the conversation. In the end, we decide that, if the board of managers does not cooperate, we will guide the workers toward a hunger strike, maybe even a sit-in at the telegraph office.

"We will mobilize the city if necessary."

The discussion turns to the "petition" and the "duration of the ultimatum."

"Three days are enough."

Everyone agrees, but I still don't understand the meaning of ultimatum.

"We need to get more workers to sign the petition," Nader says.

"We should also think of writing a petition for the oil and railway workers," the Doctor says, "because they should distribute a petition of support without any hesitation, if necessary."

Right after the meeting, I must go and find the division's boys, one by one, and have them gather somewhere and inform them of the meeting's final decision.

The Doctor, as he stuffs a fresh pipe and lights it, tells me to be strong and to act bravely. "Be in contact with Pendar at all times. If you run into a problem you can't solve on your own, let Pendar know immediately . . ."

Nader follows up on what the Doctor says. ". . . Also, report progress regularly to Pendar."

The Doctor takes a drag from the pipe and adds, "Before you start, you should know that victory is not always achieved easily."

"Especially when you have to deal with the police, you should be ready for any kind of violence," Shafaq says.

My entire body shakes with excitement. I can't wait to go find the boys and drag them out of their houses, saying, "Look here, guys! We must be strong and act bravely!"—as if it is the Doctor himself speaking through my mouth.

We sit on the oil pipes that run alongside the graveyard and all the way to the port. It is dark and midnight is approaching. Lone streetlights twinkle here and there. The weather is muggy.

"We will mobilize the city if necessary."

"The entire city?"

I nod my head. It is Nader's voice coming out of my throat: "There are numerous historical examples that are inspiring and informative."

I feel very excited. I feel as if I could move the entire city with a gesture. The headlights of a truck coming from the direction of the port illuminate the side of the road and the pipelines along it. The roar of the truck in the silence of the night is powerful.

"When should we start?"

"Tonight, before dawn, the flyers will be printed. Tomorrow, the entire textile factory should be white with flyers."

It is past midnight when I get home. The doors to the house are always open. The hinges are rusted and one of the decayed doors is stuck in the ground.

I tiptoe into our room, take off my clothes, and lie down in front of Father's room.

The sky is high above. The stars are large and bright. I hear Bolur Khanom's bed creaking.

I put on work clothes and blend in with the textile workers to enter the factory.

The entire workshop, the canteen, the hallways, and the large tree-filled yard have been showered with flyers. We have even stuck a few flyers on the director's door, the factory accountant's door, and even on the door of the board of managers' conference room.

There's no need for a strike. The director gives in. The board of managers and the workers' representatives sit around the negotiating table. It is the day the strike is supposed to start. Sitting in groups under the shade of the trees, the workers wait for the meeting to end. It takes less than forty minutes for the representatives to emerge—their faces happy—and announce, "The laid-off workers will return to their jobs, those detained will be released, and milk will be provided as usual at ten o'clock."

All at once, a unified cry of joy blasts into the air. The workers lift their representatives up on their shoulders in happiness.

In no time, the atmosphere is entirely transformed and the factory is filled with joy and cheers.

Ali the Devil has been keeping an eye on me. He shows up as I go around town. There are times that I feel he's following me. He has done such a good job pestering me that I feel his presence at all times. So far, I have managed to save my tail, but I know he's got plans for me.

"How are you, Khaled?"

He knows my name.

"You outshined everyone at the textile factory."

Who has told him?

Sometimes he is riding a bike, other times he's walking, but always under his short jacket is a bulge.

He walks past me and darts a peculiar look at me. I smile in return. I don't want to talk to him, not even a word. As much as I can, I try not to cross paths with him.

It's been a week since I last saw Black-Eyed. Since I saw her in Bagh-e Melli Park. I think it was on Tuesday. It was in the afternoon. She was with Bahram, sitting on a bench.

I'm beside myself with excitement every time I see her. She has noticed it too. I blush. My heart starts beating fast. My throat dries. My voice becomes hoarse.

I surprise her over and over. I show up as she goes about her business. We talk together.

"How are you?"

"Just fine."

"How's your ankle?"

"Good as new."

I sit down next to her, keeping quiet. We look at each other. She smiles and looks down. My heart races. How I desire to kiss her! And what a tumult goes on inside me! My entire body is warm with excitement. If I don't stop myself, I might just hug her right here and kiss every bit of her body. I want to bury my nose in her hair and smell it. I want to kiss her lips until they bleed. She looks at me again. For a second our eyes are locked together. We smile and look down again. Out of nowhere, Ali the Devil is standing right before me, his green eyes fixed on Black-Eyed, his wicked smile stretching his lips. What I want is to get up and punch him in the chin. He looks at me and says, "I didn't think a poor, wretched boy from the run-down part of town could make friends with such a cute high-class girl."

I blush up to my ears. I can't stop myself; words jump out of my mouth. "Watch your mouth!"

Not expecting this, Ali the Devil's smile disappears. "What did you say?"

Black-Eyed's face turns the color of wheat. She gets up, looks at me, forces a smile, shakes her head, and takes off with Bahram.

I grind my teeth. The veins on my neck bulge. I am beside myself with rage.

"How did you manage to fool her?"

If only I could somehow get rid of the day's paystubs in my pocket, I would fight him right here. I should control myself. The cusswords are right behind my front teeth. I swallow my anger and hold back the words.

I lean back against the bench, cross one leg over the other, and direct my gaze toward the end of Bagh-e Melli Park.

Ali the Devil shifts from one foot to the other, then sits down next to me. I bite my lip as I steal a glance at him. He lights a cigarette and plays with the smoke. I get up. He grabs my wrist. "Sit down!"

"I have to leave."

"I know . . . but wait a minute!" Then he continues on in a gentler tone. "We can be friends."

I am furious. I shake my wrist free of his grasp and say brashly, "I am a poor, wretched boy who lives in the slums downtown, and you are a government official. How do you expect us to be friends?"

He bursts out laughing.

I get up.

"That made you really upset, huh?"

I feel sweat forming on my forehead. My temples are pounding. I have a headache. The cigarette smoke drifting through Ali the Devil's blond mustache makes it look like smoldering dog poop. His eyes look like two small green sequins. His nose is red, his cheeks chubby.

"At any rate, we could still be friends."

I take off without saying a word. He really bothers me. I have to somehow find a way to avoid crossing paths with him ever again. If this goes on, one day soon I know I'll get into a fight with him and that means nothing but trouble.

It is already dark when I get home. A group of neighborhood kids dashes out of the house, booing. Rahim the Donkey Keeper comes out chasing them with a stick in his hand. Standing next to the courtyard pool, Rezvan yells, "What do you expect? It's hard not to become a cuckold when you can't even afford your own wife's daily expenses."

From the look of things, she has reached the end of her rope.

Rahim the Donkey Keeper leaves the kids alone and rushes toward Rezvan. His eyes are bloodshot. Khaj Tofiq stops him. Mash Rahim yells, "The bitch has gone wild."

Khaj Tofiq takes Rahim the Donkey Keeper aside. "Come on, Mash Rahim! This is a disgrace."

Rezvan screams, "I'll go to the police station right this minute and set everything straight, once and for all!"

"What are you waiting for, then?" Mash Rahim yells back. "Go there, go right now, go to hell. You're killing me."

The neighbors have just turned on their lanterns. Sanam helps Rezvan to her feet. Khaj Tofiq pulls Rahim the Donkey Keeper toward his room. Mash Rahim is frothing at the mouth. "She has made a laughingstock out of me before the eyes of everyone. Habib the Baker makes nasty remarks, the kids boo at me in the alleys, Mehdi the Grocer laughs sarcastically . . . What a mistake I have made!"

Khaj Tofiq takes Rahim the Donkey Keeper to his room and whispers in his ear, "In that case, let her go then . . . Why do you make yourself so miserable?"

Mash Rahim fumes, "Let her go? I'd take her life before doing such a thing."

"Then you have to get along with her."

"No matter how many times I say to her, 'Woman, don't tarnish my honor with your doings,' does she listen? No. My entire life I've had a good reputation, but now, in my old age, look what she's making of me."

Rezvan rushes into her room to grab her chador. Rahim the Donkey Keeper jumps in front of her, snatching the chador out of her hand. "You think I'll let you go?"

Rezvan tugs at her chador. Rahim the Donkey Keeper slaps her across the face. She falls down and rolls on the ground; her skirt flies up. She screams. Once again, the kids are pouring into the courtyard. Rahim the Donkey Keeper chases them out. "Sons of bitches—they won't grant you even a bit of privacy in your own home."

The kids make funny faces and boo him, then dash toward the house doors. Sanam grabs Rezvan's wrist again and drags her out of the room. Khaj Tofiq sits Rahim the Donkey Keeper in front of the room. He takes the stick out of his hand, stuffs a pipe, and hands it to him. "Mashti Rahim, this woman is no good for you."

Rahim the Donkey Keeper grumbles. Returning home from the brickkilns, Hasani leads the donkeys into the house. Behind him, Amu Bandar comes in, pushing his cart through the door as he greets everyone. Amu Bandar has gotten much thinner.

Rezvan, sitting in front of Afaq's room, cries. Squatting beside the brazier, Afaq fans the half-lit charcoals. Banu sweeps in front of Sanam's room. There's a bit of color in her face now. In three weeks, she will be marrying Karam Ali.

∽

Father has written that he'll return at the beginning of fall, and if he can find work, he will stay. But the way things are going these days, I doubt there will be any improvement in the economy and unemployment. Walk in any teahouse and you'll see groups of people with no work sitting about all troubled and worried. The oil refinery is closed, the economy has come to a halt, and the food shortage is making life harder for many.

Whenever you turn on the radio, you'll hear the shaky voice of the new prime minister asking for people's help. The government's delegation came and—as the people put it—threw the British into the sea. The British warships packed up and left, but still there is no sign of daily life getting any better. I'm considering getting a job at the textile factory. This way, not only would I be closer to the boys, I'd also be able to start attending night school in the fall. I share my plan with both Pendar and Shafaq. They make an effort to somehow get me in there, but for the time being, the textile industry is so sluggish that one of these days the factory will have to close down.

People are talking about the recent news.

"The British are sending a delegation to sign a new contract."

"You mean the delegation from the stockholders?"

"Yes . . . I think their offer is not all that bad. Fifty-fifty is a fair deal."

"How naïve you are, Brother."

"Do you see a problem with that?"

"You think we can deal with the cunning British? Have you forgotten that the taxes that company had to pay were higher than the revenue interest the usurping British government had to pay for our oil?"

But the prime minister has said he will not sign a contract with the British at all.

"Well, we will exploit the oil on our own, we will refine it on our own, and we will sell it on our own too."

"But with what vessel? With what sales agency?"

The refinery workers sit in the shade of the wall and wait for the *feydus* whistle, which marks the end of the day, so that they can pick up their empty pots of food and go home. Who knows? Most likely, sooner or later they'll be laid off in groups. I should write to Father to stay put in Kuwait and not lose his job. I should write to him about how shaky the job market is right now.

When I open my eyes, I see that it is sunset. I have slept more than five hours. The last bite of my lunch was still in my mouth as I felt my eyelids become heavy with sleep. The entire afternoon I dreamed of Black-Eyed. Just thinking about it now makes me feel elated. I should begin writing a letter to Father because I need to take off soon. I guess tonight's talk will be on the prime minister's recent speech. When he spoke you could feel the sadness in his voice. He mentioned the delegation from the stockholders that is supposed to come and negotiate with the government.

"Mother, I am writing to Father; do you have anything particular to say?"

Jamileh jumps on my lap. "Say that I miss him."

Mother says that the owner of the blacksmith's shop has asked for the late rent payments. "Write that he has said, 'If you don't make a decision soon, I'll have to go and install my own lock.'"

I write the letter, put on my pants, and take off.

The streetlights are on. At the corner of Hokumati Street I drop the letter into a mailbox and then walk toward the date sellers' market. As always, the bitter smell of cut willow branches wafts through the log sellers' alley. The Karun has risen again. The water looks murky.

Pendar and some other guys are waiting for me. I am a few minutes late. Pendar begins by reading the editorial in the paper. It's about Franco, Spain's dictator. *We must stand in solidarity with the freedom fighters in Spain. We ought to expose Spain's executioner even further, and we ought to use any opportunity to expose Franco's conspiracies for suppressing the people of Spain.*

The editorial ends. We get into a discussion about the Stakhanovites. More work by the "individual" for increase in "production." Pendar lists the great achievements of Alexey Stakhanov, the exemplary worker in the USSR. My mouth is agape. I'm surprised that tonight's discussion is not about the recent speech by the prime minister. I really wanted to know why the government refuses to accept the proposal from the stockholders' delegation. I wanted to learn more about the British attempts to con us, since it seems that this is the main issue these days. I share my thoughts with Pendar. He looks at me, pauses for a moment, then, in a gentle manner, briefly explains that this issue should be examined by the people on top. Maybe Pendar is right. After all, he knows much more than I do and understands better.

This room is on the top floor. The window opens to the Karun. I can hear the river roaring. It is very hot. The thumping sound of the doorknocker increases. Pendar stops talking. We look at each other. An old woman and a young one live downstairs. The husband of the young woman is with us in the meeting. The house is so minuscule that if they had a child, there wouldn't be enough room.

I get up and look down through the window. The knocking stops. Now it is the sound of hurried footsteps coming up the stairs. We head out of the room and see Peyman running toward us, utterly out of breath. "Come on . . . leave this place quickly . . . Quick!" And he himself turns around as fast as he has come up, rushes down the stairs, and runs out of the house.

After dividing the books and the newspapers among us, we too rush down the stairs, and head out of the house. The young woman and her husband shut the door behind us.

We can hear footsteps approaching from the log sellers' alley. We go to the end of the narrow sidewalk across from the wall. Before us stretches the long, murky Karun, all the way into the distance. The seething roar of the river is menacing. Low and high waves crash against the narrow pavement of the embankment. There's no other alternative. We jump into the water and wade toward the large cliff ahead of us. Water comes up to our knees. The sand slips out from under our feet. When a wave sweeps past us, the water comes up to our thighs. We reach the cliff and crouch behind it.

Five soldiers come out of the log sellers' alley. Their faces are not clear in the dark. One of them has a tight grip on Peyman's wrist. We hold our breath. The roaring sound of the Karun reverberates in our ears. Peyman's yelling blends with the sound of the river. "What do you want from me?"

The soldiers bang the doorknocker. The door opens. Four of the soldiers run into the house, dragging Peyman behind them. One of them stands at the door. There is another cliff behind us. One by one, we walk toward it. It is very dark. In the shelter of the second cliff, we wade toward the steep, sandy bank, and crouch as we climb up it. The sand slips from under our feet, and we slide down a few times before we reach the top. From where we are, we can barely make out the silhouette of the soldier standing at the door. We climb further up, and using the houses along the banks as shelter, get ourselves to the date sellers' street. As we stand in the dark, we observe the entrance of the log sellers' alley. Here and there the streetlights in the date sellers' street are out. A military car is parked at the head of the log sellers' alley. The soldiers come out of the log sellers' alley, Peyman with them. They linger for a few moments, let go of Peyman, and get into the car. The car turns around and heads north.

Naser Davani borrowed some money and built a four-wall on his land. He packed up his stuff and moved into his new house. They say he has bought a cow too, so that his wife can milk it and make yogurt and help him pay off the bank loan. I guess he would be willing to go to Kuwait again if making a living were harder than this.

Karam Ali has rented Naser Davani's room and is planning to whitewash it. Next Friday is his wedding ceremony. The preparations have already started. Sanam is running around nonstop. Karam Ali has bought a suit from a rummage sale. The jacket is a light brown and a bit darker than the pants, which are a sugar-and-milk color.

Afaq has had a yard of green satin tailored for Banu. In the evening, they will have the marriage ceremony, and at night the reception.

Some of the relatives have been invited for both lunch and dinner. There will also be *sorna* players. Rezvan has promised to thread Banu's face and do her makeup. Everything has been planned.

By the time I wake up, sunlight has already spread across the courtyard. I shave and put on my pants to head out of the house. The smell of Khaj Tofiq's opium wafts through the courtyard. If you let him, he'll sit by the brazier till noon. He used to go to the bazaar from time to time and make a couple of deals on rice, dates, or tea, and earned a meager sum of money, but now all he does is sit by the brazier all day long, smoking the day away and not paying any mind to Afaq's complaints.

Rahim the Donkey Keeper has gone to the brickkiln. Rezvan left the house early this morning, and who knows when she'll come back? Afaq has not been home since yesterday. I don't see Amu Bandar's cart in front of the pigeon coop, either. Mother is in our room. Bolur Khanom calls to me softly. I turn from the entryway of the house and go into her room. She closes the door and gets in my face.

"What do you want?" I ask.

"You have turned into such a bad boy, Khaled," she says, her voice trembling.

"Bad?"

"You have completely forgotten me."

I turn to walk out of her room.

She grabs my wrist with both her hands. "Wait a minute . . . I want to talk to you . . ."

I turn back around. "Let go, Bolur Khanom! The neighbors will say things about us."

"Nobody saw you come in."

"But they'll see me when I leave."

"We'll worry about that later."

She holds my wrist tightly. Her eyes are full of lust. Her voice trembles. She unbuttons her shirt. She is not wearing a bra. At her age, her breasts are still firm and perky, like those of a young girl.

My throat gets dry. "What are you doing?"

"Aman Aqa will go to Susa this evening."

"So?"

"So you have to come tonight."

I look down. "Bolur Khanom, I have made a vow not to touch you anymore."

She presses her body against my chest. Before I know it, she has put her arms around my waist, and I can feel her soft belly on mine.

"You have to come tonight, you have . . . you have to . . . ," she says, kissing my neck nonstop as she talks. "If you don't come, I'll kill myself . . . You have to come."

I struggle to free myself from her embrace. "Bolur Khanom . . . that's not good . . . If the neighbors . . ."

She won't let me finish. Filled with lust, she urges her lips on mine. I can feel her knees tremble. She presses her belly against mine, moving ever so gently, and kisses my neck, cheeks, and lips. Bit by bit, I feel aroused. I put my arms around her waist and bury my face in her bosoms. I bite her nipples gently. Bolur Khanom moans. She is begging. The words get stuck in her throat. Out of breath, we fall to our knees and lie down. With the tip of my finger, I pull up her dress. She has no panties on. My hand glides across her naked buttocks. They feel hot and smooth under my touch. I circle my arms around her hips and thighs and pull her hard against me.

Bolur Khanom has turned red and is entirely soaked in sweat. Her breath is hot. Her hand goes toward my belt, undoing it slowly, then unbuttons my pants buttons one by one. The wind shakes one of the doors, making the crack open wider. I can see the courtyard. I pull myself together. My voice trembles. "Bolur Khanom, the door is open."

She does not let go of me, and pulls down my pants.

"Bolur Khanom, the neighbors will find out."

She moves, gets up reluctantly, goes to the double doors, closes them, and bolts them. Now I am up on my feet. She comes and stands in front of me.

"No, Bolur Khanom . . . we can't do it now."

She looks perplexed and gives me a frustrated look. I buckle my belt. Her knees go limp. She sits down and cries quietly.

"Why are you crying?"

She does not talk, only sobs. I peep through the slit between the doors and look around the courtyard. Shouldering a gunnysack full of dried cow dung, Sanam comes down the roof stairs.

Sitting beside the pool, Mohammad the Mechanic's wife washes dishes, her skirt rolled up a bit, showing her slip. Her thighs are chubby. They are white, like moonlight. I step aside from the door slit. Bolur Khanom is no longer crying. Buttoning her shirt, she gets up, smooths the creases of her skirt, and in a muffled voice, says, "Get out of here."

I look at her.

"Get out of here," she says again.

"All right, Bolur Khanom."

"Now."

"Just wait a minute. Mohammad the Mechanic's wife is at the pool."

"Once you leave this room, don't ever look at me again!"

I lay my hands on her shoulders. She pulls away, disappointed.

"But we couldn't do it now."

She faces me. "We couldn't? If you wanted it, it would have been over by now."

"What if someone saw us?"

"Nobody came."

I walk up to her again and, in a gentle voice, say, "You said Aman Aqa—"

"I thought you made a vow!" she cuts me short and moves away.

I get angry. "Yes, I did . . . I still say that I made a vow . . ." And I walk toward the door. I peep through the slit between the doors. Sanam has gone into her room. Mohammad the Mechanic's wife is still rinsing the dishes. Water has splashed on her slip. I look down and see Bolur Khanom's arms around my waist, hugging me from behind. "You made a vow to do what?"

Extremely irritated, I say, "I made a vow not to touch you ever again."

There is desire in her voice. "Come tonight! Would you? Tell me you'll come. I'll wait for you."

Her voice trembles. I hear the sound of dishes being stacked. I peep through the slit. Carrying the clean dishes in her hands, Mohammad the Mechanic's wife walks up to her room. I take Bolur Khanom's hands off my waist.

"Will you come?"

I don't answer her. Unbolting the door, I gently move to the side and hurry out of her room. I tiptoe toward the outhouse and go in. I am breathless. I feel that my face has turned pale. My heart is racing. I smooth the creases on my shirt, tighten my belt, and head out of the outhouse. Banu stares at me as she stands in front of her room. Mother comes out of our room. When she notices me, she frowns. "Khaled, you haven't gone out yet?"

"No, Mother." I swallow my saliva.

Without saying another word, Mother goes to the kitchen.

I leave the house, head out for Hokumati Street, and walk north. Soon, I find myself in the vicinity of Black-Eyed's house. Now I know what high school she goes to, and I know when she gets out and what street she takes.

I have become friends with the grocer. I know what interests him and how to butter him up. We chat sometimes. We talk about the current political situation and about the British.

"Mash Baqer, what's new?"

He tells me what news he has heard on the radio.

It is still a few hours before Black-Eyed will come back from school. I walk in the direction of Bagh-e Melli Park. I stroll around a bit, then sit down on a bench. It feels cool in the shade of the palm trees. My legs crossed, I sit thinking about what happened this morning. What if someone had seen us? What a disgrace it would have been! What would Aman Aqa have done? How could I ever look into his eyes again? Aman Aqa has every right to beat her like he does. If she were my wife, I would have skinned her.

"Are you waiting for the *girl*?"

It is Ali the Devil. He leans his bike against the trunk of a palm tree and comes and sits next to me. I pull myself together.

"Just between the two of us, I have to say, not bad at all. Good tastes."

Blood rushes to my face. Without thinking twice, and in an almost muffled voice, I say, "What do you want from me?"

I will slap him across the face, come what may. I remember suddenly that I have more than a hundred books at home. I grind my teeth and bite into my lower lip.

"Nothing," Ali the Devil says. "I don't want anything from you."

His jacket is bulging.

"Then why do you keep bothering me like this?" I say quietly.

He bursts out laughing. His laughter drives me mad. I wish I could wring his neck until he turns black from pain.

He moves closer to me. "I don't think I'm bothering you."

"You don't? But that's what it looks like."

"To be honest with you, I like you."

I narrow my eyes. "You like me?"

Ali the Devil seems calm and patient. Very calm. His smile doesn't leave his lips. He cuts me short. "You are a very intriguing person," he says, and then goes on, "Look, Khaled, I'd like us to be friends. I'm not as bad as you think. I can be a lot of help to you. See, I'm in a position where I could easily move your newspapers around, and even give you news firsthand . . ."

My eyes are about to pop out. Just like a piece of brick soaked in water, I melt. I am shocked. Trying to pull myself together, I say, "I don't know what you're talking about?"

He laughs. "Don't play dumb with me!"

I should stay calm. "Playing dumb? What do you mean?"

"You know very well what I mean . . . and I know that you know that. It's just that you don't trust me yet."

I look at Ali the Devil's watch. Black-Eyed will be returning from school in a few minutes.

"Are you leaving?"

"I don't know what you want from me."

The smile leaves his lips. In a stern and dry voice, he says, "If you help me, I'll help you get the girl."

That makes me laugh. I try to control myself, thinking what a pathetic thing he has come up with. So, I tell him, "When I find out what you want from me, I might be able to help you." I take off. Ali the Devil's voice comes from behind me. "But, Khaled, I know that we'll come to terms with each other." I head out of the park. Ali the Devil passes me on his bike. "Walk a bit faster to catch her on time. The schools are closed now!"

He knows it all. He must have stopped doing everything else in his life, focusing all his attention on spying on me. I should be more careful. He is not called "the Devil" for no reason. No matter where you are, the devil appears out of nowhere, as if you have burned his hair.

I greet the grocer and pull a stool up next to the wall to sit on.

Black-Eyed shows up. I get up and greet her. "How are you?"

She buys a hundred-page notebook. I know that it's just an excuse.

"I'm fine. How about yourself?" she asks.

I can't find anything else to say. We smile at each other and look down. Finally, I say, "I hope you were not offended by what that guy said that day. Were you?"

She smiles again, making my heart tremble.

"No . . . why should I be offended?"

"Thanks."

Her lips move but words do not come out.

"Did you want to say something?"

"You know," she says, weighing what she wants to say, as if hesitant to say it, "from what that man said that day, I understand why you didn't want to give us your home address."

I blush down to my neck.

Noticing my embarrassment, she adds quickly, "But, what's wrong with that?"

My throat feels dry. It is not easy to look into her eyes. They mesmerize me. I take a deep breath and exhale noisily. "Yes . . . I guess nothing is wrong with that."

She smiles and says good-bye.

The outdoor stoves are set up alongside the donkeys' sun shelter. Firewood is piled up in front of the stoves. Sanam is busy soaking rice. The house is alive with people coming and going. Banu is sitting quietly in her room. The hired barber is in the courtyard shaving Khaj Tofiq, while Amu Bandar and Rahim the Donkey Keeper wait their turn. Karam Ali's beard is to be shaved off at the men's public baths.

The sun is high in the belly of the sky. It is hot. At dawn, Hasani took the donkeys to the brickkilns so that he could come home early in the afternoon. With one foot in Khaj Tofiq's room and another in her own room, Rezvan is preparing makeup for the bride. And Afaq cannot help but run around nonstop. The cook arrives and comes in and looks around to make sure that everything is prepared. As he checks on the stoves, the burning logs, the pots, he wipes the sweat off his forehead with the rag tossed over his shoulder. The *sorna* players come through the door. Mash Rahim, Amu Bandar, and Khaj Tofiq take their places along the wall in the shade. To make more room, Khaj Tofiq's tray of opium and smoking paraphernalia has been moved to Rahim the Donkey Keeper's room. A group of neighborhood kids pours into the courtyard behind the *sorna* players. Rahim the Donkey Keeper stuffs his pipe, the one with a long handle, and takes a deep drag. He lets the dense smoke out of his mouth in such a way that you'd think someone had poured ashes in a damp well and now the ashes have bounced back up. The beige color of the pipe's handle becomes darker in the smoke and disappears for a second. Rezvan heads out of Khaj Tofiq's room. Her chador has slipped from over her head down to her shoulders. Rezvan's hair is jet black. It shines under the sun's rays. Rahim the Donkey Keeper grumbles under his breath, "The woman does not even consider that there are strange men around here."

Bolur Khanom is beside Banu. A girlish coyness has tinged Banu's pale face. This afternoon, she'll be having her marriage ceremony, and later tonight her wedding reception. Afaq offers a round of tea to the men. Rezvan disappears into her room and comes back with a box of *sormeh* eyeliners in her hands. The cook follows her with his eyes all the way to Khaj Tofiq's room. The *sorna* players take their places in the shade of the wall, and the kids squat down on their heels in front of them.

The cook is a man of medium height, in his thirties. Wiping the sweat off his forehead with a rag, he carefully puts the firewood under the large pots, creating a makeshift kiln. Karam Ali comes in through the door. He has a big load of herbs on his shoulder. Sanam walks up to him and takes the stack of herbs from him. Once again, Rezvan comes out of her room. Standing up straight, the cook follows her again with his eyes, making Rahim the Donkey Keeper grumble, "This woman, in time, brings trouble upon myself and herself too." He empties his pipe.

Mash Rahim's pipe bowl is made of wood; it is dark beige, and as big as a three-lined Naseroddin Shah opium pipe bowl.

This time, Rezvan goes into Bolur Khanom's room, calling out to her. Bolur Khanom comes out of Khaj Tofiq's room. She has reddened her lips and rouged her cheeks. Quickly, she goes to her room and then comes out along with Rezvan. Shifting from one foot to the other, and in a low voice, the cook calls out to Rezvan. "Pardon, can I ask you for a favor?"

Rezvan stops, her face lighting up. There are beads of sweat on her broad forehead. Her cheeks shimmer.

Continuing, the cook says, "Pardon me, does anyone have a pair of charcoal tongs I could use?" He smiles at Rezvan as he says this. The cook has two gold teeth, which have turned a dark yellow.

"Whatever you need," answers Rezvan, smiling, "you should get from the groom's mother," and she indicates Sanam with a motion of her head.

Rahim the Donkey Keeper is beside himself with rage. "The woman has no shame whatsoever."

He is about to get up when Khaj Tofiq grabs his wrist. "Sit down, Mash Rahim. Today is no good for this sort of talk."

Mash Rahim is upset. "She doesn't even give a damn that there are strange men in here. Running around with uncovered hair is bad enough, and now she's laughing with that bastard too. I should at least tell her to cover herself with her chador."

Khaj Tofiq sits Mash Rahim down and calls out to Afaq to bring another round of tea. Rezvan, wearing no chador, sticks her bare head out of the room and calls Sanam. Her dress shapes all her curves. While Sanam heads toward her, Rezvan checks out the cook. Rahim the Donkey Keeper loses it at once and gets to his feet. "God damn the devil!"

He goes into his room and calls Rezvan. The cook squats down and begins a fire under one of the pots. Rezvan heads out of Khaj Tofiq's room. The low flames under the pot are mixed with smoke. Rezvan says under her breath, "God help me! The old man is calling me again."

Hearing that, the cook turns his head in her direction, and he smiles at her. Rezvan goes into her room. The flames under the pot are still mixed with smoke.

Mash Rahim's faint voice can be heard: "Woman! Cover yourself with that damn chador of yours. There are strangers in this house."

Rezvan's voice is not audible. Again, it is the trembling voice of Rahim the Donkey Keeper that is heard. "Woman, let me be today— don't make me yell at you. Pull yourself together a bit. Aren't you ashamed of yourself, laughing with that bastard?"

The cook turns a deaf ear. He adjusts the firewood under the pot. The flame blazes.

Khaj Tofiq gets up, goes into Mash Rahim's room, grabs his hand, and drags him out. Behind them comes Rezvan, covering her head with her chador. Rahim the Donkey Keeper sits down and stuffs a fresh pipe. The pipe's handle is hexagonal. Its bowl is oval. Just like a large goose egg that has been colored. Mash Rahim takes a deep drag and looks at the cook out of the corner of his eye. Afaq brings another round of tea. Karam Ali leaves the house. Mother goes into Khaj Tofiq's room, taking Jamileh with her.

Sitting on a stool, I lean against the wall of our room and cross my legs. Afaq offers me tea. "When will be the day that I come and help out at your wedding?"

"Thanks very much, Afaq Khanom."

Aunt Ra'na's son comes in through the house doors, followed by Aunt Ra'na herself and her daughter. They have been invited. The men are supposed to eat their lunch in Bolur Khanom's room and the women in Father's room. Khaj Tofiq turns to the tall man holding the *sorna* in his hands and says, "Play it up, good man!"

The tall man tightens the loincloth around his waist, stuffs his ears with cotton, and blows at the *sorna*. The kettledrum player gets up and slings the strap of the drum around his neck. The sound of the drum blasts in the air. The sun has spread its rays all over the courtyard. Before you know it, kids from the neighboring alleys gather around the *sorna* player. Rezvan comes out of her room. Her chador is down on her shoulders again. The flames under the pot are ablaze. Steam spews out of the large pot. The cook pours rice into the pot, making the boiling water froth. The courtyard is swarmed with people. The sound of the *sorna* and the kettledrum has filled the entire neighborhood. Rahim the Donkey Keeper gets up, goes to Rezvan, grabs her arm, and drags her away from the gathering. "I told you a hundred times to cover your head with that damn chador."

"Why on earth should I!" grumbles Rezvan.

"At my age, who's going to even look at me? And the same with you. What is the most that can happen? Why are you so worried about it?"

Mash Rahim's voice trembles. "Woman, be ashamed before God!"

Amu Bandar gets hold of Rahim the Donkey Keeper's arm. "Mashti, let's get out of here and take a walk."

Rezvan pleads, "Yeah, Amu Bandar, for the love of God, take him out so that I can breathe for a moment today."

Rahim the Donkey Keeper's veins bulge on his neck. The cook props the skimmer against the wall, circles around the crowd, and comes and stands next to Khaj Tofiq, watching both Rezvan and Rahim the Donkey Keeper out of the corner of his eye. At the same moment, Sanam jumps into the middle of the crowd and starts to dance. A lock of gray hair pokes out from under her scarf. Sanam's forehead and cheeks are covered with beads of sweat. The kids clap. The water is boiling in the pot, making bubbles rise up from the bottom and come to the surface and pop. Rahim the Donkey Keeper is talking, but I cannot hear him. The sound of the *sorna* and the drum travels seven alleys away. The veins on Mash Rahim's neck have turned dark blue. Shaking her arms rapidly in the air, Rezvan says something. Rahim the Donkey Keeper grabs Rezvan's arm and drags her toward their room. The chador falls from Rezvan's head. The sound of the drum is fierce. The pot is boiling.

Bubbles pop on the surface. Rezvan drags her chador behind her. Voices are jumbled up. Mash Rahim yells. The *sorna* is going full blast. Rezvan curses. Khaj Tofiq walks up to Mash Rahim. Sanam keeps dancing. The kids clap faster. The flames have swallowed the pot entirely. With both her hands, Rezvan slaps Rahim the Donkey Keeper on the chest. Large boiling bubbles gather up on the surface and explode at the edge of the pot. Mash Rahim's face has turned red down to his neck. His earlobes are white. Khaj Tofiq reaches for his arm. Sanam can't stop dancing. The heavy blows of the drum irritate the ears. Rahim the Donkey Keeper's hand slides down to his sash, Rezvan still slapping his bony chest. Flames are rising all around the pot. Mash Rahim pulls out the pipe from under his sash. Rezvan beats her own face and chest, her hair disheveled. Sanam's entire body is soaked in sweat, her cheeks red. She dances fast, to the rhythm of the drum. Rahim the Donkey Keeper shakes the pipe. Rezvan claws her own face. The boiling water rises up and spills over. Raising one arm, Mash Rahim hits Rezvan in the head with the bowl of the pipe. She falls down to the ground. The boiling water spills over, putting out the flames.

Rezvan looks as if she has been dead for years.

The drum still pounds, the *sorna* roars, and Sanam still dances, and Aunt Ra'na's son leaps up and grabs Mash Rahim's wrist.

I go to visit Rahim the Donkey Keeper. The visitors' room is jam-packed with visitors lining up in front of the bars; it's so crowded, as if this were a livestock market. The voices are muddled up. I have brought him cigarettes, because he no longer smokes a pipe. Tears well up in his eyes as he talks. "Do you see, Khaled?"

I try to comfort him.

"See what's happened to me, now, in my old age?"

His beard has grown long. His mustache is tinted yellow from the cigarette smoke. His head is shaved and his eyes are sunken. He has striped prison clothes on. "How are Hasani and Ebram doing? Do you know?" he asks.

"They're with their uncle," I say, hoping to offer him a little peace of mind.

Karam Ali's wedding has been postponed. "Sister, it's not like they sell bad fortune in the bazaar," says Sanam glumly, "an unfortunate person will be bitten by a shark, even if that person were to ride on the back of a camel."

Ebrahim came and rummaged through Rahim the Donkey Keeper's odds and ends. He took the donkeys to the livestock market and sold them. Then, he emptied the room and took Hasani with him. Hasani cried so much that it left him with no strength to talk.

It's gotten really hot. Not even a weed moves. It is humid. I finish my breakfast and get up. "Mother, I won't come home tonight."

My mother looks surprised. Her lips are pressed against each other. She looks at me inquisitively and asks, "Did you say you won't come home tonight?"

"Yes, Mother . . . I won't," I say quietly.

Coming toward me, she asks, "Where do you want to go?"

Buckling my belt, I reply, "To the port."

Mother keeps quiet, but her gaze is still on me, her lips pressed hard against each other, the lines around her mouth more defined. Her hair is almost entirely gray. As if talking to herself, she says softly, "I am worried, Khaled."

"Worried? Why, Mother? What for?" I say, surprised.

She lets out a deep sigh. "I am worried about what you're doing," she says, pointing to the shelf on the wall. "These books, your new friends. I'm fearful, Khaled."

I smile. Looking into her eyes, I say, "Why fearful, Mother? What am I doing that makes you frightened?"

Another sigh breaks in her throat. "My intuition tells me that something is wrong."

I hug her and kiss her cheeks. "Don't let these thoughts get the best of you."

"You don't know life yet, Khaled," she says in a low voice, "you're still too young . . ."

"I know, Mother, I know. God willing, I'll go to school this coming fall. 'Cause if you don't have an education, you have no place anywhere." I kiss her cheeks again. "I can't believe how many times I asked Father to let me go to school." I let her free from my arms. "Maybe I'll come home then."

"May God be with you!" she says under her breath.

I kiss Jamileh. Mother's lips move. I think she's praying. I smile at her and head out of our room.

Hokumati Street is deserted. I cannot get the image of my mother's gray hair out of my head, nor the image of my father's sunken eyes. His voice rings in my ears: "A real man is one that, when you pat him on the back, dust rises in the air."

He'll be back in less than two months. I imagine he's much skinnier now. He must look older too. "You think that you are the servant of the Arabs and the Arabs are the servants of the British . . ." Father's lips tremble with dignity. "You can make money here but with much humiliation . . ."

Naser Davani has built another room within the four walls of his house and has rented it. "You should be smart . . . smart. I told the Farangi boss, 'I good mason.' He laughed, patted me on my shoulder, and raised my wages . . . One should be smart."

Pahlavi Street is deserted. Here and there a few pedestrians walk by, their shirts soaked with sweat and stuck to their backs.

There are no customers in Mojahed Bookstore. Peyman sits there and reads the newspaper. Shafaq comes out from the back of the store. "You're here," he says, smiling.

"Yeah."

We shake hands. My hand disappears in his large palm, giving me a sense of security.

"The suitcase is in the back of the store."

Together, we walk to the back where the books are stored. Beads of sweats have formed on my neck and forehead.

"Remember! If you get caught," he says, "you deny the whole thing."

I weigh the suitcase in my hand. It's amazingly heavy. I put it down.

"Newspapers, leaflets, brochures, and a few books."

I pick up the suitcase and get going. "Good-bye."

"Good luck!"

I head out of the store. I rehearse the contact information in my mind. "When do the fishermen go fishing for shrimp?"

"If the sea is calm, tonight."

"The sea seems to be calm."

"You can never be sure about that."

I should head to the fishermen's market, in the south part of the bazaar. I go over my contact's description once again: He is of medium height; he has a swarthy complexion and curly hair. He will be wearing an azure t-shirt and a pair of dark green pants. He has wrapped a piece of yellow fabric around his thumb.

The humidity is high. I feel nervous. There are fewer and fewer people on the street. My heart races in my chest. I should keep calm; otherwise, I will lose it and, for sure, I'll get caught. I try to take my mind off the suitcase. I try hard to push away all thought of my contact. I try to think of Black-Eyed instead, but it's not possible. The suitcase's heaviness draws all my thoughts to it.

I walk along the curb as I head toward the bus terminal. It is not much of a hike. My throat feels dry. I drink a bit of iced water while standing in front of the garage. I buy myself a ticket, put the suitcase in the trunk of the sedan, and sit down on a bench in the terminal office. I wait for the driver to find more passengers for the shared trip before I get in the car.

It's crowded in front of the bus terminal. The shouts of the ice cream man, the juice seller, the fava bean seller, the iced water seller, and the terminal attendant are all mixed up. "Place for two more people to the port . . . Come on! We're leaving."

"The new spring ice cream, cardamom and rose water ice cream!"

"Iced water! Come and refresh your soul!"

"Eat beans and wrestle! Eat some more, if you fall down!"

A driver and his helper are using a rope to try and tie baggage to their beat-up bus. The terminal attendant, sweating nonstop, counts the fares and shakes his head. He calls out again, "To the port, run, come faster!"

Sitting leisurely on the ground, a few Arab women make tea in front of the terminal. Their heavy nose rings seem to pull down their noses. From the look of things, they will probably end up eating their lunches here too, and the bus will still be here, making them wait.

Sunlight has now spread as far as the paved sidewalk. The last passenger arrives. All of us get into the sedan. The car sets off. I say a prayer of Ayatolkorsi. I pray under my breath, trying not to draw anyone's attention to myself, and blow at myself and the car as protection from harm; my face turns utterly pale. My throat feels as dry as matches.

We drive the length of Pahlavi Street and pass through the square. It's not far to the inspection point at the intersection near the port. All I need to do is to pass this inspection, and the rest of the way will be safe. The most the port inspector will do is take a quick look inside the car, and then he'll lift up the wooden pole blocking the road.

The car comes to a halt.

A tall gendarme, a broad-shouldered army officer, a scrawny guard, and a short, fat, red-faced man in plain clothes are standing there.

"Open the trunk!"

The driver steps out of the car. His skin is dark, his face bony, and his hair peppered with gray. I guess him to be around fifty or so. He opens up the trunk. My heart leaps. Even the prayer of Ayatolkorsi does not have any effect at calming me down. If I could only leave the suitcase and run away.

"Everyone, please get out!"

We do as we are told. Before me stretch five long oil pipelines coming from Naftun and going all the way up to the port. Behind the pipelines lies a vast marshland extending out toward downtown and to the lower parts of the city. It is on the other side of the marshland that people have built their houses.

The stout man looks at me.

I turn pale. I think to myself that I should jump over the pipelines, run toward the marsh, and before they could make a move, I'd be gone out of the marsh and would have disappeared in the city's crowd.

"Which one is your suitcase?" asks the stout man.

I swallow my saliva and barely manage to say, "I don't have a suitcase."

People have gathered around us. I catch sight of Bidar standing in front of the teahouse next to the inspection station. A bit further down is Aman Aqa's teahouse, right at the intersection.

"Why are you so pale?" the stout man asks this time.

"Pale?" I say. My voice sounds raspy. My gaze is directed at Aman Aqa's teahouse. I wish I were there now, sitting and listening to Jan Mohammad. I hear Spider's voice: *Suddenly, you open your eyes and see that it's already too late.*

I hear the guard's voice: "Whose suitcase is this one?"

I hear Spider: *You got yourself into trouble.*

The driver looks at the suitcase. Nobody answers.

The guard raises his voice. "I said, whose suitcase is this?"

The driver comes toward me. "Wasn't it yours?"

I take a step forward, look at the suitcase, and shake my head. "No. I didn't have a suitcase at all."

The driver's eyes open up wide. He raises his voice. "You didn't? I myself took it from you and loaded it in the trunk." He turns to the guard, saying, "Can you believe it, *sir*?" and, turning to the gendarme this time, says, "The suitcase is his very own. He is just denying it."

I look at Bidar, feeling more confident now. I have taken the first step. I have denied everything, and now I have to stand by it. I tell the driver, "Cut the nonsense, good man! I never had a suitcase."

The army officer pulls the suitcase out of the trunk and puts it down on the ground. Looking at me, he says, "It belongs to you, right?"

"No," I retort with all my might.

Stepping closer, the stout man in plain clothes looks straight into my eyes. "There's no use in denying it, boy. From the first moment it was clear that you were up to something."

"Don't accuse me on any grounds that—"

The driver cuts me short, shouting, "If it's not yours, are you suggesting that it is my aunt's?"

Keeping cool, I shrug. "I don't know. You know better than me."

Bending down, the guard slashes the outside of the suitcase with a knife. Bundles of newspapers and leaflets come into view.

The gendarme whistles. The officer shakes his head. The stout man in plain clothes says, "I see now why you're denying it."

The guard grabs my wrist and shoves me into the inspection room. The stout man brings in the suitcase and sets it on a desk.

I start yelling. They don't pay me any mind. The guard sits behind the desk and places a piece of carbon paper between three sheets of white paper and starts to write the report. After writing a few lines, he lifts his eyes from the paper and asks, "What's your name?"

No one answers.

"I am talking to you."

"My name?"

The guard glares at me. "No, I mean your aunt's."

"Nightingale," I say under my breath.

"Nightingale?" He gives me a funny look.

"It's my name."

I had given Nightingale at the terminal. The ticket is issued with the name Nightingale too. The guard turns to the driver. "Where's the list of the passengers' names?"

The driver hands him the list.

"Nightingale? Who would want to have such a name—*Nightingale?*" he asks incredulously, handing the list back to the driver before starting to write again. Once finished, he gives the pen to the driver. "Sign it!"

"I don't know how to write, sir."

"Put your thumbprint here, then!"

The driver puts his ink-smeared thumb where the guard indicates.

The guard signs the paper, followed by the army officer and the stout, red-faced man.

Holding out the pen to me, the guard says, "Here, sign it!"

"What should I sign?"

"The report!"

I step back, sit down on the bench, and say calmly, "I am illiterate. I can't read."

He stares at me for a few moments, then, in a muffled but angry tone, says, "I'll read it to you." And he begins reading the report.

I look out through the window of the inspection room. The sun is beating down on the road. The oily road, dark and murky, runs patiently on to the horizon. The guard's voice echoes in my ears: "Enough already—sign it!"

"I said I can't read."

Clenching his teeth, he says, "Then put your thumbprint here!"

"I'm not so out of my head to do such a thing."

The guard's voice grows deeper. "I said, sign it, or you'll be in big trouble."

Again, I remind him that I am illiterate.

He grumbles, "All right, all right . . . then put your thumbprint."

I shake my head. "The suitcase is not mine."

The guard rises from behind the desk. He drives away the other passengers gathered in front of the door of the inspection room. Then he makes a note on the bottom of the page that I have refused to sign it and that everyone else has signed it. The driver too puts his thumbprint on it, and then gets behind the wheel. The car shakes into motion.

It is almost noon when I'm taken to the police station by another guard. It is somewhat crowded. The guard leaves the suitcase on the veranda. The veranda is cool. My entire body is soaked in sweat. I feel less scared now. As if I couldn't care less about what's going to happen next. I keep my gaze fixed on the trellis of the corridor on the second floor. A man, holding some files under his arm, heads out of a room. I look closely. It's Gholam Ali Khan. He has grown rather fat. His temples have also gone gray. Gholam Ali Khan stops and looks inside the courtyard. I hide myself behind a short man. The man grumbles, "Now where can I find a guarantor for my brother?"

Gholam Ali Khan goes to the end of the hallway. My file under his arm, the guard stands across from me. The report is in the file. The guard looks at me, hesitant whether or not to go into the room. Forcing a smile, he says, "But between us, you were clever not to sign the report."

Why is he saying this? I wonder. In a matter-of-fact tone, I answer, "But now that I'm in the police station, I'll confess to everything," and sit down on the suitcase.

The guard shoots me a look. As if he believes that I'll come clean. I glance down and give him a matter-of-fact look. Gholam Ali Khan shows up again. If he sees me, I am done for. The short man is still grumbling. The guard asks me not to move from my place.

I tell him, "I wish I had the strength to move at all."

The guard goes into the room. The short man walks up to the end of the hallway. I don't waste any time. I decide to throw caution to the wind. The door is barely closed behind the officer when I leap up. I weave through a few people standing on the veranda. The sun's rays have filled the entire courtyard. I pass by the courtyard pool and reach the hallway of the station. I grumble to myself as I walk, "Now where can I find a guarantor for my brother?"

The guard standing at the gate is sapped of energy in this heat. I grumble as I pass him by. In a fatigued tone he asks, "Where are you going, boy?"

Confident, I say, "I am going to find a guarantor for my brother. Didn't you hear what that officer said?"

I head out of the door of the police station. Quickly, I turn behind a row of short, thick mimosa trees. I reach the street. A beat-up truck is passing by. I run and climb up onto the back of it and roll in, and then sit up. My heart races in my chest. I feel it beating in my temples. Sweat is pouring down the four pillars of my body. The truck passes through a few streets, and drives along the railway mound toward Salt Mine Road. I should get off. I pull myself up onto the railing in the back of the truck; I jump over the railing and hang down from it. I put the tips of my toes down on the ground, run along with the truck a little, and then let go. The sun is extremely hot. I hurry to reach the shade of a wall. It is a long way home. I walk through the back alleys.

When I reach home, my mother, shocked, looks at me at first, then hugs me and kisses my face nonstop. I feel a tight lump in my throat. If I don't stop myself, I'll burst into tears. "What's wrong, Mother? Why are you crying?"

She holds me at arm's length to have a good look at me; she says in a trembling voice, "They came and took the books."

"They took the books?"

She nods. "They said you had been arrested," she says, squeezing my shoulders with her hands.

"That's true, Mother . . . but I escaped from the police station . . ."

She lets go of me. Staring at me, she says, "You escaped?"

I sit on the stool, resting my chin in the palms of my hands. Mother spreads the supper cloth for us to eat lunch. As if talking to herself, she says, "When they came and said that you had been arrested, my soul almost parted from my body. My knees were so shaky that I could not help but sit down on the ground . . . My legs just couldn't hold me up." She turns to me and says, "These sorts of things won't turn out good, Son. Take pity on your youth! Take pity on me and your father . . ."

She comes and stands before me. "You are young, dear . . . You should think of your future, your life . . ."

What I am thinking of now is how to inform Shafaq.

Jamileh sits at the supper cloth.

"Jamileh, can you go up to Pahlavi Street?"

She gets up from the supper cloth. "Sure, Brother, I can go."

She has not turned ten yet. Mother asks why on earth Jamileh has to go to Pahlavi Street. "She can't go . . . It's the noon rest period; at this hour of day, the child shouldn't go out."

Distressed, I press my lips together.

"Is this an urgent matter that you want to send her out for?" Mother asks.

I look at her. She has one of those looks on her face that says, I still love you, Son, with all the troubles you have caused me.

"Yes, it's very urgent, Mother. Shafaq should know that I have escaped, so that he won't send anyone after me to the police station."

She walks over to the heap of bedding and picks up her chador from the top of. "Where's his shop?"

I give her the address. She throws her chador on her head. The sound of the noon prayer call rises from the minaret of the mosque in the Abdol'amid Bazaar as Mother leaves the house. Jamileh sits at the supper cloth. I find myself drowning in my thoughts again. All kinds of things cross my mind.

I am still sitting on the stool when I see Mother come in, followed by Shafaq, who's smiling. He cannot believe his eyes. "I know what happened to you up at the police station, but after that . . ."

"I'll tell you the rest, then," I say. I tell him how I escaped.

He bursts out laughing. "Bravo . . . nice job!"

I feel proud. We sit in Father's room, where we draw the curtain hanging between the two rooms and eat lunch together.

"You should keep a low profile for a few days."

"I know."

"You should be especially careful not to fall into Ali the Devil's trap."

I think to myself that I should not leave the house for a week or so, maybe even let my mustache and beard grow, and if I have to, go out only at night.

Shafaq leaves. And I feel all the sorrows of the world pouring into my heart. I already feel like going out. Already missing the streets, the backstreets, and the alleys. I imagine how hard it must be for someone who's forced to stay home all the time and never allowed to see anything beyond his house door. The other time I had to stay home was because I had sprained my ankle. I had an excuse not to go out then . . . but what about now? Now that I am healthy from head to toe? A sudden and strong urge to see Black-Eyed takes hold of my entire body. I try to somehow occupy my mind, but I don't have any books. I remember that they came and took all of them. I get up and take down one of

Father's books from the shelf. *Qesas al-Anbia*, the stories of the prophets. It does not interest me at all. On the cover, there are a few scribbles in Father's handwriting: the date of his wedding ceremony, the day I was born, Jamileh's birth date, even the day I was circumcised.

> *Look at that green turtledove!*
>
> *I look up. I feel a sudden, sharp burning, and then it is over.*
>
> *The next day I am on the banks of the Karun. I turn over the loincloth and sit on the hot sands. The removed skin and the ring of an onion hang on a silk string around my neck.[4] The pocket of my muslin shirt is full of sugar candies. Sitting on the bank, Mother batters the clothes with a washing club to get the filth out of them. Kingfishers and seagulls smack their chests against the surface of the water and rise up again. The kids make such a racket in the water, splashing each other's faces. Using their loincloths, they catch the small fish—each the size of a finger—in the shallow water and swallow them alive so that they can learn how to swim. They bet and go under the water and stay there as long as they can hold their breath. Some of them dare to swim out to the middle of the Karun.*
>
> *"A shark attacked Mami."*
>
> *"I know . . . It took his right leg away."*
>
> *As if nothing has happened. It is summer and this kind of news is heard over and over.*
>
> *"Sharks attacked Ali the Beggar."*
>
> *"They ate his bones too."*

I put down *Qesas al-Anbia*. How I want to go and sit on the stool in Mehdi the Grocer's store and just watch people pass by.

A poor, wretched boy, living in the slums of the lower parts of town . . .

What if Ali the Devil comes looking for me? My escape must've caused an uproar in the police station. That guard, they must have taken

---

4. In some rural areas and small towns in Iran, people may put the ring of an onion in the place of the circumcised skin of a small boy, who may be as young as an infant or as old as five, immediately after the procedure to ward off the evil eye. It is believed that the onion will help expedite the healing process. In some cases, the parents may decide to have the boy wear the dried onion around his neck.

him into custody by now, and I can imagine that my description has been given to every guard. And Ali the Devil knows me inside and out. No! I shouldn't leave the house until it's dark.

I lie down, trying to get some rest, but the stray thoughts attack my mind, and I find it impossible to sleep. All I want is to think about Black-Eyed, so that I'll be free of disturbing thoughts. I hear a splashing sound from the pool. Banu must've gotten naked again and gone into the pool.

Khaled, one more time . . .

No, Banu, not anymore!

Only this one time.

Talk about bad luck. Her wedding turned into a funeral. The mullah came and married her off quietly and went away. The wedding reception has been put off till the beginning of fall. With Banu's luck, you never know—maybe that day Aman Aqa will beat Bolur Khanom to death; and bam, everything will be over. But what about that Bolur Khanom? Man, what a tough cookie she is. If you ask me, I say that she herself is to blame. From the look of things, it's like she craves a good beating now and then. If I get arrested, I imagine that I will get a good beating myself. No doubt about that. But what a sight it must have been when the guard returned and found me gone! The saliva must've dried up in his mouth. If he gets his hands on me, he'll surely tear me to pieces.

I get up and look out at the courtyard through the window. There are more shadows filling the courtyard now. I already feel suffocated being cooped up inside. I should at least take the stool and go sit in the courtyard. If not airy, at least it is larger than our room. I look at the walls. I feel a sudden angst. How could one endure a prison cell, one made out of stone—and guarded on all sides on top of that—for months and years? If I hadn't escaped, I would have surely been thrown in jail. And what suffering Mother would have had to endure! And what pain! That miserable Rahim the Donkey Keeper!

"See, Khaled, what has become of me, now, in my old age?"

"What's wrong with your cheek, Mash Rahim?"

"My tooth, Son, my tooth."

Rahim the Donkey Keeper's cheek has swollen up so bad. It's like a rotten pomegranate. Hard and angry looking.

"Then do something about it, Mash Rahim."

His toothache is nothing in comparison to the pain Ebrahim causes him.

"Ebram, why don't you go to see your father?"

"See him for what?"

"At least take two packs of cigarettes to him . . . The old man will be happy."

Hasani pleads with Ebrahim. "Ebram, let's go and see Baba!"

Finally, Ebrahim gives in. "All right, don't beg like an old woman . . . We'll go on Friday."

It's warm in the courtyard, even in the shade. The neighbors have not yet come out of their rooms. As soon as the sunlight creeps up over the wall, they'll come and sweep the fronts of their rooms, take out their stuff, and spread out their rugs to sit on.

I fan myself with a straw fan, but I still feel warm. I get up, wet the fan in the small pool, and get back on the stool. The sun is bright. It moves over the pool, creeping closer and closer to the wall. Bolur Khanom heads out of her room. Holding a pitcher full of ice under the tap, she asks, "Why are you sitting there, Khaled?"

"I got bored in the room."

She walks up to me. "You didn't take a nap at noon?"

"No."

"Are you thirsty?"

I take the pitcher of ice water from her and drink so much that I feel my stomach bulge. She takes the pitcher from me. Sweat begins to drip from the four pillars of my body. Bolur Khanom's chador has slipped down off her head to her shoulders. "What was going on today?"

"I don't know what you're talking about," I say, playing dumb.

"I'm talking about those men who came and took the books."

"Well, they came and took the books. What's wrong with that?"

There's concern in her voice. "Khaled, you shouldn't mingle with these types."

"What types?"

"The same types who came and took the books."

I answer her gently. "Well, they were their books, so they came and took them. This is nothing to be worried about."

She narrows her eyes. "It's not something to be worried about?" she says incredulously. "And the way they rushed in, taking things away, scaring the hell out of your mother. All of us figured that something was going on."

Pretending hard to be indifferent, I say, "Don't you worry! Nothing is going on."

"I really hope not," she says, and smiles. As she walks away, she adds, "You're getting worse and worse every day!"

Bolur Khanom goes back into her room. It's an hour or so before it grows completely dark. I have never longed so much to get away. Here, in the house, I feel like I'm being pierced with thousands of needles. I wriggle, shift from side to side, and get up and go back into our room. And then I come back outside again. The neighbors have begun sweeping in front of their rooms.

God knows how I suffered until darkness fell over our house.

No longer able to stand it, I head out of the house. I take a deep breath. It feels as if I have not seen Habib the Baker's bakery in over a hundred years. I turn in to Hokumati Street. Suddenly, fear sweeps through me. Especially now that I have to be wary of Ali the Devil. Even my own shadow frightens me. I look over my shoulder constantly as I check out my surroundings. Before I know it, I find myself walking in the direction of Black-Eyed's house.

The grocery's overhead light is on. In the safety of the wall, I quickly creep into the blind alley. No lights are on. It is pitch dark. I walk up to the door of Black-Eyed's house. It is closed. There's light coming from the window, visible through the curtain. I crane my neck. It's a thick curtain, making it hard to see through. My hand reaches for the knocker. I feel my pulse beating in my temples. My entire body burns. I don't have the courage to knock on the door. My hand comes down. I turn to leave the alley. I have barely reached the head of the alley when I hear the sound of the door opening. I turn and see the shapeless silhouette of Bahram's body in the doorframe. He starts to run. I stand in his way. Once close, I greet him. He greets me back and slows down his pace. He looks at me. "Is that you?"

"How are you doing?"

"Fine."

"Where are you going?"

"I am going to buy a pack of chewing gum."

I walk alongside him. "Let's go together."

He buys the gum from the grocery. I stand back so that the grocer won't see me. Otherwise, I will have to put up with his chattiness for the rest of the night.

Did you listen to the prime minister's speech? he asks, and soon begins an analysis. He is such a chatterbox.

I part ways with Bahram. He rushes toward his house at the end of the alley. I stand in the dark for a short while; then I walk away. Not too far from the grocery, I stop and linger, leaning against the wooden light pole. I don't want to stand in the light, but I have a feeling that Black-Eyed will come. I think that I should stand in the light so that when she comes out, she will be able to see me. Impatient, I shift from one foot to the other. The thought of Ali the Devil storms my mind. I move out of the circle of light. I see the silhouette of a woman taking shape at the head of the alley. It must be Black-Eyed. I walk fast, getting closer to her. It is her. I slow down.

"Salaam."

"Salaam."

"Is that you?"

"Bahram told you?"

She doesn't say anything.

"Thanks for coming out."

She smiles. "I just came out, not for any particular reason."

I know she is lying. It's obvious that Bahram told her.

"I wanted to see you."

"What for?"

"I need to talk to you."

"Talk to me now."

"No, not now."

"Why not?"

"Because I have a lot to tell you."

She begins to walk back toward the alley. I limp along. My entire body is burning. I hear my heartbeat in my temples.

"What do you want to tell me?"

Hastily, I say, "I guess, I wanted to explain why I didn't give my home address that first day. I want to tell you why Ali the Devil doesn't leave me alone—"

"Ali the Devil?" she cuts me short.

"Yes, Ali the Devil . . . the man you saw in Bagh-e Melli Park the other day . . ."

She laughs. "What a strange name."

"That's what the boys call him."

At the entrance to the alley, she shifts from foot to foot. "Don't walk with me any further!"

"But I need to see you . . . I am a fugitive now. I can't come out of the house during the day . . . I should tell you a lot of things." My words are rushed, choppy, and confused.

"What are you escaping from?" she asks, surprised. Her tone is gentle. It calms me.

"That's what I want to tell you."

She keeps quiet.

"I want to say that . . ."

"Why do you want to tell me these things?" she says in a cool tone.

I feel like a deflated ball. I fall silent, losing my sense of eagerness and excitement. I must look pale too. Embarrassed, I say in a faint, raspy voice, "I am sorry to bother you." My throat is dry.

I begin to walk away.

"Please wait!"

I stop.

"You don't bother me."

I am filled with passion again. Finding my courage once more, yet still in a broken voice, I say, "So, can I see you?"

She is quiet for a moment, but then she says, "All right."

"When?"

"On Tuesday."

"What time?"

"At half past three in the afternoon."

"Where?"

"The oil company bus station."

My body is brimming with excitement. I want to fly. Without realizing it, I reach for her hand and bring it to my lips. My lips are on fire.

I part with her. "Good-bye," I say.

"Good-bye."

∼

It's still awhile until three thirty. I think I should go to the barbershop first and have my hair cut short. I will tell him to shave my beard too.

The weather is not that hot. It smells like autumn. After I see Black-Eyed, I'll go and have my shoes stretched. They're irritating my feet badly. After years of not having new shoes, I got myself a pair of new dress shoes, and, with my bad luck, they've turned out to be tight. I don't understand how; when I tried them on in the shoe store, they fit me perfectly, but now . . .

From the look of things, it seems like no one is searching for me after all. These past few days nothing unusual has happened either.

I get dressed. Mother wants to know where I'm going.

"I'll be back soon, Mother."

She looks worried. "Don't go out, dear!"

"I won't be long."

I head out. In my mind, I go over all the things I want to tell Black-Eyed. I should be more confident. This time, I must tell her that I love her.

I walk through backstreets and alleys to get to the barbershop. If it weren't for Black-Eyed, I wouldn't be wearing these damn shoes. Cotton shoes sure are something else. I can walk in them however I want.

The heels of my feet already sting. I'll be lucky if I don't get any blisters. Tuba the Liquor Seller's saloon is not that far from here. When I was leaving the house, I saw Karam Ali getting his cart ready to take the pot of cooked beans up to Tuba's saloon. The barbershop is one alley north of Tuba's. Mohammad the Barber, whenever he has no customers, comes down and gulps a shot of liquor, and quickly goes back to his shop. The wind today is not a summery wind at all. The weather has changed unexpectedly. Impotent cumulus clouds have gathered in the belly of the sky. The weather is still warm, but it smells like cool air is on its way. It smells of autumn.

The oil company bus station? Why at the station? Maybe she wants us to go to the oil company club, or maybe she'd rather we stand in the bus line so we'd appear to be passengers talking.

I head out of the alley. The barbershop is across from me. To get there, I have to cross a thirty-meter-wide street. So far I have managed to zigzag through the backstreets and alleys. I cross the street and sneak into the barbershop.

"Salaam, Khaled."

Mohammad the Barber always has a pocketful of brags and boasts to tell you. You're hardly in your seat when he begins chewing up your head with his chattering. He knows all the gossip about everyone in town. He eavesdrops on people until he finds out who they are, where they come from, what they are doing, and what they want to do.

"Do you see that guy?" he asks, honing the blade on the stone as he talks. "When he came into this town, he was wearing a pair of patched-up pants and holding an empty suitcase in his hand. Now look at him—he's rolling in it . . . That's God's will."

Then he smiles and asks, "It's God's will, isn't it? Isn't it?"

He laughs, showing his large yellow teeth.

I sneak into the shop.

"Salaam, Khaled."

"Salaam."

"Long time no see."

"At your service."

I take my seat when he begins his gossiping.

"I hear you're thinking of quitting the teahouse—is that right?"

I look at myself in the mirror. These last few days have made my cheeks look a bit flaccid. The skin under my eyes is puffy.

Mohammad the Barber asks, "I hear you're thinking of working at the textile factory, right?"

I look at him in the mirror. The smallpox scars make his face look like honeycomb.

"No, I have no such intention."

"This is what I heard."

I try to change the subject. "Don't cut it too short. Just make it even . . . Shave my face too."

The comb and the scissors get into motion. I can see the wall behind me in the mirror. Right above the sink, there is a mantelpiece, upon which an alarm clock is placed. Six minutes after two. "Look, Mash Mammad, don't touch my mustache at all. Just darken it with a black pencil!"

As he works through my hair, he says, "Do you know what happened the day before yesterday?"

"No."

"Javad made such a scene."

He talks about the smugglers and how a patrol chased them, and how the smugglers raced through the thirty-meter-wide street, and how their buddies blocked the patrol by throwing the benches from the teahouse onto the street. He talks with such excitement, as if he himself were one of the smugglers.

"Mash Mammad, wait a second."

He pauses.

Bending down, I take off my shoes. My heels throb. "Do me a favor and call that shoeshine boy for me?"

He opens the door and calls out to the shoeshine boy. It is muggy inside the shop. The ceiling fan is creaking. The shoeshine boy comes in.

I give him the shoes. "Look, Brother, stretch these shoes real good. They're killing my feet."

The shoe shiner takes the shoes and leaves the shop, closing the door behind him.

Fifteen minutes past two. So much time still till three thirty. The most my haircut will take is about twenty minutes. Mohammad the Barber works his scissors through my hair as he talks his usual nonsense. I sink deep into my own thoughts, thinking of what I want to tell Black-Eyed. I close my eyes slowly, thinking that I should tell her everything today, or . . .

Mohammad the Barber's voice breaks my train of thought. "Dozing off?"

I open my eyes. "No, I'm just a bit tired."

I close my eyes again. Mohammad the Barber doesn't talk anymore. The monotonous sound of the scissors reverberates in my ears. *I should tell her that I love her. If I don't tell her today, I won't ever be able to tell her. I don't know why I don't have the courage to talk to her.* I hear the door open. I open my eyes. It is Ali the Devil. My face turns pale. My heart thuds. *Damn you. Don't you even take a break for a midday rest?* Our eyes meet in the mirror. I smile at him. His face lights up with a smile. His thin, pointed eyebrows have stretched all the way to his temples, just like the devil's. His lips move. "Long time no see."

I force a smile. What other choice do I have but to pretend to be friendly?

Mohammad the Barber greets him. Turning his face to me, he says, "I swear on the lives of all worthy men that I have never seen a man as gentlemanly as Ali Khan. I'm at your service, Aqa."

Ali the Devil positions himself in such a way so that we can see each other in the mirror. The clock is right above his head. It is two thirty now.

"How are you, Mash Mammad?"

"Doing good, doing good," responds Mohammad the Barber, smiling. He goes on, "Ali Khan, do you want me to order you a good cup of tea?"

Ali the Devil says coolly, "It doesn't matter."

Mohammad the Barber sets down the comb and scissors on the table, sticks his head out of the door, and calls the errand boy from Mahtabi Teahouse.

Facing me, Ali the Devil says, "I haven't seen you around these past few days."

Since no one responds to Mohammad the Barber's call, he walks out of the shop.

"No answer?" says Ali the Devil.

I sink further into the chair and say, "I've been around."

The menacing smile does not disappear from his face as he goes on in such a way as if to let me know that I am in his claws and that there is no way out of his grip. "Well, I haven't seen you around recently."

"It happens sometimes."

"And sometimes one makes it happen that way, isn't that right?" he asks bitingly.

Mohammad the Barber comes in. Bringing the cup of tea from the teahouse himself, he offers it to Ali the Devil. He picks up the comb and the scissors and resumes fiddling with my hair.

"Mash Mammad," remarks Ali the Devil, "give him a good haircut. He is a nice boy!"

Mohammad the Barber grins, showing his yellow teeth. "At your service, Ali Khan!"

Ali the Devil stirs the cup of tea in his hand. As he slowly sips from the rim of the cup, he talks, pausing between words. "You know, Mash Mammad, sometimes you envy some people . . . for being so clever."

My heart drops. Mohammad the Barber takes over. "You said it, Ali Khan . . . I envy the cleverness of these smugglers. Do you know what a spectacle they put on the other day? This guy, Javad, with Khodabakhsh—"

Ali the Devil cuts Mohammad the Barber short. "Or for instance . . . Nightingale."

Mohammad the Barber's eyes narrow. "Who is Nightingale?"

Not paying him any mind, Ali the Devil goes on, "How clever and quick he must've been to find his way out of the police station and run away despite a million guards around."

Mohammad the Barber looks perplexed. I get the whole picture. Ali the Devil knows every little bit of the story. Obviously, he has every intention of letting me know that he knows. Today is not a day where he will let me off the hook that easy. I feel all the sorrows of the world in my heart. Mohammad the Barber's puzzled gaze is fixed on Ali the Devil's mouth.

Ali the Devil says all this in a cool manner. The smile doesn't leave his lips. "Mash Mammad, can you imagine, in broad daylight? . . . You know, Mash Mammad, one would have to be very quick to do that."

I have no choice but to look at him and smile. No longer able to stand the confusion, Mohammad the Barber loses interest in what Ali the Devil is saying. Turning to me, he asks, "Did you say you didn't want me to trim your mustache?"

"Yeah . . . leave it . . ."

As if talking to himself, Ali the Devil says, "It's not a bad idea to make a change. One cannot always keep the same style. It gets boring . . ."

Mohammad the Barber soaps my beard and begins sharpening the razor. It's six minutes to three. The walk to the Petroleum Quarter is about fifteen minutes. If I take a taxi, it'd be only five minutes. However, freeing myself from the grip of Ali the Devil is not a trifling task. Today he has every intention of getting even with me for all those times I did not pay him any heed.

Mohammad the Barber dabs my cheeks with eau de cologne. He darkens my mustache with a pencil and holds the mirror at the back of my head.

"Thanks very much."

He unties the cape from around my neck.

"Mash Mammad," I say, "would you call that shoeshine boy to bring me my shoes?"

The shoeshine boy comes in, bringing my shoes. I get out of the chair. Mohammad the Barber offers the chair to Ali the Devil.

"No . . . I don't need a haircut."

He insists. "Let me at least brush and fix up your hair for you."

I take Ali the Devil's seat and he takes mine. I bend down to put on my shoes. My foot is blistered. Mohammad the Barber begins to comb Ali the Devil's hair. I get up and walk toward the door.

"Wait a minute!" says Ali the Devil. "I've got to talk to you."

The smirk does not leave his lips, not even for a second. There is a bulge under his jacket. It is two minutes before three. My heart races like that of a scared sparrow.

Mohammad the Barber is busy clipping the hair inside Ali the Devil's nose. He combs his eyebrows too. Without moving in his seat, Ali the Devil turns around and stares right into my eyes. "All right?" he says.

His tone is such that I know I have no choice but to wait. If only I could punch him in that big mouth of his and smash all his teeth. I'm not so much bothered by my bad luck today as I am by his incessant smirking. He stares at me for a few moments without saying anything. Then he turns to Mohammad the Barber. "Can you leave us alone for a moment?"

"Of course," says Mohammad the Barber, who then leaves his shop, shutting the door behind him. Ali the Devil coughs and, without wiping the smirk off his lips, says, "All right, buddy!" stressing each word.

"I am not going to keep you, or waste my own time." He spells it out. "I'll be very frank with you . . . only if you are a nice boy and give the right answers . . ."

The smirk has left his lips.

My gaze stays focused on his green eyes, which seem perfectly still and unmoving.

He carries on. "I know that five days ago you escaped from the police station. Of course, I like your cleverness, but I don't like you playing smart games with me," he says, measuring his words with intention.

He waits for me to say something. But I think it's best that I not say anything.

He goes on, "I also know that you were taking a suitcase full of newspapers and leaflets to the port, but you got caught. The guard put in charge of you is now in custody. His wife and children are sleepless with worry. Your description has been given to more than ten officials in order to find you. But you know that none of them know you better than I do . . . You know that! From the very moment I heard that he was wearing a blue and red plaid shirt and a pair of blue linen pants, I had no doubt that it was you. Now I can easily take you to the police station."

Finishing his sentence, he slips his hand under his jacket and takes out handcuffs, which causes the corner of his jacket to turn over, revealing the brown butt of his pistol. I know he's doing this on purpose so I'll know that he's armed. My eyes move from the butt to the clock on the wall. It's five minutes past three. Putting the handcuffs back in his pocket, he smooths the side of his jacket. I am stunned. If I didn't have to go see Black-Eyed, I would have more time to somehow think of something to free myself from his clutches. Ali the Devil looks at me. Victory beams in his green eyes and in his smile. I feel as if nailed to the chair. Like I can't move.

I hear Ali the Devil's voice: "So . . . what's it gonna be?"

I wish I hadn't put on my shoes. Then there would at least be some hope of escape. But now, with these shoes, I cannot run, not even a few steps. I wish I had my tennis shoes on.

"Say something!"

I smile involuntarily. "You're mistaken," I say.

"What do you mean?"

"I mean it wasn't me."

I see it clearly, that he is taken aback. He was expecting me to agree to everything he said. His tone was so self-assured, as if I had already accepted everything.

His voice drops. "Are you saying that I'm mistaken?"

His eyes narrow. I nod. Mohammad the Barber taps on the window. We look at him. He's standing behind the door with another person, motioning with his hands and eyes that he has a customer. Ali the Devil gestures back, telling him to wait. Mohammad the Barber gets upset. Turning to me, Ali the Devil says, "You mean, you want to say that you didn't escape from the police station?"

"Yes."

"All right! We'll try it."

He gets up from the chair.

"Try what?"

In an indifferent tone, he says, "Yes, we'll try it. We'll go to the police station together. All the police officers who arrested you at the harbor intersection are there . . . The officer who watched over you is also there . . ."

His hand searches under his jacket.

"Get up!"

I don't move.

"I said, get up!"

Blood rushes to my face. I look at the clock. It's ten minutes after three. My voice is hoarse now. My parched throat makes it hard for me to speak. It feels real dry.

"What do you want from me?"

"Nothing."

He grabs my wrist, wanting to put the handcuffs on me.

I resist. "Why should I go to the police station with you?"

"Because you are a fugitive, and I am in charge of arresting you."

I can't pull my hand free from his grip. Without speaking or looking at each other, we challenge one another. The steel ring of the handcuffs clicks around my wrist.

"Now, get up!"

A tremble replaces the smile on his lips. His thick blond mustache quivers. He tries to make me get up from the chair. I feel as if I'm stuck to the seat. There is a storm stirring inside me. After yearning to see Black-Eyed, now that I can, I have fallen into the clutches of Ali the Devil. The handcuff is around my wrist. I think to myself that I should jump up, pull the pistol out from under Ali the Devil's jacket, whack him in the temple with the butt of it—just like Rahim the Donkey Keeper hit Rezvan in the head with his pipe—and run away; and then come what may.

Ali the Devil's tone turns authoritative. "I said, don't keep us!"

Still shifting from one foot to another, Mohammad the Barber looks at us from behind the door. He holds on to the customer's wrist and does not let him go. The customer is a tall man wearing a keffiyeh on his head and peeking inside the barbershop like an innocent lamb. Mohammad the Barber is getting mad. With the palm of his hand, he hits the glass window, now more curious to find out what's going on between me and Ali the Devil. Ali the Devil doesn't pay Mohammad the Barber any mind. All he cares about is getting me out of the chair and taking off. I should come up with something. Time is running away from me. I look down and speak in a tone that makes it sound like I am giving in. "Let's say I go to the police station with you and it becomes clear that it was me who escaped. What will you get out of this?"

Ali the Devil's tone is anything but friendly. There is not even a trace of softness in his voice like there was before.

"It's not about me getting anything out of it. I am just an official doing my job."

With my head still bowed, I look at the tips of my shoes. I wonder how long I saved so as to afford to buy these shoes for today's rendezvous. Without any further resistance, I let him take hold of my handcuffed wrist and tell him, "What if I do whatever you want me to do?"

He turns soft. Unlocking the handcuffs, he steps back and sits down in his chair. I look at him. He has that same deceptive smile on his face again.

"I take it you've come to your senses and will do the right thing?"

I murmur, "Well, it's not like you're leaving me any other choice."

I feel helpless in his claws. I have to come up with something.

"So, you're ready?"

I have no idea what it is that I should be ready for. I look at the clock. If I walk there now, I will be right on time. "What should I do?" I ask.

He does not mince his words. "Cooperate with me!"

"Cooperate?"

"And I'll help you in whatever way possible."

I struggle to find something suitable to say. Whatever I say, I'll give myself away. He is one of those bastards you cannot bullshit. Time is running out and this alone is driving me crazy. I throw caution to the wind and say what I want to say. "Look, today I don't have the time to sit down and talk with you. There's something I have to take care of."

"Late for a *meeting*?" he asks.

"A meeting?" I respond, surprised.

"Then what?"

I dodge his question. "Let's set up a time when we can sit down and talk without worrying about time and being late."

I can see in his face that he's considering the idea. A few moments pass in silence. Mohammad the Barber still hasn't let go of the customer's hand, and the customer is growing more and more agitated. The barber keeps hitting the glass door with the palm of his hand. Ali the Devil ignores him. All his attention is on me. I know I have to somehow get rid of him.

"Would you accept this offer if you were in my shoes?" he asks.

I assume the self-assured tone of someone who is very confident and say, "If I believed you and trusted your word, yes, definitely."

He looks me straight in the eye. "Should I trust your word?"

I shrug my shoulders. "I don't know."

Pressing his lips together, he falls silent, obviously thinking over my words. His gaze is fixed on the ground. I look at the clock. If I don't act quickly, I'll be late. I finish with absolute confidence. "Today, I'm not in the mood for talking. I'd rather you take me to the police station."

He looks up. It seems like my words are having an effect. So I go on, "Yet, if you let me go, next time . . ." I shift the direction of my words, even changing the tone of my voice. "Besides, where can I go, anyway? I am always in your clutches. If I can manage, the most I can hide from you is, let's say, ten to twelve days . . . What about after that?"

I can read signs of confidence in the wrinkles of his forehead. "All right!" he finally agrees.

I let out a deep breath.

"When will we meet again?" he asks.

I shrug my shoulders. "It doesn't matter to me."

"Tonight?"

I shake my head. "No!"

He gets up from the chair. "Then when?"

Mohammad the Barber's patience is gone. The customer still struggles to free his wrist from the grip of the barber. Not minding Ali the Devil anymore, Mohammad the Barber pushes the door open and comes in grumbling.

"Friday morning," I say.

Looking at me, Mohammad the Barber pulls the customer forward and sits him down in the chair and ties the cape around his neck.

Ali the Devil agrees. We walk out of the barbershop together, arranging the time and place of the meeting.

"Right behind Richie Gardens, on the bank of the Karun, at 10:00 a.m."

I cannot find a taxicab. I am a few minutes late. The bus is about to take off. Black-Eyed's eyes are wandering. By the time I get there, I am completely out of breath. My forehead and cheeks are drenched in sweat. Black-Eyed smiles at me. She is wearing white cotton shoes. Her skirt is short and pleated. She has tied her hair up with a thick piece of yellow woolen string. In one hand she holds a tennis racket, and in the other a long tin can. I greet her. We get on the bus. Pointing to the can, I ask, "What's that?"

"Tennis balls."

We sit next to each other. Her thigh is touching mine, filling my body with excitement.

I hear her voice. Everything seems to be happening as if in a dream.

"The mustache doesn't suit you," she says.

I don't know what to say. I forget all the words I have memorized. The conductor shows up. She gives him a ticket for me and shows a card for herself. I take the card from her hand and look at her picture. Her lips are parted, as if they have just been kissed. Her hair cascades over her shoulders, her bangs curve over her eyebrows. She appears to be looking at something that does not exist. You cannot guess what direction she is looking in. Her neck is so perfect in size and so beautiful that you just want to suck on it.

"Why do you look so surprised?" she asks, startling me.

"It's nothing. I was just looking at your picture," I say, handing the card back to her.

"Well, what was it you wanted to tell me?"

I feel rushed. "Not here," I say. "This is not the right place."

There are not that many people on the bus. A few old men and women and a few boys and girls sit here and there. They are all well dressed. My clothes are not all that bad but very different compared to theirs. I am wearing my blue linen pants and my plaid shirt.

The bus leaves behind the houses at the edge of town and reaches the first row of the oil company's white houses. We pass under tall mimosa trees and tall, lush willow trees. The bus makes a few easy turns and passes through the oil company housing, which is secluded by green walls of ivy, and stops in front of the sport club. The air here is much different from the air you breathe in the city.

We get off the bus. She shows her card. We walk into the club. We pass by the large covered tennis court. At the back of the building, a vast area of lawn stretches all the way to the bank of the Karun. No one is swimming in the pool. The tennis courts are right behind the pool. A cool breeze blows in from over the Karun. We go around the pool. Black-Eyed's voice fills my ears: "Say something."

My voice trembles, "I will."

We pass by the screened fence of one of the tennis courts. A man and a woman are playing tennis. The man is fat, short, stout, middle-aged, bald, and has a big nose.

"He's my coach."

"Coach?"

"He teaches me tennis."

The man catches a ball in the air, looks at us, waves his hand, and comes toward us. We wait behind the screened fence.

"How are you?"

Black-Eyed smiles and greets the bald-headed man.

"It's been a long time since I've seen you," says the fat man, "about ten sessions or so."

"I have a lot of studying to do."

The fat man turns to the female player, who's just standing there, not sure what to do. "I'll be with you in a second," he tells her, and, giving us a smile, he says, "She bores me."

The woman is tall and scrawny, with a touch of yellow to her skin and wide puppy dog eyes that are not appealing by any means.

The bald man does not look at me at all. From that very first look he gave me, I got the message that I was not welcome in a place like this.

"You will be here, right?" he asks Black-Eyed.

"I'll be here, but I don't think I'm in much of a mood for playing today."

"Not in the mood?" he says, surprised, and adds, "You shouldn't be talking about 'mood' at your age."

Black-Eyed tries to dodge his comment. "I mean . . . I feel tired . . . I've had so much to study."

The bald-headed man gazes at the racket in Black-Eyed's hand.

"I'll be done in a minute," he says as he walks away. "Stay put and don't feel so lethargic."

What luck! I got rid of Ali the Devil only to fall in this hyena's trap.

The bald-headed man starts to play. We start to walk. We walk behind the second tennis court and toward the bank of the Karun.

The shoreline is rocky and elevated. Gentle waves hit the cliffs and roll back on the shore. We sit down on one of the benches. The bench is the color of a green lawn. Before us lies the Karun, vast, tranquil, and mysterious. We are both quiet and do not know how to start.

"So . . . tell me!"

Mumbling, chewing my words, I say hastily, "You see . . . I wanted to see you to tell you that I might be getting arrested any moment . . ."

I have no idea why I start to tell her this so bluntly.

"Arrested?"

And before I know it, I'm telling her the entire story of my escape from the police station in detail. I am drenched in sweat. I look down as I talk. My tone of voice has the ring of both hesitancy and pride. Once I'm done telling her what I wanted to say, I lift my head up and look at her. Black-Eyed's mouth is half open. She looks at me, unblinking. Beads of sweat trickle down my forehead. The Karun's roar fills my ears. The bitter smell of willow trees, the acrid smell of mimosa trees, and the smell of grass all fuse together and fill my nostrils.

Black-Eyed brings her hand to her mouth and gasps with such excitement. "How amazing!"

The color of her eyes has become like that of black olives. Surprise has colored her face. Her eyes then take on a different shade of black. She bursts out laughing. I laugh with her.

I feel bold enough to lay my arm along the edge of the back of the bench. If she leans back, my arm will be resting against her shoulders. I find myself in such sweet bewilderment. I hear her voice, but it sounds as if it's coming from far away. It sounds as if it's coming like a spring breeze, filling my ears. "So that day, when you rushed into our house, you were running away from something then too?"

I feel a desire to enchant her. I want to make up a heroic story and amaze her even more. But I am afraid. I'm afraid to give myself away. So, I say quietly, "No, that day I was just attending the demonstration."

The sun is setting on the banks of the Karun. The skyline has turned orange. The sun's rays have blended in the tiny lead-colored waves on the surface of the Karun. The sky is especially clear. A soft breeze blowing through the faraway palm groves brings the scent of newly blossomed dates. The air grows cooler.

"Tell me more!"

Gaining confidence now, I start to talk. Utterly wrapped up in my story, I tell her about the night when Peyman came and warned us right before the soldiers arrived, so that they saw only the smoke but not the fire, so to speak. I tell all that went on inside Mohammad's barbershop. "I was so anxious. All I was thinking was what if I couldn't get myself free from the grip of Ali the Devil in time to come and see you."

It's getting darker by the minute. Here and there on the lawn, the milky florescent lights have come on. Black-Eyed's eyes sparkle. I bring my arm down from over her shoulders. I realize that I am holding her hand. We are silent. The roar of the Karun is strong. I hold her hand gently. A smile blossoms on her face like a rosebud.

"Now, you tell me," I say in a low voice.

"About what?"

"About yourself."

She looks down. Her cascading hair falls over her shoulder. "I love you," she says so quietly that I can hardly hear her.

I feel my heart leap against my chest. This is the last thing I expected. I feel hot. My temples pound. I reach out my hand and take hold of her chin gently. She lifts up her head. We look at each other, exchanging smiles. I don't know how, but suddenly I feel the warmth of her lips on mine. I pull myself away from her. Everything seems to have happened as if in a dream. I can't believe my eyes. The intoxicating warmth of her lips is still taking hold of me when I hear her say, "Why did you pull away?"

I am filled with a joy for life. I get closer to her and ask, "Can I see you again?"

"I'd like to see you for always."

She talks so softly, so gently, as if the fragrance of all the flowers fills the air as she exhales.

I am intoxicated by the way she looks, by the tremble of her lips.

"But you know, I can only come here on Tuesdays," she says.

Still holding each other's hands, we get up and start walking, until we reach the clubhouse's courtyard, which is lit by large lights. In front of us, the small shoot of a palm tree spreads along the ground. We walk on the lawn. I feel as if I am weightless. I want to fly. I squeeze Black-Eyed's hand. We reach the palm shoot. Its leaves are like intertwined spears. I walk on the left side of the palm shoot, and Black-Eyed on its right side, our hands reaching above it. A few pointed leaves have risen to meet our palms and wrists. The palm shoot's branches spread out, causing our fingers to separate. The pointy leaves standing upright sting the palms of our hands. The tips of our fingers touch. I want to hold her fingers. I do not wish for our hands to be separated. The leaves spread upon the ground sting my right shin through my linen pants. I try to hold on to Black-Eyed's fingers, but I fail. The tips of our fingers touch, but then we let go of each other's hands.

Mullah Ahmad has rented Rahim the Donkey Keeper's room. It's not even sunrise yet when Mullah Ahmad, his wife, and his five daughters, carrying their stuff on their shoulders, move in. He has rented the room provided that the landlord will let him use the donkeys' sun shelter as his *maktabkhaneh*. His daughters are all pale and skinny. They range from eight to eighteen years old, and they don't care as much about covering themselves as the daughters of a mullah should. Not to mention Mullah Ahmad's wife, who doesn't even bother wearing a chador when there are other men around in the courtyard. She doesn't count me and Karam Ali as men to begin with. Gray hairs run through Mullah Ahmad's beard. His beard moves as he talks nonstop, spewing orders around. The daughters get to work, sweeping the room clean and unpacking their stuff. They tumble down the donkeys' manger and Sanam's half-ruined oven, and use a busted wheelbarrow that had been left in the pigeon coop to take the rubble out into the alley. Then they smooth the rough ground under the sun shelter, sprinkle it with water, and spread out a straw mat.

Mullah Ahmad's daughters, in spite of looking pale and weak, work like day laborers.

By noon everything is taken care of.

Mullah Ahmad's beard moves. "All right, kids, now do the dishes at the pool."

The girls bring the large pots, the small pots, the spatulas, the plates, and the bowls, and sit at the edge of the pool.

Until recently, Mullah Ahmad held his *maktabkhaneh* on the pavement in front of the mosque in the produce market. He lived with his wife and five daughters in Nasim Baqlai's large house.

Leila, the oldest of Mullah Ahmad's daughters, has a very daring gaze.

∼

I have borrowed a few books to read while I'm hiding at home. I have made a hiding place for the books too. I bear in mind what Shafaq said: "You should expect to be arrested at any moment."

And I remember what Pendar said: "You should try as much as possible not to keep anything at home or in your pockets."

I have dug a hole under the back storage room, placed a clay pot in the depression, and covered it well with mud. Once I've put a brick on the pot and covered it with a piece of kilim, I think to myself that no one will be able to find it, even if they have extrasensory powers. I keep just one book at a time out, and the rest I keep hidden in the pot.

I wake up late in the morning. The commotion of the kids at Mullah Ahmad's *maktabkhaneh* wakes me up. The mullah has placed his cushion in what used to be the donkeys' manger, and sits on it cross-legged. Plunking their Koran holders before them, the kids also sit cross-legged. One by one, they go and sit on their knees in front of Mullah Ahmad and read to him.

Mullah Ahmad wears a milk-and-sugar-colored turban around his head. His shirt is white, the collar of which he keeps unbuttoned. His thin robe, folded, rests beside him. Leila fetches him a water pipe; as she passes by me, she looks at me boldly. There are twenty or so kids. I sit at the pool to wash up. Khaj Tofiq comes out of the outhouse, his ewer in his right hand. He's holding his left hand away from his body as if it were something soiled. He sits beside the sun shelter and talks to Mullah Ahmad.

I go back into our room. Bolur Khanom is whispering words of complaint in Mother's ear. "This place has turned into a caravansary . . . from dawn to dusk we have to put up with the racket of thirty, forty small kids."

There are not even twenty. All of them must be less than ten years old. There are even six-year-olds among them. Runny snot has turned the skin above some of their lips all red and crusty.

Mullah Ahmad's *maktabkhaneh* is closed in the afternoons. During the winter, when he held his class in front of the mosque in the produce market, he sat the kids in one of the porches of the mosque and set up two charcoal braziers for them. This winter, he must be planning on accommodating the kids in his own room. It's a long way until winter.

I place the stool in the shade of the wall and start to read a book. In the midst of the kids' noise, a familiar voice catches my attention. I lift my head up from the book and look around. Pendar is standing on the threshold of the house. I wave at him. He comes in. Together we go into Father's room. I draw the curtain between the two rooms and place the stool so Pendar will sit on it.

"I have come to talk to you."

I lay a pillow next to the wall, lean against it, and hug my knees. "I'm listening."

He looks hesitant, or perhaps he doesn't know where to start. The high-pitched clamor coming from the class is deafening.

"Is there something wrong, Pendar?"

"No," he answers quickly, "nothing in particular."

The teapot we used for breakfast is still on the burner. "Do you care for some tea, Pendar?"

He shrugs, and in a subdued manner says, "Sure."

I get up, fetch two cups of tea, and return and sit down.

"All right then . . . tell me what you wanna say."

Pendar's silence and hesitation make me nervous. Finally he starts to talk, his eyes fixated on the rug. "You are seeing a girl, right?"

I am taken aback. Thousands of stray thoughts cross my mind. Ali the Devil must be double-dealing. He must have told them all kinds of lies about Black-Eyed, or perhaps they themselves have found out some things on their own.

"I'm sure you know that the organization would not just admit someone in without tapping into his background and trying him out." He adds, "We monitor anyone who requests a membership for more than two months."

I don't know what to say.

Pendar's voice brings me back to my senses. "You didn't answer!"

"Yes, that's true," I say in a low voice. "I am seeing a girl. But before we discuss the matter, I'd like to know who told you this?"

"Does it make any difference to you?"

Looking down, I say, "I think it does."

Pendar starts to speak, not bothering to mince his words at all. "If it does matter to you, then I should tell you that it was Ali the Devil."

My jaw drops. Looking into Pendar's eyes, I say, "Ali the Devil?"

"Yes, Ali the Devil."

There is a hint of mistrust in Pendar's voice. He pauses for a moment, then continues, "And he knows a lot more about you."

I think Ali the Devil has every intention of tarnishing other people's trust in me. He has used whomever he could to get his manipulative words to the ears of the guys. People like Mohammad the Barber, for instance.

"What went on between you two that day in Mohammad's barbershop?"

Without missing a beat, I tell him the entire story. I tell him about all of Ali the Devil's threats and promises, and the appointment we set up to see each other on Friday. Pendar, pressing his lips tight, just looks at me. I cannot read his face.

"And then?"

"I didn't go on Friday."

"Did you hint at anything in particular by accident that may cause others trouble?"

I shake my head. "No, I didn't mention a thing."

"Why didn't you discuss this with Bidar?"

"I didn't think it was necessary."

It seems that Pendar believes what I'm saying. The hint of mistrust in his voice fades away. His words are now more like advice. "Apparently, Ali the Devil has some plans for you," he says. "He thinks he can influence you and then use you... Especially now that you have two major weak points."

"Weak points?" I repeat quickly, "Two major weak points? What does that mean?"

Nodding his head, Pendar says, "One is that you are a fugitive, the other is *that* girl."

I don't quite understand, so I ask, "What does loving a girl have to do with it?"

Pendar's dark, piercing eyes take away all of my confidence.

"You... you're still inexperienced... There might come a time when you'll have to pay a hefty price, either to protect that girl's honor, or... for your own emotions and feelings for her, or whatever else that will somehow be related to that girl. And it's not like you'd only harm yourself. Most likely you'll end up harming others, others whom you have never even met."

Flabbergasted, I murmur under my breath, "I'm completely confused."

"Well, you may have to experience it to understand. But then, it'll be too late."

I am fixated on Pendar's mouth. "What should I do?"

"You should learn, in the course of battle, not to allow your emotions to take over."

"You mean—"

He cuts me short. "Yes, I mean you have to forget the girl."

I cannot even imagine the thought of it. I plead with Pendar. "But it'd be very difficult for me."

"But it's possible," he answers without any hesitation, and gets up from the stool.

I take the books I have already read out of the large clay pot and give them to Pendar. He takes a folded newspaper out of his back pocket and hands it to me. "Once you've read it, drop it into one of the houses nearby; it doesn't matter which one."

I walk him to the house doors. We shake hands. In a friendly yet stern tone, he says, "Remember what you've got to do!"

The kids in Mullah Ahmad's *maktabkhaneh* are spelling out words together. I pass by them. Leila looks at me. I go to Father's room, sit down, and think over Pendar's words. Mother draws the curtain aside and comes in. The corners of her mouth are drawn. "Khaled, I am getting more and more worried about you," she says in a sympathetic tone.

I feel apprehensive. I wish I had someone who could help me. I get up and hug Mother. "Don't you worry about me, Mother." Unexpectedly, I add, "When Father comes back, I'll go with him to Kuwait."

This calms her, as if the relief takes away a bit of her restlessness. She drops the curtain and leaves Father's room. In his last letter, which arrived a few days ago, Father wrote that he would come back at the beginning of fall. "Tell the blacksmith shop's owner that the world hasn't come to an end. I'll come back and pay all my late rents." To escape from the chaotic thoughts attacking my mind, I allow the idea of going to Kuwait to take hold of me. My intention was to start night school this fall. The kids' noise has quieted down. I lie down, place my hands under my head, and look at the ceiling, thinking. No! I can't stop seeing Black-Eyed. I love her with all my heart. I cannot comprehend why feelings and combat don't go together. Why not? I close my eyes. No! No to Kuwait. I'll stay and fight. Stay and see Black-Eyed every day. And come fall, I'll attend night school. No! I won't go to Kuwait. Never!

~

I have not left the house for four days. I am dying to go out. Leila, Mullah Ahmad's oldest daughter, would like us to be friends. She gives me bold looks, but there is a sort of kindness in the gleam in her eyes. She has tried to start up a conversation with me a few times. She wants to know why I stay home and don't go out. I dodge her questions. "I just don't feel like going out in this heat."

Obviously, she doesn't buy it. She just smiles as if she suspects something. She has warmed up to the women in the house, especially Bolur Khanom. Already she has bewitched Bolur Khanom, suggesting that she should learn how to read and write. She has told her that if a woman is educated she can understand many things in life better. "There is no difference between men and women," she has told her. "Why shouldn't women have the right to work like men do? Why shouldn't they participate in everything along with men?"

Leila's words make you think. Her attitude and her words are so different from those of her father.

Mullah Ahmad and Khaj Tofiq have become buddies; it's as if they've known each other for years. When night falls and Khaj Tofiq's smoking opium, Mullah Ahmad sits facing him, chatting. "It's such a bad time."

Khaj Tofiq agrees with him.

"Today's schools, they teach kids antireligious stuff . . . They don't teach them good manners or how to perform their religious duties." Sticking a finger in his nose, Mullah Ahmad goes on, "All the learned of the world are the product of *maktabkhanehs*. Avicenna was a pupil at one of these religious schools. Amir Kabir too studied at one of these sorts of schools, which these days only a few godly Muslims send their kids to. And with all this happening, you won't see any *maktabkhanehs* left in ten years."

Khaj Tofiq sticks a tiny bead of opium to the pipe and offers it to Mullah Ahmad.

Mullah Ahmad hesitates to take the opium pipe. Khaj Tofiq blows his nose into his checkered Yazdi handkerchief and talks about the benefits of opium: "Especially for people our age, it's a must. Besides, if opium was harmful to the body, or would lead one astray from the path of God, the Holy One would have forbidden its use."

Mullah Ahmad is hesitant. Khaj Tofiq goes on as he melts the bit of opium on the pipe. "It's the remedy for all pains. It makes one live longer."

Mullah Ahmad finally gives in and moves closer. Khaj Tofiq helps him smoke the pipe.

Mullah Ahmad's wife prepares a water pipe, puts it in front of him, and walks away, grumbling, "It's like the only thing he lacked was to start smoking opium at this age. Not to mention that God has granted him five ill-fated girls who are born paupers."

Yet she doesn't dare to raise her voice in front of Mullah Ahmad.

I head out of the house to see Shafaq. He needs to sit down and make me understand why I cannot love Black-Eyed. I don't see any problem with it. Pendar's words have not convinced me. I walk through alleys and backstreets toward Pahlavi Street. It's just gotten dark. Pahlavi Street is alive with people. As soon as night falls, all the people of the town swarm to Pahlavi Street. I try to walk in the protection of the dark shadows of the walls. Hesitant, I stand at the back of the wooden kiosk of the National Lottery. I watch a middle-aged man taking out a crumpled two-toman bill from the waistband of his pants to buy a lottery ticket. The man closes his eyes, says something under his breath, and draws a ticket out from the stack.

I wait in the hope that someone familiar will pass by, to send after Shafaq. I should've just stayed put at home and sent someone after him. Fear and panic dart through my body. It was such a terrible mistake to come to Pahlavi Street, where anyone could show up.

You should learn how to disguise yourself in a crowd of people, Pendar said.

Everyone passes through this street, and as Ali the Devil said, there must be more than ten people who are after me.

Mojahed Bookstore is not far from here. About a three-minute walk. Maybe even less. I don't think that it's safe to leave the shelter that the National Lottery kiosk offers me. Not only do I think it's unsafe, but I am rooted to the ground. I decide to pull myself together and shake free of the wooden shack; I step back and slide into the darkness of an alley. It's best that I go back home and send Omid to fetch Shafaq. If not, perhaps even Mohammad the Mechanic himself; he'll do it for me if he's home.

"I am happy that you have found your own way." Mohammad the Mechanic's lips move under his large mustache. "People are all looking to the young."

I can walk in the shadows back to our neighborhood. There are enough patches of darkness here and there that I can easily avoid walking under the streetlights. It's only near our house that the kerosene lanterns at Mehdi the Grocer's shop and Habib the Baker's bakery illuminate the entire alley, which extends forty to fifty steps more at the most.

I pass by the abandoned building behind Habib the Baker's bakery. I reach the corner of the street leading to our house. I shift from one foot to the other. I look around the entire street carefully. Khalifeh is sitting next to the rice pudding seller. Mehdi the Grocer is tending to his customers. Standing in front of our house, Mullah Ahmad talks with Amu Bandar. Mullah Ahmad's little daughter, holding a plate in her hand, stands beside them. It looks as if her father is giving her some change; he's reaching deep into the large pocket of his robe. His shadow is cast on the wall. There's hardly anyone in front of the bakery. A limp and scrawny stray dog lies in the slimy gutter along the street. There are fewer and fewer people around. I head out of the alley and hurriedly stride along the street toward our house. As I reach the front of the bakery, I hear someone calling me from inside. I pause for a moment. The voice is so familiar that I have no doubt who it belongs to. It is Ali the Devil himself. I turn pale. I know that Ali the Devil will not leave me alone under any circumstances, not this time. I hear his voice; I pause for another second, and then I quickly start to run. I have my tennis shoes on, but the blisters still burn. I run into Mullah Ahmad's daughter standing in front of the rice pudding seller's shop. She goes sprawling onto the street. I jump over her. Ali the Devil runs out of the bakery and comes after me. I know that Ali the Devil always carries a gun.

"There's no use in running away."

I pay him no mind. I dart past our house. Ali the Devil's footfalls fade away. Obviously he's fallen behind. A circle of light spreads out before me. If I run another hundred steps or so, there will be no chance for Ali the Devil to catch me. I dart into the alleys and backstreets, where you can find a thousand passageways. The blister on my foot stings terribly. A gravelly voice, coming out of nowhere, roots me to the spot. "Don't move!" it commands.

A tall, broad-shouldered man, who's chasing me on a bike, quickly let's go of it, jumps onto the pavement, and points his pistol at my chest. The bike swishes ahead and turns toward the pavement, its front wheel plunging into the mud alongside the street, and its rear wheel still turning.

The tall man steps closer, reaching to grab my wrist. Drenched in sweat, I'm breathing so fast that I can hardly talk. "What do . . . you . . . want from me?" I ask him haltingly.

I know that I'm talking nonsense, and I know all too well what he wants from me. Ali the Devil arrives in no time. First thing he says is, "You dirty liar." Grinding his teeth, and holding metal handcuffs in his hands, he orders, "Put your hands together!"

I have to put my hands together. There's no way around it.

As soon as the handcuffs have been locked around my wrists, everyone gathers around me; Mehdi the Grocer, Habib the Baker, the bakery workmen, Mullah Ahmad, Leila, Khaj Tofiq, and Khalifeh are all here.

Now comes Bolur Khanom, holding up the skirt of her chador as she runs. Behind her runs my mother, leaving the house for the first time ever without putting on her chador. Jamileh follows her. Mother elbows the men aside, breaks into the crowd, and hugs me. "What do you want from my child?"

She has done all this in such a rush that Ali the Devil is taken aback. "Step aside, Sister!"

Furiously, my mother retorts, "What's that bangle you've put around his wrist?" She clenches her teeth like a she-tiger.

I whisper into Mother's ear, "Don't trouble yourself, Mother. They won't listen to you. Please, calm down!"

She then falls to one side and tears well up in her eyes.

Leila takes hold of Mother and says, "Don't worry, Khaled! These things happen to a man."

I plead with Mother, "Please, go home, Mother! They might insult you. These people have no honor."

Mother steps aside.

Bolur Khanom says hastily, "Don't worry, Khaled! I'll send someone after Aman Aqa right away." And facing Ali the Devil, she says, "What are you thinking? Do you think it is a nonbeliever you're dealing with?"

I know that it's out of Aman Aqa's hands. It's not like last time, breaking Gholam Ali Khan's window. This time, it's another story altogether.

Ali the Devil searches my pockets. He doesn't find anything. I feel the weight of Leila's gaze on my handcuffed wrists. I walk along with Ali the Devil. Mother and Jamileh follow close behind.

I feel like I am suffocating in the heat. The solitary confinement cell is three meters in length and two meters in width. The ceiling is very high. It is terribly dark. Only a thread of light peeks through the keyhole in the iron door, casting patterns on the kilim rug. The only thing Aman Aqa managed to do for me was to get me a pot of food. I was given a message that he would bring me candles but there are none as of yet.

"Let's take a taxicab," I say.

Ali the Devil is a changed man entirely. He cusses at me so much, as much as he wants to.

"You have to walk all the way to the police station. In handcuffs."

"But what'll you get out of it?"

In a gruff voice, he says, "So that all the people of this town get to know a motherfucking liar like you."

"All right, let them know me. It's not like I'm a thief or something."

Raising his voice, he barks, "Thieves have honor, but you, motherfucker, don't have anything."

My head is burning. He is mad at me because I stood him up on Friday.

"You kept me waiting for two hours. Grass grew under my feet. You're such a bastard."

He shoves me into the solitary cell and shuts the door behind me. It is a two-by-three-meter cell, hardly enough room to breathe. It is insanely hot. Its tall ceiling makes my stomach churn.

"You stay here till I have them shove a baton up your ass in the morning."

Can a person be this vulgar? He closes his eyes and curses me and my family, dead and alive. Shutting the iron door, he leaves. I can still hear him. "Watch this motherfucker. He'll slip through the keyhole and run away . . . already has escaped from the police station once."

All my thoughts right now are on Mother. I think about Black-Eyed, but not so much that it bothers me. I know that Mother won't sleep tonight. She will sit in front of the kerosene lantern shedding tears quietly and singing under her breath. This is what she did when she heard the news of her brother's death. When they went and got her brother's body and brought it home, she was shocked at first; then she sat down, wept, and sang quietly:

> *Where is the grief caravan driver to carry my griefs away?*
> *I'll mount the caravan, roaming around the bazaar and the alleys.*

The thing that makes me suffer the most right now is the thought of my mother. She burns from the inside and weeps. I know her well.

I sit in the corner of the solitary cell, hugging my knees. I stare at the small patch of light casting rays on the dusty kilim. I can't sleep at all.

Suddenly, the door opens violently and a small young man is thrown down on my head. I put my hands under his body and rise to my knees. The door shuts. The small young man starts to cry. "I swear to God, I was set up, I was trapped . . ."

He cries and swears. I try to calm him. He doesn't pay any attention. He cries as if he were a young woman who has lost her child.

I grab his shoulders. "Stop crying, man! If nothing else, you're a grown man."

He doesn't mind my advice at all. He's driving me crazy, really getting on my nerves. I let go of his shoulders, put my hand over his mouth, press it, and tell him in a threatening tone, "If you keep on crying, I'll strangle you."

He struggles to get himself free of my grip.

I remove my hand from over his mouth.

He sits in a corner of the cell and, instead of crying, starts to whimper.

I talk to him and try to calm him down.

"Why were you arrested?"

He doesn't respond. He just keeps whimpering.

I lose my patience. So I grab his arms and shake him. "I'm talking to you. Why are you here?"

Finally he talks, his speech halting. "The lady . . . she, she says . . . I have stolen . . . her necklace."

The little I can make out tells me that he was the servant of one of the high-ranking oil refinery employees.

Again he stutters. "They'll . . . kill . . . me. They'll hang me."

I lose my cool. "Shut up, man! What have you done to hang for?"

He stops whimpering and hugs his knees.

We sit facing each other. There is not enough room to stretch out our legs. Our legs are folded against our stomachs. I feel anxious. I feel suspicious. Something fishy is going on. I cannot see his face all that well in the dark. He moves a bit and draws his legs closer. I don't know why, but I am frightened. I shift my body. Thousands of stray thoughts swarm my mind.

"They terrorize you from the very first moment . . ."

Pendar's large black eyes sparkle. His voice echoes in my ears: "They try to break your spirit . . ."

The man is now sitting alongside me, and looks as if he's fallen asleep. Suddenly, Mother's face fills the entire cell. I can even hear her crying. I hear her singing softly too.

> *I will reach my hand to my heart and pluck it out.*
> *With my bloody hand, I will reach for your throat.*

It should be around midnight. All the noise has died down. I get up and look out through the keyhole. Two guards sleep on cots alongside each other. I can see a large door.

It's bright in the courtyard. It's bright in the hallway. A tall guard, leaning against the doorframe, has placed the stock of his gun on the ground. He seems to be drowsy. I sit down again. The small young man is asleep, snoring quietly. I lean back and stretch my legs. My neck and chest are entirely drenched in sweat. I unbutton my shirt. I was wearing this same shirt when I went to see Black-Eyed. Ali the Devil's voice rings in my ears: "From the very moment I heard that he was wearing a blue and red checkered shirt and a pair of blue linen pants, I was sure that it was you . . ."

My head feels heavy. I close my eyes. Sleep eludes me. My eyelids burn. I breathe rhythmically but noisily. I hear a rustling sound. The small young man is wriggling around. Without moving, I keep watching him. He moves a bit; then he starts to snore again. It will be a long night. My body feels sore all over. I hear the small young man wriggling again. Abruptly, he jumps to his feet. The nails on his right hand pierce my neck. His brings up his left hand. I see the gleam of something in the shaft of light that provides what little illumination there is in the cell. His voice grows coarse. "I'll kill you . . ."

"They'll create a mood of terror . . . ," Pendar says.

"I'll cut your vein with this razor!" yells the small young man.

I grab his wrist. He clenches his teeth.

"Take pity on your youth . . ." I hear Mother's voice.

Spider's laughter echoes in my ears: "You open your eyes and see that it's too late . . ."

Struggling, we twist around each other.

I kick the iron door and yell out, "Open the door!"

Spider keeps laughing. "It's still too soon for you to understand what making a mistake means."

We roll around.

I hear Pendar's deep voice: "An atmosphere of terror, terror, terror . . ."

Mother's voice comes from the deepest sorrow of her heart: "I'm worried about you, dear . . . I'm getting worried . . ."

Ali the Devil's green eyes have filled the entire room. "You are such a bastard, a liar."

Before the door is opened, we roll around a few more times. The light from the lamps in the yard illuminates the solitary cell.

"What the hell is wrong with you two?"

"This guy is crazy, Guard."

The blade flashes in the small young man's hand. His eyes are like two balls of fire. The guard grabs the small young man's shoulders and drags him off me.

The young man continues to make threats. "Let go of me. I wanna kill this motherfucker."

They drag him out of the solitary cell.

"He thinks I'm a sissy boy . . . He thinks I'm one of those boys . . . !"

I am shocked.

Still shouting, he says, "He was about to undo my belt . . . !"

The guards seem to believe him.

As one of the guards closes the door of the solitary cell, he calls me all sorts of names that really only suit him. I am totally shocked. I can't talk at all. My mouth is as dry as a matchstick. Could it be that they have set all this up themselves? Or maybe the boy is really mad!

The guard keeps cursing. "The motherfucker has no shame . . . I'll show you in the morning what it means to mess up like that."

Not knowing what else to do, I shout, "He's lying, Guard!"

The guard's face fills the round hole in the door. "Why on earth would he want to make up such a thing?"

"I swear by your life that . . ."

In a gruff voice he says, "By your own fucking life . . . The bastard talks like he has breastfed me."

I fall silent. I should have kept quiet. There is no use in talking. It's like a sewage pit: the more you stir it, the more it stinks. I lean back against the wall, drawing my knees to my chest. What a place I've gotten myself stuck in. There's trouble all the time. The guy was nuts. His eyes told me that. Like two balls of fire. Come to think of it, his mouth smelled of liquor too. I feel so numb that I don't want to move at all. My mouth tastes bitter, just like snake venom.

If only I could fall asleep. I lean my head back. My head feels larger by the minute. I start to count. Maybe it will help me stop thinking. The numbers bang on my brain one by one. It's such a vain attempt. What a long night!

The hot sun is beating down on the iron door. It's humid and suffocating inside the solitary cell. The police station employees are showing up. I'd die for a cup of tea. A man with a bent back sits in the shade of the opposite wall. I call out to him. From the look of his clothes, I can tell that he is a server. He gets up from the chair and comes over. He is deformed, just like a midget. His head is large, yet his body is like that of a ten- to twelve-year-old boy. He walks with his back bent. He's an older man.

"What do you want?"

His tone of voice is kind.

"Father, what can I do to get a cup of tea here?"

"You got money?"

I give him two tomans.

"You want bread and cheese too?"

"I'd appreciate it if you'd do that."

Before he comes back, I peek through the hole in the iron door and take a look at the police station. Gholam Ali Khan walks in through the large gate. His stomach has become fatter. His head down, he walks into the hallway. I can't see him anymore. The dwarf is here. He hands me some bread, a slice of cheese, and a glass of sweetened tea through the opening in the door. I figure that there must be a teahouse in the police station.

I cannot swallow the bread. I force myself to eat two bites; it's as if I'm chewing on my own flesh. The tea is refreshing. I savor every single drop. The police station is getting more and more crowded by the minute. The noises are all jumbled up. Just like in the livestock market. I'm sipping the last drops of the tea as the door flings open. Ali the Devil is standing there, looking stunned. He freezes for a second, and then yells, "Who has brought breakfast for this motherfucker?"

Sitting on his chair, the dwarf looks at me, shaking his head to the right and left.

Ali the Devil's voice is filled with loathing. "They gave you food last night too, huh?"

I have the urge to tease him. I point at the pot lying empty in the corner of the solitary cell and say, "I had steamed rice and kebab. Too bad you missed it. There's the empty pot."

Blood rushes into his face. "Who gave you breakfast?"

I doubt he can read the mocking expression on my face. He is fuming. I smile. He gives in, realizing that there is no point in arguing. "Come on out!" he orders.

I get up, shake the dust off my pants and shirt, and head out of the solitary cell. It crosses my mind that it's Tuesday and that Black-Eyed is expecting me at three thirty in the afternoon.

Ali the Devil has my wrist tight in his grip. We weave through the people crowding the hallway and walk up the stairs. A few rooms stand in a row on the second-floor hallway. Ali the Devil opens the door to one of them. We walk in. A ceiling fan turns gently. The air inside is cool.

"Sit!" He points at a bench against the wall.

I choose not to greet anyone. I sit down. There are two desks in the room, a person sitting behind each one of them. Both are middle-aged and in gray civilian clothing. One of them is so skeletal that if you were to pinch his nose, his soul would part from his body. He is even skinnier than Khaj Tofiq. It looks like he smokes away a good three to four *mesqals* of opium every day. The second one, whose desk is larger and taller, is so fat that you'd think he might explode at any minute. Both employees have mustaches just like Gholam Ali Khan's—as thick as the tail of a rat. They both look at me. The suitcase holding the newspapers and pamphlets is on the bench.

The fat man turns to Ali the Devil and asks, "Is that him?"

Ali the Devil sits on the bench and says, "Yes, sir, it's him."

The fat man wants to see the report filed by the checkpoint at the harbor intersection as well as Ali the Devil's. The skeletal man picks up a file from his desk and hands it to the fat man. There are also a few books and newspapers inside the file.

The fat man examines the books and newspapers carefully. He then reads the reports.

The only sound inside the room comes from the ceiling fan turning gently. Ali the Devil sits down, crosses his legs, and lights a cigarette. As always, there is a bulge under his jacket.

The fat man takes more than ten minutes to read the reports and seems to be going over some of the details a few times. I grow more impatient by the minute as the silence that has fallen in the room continues. I shift in my seat and yawn. The fat man lifts his gaze from the file and looks me over. His eyes are just like an elephant's. Tiny and narrow. They do not match his wide and ruddy face at all.

Ali the Devil gets up from the chair. "Is there anything else, sir?"

"I'll call you if you are needed," answers the fat man.

Ali the Devil leaves the room.

The fat man shuffles the books and newspapers once more and then starts his questioning. His voice does not match his bulky figure by any means. It's delicate and high-pitched. "I am sure you don't want to get yourself into trouble, right?"

I can't figure him out. I am already in trouble, and now he says that I shouldn't get myself into trouble. I keep quiet.

"Don't you have a tongue?" he remarks.

The pitch of his voice makes me laugh. Such a big guy with such a girly voice!

"You're amusing too."

In a muffled voice I say, "I don't understand what you mean."

He is taken aback. You wouldn't expect such a relaxed man to be surprised so easily. "What did you say?" he asks impatiently.

In a low voice I repeat, "I said, I don't understand what you mean."

"You'll understand soon," he retorts harshly.

He hands the files, books, and newspapers to the skeletal man so that he can interrogate me.

The skinny man puts half a Homa cigarette into his wooden cigarette holder, examines the papers in order, ignites a match, and lights the cigarette leisurely. When he takes a drag of his cigarette, his cheeks sink so deep that you'd think he had no teeth inside his mouth. In a nasally voice he says, "Come on and sit here!"

Rising from the bench, I go and sit on the large, hefty chair he points to. He asks for my first and last names, my birth certificate number, and my date of birth. His pen is attached to the table with a piece of string. He writes a few lines and turns to me again. "Are you literate?"

"Sort of."

Scratching his nose, he says, "Give me a proper answer!"

"I am sort of illiterate."

Looking straight at me, he says, "If you are sort of illiterate, how can you read these sorts of books that one has to use black magic in order to read their titles?"

"But when did I say I read such books?"

He rolls his eyes. The whites of his eyes are tinted yellow. The blackness of his pupils had faded. The skin at his temples looks dried up. Looking at me, he says, "Are you saying that these books aren't yours?"

The fat man listens to this conversation.

"Were these books supposed to be mine?"

Disappointed, the skeletal man turns to the fat man. "Do you see what a quick-talker he is, sir?"

The fat man squeaks, "These types know how to play their cards."

Taking a drag of his cigarette, the skeletal man starts to write. The ceiling of the room is low. The walls are a chickpea color. A fading kilim rug covers part of the floor. A number of digits, large and hideous, have been written on the surfaces of the desks. The fan keeps turning gently, drying up my sweat-drenched body. My entire body feels sore.

"Read it and then write a response!" commands the skeletal man.

He places a transcript of the interrogation with a list of accusations in front of me. It's written that when Ali the Devil arrested me, I had the books and newspapers with me. He has scribbled down the titles of the books and newspapers. If I didn't already know the titles of the books, there would be no way I could read them. I slide the pages back toward him. "As I told you, I am sort of illiterate . . . I can't read what you have written."

He lifts his head up. His Adam's apple shifts. "Well, aren't you cheeky?"

I have no idea what illiteracy has to do with cheekiness! So I tell him, "Say what you wish. I am not literate enough to read this."

He pulls the pages toward himself, reads them out loud, and waits for my response.

"It's all lies."

I don't know what has come over me that I feel so calm. It is as if I have been drowned and it no longer matters to me that I will sink deeper and deeper. "Of course it's all lies. Call him and let us confront him. All the people who were there know that I didn't have anything with me. Besides, what good are these books to me when I can't even make out their titles?"

The fat man shifts in his seat, then gets up and walks around the table. He's all one big giant torso. His legs are short and thick, like two dumbbells. Like a crocodile, he slithers toward me. "You're saying it's all lies?"

"Yes, it's all lies."

Pointing at the suitcase with his plump, short finger, he says, "What do you say about that suitcase, then?"

Looking surprised, I say, "Well . . . that's a suitcase."

"And it's ripped too, right?" His voice is muffled and trembling.

"Yes, it's ripped."

Suddenly, he yells, "How dare you talk back?"

I enjoy messing with them. It's good to get back at them. "Believe me, I have no idea what you're talking about."

"You mean to say that that is not your suitcase?" He's yelling again.

I shake my head.

His tiny eyes are fixed on my face. His voice drops. "You're a boorish one!"

I throw caution to the wind. "And of course, if I said that the suitcase belongs to me, I'd be a good guy, right?"

His ruddy face turns dark. Quietly, he slithers back to his desk and sits down. His shrill voice breaks in his throat. "Evidently, you wanna say it wasn't you who escaped from the police station."

I play dumb. "If it was me, I wouldn't be here before you now."

The fat man, like a hen hit by a stone, screeches. "Shut up!"

He keeps quiet for a while and puts his hands under his chin and stares right at me. The skeletal man stubs out his cigarette butt. The fat man shifts in his seat, lights another cigarette, inhales its smoke, and rings a bell.

The server comes in.

"Tea!" he orders.

The server leaves. A heavy silence falls in the room. The soft turning sound of the fan makes me sleepy. My eyelids feel heavy. As he smokes, the fat man keeps his gaze on me, unblinking. The skeletal man constantly scratches the tip of his nose. Khaj Tofiq does the same after he has smoked a hearty portion of opium and gotten high. He will keep scratching his nose until his eyelids close.

The server brings in a cup of tea, puts it in front of the fat man, and leaves. His cigarette has burned halfway down. He starts to talk. His voice takes on the tone of one giving advice. "Look, young man . . ." He takes a drag. The tips of his fingers are yellowish from the cigarettes. "You can easily save your life, and you can . . . ," he takes another drag, "get yourself into trouble."

Stubbing out the cigarette butt, he continues, "All right! Let me tell you how you can get yourself into trouble . . ."

I try to look as if all my attention is on him, as if I need his advice.

Putting his elbows on the desk, he closes his eyes and goes on, "We all know that a few days ago you were arrested at the harbor with that suitcase . . ."

Opening his eyes, he points at the suitcase placed on the bench with his chin.

"There's the report too. The people who signed the report are also here. The officer who brought you to the police station from the checkpoint is also alive. And I have sent for him. It's not clear how you distracted the officer and got away from the police station. And you had a lot of newspapers and books with you when you were arrested . . ."

"That's a lie. I didn't have anything with me."

Paying no mind to my words, he continues, "Everything is clear to us. There's also no need for us to interrogate you or have you confess. As far as we are concerned, this file is complete. All we need to do at this point is to send you to court and then to jail. This is one option, and it will cost you at least five years of your life behind bars."

I feel sleepy. A knock on the door shakes me awake.

"Come in, please," says the fat man.

The door opens. Gholam Ali Khan walks in, greeting the men. As he catches sight of me, he freezes on the spot, looking surprised. A sour smile sets on his lips. He says hello in such a way that's worse than a hundred cusswords. I ignore him. He's become a bit fatter and his stomach is sticking out farther too, making him look older.

His cheeks and his chin are somewhat plumper. But his meticulous tie knot, his trimmed mustache, and his shaved face are no different. The only exception is the now-fading color of his raisin-green eyes.

"You know this guy?" the fat man asks Gholam Ali Khan.

"Do I know him, sir?" says Gholam Ali Khan in a bitter tone. Then he asks, "What are the charges?"

The skeletal man points at the suitcase, the books, and the newspapers.

Gholam Ali Khan's eyes pop out. "So, it was you who got away from the police station?"

Interestingly enough, no one says, "you escaped," or "ran away." They all say, "got away."

"I always knew that a boy like you from the slums would end up here at the police station."

It seems like everyone knows the story of my escape.

Turning to the fat man, Gholam Ali Khan says, "Sir, if you ask me, he was a problem child to begin with. Everyone in the neighborhood was bothered by him. There was not a window he hadn't broken. He even disgraced people's honor."

I get so furious that I lose it. "By 'people's honor,' you mean the whores that you brought to your house at noon?"

The fat man's voice explodes. "Shut up, you motherfucker!"

When the occasion demands it, he is a match for Ali the Devil in the use of vulgar language.

Gholam Ali Khan darts an angry look at me, and noisily lets out his breath. His face has turned pale. His lips are tightly pressed against each other. Putting down the file under his arm on the fat man's desk, he asks in a raspy voice, "Am I released, sir?"

"Certainly!"

Gholam Ali Khan leaves, and silence returns to the room. It is not long before the silence is shattered by the fat man's squealing. "From the look of things, you don't have all that clean a record. Bothering people even as a child . . ."

Everything comes back to me: the droshky driver has stuffed cotton balls into the bells around the horses' necks; the muffled sound of the wheels and the horses' hooves on the dust-filled street; the quiet streets are empty of passersby; the weather so hot that even dogs don't dare come out of their holes.

"What do you say, Khaled, we make a ball out of rags, pour some oil on it, set it on fire, and hurl it at his mistress when she comes out?"

I am ready for anything, but I say, "Ebram, let's get all the boys in the neighborhood together and boo her all at once when she is about to leave."

The droshky arrives and stops in front of Gholam Ali Khan's house. Gholam Ali Khan opens the door quickly, and the woman walks up the steps. Astonished, all of us are standing still, staring, when we hear the sound of glass shattering. I see Ebrahim running away . . .

"My duties obligate me," blabbers the fat man, "to guide you and show you the right path. You're young and you can change, after all . . ."

I mumble a thank you under my breath.

"There's another way," he says.

I listen carefully.

"Just give me the names of the people who gave you these books and newspapers, and I promise, I'll fix up your file in such a way that you will be released as soon as you set foot in court."

He pauses for a few moments. His eyes narrow even further as he looks straight at me. He tries to read my face and weigh the effect of his words on me. His blood-colored lips move again. Chirping, he goes on, "And it is in your best interest, because those who have given you these things are really your enemies."

Then he's quiet. I don't say anything either. He waits for me to choose. He searches around his desk, picks up his pack of cigarettes, and lights another one, inhaling the smoke leisurely. "What do you say?" he asks.

"I don't even know what you're talking about," I respond calmly.

His fleshy face suddenly darkens. His voice breaks in his throat. "Do you really intend to deny that the suitcase and the books belong to you?"

"They were not mine to begin with, so I'm not denying anything."

He rings the bell.

The only sound audible in the room is the soft whirring of the ceiling fan.

The server comes in.

"Have Shahri come in!"

All I hear now are Pendar's words. I have heard this beast's name: "He wouldn't even have mercy on his own mother."

My throat becomes awfully dry. Fear sweeps through my body. I know that giving the guys' names would save me from a good five years behind bars. The sound of a door opening jolts me. I turn around.

"Yes, sir?" says Shahri as he walks in.

He's not all that scary looking. Just a man of medium height, with bony cheeks, a long nose, and an unassuming presence.

"Teach the kid what's good for him," the fat man says as he points at me.

There is no hint of cruelty in Shahri's voice as he says, "Your wish is my command." It is not until he motions to me and barks "Get up!" that I see something in his eyes I have rarely seen before. A sort of absentmindedness, a sort of idiocy and powerlessness, or even frozenness, that you find in the eyes of a dead man.

I have heard that he takes pleasure in torturing people. Time to find out.

I get up from the chair.

A smile spreads over the skinny man's dried-up face. He scratches the tip of his nose. Shahri grabs my arm. "Come along!"

I feel exhaustion spread through my entire body. The motion of the fan has dried my sweat. I walk along with Shahri. We leave the room and go down the stairs. The outside heat wraps around my body once again. Shahri doesn't talk at all. We pass through the hallway and the courtyard of the police station; then we go behind the row of solitary cells, till we reach a small, grungy yard. There's a detached room in the corner.

"Get in!"

The moment I set foot in the doorway, I feel Shahri's fist hit the back of my neck. Before I know it, I am thrown into the room on my knees. Behind me, the door shuts violently. I feel dizzy. Everything turns black before my eyes. I come back to myself bit by bit. My neck aches. The veins in my neck throb. I pull myself together and crouch on my knees. Pendar's husky voice echoes in my ears: "He's one of those sick bastards, taking such pleasure in torturing people." I get up from the ground. For a second, I feel like I'm about to faint again. "You won't believe how much he enjoys watching people writhe under the blows of his whip. You can see his eyes sparkle with delight."

The room is square-shaped. Its walls are white. There are no windows. The black iron door is solid. A very small vent, the size of a plate, is installed in the high ceiling. Right next to the vent is an iron hook in place of a ceiling fan. Through the vent, a cluster of the sun's intense rays pours inside, making the room bright. The stench of urine fills the entire room. I walk around. My head feels very heavy. There is a crack in the corner. I crane my neck and peek through it. There is a pit full of shit and flies. Terrified that the flies might swarm me, I step back. I walk to the door. Even the cracks around the doorframe are sealed. I hear footsteps getting closer. I step back. The door opens noisily. It is Shahri, bringing the guard I ditched at the police station. His face darkens with rage the moment he sees me. I look down and keep quiet. These past few hours have been enough to teach me that I'm better off keeping my mouth shut.

Shahri twists my ear. "What do you have to say now?"

I keep silent.

He wrings my earlobe. "Will you come clean now?"

I shake my head.

"Talk!" he yells, letting go of my ear.

"What should I say?"

I can see his gold teeth, discolored and grimy, as he talks. "Say that you escaped from the police station and that the books and newspapers, and that suitcase, are yours!"

I can't help feeling agitated. I can't stop myself from talking back. Words jump out of my mouth. "What else should I confess to?"

Shahri gawks at me. His stare is even more hostile than a rabid dog's. Next thing I know, light flashes before my eyes. "Say that you're a motherfucker!"

I have to stomach it. He's the same as the rest, no better. I just smile. There is still a smile on my face when Shahri's heavy hand comes down on my skin like a whip. My ears ring. Once the dizziness leaves me, I can make out Shahri standing in the doorway. "Give it some serious thought," he says.

The bitterness in his voice bites me. Something about his tone would make even the most pleasant words sound like cusswords or insults.

"I'll be back right at three thirty. I want to see you come to your senses by then," he says, stepping off the threshold and shutting the door behind him.

I lean against the wall, hugging my knees. Shahri's voice rings in my ears: "Three thirty."

Suddenly, the memory of Black-Eyed makes my body tremble. "What are you thinking about?"

I am filled with joy. The hum of the Karun is pleasant. The bitter smell of the palm trees is gratifying. I move closer to Black-Eyed. "Can I see you again?"

She speaks so softly, as if the fragrance of all sweet-smelling flowers springs forth from her breath. "Only on Tuesdays."

I hear Shahri's voice: "At three thirty."

I hear Black-Eyed's voice: "At three thirty."

The patch of light spread on the ground has crept toward the wall. I feel hungry. I wish I'd eaten a few more bites of that bread and cheese this morning. Both my cheeks burn. So does my earlobe.

The whip must be barbed. It pulls up. Makes the slashes open wide. Comes down. Lands on the skin. Feels like it's licking the slashes. A thousand teeth take hold of my flesh. A pair of pliers tugs and pulls at my flesh.

The door of the room opens up violently.

I'll be back right at three thirty.

Shahri appears in the doorway. I know that Black-Eyed is now waiting for me, her eyes searching everywhere for me, those same eyes that fill me with ecstasy.

The patch of light has crept up the wall. The flies swarm out of the pit. The room darkens. Two people bring in a bench, each holding one side of it. The flies swarm toward me and sit on my face and head, pestering me. Shahri doesn't give a damn. He shuts the door. I feel feverish from the buzzing sound of the thousands of flies.

"Sit down on the bench!" orders Shahri in a vengeful tone.

I sit down.

He stands in front of me. His pants pocket bulges. "All right, *comrade!*" he says, stressing the word "comrade."

"Are you ready to give the names of those who gave you the suitcase and the books?"

Everything appears threatening. The shadows standing behind me feel heavy on my neck. I have to say something. "The suitcase is not mine," I say under my breath.

Shahri comes closer. His hand digs into his pocket, producing a twisted whip. It's gray and thick. Shahri's voice is repulsive. It sounds fevered. "Will you give the names of those damn motherfuckers who gave you the books and newspapers?"

"They're not mine . . . I am ready to face my accuser."

Shahri's eyes narrow. Next thing I know, I am being laid down on the bench. One man sits on my neck and another on my legs. They roll my shirt up to my shoulders. I feel suffocated. I fold my arms and lay my hands under my chin. I hold my mouth upward, away from the bench. An annoying gadfly sits on my nose. I can't move my head. The gadfly moves up my cheek, tickling me. I hear a hissing sound. Just like the hiss of a provoked rattlesnake. My back is set on fire. It feels as if a red-hot iron rod has suddenly been put to the skin of my back. Again comes the whistling sound, and again my back feels like it is on fire. I want to scream. I feel suffocated. Pendar's voice echoes in my ears: "If you can just tolerate the pain . . . You got to tolerate it." I bite into the softness of my palm. My teeth sink into my flesh. There is a salty taste in my mouth. It's blood. The whistling sound of the whip and Shahri's breathing blend together. The whip feels jagged. When it lands on the skin, it burns, jerks, and, with thousands of little teeth, pulls back the skin bit by bit.

My entire back feels numb now.

I feel like fading away. My teeth loosen their grip on the palm of my hand. A moan is muted in my throat. My lips taste salty. I hear Shahri's breathing. I hear the whistling sound of the whip coming from far away, from the bottom of a deep valley. Now it feels like the whip comes down on a mass of cotton. My entire back is numb. I realize that Shahri has stopped whipping me. I cannot move. I hear the sound of a door closing coming from miles away. My arms drop off the bench and just hang there. My right leg falls from the bench too. The buzzing sound of the flies echoes in my ears.

It must be midnight. It's completely dark in the room. Coming back to myself, I find I'm still lying on the bench, like a corpse. I try to use my hands to prop myself up. My entire back jerks and aches as I move. Blood has congealed wherever the whip left its marks. With every move thousands of needles pierce my back. I struggle desperately until I finally manage to slide my hands under my chest. I can breathe a bit more comfortably now. I feel dizzy. I feel like vomiting. My stomach is empty. I did not eat anything for lunch or dinner. I feel a gnawing sensation in my stomach. Any minute I will vomit. My guts heave up into my throat, leaving a bitter taste behind. My mouth is dry. My head spins; it feels swollen and as large as the room itself. I try hard to pull my leg up. Flakes of dried blood crack and shift. I am on fire. I think it's best not to move. Pendar's black eyes overwhelm my mind. I hear his voice: "If you can stand it for just two days, it will be over . . . but it really takes a man to stand those two days." My chest, ribs, and stomach ache from lying too long on the hard bench. What I really want is to sit myself up somehow, so that I might feel better. Maybe I would feel less of this pain. I clench my teeth, close my eyes, and quickly push myself up and sit at the edge of the bench. The layer of congealed blood cracks. Fresh blood oozes out through the tears. My shirt slides down over the wounds. I die a thousand times before I am able to remove my shirt. My head feels as heavy as lead, wobbling on my neck. I fall off the edge of the bench. If only I could find something to hold on to. I cannot hold myself up. I lay both my palms on the edge of the bench and cautiously slide down to my knees.

I lay my hands against the bench and place my forehead on them. The throbbing in the bones of my chest subsides, but my back is still ablaze, as if it is tied to the dome of a burning oven. My ears start to ring. A cool breeze blows in through the vent in the ceiling. Summer is winding down, and the smell of fall comes at night. It gets chilly after midnight. Mother's sad eyes fill the entire room. I hear her voice, soft and sad. "You're still too young to understand what it means to make a mistake in life . . . You don't know the ways of the world yet."

"I know, Mother," I answer quickly. "God willing, I'll start attending school in the fall."

I feel a bit better. The breeze blowing in through the vent in the ceiling helps. I would feel less pain if I could just hold still. Suddenly, my heart leaps. "Three thirty in the afternoon." She must have thought a thousand crazy thoughts when I didn't show up. Her eyes, those eyes that bring one to one's knees in submission, must have wandered around the entire thirty-meter-wide street.

"I might get arrested any minute."

I'm glad that at least I told her what I've been dealing with.

How agitated and anxious I am. If I could stand the bench upright and get out of here through the vent in the ceiling—hit the road, as they say—how pathetic Ali the Devil would look.

I lift my head up. The vent is as big as a plate. I shouldn't even think about that.

The sky is a dark blue. Through the vent I can see a few stars. I wish Black-Eyed and I had made a vow that whenever we are apart from each other we will both look at the moon. My neck becomes tired. I take my eyes off the vent and lay my forehead on my hands. The cold breeze coming in through the hole in the ceiling drifts over my neck. I hear footsteps. I prick up my ears. The footsteps are getting closer. They are heavy. My body begins to tremble. The footsteps have reached the door.

If there's whipping again, if there are handcuffs again . . . I hear Pendar's voice: "Sometimes they hang a few weights from the handcuffs."

I lose all of my fortitude.

"Weights?"

He encourages me, reviving my confidence. "But one can endure anything."

The door opens slowly. The silhouette of a man appears in the frame of the door. He's holding a lantern in his hand. He is lit up to his waist. He looks like Ali the Devil. Stepping forward, he shuts the door behind him. It is *him*. If I could, I would jump on him and tear his throat out with my teeth.

He puts the lantern down on the bench, shifts a bit from one foot to the other, then sits on the edge of the bench. I lay my forehead on my hands, determined not to talk to him at all. He is not armed. This is the first time I've seen him without his jacket. He starts to talk, as if to himself. "If I knew you were going to end up dealing with that bastard, Shahri, I would have come to an agreement with you somehow."

They even curse each other, apparently. With those foul mouths of theirs, I wouldn't be surprised if they even cuss out their own wives.

My forehead still rests on my hands. My lips, like two pieces of lead, are sealed. I have every intention of resisting.

He lights a cigarette. "Do you smoke?"

I keep quiet. Holding up the light and looking at my back, he says, "Oh, oh, oh . . . look what the bastard has done to him!"

Putting the light back down on the bench, he takes a deep drag of his cigarette and asks, "You don't wanna talk to me?"

I just keep quiet.

He says, "Look, I'm not as cruel as you think. I never wanted this to happen to you."

"Leave me alone," I grumble deep down in my throat.

His voice is fatigued. In a gentle tone he says, "I've just come to help you. I have brought you food . . . I wanna teach you how to get rid of that bastard. I know the trick."

I am still quiet.

He goes on, "It hurts me when I see your back like this. Don't let things get worse."

I lift my head up and breathe noisily. His eyes look dark in the faint light of the lantern. "What do you want from me?" I grumble deep down in my throat.

He blows smoke out and says, "You can't do anything for me right now." He pauses and takes another drag of his cigarette. I keep looking at him. He continues, "Now, it is me who is able to help you in a thousand ways. I can get you out of here and let you go, without expecting anything from you."

I cannot read his face in the faint light of the lantern.

He lingers a bit, takes another drag from his cigarette, and plays with the smoke. I am filled with so much hate.

"You are free."

The man is incredulous.

The prison guard's tone is kind. "You are free to go wherever you'd like to."

The man moves a bit. "Can I really go?"

The prison guard smiles.

The man is skinny. His beard is long and his eyes are sunken.

"Of course you can . . . Get moving!"

The man breathes noisily. Fresh air entices him. He looks at the deceptive eyes of the prison guard. The prison guard's tone is kind. "Come on, I brought you out of the cell for this . . . Come on, get moving."

The man starts to limp away hesitantly. Straightening up his bent back, he turns around and looks at the prison guard. The prison guard presses the cold barrel of the gun against his hand. The man picks up his pace. The prison guard stands still, without blinking an eye. A smile lights his face. The man starts to run. Next comes the sound of a shot. The muffled sound of a slug landing in flesh. The man falls to his knees. The prison guard darts toward him. Blood oozes out of his chest.

"He was running away; I warned him . . . I had to shoot . . ."

Ali the Devil's sleepy voice pulls me out of the story.

"Aren't you going to say something?"

I shake with hatred. Words claw at my throat, tearing my mouth open to find their way out. "And there must be a few gunmen waiting for me outside the police station . . ."

Ali the Devil's eyes pop out.

"You have an excuse too," I add.

He takes a deep drag of his cigarette and just listens.

"He was trying to run away . . . We warned him . . . He paid no mind . . . We had to shoot him . . ." I hold the rest of my words and breathe noisily. I lay my head on my hands. I hear Ali the Devil's voice. "You are so paranoid."

"Leave me alone," I mutter.

He lights up another cigarette with the end of the burned-out one between his fingers. "You might have every right not to trust me, but to this extent?!"

The smoke is suffocating me. The breeze coming in through the vent has become colder.

"In that case, if I bring you food, you must think that I have poisoned it too," he adds.

"How can I trust you with food when you made such a racket over the cup of tea they brought me in the morning?"

He gets up from the bench, and without saying a word, picks up the lantern and walks away, grumbling.

He stops at the door. "You're not sensible at all. But if you think you're hungry, I can bring you food."

I have no idea what he is up to.

He opens the door.

"I might wanna eat something," I say.

He walks out of the room and closes the door.

Now I can only see a small patch of the sky, and while it is empty of any stars, it is illuminated with pale moonlight. The moon should be close to the vent in the ceiling.

My knees are aching. They would maybe feel better if I could sit cross-legged. I use my left hand as support and drag my right leg from under my body. I pull out my left leg and sit cross-legged. My thighs, my bottom, and knees feel more relaxed. I let my bare arms fall onto the bench and lay my cheek down on my left arm.

The door opens. Ali the Devil comes in holding the same lantern as before in one hand and a pot of food in the other. I eat a spoonful. It tastes like cold noodles and vegetable soup. I choke on the first bite, so I roll it around in my mouth. I have such a hard time swallowing it. I try to eat a few more spoonfuls quickly. It is making me sick. It's spicy. I stop eating.

Ali the Devil sits on the corner of the bench. "Do you want me to eat it to convince you that it's good?" he asks.

"I can't eat it . . . It's making me sick," I say, pausing as I speak. The food is in my throat.

"It feels like that when your stomach is empty . . . Wait a minute and then eat it."

My bowels grumble.

Ali the Devil begins to talk. He brings up Shahri again. "If you fall into his hands again, he'll make you wish you were dead." He pauses for a few seconds, then carries on. "I am sure the last thing you want is to die under the bastard's whip . . . He'll be back tomorrow, no doubt about it."

He pauses for a few seconds. I feel a bit more at ease now. He rambles on. "There's not a grain of mercy in that bastard's heart."

I start to eat again. Next thing I know I am cleaning out the bottom of the pot. My stomach feels like it's bulging.

Ali the Devil keeps at it. "There's no reason why you shouldn't trust me. You made a mistake not showing up on Friday."

I rest my cheek on my hand and look at him. His words are jumbled. "What do you think I want from you? Huh? . . . You think I am happy with what I'm doing? There's no such thing . . . You should consider me one of your friends. If you'd trust me, I could help you a great deal."

I feel much better. The bitter taste in my throat and the dryness in my mouth are gone. All I can think about is the fact that I must stay as still as possible in order to avoid disturbing the dried blood and wounds.

Ali the Devil is garrulous. "If tomorrow Shahri were to get your hands in the handcuffs, I doubt you could stand it for an hour . . . The bastard will torture you so much, until you come clean."

I know he's trying to puncture my confidence. I take a deep breath and ask, "Man to man, why is it you feel sorry for me and wanna help me?"

He doesn't respond. Just thinks his words over. His green eyes have taken on a much darker shade in the pale light of the lantern. Finally, he says, "I am just thinking of why you should go through pain when you can avoid it!"

"Do you also realize that you caused me this pain in the first place?" My words bite. I close my eyes. Now that I have eaten, my eyelids feel heavy with sleep.

Ali the Devil doesn't let go. "I never thought you were going to end up like this."

I get the urge to make him feel guilty. "Now that I have ended up like this, your conscience must be bothering you."

He murmurs to himself a bit, then says, "Maybe . . . I don't know . . . I feel like you're making fun of me . . . but to be honest with you . . . that's true. I am unhappy about that."

He speaks in such an intimate and kind tone that it leaves me with no choice but to believe him. "So you wanna help me to appease your own conscience?"

Either he believes it or he sees fit to pretend he believes it. "Yeah, you could put it that way, if you wanted."

My voice grows husky with sleep. "You know . . ." I move my head a bit on my arm and say, "I am sleepy now . . . I can't think at all about what I'm supposed to do or what I'm supposed to say—"

"But it's not like I want much from you," he cuts me short.

"If you give me some time, till tomorrow, I might be able to understand what exactly you want from me."

"But you have only tonight!" he snaps.

I am surprised. "What do you mean?"

"I mean, if you agree to my offer, I won't let Shahri come to you again tomorrow," he says.

I look into his eyes for a few seconds. And without saying anything, I close mine. I hear him say, "You don't wanna answer me?"

My lips part from each other slightly. "Tomorrow."

"As you wish." There's disappointment in his voice. I hear a match being struck. "But tomorrow . . . ," he adds—the smoke of the cigarette hits my nose—"before expecting me, you should expect Shahri to come."

I draw my right hand forward and hide my face between my arms.

He gets up from the bench and picks up the lantern. First, I hear his footsteps, then it is the sound of the iron door opening and closing. Once the door is closed, I look at the vent in the ceiling. It is dawn. I take a deep breath and close my eyes.

I wake up to the sound of the door opening. I have spent a few hours half asleep and half awake. When the door opens, the morning sunshine pours into the room, striking my eyes. The hunchbacked old man is standing in the doorway. His large head wobbles on his neck as he drags his small, bent body forward on his lame legs. He has brought me bread and cheese, as well as a cup of tea. He lays the tray down on the bench. From what he tells me, I gather that Ali the Devil had him bring me breakfast.

"You can't ever be sure what he's up to," he mumbles, catching the fly sitting on his nose. "One day he makes such a fuss over why you have given him food," he says, squishing the fly and then going on, "and next day he himself comes and asks me to give him breakfast."

He looks at my back. The wrinkles on the old man's face become more pronounced. His old eyes narrow. "Those unbelievers!"

He goes to close the door. The sun's rays vanish. Having shut the door, he comes and stands over me. "Take a gulp of tea, it'll soften your throat."

I lift the cup from the tray. I feel full from the soup I ate last night. I sip the tea bit by bit.

"Don't you want to eat some bread and cheese?"

"I can't." I shake my head.

The hunchbacked old man's voice trembles as he talks. His tone is very kind. "So how do you expect to get any strength now?"

He sounds like Amu Bandar. It makes me sad, remembering him. "It's the beginning of winter, and Oussa Haddad is still in a foreign land . . . alas!"

My father stands before me. His Adam's apple shifts up and down, as if he's swallowing his saliva. He doesn't speak. He just stares at me. Amu Bandar takes a drag from his pipe. His voice trembles. "But, Son, just remember, if you ever need anything, don't hesitate to let me know."

The hunchbacked old man sits on the bench. "Do you have a message for anyone?"

Again it is Amu Bandar's voice. "You know what, Khaled?" he says, gulping down the over-brewed tea, "We, the poor, should help one another. If we don't help each other stand, we'll all fall down."

I look at the pale eyes of the hunchbacked old man. I hear him ask again, "You don't have any message for anyone, any family?"

My heart trembles. His large head wobbles as he talks. I am touched by his sense of compassion. I am about to say something, but Pendar's voice echoes in my ears: "You should learn not to get carried away by emotions when you are engaged in combat." My lips stay sealed.

The old man is waiting. A bulging vein runs from his elbow down to the back of his hand. His temples are dry.

"Why do you want to do such a thing for me?" I ask him.

"Why shouldn't I do it?" he answers kindly.

What if Ali the Devil has instructed him to get some information for him? Then again, what about yesterday, when he gave me breakfast and Ali the Devil made such a big fuss over it? Besides, what message can I give him to take for me? Mother must have died a thousand times over by now. It's best that she not know anything about what has happened to me. And I can't give the old man a message for Black-Eyed. And the guys, for sure, must have found out about everything on their own.

"Think of me as your father," I hear the old man say. The skin under his right eye pulses. "If you have a message, I can take it for you. I have done this for others too."

"No, Father, I have no message for anyone."

"You have no one to pull strings for you?" His dry lips part from each other.

"Nobody." I shake my head.

I sip the last drops of the sweet tea.

Again, he says, "Take a bite at least."

"I don't feel like it."

I put the cup down on the tray. The old man looks at me for a few seconds, then rises, picks up the tray, and leaves the room.

I pull myself up and sit on the bench. My knees are stiff. The burning pain of my back is a bit more tolerable. I let myself drown in stray thoughts. "You think I am happy with what I'm doing?" Ali the Devil's voice rings in my ears. "You should consider me one of your friends." The sound of footsteps catches my attention. I hear the sound of the door opening. Ali the Devil stands on the threshold, smiling. He comes in. "Hope you slept good!"

Already he's pushing it. I know he won't let go. I shrug my shoulders.

"Did they bring you tea?" he asks.

I nod. I have decided to avoid talking as much as possible. He sits next to me. The smile doesn't leave his lips. "So, this is tomorrow."

"I thought I was supposed to expect Shahri." The words spring out of my mouth.

The smile on his lips withers away. "You can't wait for that?"

"No!"

He yawns, looks straight at me, and says, "You know, Khaled, it's very simple what I'm offering you." He gets quiet, as if searching for the right words. "If you promise me to keep me informed of your plans, I promise you I'll have all the evidence against you destroyed, and you'll walk out of the police station by noon."

I stop myself from laughing. "Do you have such power at the police station?"

He exhales loudly. "If you cooperate with me, yes, I do."

A smile sets on my lips.

Ali the Devil continues with what he was saying. "I don't know how I can make you trust me!" He changes the course of the conversation.

"Look, Khaled, I'm not asking too much. I don't even want you to give me anyone's name."

A gleam of sunlight shines on the wall through the vent in the ceiling.

"I give you my word of honor that nobody will ever know of our agreement . . . ," Ali the Devil says, buying into the hope that I am falling for his words. "I promise to keep it between us . . . and in return, I'll support you directly or indirectly. And nobody will be harmed."

He presses his lips against each other for a second, trying to read the impact of his words in my face. He then goes on, "I don't think I can be more frank than this."

"Yes, of course." I nod.

"So you agree?" he asks hastily.

He looks foolish. An idiotic smile has spread across his lips. He struggles to give his words a tinge of wittiness. In a friendly manner he says, "Of course, this time I will not be fooled. You fooled me once, and that's enough for me not to ever be fooled by you again."

He wriggles in his seat a bit and lights a cigarette. He is trying hard to express his words in an intimate manner, to have them sound funnier and less threatening. "This time you should guarantee your word." He bursts out laughing, a fake laugh. "All right?" he says, laughing again. "I don't mean guarantee . . ." He takes a drag of his cigarette and blows the smoke into my face. "I mean to say that we'll write something on paper promising not to ever betray each other's trust again, and we'll both sign it."

He looks so credulous that foolishness exudes from every pore of his body.

I crave a cigarette, so I ask, "Can I have a cigarette?"

"Cigarette? Ask for my life!"

I laugh.

He offers me the pack of Homa cigarettes. I don't know why everyone in the police station smokes Homa cigarettes.

"Take it!"

I take a cigarette. He strikes a match for me. I roll the smoke in my mouth and let it out. The patch of light creeps down the wall, making the room even darker.

"You are quiet!"

I play with the smoke. The few flies that have come out from the pit are hovering around my back.

"You are quiet!?" he repeats.

I look at him. "What do you mean?"

He looks surprised. His eyes are about to pop out. "What do *I* mean?" Taking a drag at his cigarette, he continues, "You know exactly what I mean." His voice has lost the vigor it had a moment ago. "I mean about my offer."

I keep quiet for a few seconds. But my stubborn nature won't let me be. "What offer are you talking about?" I ask calmly.

And I say it in such an indifferent manner that I can imagine what it would be like to suddenly turn on an icy cold shower over Ali the Devil's bare body. It's clear that he's bowled over. The flies sitting on my neck are pestering me. I shake my shirt slightly. The flies fly. Ali the Devil stares at me. He looks so foolish. Embarrassment has colored his lips. Bending down toward me, he grumbles through his clenched teeth. "Have I been rambling on to deaf ears all along?"

I can't stop myself. I burst out laughing. Ali the Devil is frozen, just like a statue made of stone. He is staring at me, his mouth agape. He throws away the cigarette butt and lights up another mindlessly. He stands up, looking completely dazed. He looks like he doesn't see me. As if talking to himself, he mumbles, "I am such a fool to pity you."

He walks out of the room. As he closes the door, fear sweeps over me. I should expect Shahri any minute.

Shahri is before me, sitting on a stool. His eyes are motionless. Just like the eyes of a slaughtered sheep. I feel the heavy shadows of the two stout men standing over me. The very same men who laid me down on the bench. I haven't seen their faces in full view yet. But the image of their tall and hefty bodies, bony cheeks, large black mustaches, and dark complexions is burned in my memory. They look as if they are twins.

Shahri plays with a whip made from the woven hair of a cow's tail. His long nose covers his lips. I can't read anything in his expression. The whip he has in his hand is different from the one he shredded my back with. It's short, and thicker as it moves upward, with two wide strips of leather attached to its end. The whip that shredded my back was gray; this one is brown.

"Who gave you the suitcase?" Shahri demands.

I know very well that there is no point in answering. I know very well that even if I repeat a hundred times that the suitcase is not mine, he still won't accept it.

He winds the whip around his hand as he talks. There's something in his tone that chills my body.

"You don't wanna talk?"

"What should I say?" I reply under my breath.

This time, there's fire in his tone. "I hope you know that we've detained that pretty girl!"

I am on fire with rage.

"I mean," he goes on, "that pretty girl of yours."

Blood rushes to my face. Is it possible that Ali the Devil has done such a thing? Is it possible to arrest a girl without any reason whatsoever? What if they have arrested Black-Eyed? What if she has told them everything I told her at the oil company sports club? I lose all hope entirely. The bastard has touched my weak spot. I have no doubt that if he focuses on this weak point of mine a bit more, I'll give in. To save Black-Eyed, I'll tell them whatever I know.

My entire body is shaking. How would I ever look into her reproachful black eyes? No! . . . Leave her alone . . . Swiftly, I come to my senses. They must be bluffing. I try to calm myself. I have to be strong. I can't lose it, at least not until things are clear. I mustn't be fooled.

"You're quiet, kid?!" remarks Shahri.

"What?"

His eyes look like those of a cat. A ridiculous smile reveals his nasty gold teeth. My throat is as dry as a matchstick.

"Why don't you say anything?"

"What should I say?" My voice has become raspy.

Tickling my forehead with the tip of his whip, he says, "I'm sure you don't want me to slash the pretty hips of that pretty one, do you?"

It's hard not to spit in his face.

"Ha . . . what do you say, what?!"

Somehow, words find their way out of my choked throat. "I don't want a lot of things." I know I should not have said it, but I did.

"Then talk if you don't want that!"

The flies are sitting on my neck. I shift my position to shoo them away.

"Say something!"

"If I had anything to tell you, I would have told you yesterday."

I see stars before my eyes. The whip leaves its mark on my neck. I don't even scream. The pain is not worse than yesterday's. I look straight into the frozen eyes of Shahri. If he has any sense of decency, he will see the hatred in my eyes. I bite the corner of my lip. The whites of Shahri's eyes look yellow, just like the eyes of a wolf suffering from jaundice. I can see his grimy gold teeth.

"But you got a lot to tell, and you will."

I feel like my face is revealing signs of my humiliation. I'm afraid that I'll spit into his face any minute.

"Do you want me to bring the pretty one here?" He is at it again.

"You can do anything you want to," I tell him.

Shahri squints his right eye. My neck is pushed down toward my chest and a fist comes down on it. The small wrinkles in Shahri's face deepen, as if he's about to laugh. I feel the burning sensation of red-hot iron rods piercing my heart as he talks.

"Do you enjoy her alone, or do you share her with your friends too?"

I bite my tongue to stop myself from talking back. I am filled with rage. My earlobes have turned red. My temples are bursting. I struggle to control myself. If he finds out how weak I am about Black-Eyed, he'll make me feel miserable. There's a tumult going on inside me. I want to cry out. The bastard is torturing me too much. I would have been better off being slashed by his whip.

"Come on, already, say something!" His voice breaks in his throat.

I press my lips together. Once again, he squints one eye, and so my neck is pushed down against my chest.

This time Shahri's voice is filled with ridicule. He obviously enjoys playing with me. Just like a cat that has a shocked mouse between its claws.

"What would you say if I had them bring the pretty one here so you could sleep with her right here, till tomorrow morning?"

My heart is on fire. I can no longer control myself. "Do you do these sorts of things too?" The words spring out of my mouth.

He leaps at me from the stool. His whip lashes my cheeks and face. "You motherfucker! How dare you talk back?!"

I feel good. He continues to strike me nonstop. I writhe under his blows. The dried blood crusted on my back and neck opens at a thousand spots and fresh blood oozes out.

He stops beating me and starts to pace and curse, all the while calling me names that I have never ever heard in my life. I realize from all his agitation that he has lied about Black-Eyed. If they had their hands on her, he could have easily brought her before me so he could do whatever he wanted to do to me.

He doesn't stop pacing and cussing.

Suddenly, he's standing in front of me, shaking the tip of his whip in my face and calling me all kinds of names more suitable for himself.

"I'll have a donkey fuck your mother. I have never seen a brash motherfucker like you."

I have never heard such a foul mouth in my life. Now I know why he has such a bad reputation. It is for the things he does that others won't. Compared to him, I hail Ali the Devil.

Shahri walks toward the door. He motions to the men standing behind me. All three of them leave the room and slam the door behind them.

I draw my hand over my cheeks and neck. They're swollen from the whipping. They're burning. But however great the pain may be, it's less than the pain he instilled in me with his words.

I think he went to fetch the heavy manacles.

"One can stand anything in life."

Finally, it's happened to me too. I've withstood it so far. I'll withstand the rest too. But I know that the torment my silence inflicts is worse than all the whippings my face, neck, and back have received.

I hear a jumble of footsteps. The iron door is flung open violently. All three of them come in. Shahri is holding a looped piece of rope in his hand. They have brought a two-sided stepladder too. I have no idea what they are up to. I sit on the bench, looking at them. The flies bite my shoulders. The patch of light has crept further down. It won't be long before it drops from the wall to the floor. Noon is about to arrive. The three of them are busy, working at such a fast pace that they must have done this a thousand times.

They place the ladder in the middle of the room, right below the vent. Shahri climbs up quickly. He loops the rope around the hook next to the vent and pulls it down. Are they going to hang me right here? There is a noose at the end of the rope. Is it possible that they could just hang me, without any trial? I am baffled as to what they're really up to. Pulling down the end of the rope, they put the ladder aside.

Shahri comes and stands in my face. The shadow of the angel of torture is weighing heavily on my shoulders. My eyes are fixed on the noose at the end of the rope lying on the floor, which seems as if it's slithering its way toward me like a snake.

Shahri's voice explodes out of his mouth like a shot. "Blindfold him!"

A piece of black fabric covers my eyes and is tied behind my head. I hear the heavy sound of Shahri's footsteps. It sounds like he is pacing. He walks to the end of the room and comes back. The sound of his footsteps amplifies my apprehension. If only I knew their intention, it would be much easier to go through this. The sound of the footsteps grows fainter.

"All right . . ."

He pauses for a second and then continues. "Who gave you that suitcase?"

I feel the noose lying at my feet. It feels like it's ready to strike, like a snake, moving its needlelike tongue in and out.

"Who gave you the suitcase?"

"I've told you a hundred times it's not mine."

"It's yours and you'll admit that . . ." His voice becomes gruff.

"It's not."

My neck is on fire. He has struck it with the whip.

"You're playing with your own life."

I don't respond.

"I can easily hang you right here and dump your body in a sewage pit."

I feel like the noose is dancing over my head.

Shahri goes on, ". . . And I can also let you go and live your life."

He sounds like Ali the Devil now.

"What I am offering you is very simple . . ." Shahri keeps talking. "You've wasted so much of my time."

Ali the Devil's voice is in my ears: "Just promise me that . . ."

"They will put you in such a state of terror . . . ," Pendar's voice rings in my ears.

"If you don't wanna talk, then write your will." Shahri's voice comes from deep in his throat.

I wish I could shoot at him all the curses in the world.

He grabs my earlobe. "You don't wanna come clean, huh?"

I just keep quiet. He lets go of my ear. I hear a rustling sound. Then Shahri's voice rises again. "I will count to ten."

He paces and goes on talking. "I just want the names of those who gave you the suitcase. That's all!"

He paces to the end of the room and comes back. The sound of footsteps ceases.

"I'll count to ten." He starts to count: "One, two . . ."

I hear Aunt Ra'na's voice: "Sister, how stubborn is this kid?!"

"Three . . . four . . ."

It is Father's voice: "If you hadn't covered up for him so often, he wouldn't have become this unruly."

Mother weeps quietly.

"Five . . . six . . ."

I know that when I become stubborn, there's no stopping it.

"Seven . . . eight . . ."

Past memories come alive. I am rolling on the ground. I have ripped my shirt, and I am hitting my head against the wall. I have made up my mind not to go to Aunt Ra'na's house.

"This child is so spoiled," Father's voice reprimands.

Mother weeps as she answers him. "He gets worse if you try to stop him."

"Nine . . ."

Shahri hovers right over my head. "Still don't want to talk?"

My lips are pressed against one another like two rocks.

Shahri's voice explodes: "Ten."

Before I can make a move, the noose is pulled tightly around my ankles, and I am being pulled up. Just like the body of a slaughtered sheep hanging from a butcher's hook. My arms dangle. I lift my head up. My neck gets tired quickly. I feel the blood pooling in my skull. I try to hold my head up again, but my neck soon gets tired. My ears start to buzz. The pooling blood is forcing my eyes to close and my temples to throb. I feel like my face has lost all its color. I hear Shahri's voice, but it sounds like it's coming from a deep well. "I can do these kinds of things too."

The buzzing in my ears grows into a whistling sound.

Do you want me to have the pretty one sleep with you till tomorrow morning?

Do you do these kinds of things too? The words spring out of my mouth.

"I can do these kinds of things too." Shahri's voice comes from the bottom of a well.

They untie the black fabric over my eyes. I cannot see at all. Everything is dark. My head feels swollen. Blood ripples inside my skull. My head has become the size of the room, the size of the police station, the size of the entire town. My temples are being pounded with a hammer, with an ax, with a club.

All the voices, the talk, the memories are soaked in waves of blood. My temples are bursting. The veins running through my neck have swelled so much that I am about to choke. Suddenly blood squirts out of my nostrils like water coming from the spout of a ewer.

The swarm of flies brings me back to myself. I open my eyes. The room spins around my head. I find myself lying on the ground like a corpse. Dried blood covers my nose and mouth. The smell of alcohol wafts through the room. They have given me injections. I can feel the swollen injection sites, three puffy spots on my hip, close to each other. I must have been struggling with death before they saved me. I have no idea what time it is. I close my eyes. The flies are pestering me. They bite me through the dried blood caked on my shoulders. I can't move. I wish I could turn over and lie on my back. Hunger, pain, and dizziness annoy me. My ribs are killing me. I draw my left arm under my chest. I struggle. My arm is no good. I struggle again. I manage to lift my chest off the ground. I gather all my strength in my arms and lift my chin up. The bench lies before me. The dizziness diminishes a bit. I try to grab the legs of the bench. I might feel better if I could sit up. I catch sight of the patch of light on the floor. It should be before noon. A day must have passed. When they hanged me the patch of light was in that same spot. My mouth is so dry that I can hardly open it, as if I had eaten colocynth. There is a sour taste in my mouth. I grab the legs of the bench and pull myself up. I manage to sit on my knees and stretch my arms on the bench. I lay my forehead on my arms. My ears start to buzz. The flies buzz around me. I feel like there is a beehive in my ears and that hive has been set on fire.

The door opens. Someone comes in. I don't even look up. I have no energy. My face is hidden in my arms. The bench shakes. He must be sitting down. Silence dominates. The smell of smoke turns my stomach. His voice mixes with the buzzing in my ears. A very familiar voice. "Why are you so stubborn?"

I don't respond. Now that I have made it to this point, I won't part my lips to confess even if I am being butchered.

"Aman Aqa has asked me to help you," he says.

I realize that it's Gholam Ali Khan. His voice comes from far away, deep in my memory: "He was mischievous from childhood, sir . . ."—his blond mustache moves—". . . everyone in the neighborhood was bothered by him . . ."

He must have come to dig something out of me just like Ali the Devil. His raisin-green eyes glare in their sockets. They have all joined together to make me confess. His words find their way through the buzzing of thousands of bees. "It's such a pity that a young man like you should sacrifice himself for no reason."

I should hurt him good by being silent.

"I feel bad for you."

Memories of the past come to my mind. It is sunset. Mehdi the Grocer is pleading with him. "Gholam Ali Khan, forgive him, please."

Khaj Tofiq begs: "Gholam Ali Khan, he made a mistake; you should forgive him."

Habib the Baker kisses his cheek. "He won't do such a thing again."

His raisin-green eyes are cold. He pays no mind to any of them. The police officer has taken hold of my hand. Gholam Ali Khan is clean shaven. Habib the Baker has just lit the kerosene lamp. Standing at the door, Mother weeps. Khalifeh tries to stop him, but to no avail.

In my mind, I fire at him all the filthy names he's called me.

Gholam Ali Khan's voice mingles with the buzzing sound in my ears. "Aren't you hungry?"

He starts the same way Ali the Devil did.

"Aman Aqa had me promise him I'd do anything I could for you."

I wish I could yell at him. I want to tell him to go to hell.

"Do you want me to bring you some food?" He speaks very softly.

The smell of cigarette smoke clings to him, making me sick.

"Don't you want to talk to me?"

I refuse to answer him.

Shifting his position on the bench, he says, "Don't be stubborn, Khaled!"

Words find their way out of my dry throat. "I have nothing to tell you."

He doesn't say anything.

I add, "Shahri knows this all too well."

He rises from the bench. There's a trace of embarrassment in his tone. "I thought you'd like me to help you."

I feel good. I know that the fact that he has become embarrassed is bugging him. He walks toward the door, saying, "Look who I pity."

I hear the door open and close. I don't even bother to look at him.

I lift my head up from my arms and look at the patch of light. It has crept down to the foot of the wall. It should be Thursday—that is, if I'm not mistaken. Ali the Devil arrested me on Monday night. They whipped me on Tuesday. And then I was hung like a chunk of meat at the butcher's. I must have been completely unconscious through an entire day and night.

I look at the iron hook in the ceiling. They have taken the rope off it. Here and there on the floor, patches of blood have dried. I imagine that there must have been more blood on the floor—blood gushed out of my nose like water from a fountain. They must have wiped it clean.

I lay my head on my arms again. If Shahri doesn't show up today, he won't come tomorrow either. Hunger and weakness are killing me. I wish I had accepted Gholam Ali Khan's offer to bring me food. I am mad at my own stubbornness. Maybe Gholam Ali Khan was telling the truth, and Aman Aqa has asked him to help me after all. I know that Bolur Khanom has done everything she can for me. I know that she has been bugging Aman Aqa over the past few days. I know that she has been complaining to him day and night. As long as Mother has not parted from her soul by now, I will consider myself lucky.

I hear footsteps approaching. I lift my head up from my arms. The door to the room opens. Someone pushes a copper bowl inside and then closes the door again. It must be food.

I use my hands to support my body and drag my butt toward the bowl. My mouth has started to water. The bowl is brimming with lentils and rice. I rub my fingers clean against my pants and start to eat. The rice is full of gravel. The hair on my body stands up at the crunching sound the gravel makes between my teeth. It seems like they have poured a handful of the stuff in the rice. It doesn't go down my throat. I grind the first bite until it becomes like soup. Then I swallow it with all the tiny bits of gravel mixed in. I don't grind the next morsels. I just roll them inside my mouth and send them down my throat. I eat half of the bowl of rice. My stomach starts to grumble. I drag my butt back to the bench. I rest my shoulders against the bench and stretch my legs. Soon, my eyelids feel heavy. The buzzing inside my ears has gradually ceased. My eyelids fall down.

I open my eyes to complete darkness. I cannot see anything. I don't know how long I have been asleep. I look up. I can see a small patch of sky through the vent in the ceiling. A bright star twinkles over the vent. My heart fills with sadness. I long to see Black-Eyed. I become restless. I want to shout. I want to beat my head against the iron door until I pass out. The star is moving out of my sight. My heart is heavy with sorrow. I feel like walking. I think it might help me calm down. I get to my feet. Eating food and sleeping have made me feel a bit better. I am dizzy for a brief moment, so I sit down on the bench and hold up my right leg. I bend my knee a few times, taking pleasure in the motion, forcing pain and exhaustion out of the joint. I try to stand up again. This time I am able keep myself upright. I start to walk slowly. My legs tremble. I limp to the iron door. I press my ear to the door and feel its coolness. I turn around and walk to the other end of the room. I am about to vomit. I think it's best if I sit down. I squat down next to the wall. The breeze coming in through the vent carries with it the scent of fall.

Over the past two days, I have devoured all of the lentils and rice. Gravel is stuck between my teeth. "If you are hungry, you'll eat rocks too," I remember Mother saying. Only God knows what's going to happen to me. After Gholam Ali Khan left and the bowl of lentils and rice was pushed inside the room, nobody has come at all. The patch of light from the vent in the ceiling has just fallen on the wall. I pick up my shirt, shake the dust off it, and sling it over my shoulders. It no longer hurts as much when the shirt rubs against the wounds. I have walked around so much inside the four walls of this room that my legs are beginning to ache. The patch of light slides down the wall to the floor. I want to talk to someone so bad that it's driving me mad. My heart feels heavy. The walls of the room weigh on my heart like a mountain. I sit in the patch of light and look up. I breathe in the sunlight. I stuff my lungs and then exhale noisily. I stare at the sky through the pleated tresses of the sun's rays. A moving black spot has marked the blue of the sky. I imagine a pigeon soaring or a hawk flying into the heart of the sky. The black spot gets smaller. It disappears from the circular view of the vent. Again, the bright patch of sky shines like transparent turquoise. I hear two sparrows chirping beautifully, playing on the edge of the hole. They peek in. The sun is burning my forehead and cheeks. The sparrows step back from the edge of the vent. I can only hear the sound of their lively chirping echoing inside the room. Again I can see the black spot in the sky. It's plunging down, becoming larger. It's not a pigeon. I feel dizzy. I close my eyes. I want to get up and shout. I hear the door to the room open. I move a bit, but I don't dare turn around. Someone steps inside. The sound of footsteps ceases. "Get up!" The voice is not familiar. I don't move. The voice gets huskier. "I said, get up." I can see the sparrows once more. The black spot has soared again. The sparrows are craning their necks and making a lot of noise for no reason. The black spot has flown so high that it's invisible. The person standing behind me pokes my hip with the tip of his foot. "I am talking to you."

Using my hands for support, I get to my feet. A tall man stands before me, his eyes like two balls of fire. His mustache is as thick as a fox's tail. His cheeks are chubby. "Come with me!" Thousands of stray thoughts cross my mind. The image of the heavy manacles haunts me. I walk out of the room with him. It lifts my spirits to see sunshine spread across the police station courtyard. My body shivers with joy. I enjoy the color of the sun. We ascend the stairs and then walk into a room. The fat man is smoking. The skinny man is fidgeting with the papers in a file. They both look at me. The skinny man is busy scratching his nose. He motions for me to take a seat. I sit in a large chair beside his desk and look down. I hear the papers in the file being turned over. I hear the fat man chirp like a songbird. His voice sounds like it is coming out of his stomach. "Finish his interrogation and send him to court!" I take it I am no longer in Shahri's hands. I feel relieved. I feel like heaving a loud sigh of relief, but I refrain from doing so. From the corner of my eye, I look at the skinny man, busily writing. When he takes a drag of his cigarette, his cheeks sink in so much that I'm certain he has no teeth. The tip of his nose is red from too much scratching. The skinny man slides a sheet of paper toward me. "Read, and write your answers!" I remind him again that I am not literate enough.

I hear the fat man chirp to him, "You read it to him yourself!"

I look at the fat man. He asks, "You can sign it, can't you?"

"Hmm," I say.

The skinny man proceeds without waiting for my answer.

"Question number one: who gave you the books and newspapers that were in your possession at the time of your arrest?"

I refuse to answer.

His weak eyes become smaller. The whites of his eyes look yellowish. "Don't you have a tongue?" he says.

"The whole thing's a lie," I say under my breath.

Words come out through his nose. "Do you want me to write 'It's a lie'?"

"Of course I do . . . because I didn't have any books and newspapers on me."

He makes a note of my words, and then reads the next question. "At the harbor checkpoint a suitcase containing deviant material was seized from you. Whom did you want to deliver the suitcase to?"

Again, I refuse to answer.

He stares at me, asking again if I have a tongue.

I tell him that I don't understand what he is talking about.

He glares at me. Words get tied up in his throat. "Are you denying that the suitcase is yours?"

"The suitcase wasn't mine to begin with, so I'm not denying anything."

The fat man moves and looks straight at me. He takes such a deep drag it's as if he wants to swallow the entire cigarette. The skinny man, having stopped writing, glares at me. He then lights a cigarette and asks the fat man, "What do you command, sir?"

The fat man has grown impatient. Stubbing out the cigarette butt, he waves his short white hands. "Write, write whatever he says!"

I am about to burst out laughing. I have to try hard to stop myself. I look down and bite my lip. I hear the skinny man ask, "What was your intention in going to the harbor?"

I lift my head up and say, "Are you asking me?"

Beside himself with rage, he screams, "No, I am talking to your sister!"

Blood rushes into my face.

He yells again, "I said, what was your intention—"

"Why should I go to the harbor?" I cut him short.

There is a moment of silence. The empty eyes of the skinny man are fixed on the suitcase. "What do you have to say about the report in your file?" he asks.

"Report?" I shake my head. "What report are you talking about?"

He promptly draws the report out of the file, and, as if he wants to slap it in my face, he holds it out to me violently. "I mean this . . . this report."

He holds the report with his trembling hand in front of me for a few seconds.

"I told you . . . I cannot read," I say calmly.

He draws his hand back quickly and starts to read. His Adam's apple moves up and down constantly. His lips look bruised. He's in no mood to read. Once done reading through it, he looks at me. I keep quiet. He picks up his cigarette from the ashtray and takes another drag, still waiting for me to speak. Then he says, "Well?"

I try to look surprised.

"What do you say?" he asks.

"You just read it yourself . . . It was someone by the name of Nightingale," I say.

"Then you gave a fake name," he says.

"Write whatever you'd like," I respond.

The veins on his neck bulge. "But what do you say?"

"These are all just accusations."

He lays down the pen on his desk and starts to scratch his nose. As he looks at me, his eyelids close, hiding his eyes. Obviously, the opium is starting to take effect. Just like Khaj Tofiq after wasting three *mesqals* of opium.

The skinny man's voice has become softer and raspier. "You say these are all just allegations?"

I don't respond.

He talks softly. The opium must be having an effect, calming him. "What do you say about the signatures at the bottom of the report sheet?"

"False statements."

His eyes take on their usual expression. "What about running away from the police station?"

"It's a lie."

His voice becomes louder. "The officer who confirmed it was you is also a liar?"

"It was all made up. You yourself instructed him."

The fat man lets out a sudden squeal. "You are trying my patience."

I don't know if he means me or the skinny man. I give him an indifferent look, trying hard to keep myself from laughing. His bloodred cheeks, narrow mustache, and tiny eyes make me laugh to myself.

The skinny man starts to write again. He is so angry with me that if you were to stab him with a knife, he would not bleed.

"What do you have to say about this?"

"It's a lie."

"What about that?"

"It's a lie."

He's done with his interrogation. Resting his pen on his desk, he just stares at me. As I begin to sign the paper, the fat man rings the bell. The servant comes in. He asks him to go to the guards' office and ask for two guards to come and accompany me.

"Sign here too!"

I sign it.

"Here too!"

I sign again.

The guards load their shotguns. The handcuffs are placed on my wrists. They've been informed of my escape from the police station, so they act very rigid and stiff, with their faces empty of any sign of empathy. We leave the police station, pass by the boxtrees, and walk in the shade of the mimosa trees as we head in the direction of the town's main square. The butt of a gun is jammed against my waist. "You got money on you, so we can take a cab?"

I'd rather walk to the courthouse. I was about to suffocate in that cage of four walls. I yearn to see people. I want to look at the shops. It's a sunny day, warm, but not uncomfortably so. To get to the courthouse we need to pass over the White Bridge. I yearn to see the Karun. The water of the Karun is so clear now that you can see the fish swimming. It's so clear that its small waves sparkle silvery under the sun's rays.

"Hey, I was talking to you."

"I don't have a red cent," I grumble.

"Then you have to walk to the courthouse."

It is not long before we get to the main square, opposite the bridge.

By the time we reach the office of the public prosecutor, and by the time an examiner gets a chance to look through my file, it's already one thirty in the afternoon. Just about two and a half hours into the afternoon, I find myself in the prison's office, and before I know it, fingerprinting and all that stuff is done and I'm behind the iron door of a solitary confinement cell.

The solitary cell is five paces long and three paces wide. Yet it is still larger than the solitary cell in the police station. Its ceiling has a square vent that is covered with iron rods and mesh wire. The cell is off a covered hallway. A short guard paces along the hallway. Its floor is covered with stone tiles. The only sound that disrupts the hot and humid silence of the hallway is that of the guard's footsteps.

The public examiner was not in the mood to talk. God knows how many people he had to deal with before me today.

"What are the charges?" he asks.

Irritated, he opens the file and looks through the report and the interrogation transcript perfunctorily. As he lifts up his head, he shakes it and gives me a look. His eyes shout that he's craving opium. I must have seen the same expression more than a thousand times on Khaj Tofiq's face. The examiner takes another look at the papers. Half the hair on his head has gone gray. His temples are dry. Still looking at the file, he says in a nasal voice, "What does your kind wanna get out of these sorts of adventures?"

He assigns me temporary detention and sends me to the prison.

I call out to the guard. He walks toward me from the end of the hallway. Resting his hands against the iron door, he fixes his pale eyes on mine through its round hole. "What?"

"I am hungry," I tell him.

"God bless your aunt's soul."

Laughing, he goes on, "He's just arrived, and he already wants to eat."

His decaying teeth make me sick to my stomach.

I close my eyes and say, "But I haven't eaten for two days."

Laughing, he says, "You don't get a ration until you're here at least twenty-four hours."

I am surprised. "I don't?"

His voice is raspy. "No, of course not."

He coughs and continues, "It's not like you've been invited to your aunt's home." He starts to walk away.

"Wait a second, Guard."

He stops, and before I can say a word, he asks, "You got money?"

I dig into my pants pockets. I find four crumpled-up two-toman bills in the corner of my pocket. "I do."

Looking around, the guard mumbles, "Give it to me, then. I'll have someone bring you food from the teahouse."

I figure that, just like in the police station, there is a teahouse here in the prison too.

A short man in prison clothes brings me food: a piece of stale dark bread with four small boiled potatoes, each the size of a walnut, and a pack of salt the size of a thimble.

I devour the bread and the potatoes. The hot weather and the silence of the afternoon on top of my full stomach make me drowsy.

I rest my shoulders against the wall and stretch my legs. There is so much dust on the kilim that at first I didn't even notice that there was a rug at all. My back doesn't touch the wall if I sit this way, but soon I grow tired, so I lie down and roll over on my right arm. My eyes begin to droop. But sleep eludes me. Random thoughts won't leave me alone. For no reason, I think of Rahim the Donkey Keeper. I get up and call the guard. He walks toward my cell from the end of the hallway. He doesn't strike me as a mean person. Now that he has removed his cap, I can see that he is bald except for a few strands of henna-colored hair behind his ears and on the back of his head. "What is it this time?"

His eyes are faded, as if two black buttons had lost their color.

"Do you know Rahim the Donkey Keeper?" I ask.

Staring into my eyes, he asks quietly, "The one who killed his wife?"

I am beside myself with joy. I feel like I have been given all the goodness of this world. "Yes, the one who killed his wife, that's him."

The guard's long, plaque-crusted teeth are visible. "Why? You know him?"

"Yes, I do . . . I know him . . . We were neighbors. We lived in the same house," I say with excitement.

The guard scratches his bald head with his nails and says, "Then you should know Aman Aqa too."

I want to jump at him and kiss his smallpox-scarred cheeks. "I do know him . . . I used to work in his teahouse."

"Then I should take good care of you," he says.

Yet doubt and distrust quickly sweep through my mind. Pendar's voice echoes in my ears: "Sometimes, they build up trust and make friends with you just to get something out of you."

I feel hesitant. This might be a trick. What if they have asked him to become friends with me so they can misuse my trust and get whatever information they're looking for? The excitement leaves my voice. "Guard . . . is it possible that I could see Rahim the Donkey Keeper?"

The smallpox scars on his face jerk. He laughs. "You're not allowed to see anyone."

I am surprised. "I'm not allowed?"

In a gentle voice, he says, "Didn't they tell you that? You're in temporary detention. Until the interrogation is over, you're not allowed to see anyone."

Disappointed, I sit down, and then lie down. I hear the guard say, "My shift will end at four—if you have a message for anyone, I can take it for you."

I don't answer him. I am beginning to doubt myself. I hear him say again, "I'll let Aman Aqa know that you're here. I'll tell him to at least bring you a bedroll."

He walks away. The sound of his footsteps echoing off the ceiling adds to the silence and solitude. Sweat has rolled down over the dried blood caked on my back. The whip marks burn. I sit up, take my shirt off, and fan myself with it. It's no use. Too humid. The prickly heat creeps all over my body, piercing me with needles. Above me, the vent is suddenly shadowed. I look up and see a pair of blue legs and the loose crotch of a guard's pants covering the mesh wire. From between the legs, I see a long, old face bending over the vent. The brown stock of his gun leans against one of his blue legs. Above the stock is the breech, which gleams darkly in the sunlight. Two round eyes wander in the guard's wide face. I can't stand those eyes. I can't stand that long nose and bony cheeks. I lower my head, lie face down, and place my cheek on my hand. The vent in the ceiling is still obscured. The guard's gaze weighs heavily on me. I look up again and see him still staring down into the solitary cell. I hide my face between my arms. The sound of the other guard's footsteps is monotonous. The floor of the hallway is covered with flagstones. And the soles of the guard's boots are studded with nails. He walks the length of the hallway, back and forth, without a pause. Back and forth. I imagine there must be a row of solitary cells along the hallway. When I came in I was so discombobulated that I didn't pay any attention. I was completely distracted. The sharp ringing sound of a bell, just like that of a school, fills the hallway. I get up and look out through the hole in the door. The ringing has ceased. A humming sound comes from the end of the hallway. It is the confused voices of people. I call the guard; he comes toward me. I ask him what is going on.

"They're getting lunch," he says.

It must be past three in the afternoon.

"It's past lunchtime," I say.

The guard laughs. His long black teeth make me want to vomit. "This is not home . . . or a restaurant."

The prisoners, in single file, pass by my cell. I look carefully to see if I can find Rahim the Donkey Keeper. I see all kinds of people wearing yellow- and black-striped clothes made from canvas. But before I get a chance to look them all over, they have passed out of my sight. They each carry a copper bowl. After getting their ration of food, they return, walking slowly. Steam rises from the yellow water inside the bowls. An old man with a bent back holds on to his bowl as if it were his life. The old man toddles along. His nose is as big as a carrot. His eyes are watery. He passes by me. Suddenly, I spot Rahim the Donkey Keeper, carrying a bowl under his arm. His head is shaved. His forehead is creased. His mustache looks yellow. It must be from smoking. Ever since he killed Rezvan with the bowl of his pipe, he hasn't smoked one. I call him. He stops for a second and looks around. I call him again. "Mash Rahim . . . it's me . . ."

I don't have a chance to say my name before the guard takes his shotgun and pushes Rahim the Donkey Keeper along. "Walk on, old man!"

Then the guard comes toward me. His face is kind. His pale eyes exude patience. There is a tinge of criticism in his tone. "I told you you weren't allowed to talk to anyone."

Again the legs and the crotch of the blue pants and the stock of the gun cover the vent.

I press my forehead to the iron door and look out at the hallway through the round hole. Some of the prisoners' faces look familiar. I feel like I have seen them somewhere. In just one evening, at sunset, if you walk on Pahlavi Street, you'll see all the people of the town.

Rahim the Donkey Keeper comes back and stops in front of the solitary cell. The guard is at the end of the hallway.

"Mash Rahim, it's me," I call out to him.

He looks baffled.

"It's me, Khaled. I am in the solitary cell."

He looks at me, his old face drowned in sadness. His voice comes from far away: *Do you see, Khaled, what's happened to me at the end of my life? . . . Do you see?*

He looks bewildered. His lips tremble. He has yet to say anything when the guard shows up. "Not again . . . Come on, old man, walk away!"

Rahim the Donkey Keeper looks down and walks away.

I sit down in the corner of the solitary cell. The buzzing of the prisoners has now ceased. I hear the doors of the cellblock close. Silence takes over the hallway. I hug my knees and rest my chin on them, letting myself become lost in thought. The memories rush back. Rezvan's voice is loud and clear: "What could I do, Sister . . . People talk so much nonsense behind the back of a woman without a husband."

Rezvan has an expression of self-righteousness on her face. Her words are convincing. "He came and persisted that he has two kids without a mother . . ."

Her pitch-black hair is shining. She has rubbed black *sormeh* onto her eyelids. "I pitied his children . . . but as for him, his time has passed . . ."

She has reddened her cheeks. Her long forehead creases. "To be honest, my time has passed too."

The women in the neighborhood whisper among themselves: "She is one of those whores who will have Mash Rahim wrapped around her little finger . . ."

Hajar pokes her nipple into her sickly child's mouth as she says through her nose, "She has ten lovers waiting for her, Sister . . ."

Roqayye sticks her finger into her nose, and while moving it around, she says, "Being an old man, and being a cuckold?"

The pounding of the drum and the piercing sound of the *sorna* shake me. Mash Rahim yells, "Woman, you should be ashamed of yourself before God!"

Amu Bandar grabs Mash Rahim's arm. "Mashti, let's go out for a walk."

Rezvan is begging him. Beads of sweat have formed on her forehead. Sanam is dancing. The water in the pot is boiling. The veins in Mash Rahim's neck are bulging. I can't hear his voice. The *sorna* is playing at full blast. Rahim the Donkey Keeper is shaking the pipe in the air. The sound of the drum explodes with each beat. The pipe's bowl comes down on Rezvan's temple. A wide red face fills the round hole in the iron door. "Is he the new guy?"

A new guard begins his shift in the hallway. It's four o'clock. I hear the bald-headed guard say, "Yeah, he arrived today . . . He's not allowed any visitors."

I am filled with sadness. If only I could have talked to Rahim the Donkey Keeper, I would feel better.

The guard passes by my cell. The meshed square of sunlight has crept up the wall. All the sorrows of the world have crept into my heart. I can imagine the neighbors sprinkling the fronts of their rooms with water, sweeping, and spreading their carpets. Khaj Tofiq will be squatting beside his brazier, fanning the charcoals gingerly. And Mother—ah, Mother!—will be hugging her knees, staring blankly.

Just like a pot of water boiling over, suddenly, my heart boils over. I want to get up and shout. I want to get up, put my mouth on the round hole, and shout my love for Black-Eyed. "How lovely you are . . . How I

cherish the thought of you . . . How soft and warm is the sound of you
. . . I love you . . . my beautiful Black-Eyed . . . my darling." I realize that I
am talking to myself. The red face of the guard fills the round hole again.
"Did you want something?"

"No."

He is about to walk away.

"Wait a minute!"

"What?"

"I want to use the restroom."

He goes and fetches the keys. He returns and says, "Get up!"

The door of the cell opens.

"You only got five minutes!"

A guard with a swarthy complexion walks with me. I feel like I have
seen him before. For sure he's one of those boatmen. I talk to him. I hear
his Arabic accent. His voice rings a bell. He must be the guy I know. I
tell him so. In a bitter tone he retorts that I'm talking nonsense, and then
opens the door of the cellblock so we can go into the courtyard. The
brick-walled stalls are lined up in a row at the end of the block. Sunlight
has crept up the stone wall. At the edge of the roof, a tall guard, his gun
slung over his shoulder, paces behind barbed wire. He has pushed his
cap up on his forehead. The prisoners, sitting in groups, chat. There are
a good hundred or more of them. Here and there, Primus burners are
lit, a kettle on top of each one. They must be for making tea. There are
pots on top of the enameled burners. An elderly man is squatting on the
cement steps in front of the stalls. Hugging his knees, he looks intently
at the sky.

I walk out of the latrines. All of my muscles feel stiff. My bones are
aching. I can barely walk. My steps are very slow. I want to get a look at
the prison. The rooms are set in a row. All of them have a window that
opens to the yard. I count them. Eleven sprawling rooms.

"Get moving!" orders the guard.

I stop. "I can't walk."

"Why? It's not like your legs are broken."

"No . . . but my back is smashed."

Some of the prisoners' eyes follow me to the door of the block.
Back in the hallway, I become gloomy again. It is suffocating here. And
humid. I imagine that behind the holes in some of the doors pairs of

eyes wander. In front of my cell, I see a bedroll sprawled on the ground. I recognize the small rug.

Someone asks, "Are you Khaled?"

I turn around. He is short and stout. His arms are like two rocks. His gaze burns me like fire. "Hand it over!"

I am completely confused.

He spells it out: "I brought you the bedroll. It costs two tomans."

I dig into my pockets and hand him a crumpled-up two-toman bill. I pick up the blanket, the pillow, and the rug and walk into the cell. Father's scent and the smell of his tobacco permeate every knot in the threadbare rug. I spread it out, put the pillow on it, and lie down. I rub my face against the rug. I feel like crying. It's Mother's pillow. I press my cheeks into the pillow and sniff it. I feel a lump in my throat. It would only take someone coming over and talking to me right now for me to start bawling my eyes out. I have never been so vulnerable. I can imagine my mother's hair spreading over the pillow. I can see Father sitting on the rug, rolling a cigarette. I hear his cheerless voice coming from a distance, from the bottom of a well: "The blacksmith business is slow . . . It's not thriving at all. These days, even hobnails are imported from abroad."

I turn the pillow over and sniff it. It smells of Mother. I can hear a reprimand in her voice: "You're still young, my son . . . You should think of your life, your future."

I sink my face into the pillow. Something hard pokes my cheek. I sit up, put the pillow on my knees, and search it. I feel something resembling a matchbox moving among the feathers. I undo some of the stitching and thrust my arm up to the elbow into the pillow. I find it. It's a prayer paper wrapped in a green piece of fabric. I rip the green fabric open and pull out the prayer paper. It's in Mirza Nasrollah's handwriting. It smells of perfume and rose water. The writing gleams like black mica. I wonder what I should do with it. I want to rip it up, but Father's glaring eyes fill my mind. My hands go limp as I fold the prayer paper, wrap the green fabric around it, and shove it into the feathers inside the pillow. I figure even if no good comes from it, it can't hurt either. I lie on my arm. Only God Himself knows how much Mother must have begged Mirza Nasrollah to write the prayer for her.

I hear someone say in a violent, bad-tempered voice: "Shave his head!"

Someone else responds: "Your wish is my command, sir."

The door opens and a guard appears. He has large bloodshot eyes, a wide, strong chin, and is of medium height.

"Get up!"

I stand up.

"Come out!"

I walk out of the cell.

The guard walks past the other cells in solitary, peeping in each one, then walks into the block. I walk along with him. A chair is placed in the middle of the hallway. The guard motions for me to sit down. I sit on it. All I can see is the guard's wide bloodred face. His coarse voice reverberates under the ceiling of the hallway: "Ali the Barber!"

I hear footsteps.

A middle-aged man appears from around the corner of a side hallway that leads to the kitchen. He staggers along just like a pregnant woman due any minute.

"Come and shave his head!"

He walks off slowly, and then returns at the same pace, holding a rusted shaver in his hand.

The shaver must have pulled my hair more than a hundred times. It brings tears to my eyes before it's over. I am soaked in sweat, and the perspiration burns the whip marks.

I nearly die before they finish shaving my head. Hair is all over my neck, my shoulders, and my chest, poking my skin. I get up and walk back to my cell. The door shuts behind me. I spread the blanket over the rug, and take off my shirt and shake it. I feel like sleeping. The light from the bulb in the ceiling annoys me.

I have no idea what time of day it is. The sky above the mesh vent in the ceiling is sunny. The ceiling light has been turned off. I yearn for a cup of tea. I know now how things work here. I call the guard. He's not the same guard from last night. This one is bad-tempered; ugly too.

"Guard, is there any way I can get a cup of tea from the teahouse?"

"Sit your ass down for now."

He is foulmouthed too. Some people sure do have it all.

My mouth tastes as bitter as snake venom. I hug my knees. The walls press against my heart. I feel tense, with a kind of anxiety that pains me. It stings. All the familiar voices, words, smells, and looks of the people I know blend together.

Banu appears before my eyes. She is naked. Her saggy breasts, like those of a bitch just finished feeding its litter, hang about each other. She grabs my hand and begs me: "One more time, only once . . ."

Father is sitting on his prayer rug, reciting the Tasbihat prayers: "Glory be to God. Praise be to the Lord of the universe. There is no god but God. God is the Greatest!"

My heart trembles at the sound of his voice. Father prostrates himself. Rahim the Donkey Keeper's wife lies dead. The last beads of the cold sweat of life have dried on her forehead. Rahim the Donkey Keeper is panicky. Smacking the back of his hand helplessly, he laments: "What am I supposed to do now?"

Khaj Tofiq's voice is husky: "There's no god but God!"

The smoke coming from Khaj Tofiq's opium pipe darkens my vision.

Gholam, Aunt Ra'na's son, asks: "Dear Aunt, Uncle Haddad hasn't sent money?"

Bolur Khanom quickly throws her muslin undergarment into a corner of the room. She presses her tight belly against mine.

Black-Eyed's reproachful eyes—the eyes that have now taken on the color of black olives—send shivers through me. The smell of freshly ripened dates fills my nose. The pungent scent of fish fills me with the cool water of the Karun. The acrid, bitter taste of unripe dates adds to the bitterness in my mouth. The Karun is fuming, pounding the concrete pillars of the bridge. Pendar's voice, mingled with the roar of the Karun, echoes in my ears: "You can't love anyone . . . You can't . . . just can't . . ."

Black-Eyed's warm lips give life to my dry, dead lips.

Mother is pleading: "What do you want from my child?"

Leila's daring gaze pierces the darkness. I hear the irate hiss of a snake. It's the whistling of the whip writhing in the air. Black-Eyed's head rests on my chest. The fragrance of her hair intoxicates me. It smells like fresh date molasses wafting through the humid air on the banks of the Karun. Ali the Devil's mocking laughter explodes. "I didn't know a poor, wretched boy could . . ."

The whip comes down on a mass of cotton. I am soaked in sweat. Bolur Khanom is struggling. Her body is hot. Her lips quiver. She is soaked in sweat. Aman Aqa's voice fills my ears: "Hurry up, my son . . . get a water pipe over there . . . Hurry up . . ."

Light passes before my eyes. I see stars. I see Gholam Ali Khan. His scorpion-tail of a mustache trembles. "You motherfucker, you dared break *my* window?"

Mother's humming heaps all the sorrows of the world on my heart:

> *If I knew that my fate would be like this,*
> *I would've drunk poison instead of my mother's milk.*

Rahim the Donkey Keeper's forehead fills my vision. His voice is heartrending. "Do you see, Khaled? Do you see what's happened to me at the end of my life?"

Rezvan has pushed Sanam aside and is dancing. She has dropped her chador, letting her pitch-black hair fall around her shoulders. Stretching out her arms, she pushes everyone aside. The drum and the *sorna* are playing at full blast. Rahim the Donkey Keeper is yelling. The dark veins on his neck inflate and deflate. Rezvan is laughing out loud. She is dancing merrily, just like a little girl, gleeful and happy.

Beads of sweat glide down her forehead and cheeks. The cook's mouth hangs open. His gold teeth glitter. Lines have appeared under his wide cheeks. Hajj Sheikh Ali's index finger waves in warning, just like a dagger dancing over my face, ready to slash it at any moment. Two bony hands clutch Hajj Sheikh Ali's throat. I recognize the hands. I know the bulging veins running through them. Hajj Sheikh Ali's bloodred cheeks have turned gray. Spider's languid voice gets raspy in his throat: "Khaled, pick up those cups!"

A coarse voice rises from a corner of the teahouse: "Hey, boy, give me a cup of tea with sugar cubes."

I turn around and look at him. Someone else calls me. It's from behind me. "Hey, I'm talking to you."

The sounds are muddled.

"Hey, boy!"

"Hey, you!"

"Hey!"

The sound of the iron door rattling startles me back to reality. The bad-tempered guard's voice rushes in. "Hey, I'm talking to you!" he yells, pounding the iron door with his fist. "Hey, boy, I'm talking to you. Have you lost your mind?"

I get up. The guard is in a bad mood. "Are you deaf or something?" I don't answer.

"Give me money and I'll have them get you tea," I hear someone else say.

I hand him two crumpled two-toman bills through the hole in the door. Two sharp eyes gaze at me, just like two red-hot drills, two balls of fire. He is the same guy who brought me the bedroll.

I barely have time to fold the blanket and put it on the pillow before he is back with the tea. He hands me a teapot that has been broken and glued back together, a teacup with a saucer, a piece of stale bread, and four sugar cubes through the hole in the door.

I sit down and lean on the blanket and pillow. I devour the first cup of tea. The teapot is so tiny that it holds only three cupfuls. I bite off a corner of the bread, but it won't go down my throat. I force it down with tea. The teapot runs out of tea. I stretch my legs and lift my head up. I notice that some things are scribbled on the wall. How could I not have noticed them before? The scribbles have been carved into the plaster of the wall either with nails or matchsticks. The plaster is soft, ruined. I get up and look at the walls. The scribbles are jumbled. Some are readable, others are not. Most of the writing is cusswords directed at the chief of the prison and his wife and daughter. In the scribbles, both the inspector's and the prosecutor's relatives and ancestors—dead or alive—have been cursed beyond disgrace. There are a few words on love, a few hearts pieced with arrows, the image of a woman with hips the size of a millstone, and poems of all sorts:

> *The beauties of the earth have no mercy,*
> *There's no choice but to fuck and then dump them.*

Reading some of the poems makes me blush. I look at the carved woman. It can't get any uglier. I entertain myself by reading the scribbles. I want to forget about everyone and everything. I feel like pouring everything out of my heart. I want to be emptied of theses burdens.

The guard on duty picks up his pace. His footfalls are heavy. He walks to the end of the hallway and comes back. Back and forth. Abruptly, the iron door to the block opens with a clanging sound that echoes through the hallway. A man's coarse voice fills the hallway as he cusses out all the guards and officers. His bellowing sounds like that of a wounded bull. I peep through the hole. The man is tall. A few guards make it up to his chest. His curly hair is disheveled. Blood is running down from above his upper lip. The guards are shoving him. He resists, dragging his feet. His shirt is ripped down to his navel. Blood dribbles from his nose onto his chest.

I call to the guard on watch. He ignores me. I call him again. He frowns. "Spit it out!" he reluctantly commands.

"Guard, what happened to him?" I ask.

"The motherfucker has messed up the block again," he replies in a bad-tempered manner.

The tall man's eyes are like two balls of fire. His feet are glued to the ground—firm and unyielding. The guards struggle to shove him along. Two guards are holding on to each of his arms, just like a whale being hauled out of the sea.

The guards are completely out of breath by the time they manage to shove him out of the hallway. The door shuts behind the tall man. His bellowing dies down. The short man comes to fetch the teapot and the cup. I can't look into his eyes. "Who was that man?" I ask without looking up.

"It was Sadeq, Sadeq the Kurd," he says, deepening his voice.

The short man's voice is raspy. It's bothersome to the ears. I'd like to know his name too. "What's your name?"

He looks at me, smiling. A gentle smile.

"At your service. Naser, Naser the Lifer."

Taking the teapot, the cup, and the saucer, he walks away. Silence swallows the hallway. Once again, the sound of the guard's footfalls hammers my temples. Suddenly, a long streak of light falls on the wall through the vent in the ceiling. I sit down and watch. Creeping down, the sunray gradually grows into a square crisscrossed with mesh wires. The shadow of a bayonet attached to the barrel of a rifle slithers over the mesh wires and passes by. A guard must be walking above my head with a gun slung over his shoulder. The shadow of the bayonet comes back and pauses on the meshed patch of light on the wall. I imagine that the guard watching over the roof has experienced this a thousand times before, and must have learned exactly where to stand so that he casts the shadow of his bayonet on the wall inside the solitary cell.

It's getting hot. I take off my shirt. Sweat beads on my shoulders. I wipe it off with the hem of my shirt. The door suddenly opens. "Take it!"

It's a copper bowl. I take it. The guard closes the door. I am entitled to a ration of food starting this afternoon. I decide that when it's my turn to go get my food, I'll linger until Mash Rahim shows up.

I put the bowl in a corner of the cell and sit on the pillow. I hug my knees and stare at the shadow of the bayonet cast over the pattern of the mesh wires.

Gholam, Aunt Ra'na's son, is waiting for me in the hallway of the courthouse. His mustache glistens. He is wearing his cap at an angle. As soon as he sees me, he rushes toward me through the crowd. He is running so fast that on his way he shoves a woman and knocks an old man down, making them both yell in return. Just as I reach the glass double doors of the courthouse's main hallway, Gholam catches me, embracing and kissing me. He has never been this friendly. The guards on duty do not protest my cousin embracing me. I imagine it's out of respect for his army uniform. Gholam has twisted his mustache upward, just like that colonel, the same colonel whose fat-ass wife Afaq used to take satin fabrics to when her husband was still a captain. Cousin kisses my cheek again. The edge of his cap hits my eye. Together, we walk along with the guards, one on either side of us. Aunt Ra'na's son starts lecturing me, to which I turn a deaf ear. He talks nonsense. I wait for a chance to shut him up. Suddenly, I see Mother. Weaving quickly through the crowd, she rushes toward me, dragging her chador behind her on the floor. A lock of her hair has fallen on her forehead. Everyone's eyes are on us. Mother's face is on fire with rage. She is drenched in sweat. Who told her, I wonder? She must have been searching for me day in and day out, trying to find out what had happened to me. Mother draws me to her, hugging me. Her hands touch the lash marks. I tolerate the pain and try to stay calm so that she will not suspect anything. She covers my face with her kisses. The scent of her body chokes me with sadness. I am scared to talk. I know that the first word that comes out of my mouth will be followed by tears. The guards try to unwind Mother's arms, but they fail. Aunt Ra'na's son pulls the guards aside and reasons with them. They agree to let Mother and me talk for a bit, but Mother cannot speak at all. She just cries, especially when she notices the handcuffs. Upon seeing them, she begins to sob. I sit on the bench in front of the inspector's room. The courthouse is so crowded that it even beats the livestock market.

Reza the Dealer wanders in and out of the crowd. I know he is after his prey. I have heard about him from Aman Aqa. God forbid if you happen to have some business in the courthouse and you cross paths with Reza the Dealer. Before you know it, you will be deceived out of an arm and a leg.

Mother sits so close to me that I can hear her heartbeat. Her head rests on my shoulder, and her arms are looped around my waist. The guards, who are hovering over us, unlock the handcuffs. Aunt Ra'na's son keeps talking to the guards, telling them about the sergeant-training classes. From the middle of the crowd, Reza the Dealer's sharp eyes set on mine. I can hear him saying, "Get me a water pipe, young man!"

"Right away, Aqa Reza."

"Why don't you go to school, young man?"

"I'm planning to attend night school, Aqa Reza."

Smiling, he comes toward me. He must have remembered that I used to serve him in Aman Aqa's teahouse. His belly moves ahead of him. He has fastened his belt on his pelvis. His drumlike belly is likely to burst his shirt open any second.

"How are you, young man?"

"Good, thanks, Aqa Reza."

Rolling the prayer beads in his hand, he asks, "Did you get into a fight?"

"Kind of."

Sticking a finger into his nose, he says, "If you're ever in trouble, Uncle Reza here can take care of it."

Mother opens her mouth to speak. I beat her to it, though, and say, "No, Aqa Reza. It's not a big deal."

He narrows his eyes. "As you know," he says, as he points to himself, "everyone's like wax in Uncle Reza's hands."

"Can you please—," Mother starts to say (or, rather, sob).

Reza the Dealer pulls his finger out of his nose, cuts Mother short, turns to me, and asks, "Is your case in Division Three?"

"Division Three?" Mother asks.

Reza the Dealer points the same finger he just had up his nose at the door we're sitting next to, and says, "I mean this division." He continues in the same breath, "If it's Division Three, it's taken care of. I mean, Uncle Reza has the inspector of this division wrapped around his little finger. But let me tell you that I am doing this for Aman Aqa's sake . . ."

I hear my name called. Before I walk into the examiner's office, I make Mother understand that she must not take Reza the Dealer's words seriously. "Look, Mother, if there's any chance that I can get out of here, I can assure you that he's not the one who can get me out."

By the time I get out of the examiner's office, it's almost noon. Bolur Khanom has arrived. So has Aman Aqa. Reza the Dealer has hit the road. The courthouse is less crowded now. My hands are still free of the handcuffs when Bidar quickly comes down the hallway, embraces me, and kisses me on both cheeks, taking the guards by surprise. He asks how I have been doing, shakes my hand, and presses a folded paper into my palm. The guards move Bidar away from me. I hold out my fisted hands to be handcuffed. Bidar says good-bye. As he leaves, he winks and tells me, "Don't you worry, it'll be over soon!"

We head out of the courthouse. The sun's rays are everywhere. It lifts my spirits. I cherish everything I lay my eyes on. It feels as if I haven't seen the row of mimosa trees in front of the courthouse for years. We take a taxi. Aman Aqa has talked the guards into letting us all go to lunch together before going to the prison. We pass over the White Bridge. I watch the boats gently gliding on the surface of the water. I listen carefully to the words being spoken around me. The Karun's surface shimmers like silver under the sunlight. Jamileh is not feeling well. Her throat is sore. I miss her.

The island sitting in the heart of the Karun is lush and green. The dark green branches of tamarix trees have covered up the entire island. A letter has arrived from Father. If only I could see him. The sky is stunningly clear. The tall crescents of the bridge reflect the sunlight. The neighbors are worried about me. Aunt Ra'na's son brags, "I'll ask our first sergeant to do something for you."

In my heart I laugh at him. Mother insists on knowing what happened to me at the police station. I don't tell her anything about the miseries I have been through. I know if I tell her, her soul will part from her body on the spot.

"I'll have you released on bail," Aman Aqa says.

The driver looks at me in the mirror. "Did you knife someone?" he asks.

I give him a smile. "No, Brother, I was on my way to the mosque to pray when they took me."

A surprised expression seizes the driver's dark face. "To pray?"

Aman Aqa bursts out laughing. The driver purses his lips.

We get out of the taxi in front of a kebab eatery in the main square of town. The guards unlock the handcuffs. I shove the paper into my pocket. We all sit at a table, along with the guards. Aman Aqa sits beside me. I sit in such a way so that I can see the square. Aman Aqa shoves three ten-toman bills into my pocket. Statue Square is full of sunshine. It feels like I haven't seen it for ages. I enjoy watching people come and go. I enjoy looking at the lush lawn in the middle of the square. I can see as far as the junction, past the square. I keep my eyes fixed on the junction for so long that it draws Bolur Khanom's attention. "What are you looking at, Khaled?"

"At the street . . . the square . . . It feels like I haven't seen them for ages."

Mother bursts out crying, tears covering her face.

The morsel of food congeals in my mouth. "I didn't mean anything by that, Mother."

Bolur Khanom comforts Mother. Aunt Ra'na's son glares at me, then shoves a bite as big as a cat's head into his mouth.

The guards are in a hurry. "This is our responsibility. Make it quick!"

As we wait for the tea to be brought to us from the teahouse next to the kebab eatery, I go to the restroom in the company of one of the guards. Inside the stall, I take the paper out of my pocket. It is moist from the sweat of my palm. The ink has smeared. I read it. It is a contact code:

"Your eyes tell me that you are not from the south, so does your complexion."

"As a matter of fact, I am."

"Then you should like *hilsa* fish."

"But I prefer the *bon-e nay* fish of the Karun."

~

Sunlight is climbing up the stone wall of the block. When I returned from the courthouse at noon, I placed the bedroll under my arm, picked up the copper bowl from my cell in solitary, and walked through the block. My place is next to the door in the fourth room. It must be around five in the afternoon now. Shadows spread everywhere. Some of the prisoners are sprinkling water on the floor and sweeping so they can lay out a carpet. Some are walking in pairs. They pace back and forth. The contact code is all that's on my mind. I look at everyone passing me by as if they are about to get in touch with me. I haven't met anyone yet. I just got my dinner a few minutes ago and left it next to my bedroll. Three boiled potatoes with a few black dates. I am already bored to death. I still haven't gotten used to the guard pacing across the roof. He has unbuttoned the collar of his uniform shirt and pushed up his cap off his forehead; with a rifle slung over his shoulder, he trudges along languidly. Reluctantly, I count the rows of stones in the walls. There are twenty-nine of them. Time passes slowly. If someone contacts me, I might be able to get rid of this boredom and confusion. The guard on duty monitors the block by leaning against the wall and rolling his baton around in his hand. I think he's looking at me. I hear someone's voice: "Are you new?"

I turn around. A tall young man with a pleasant look and a pale face stands before me. My heart leaps. I stare at his mouth. He sits beside me. I wait for him to say, "Your eyes tell me that you are not from the south . . ."

"Are you new?" he asks again. A smile brightens his face.

"Yes, I came in today."

"On what charges?"

"I don't know."

The tone of his voice is pleasant. "Oh, we're in the same boat. You're like me. They tell me—with no evidence—that I have killed someone."

I feel dejected. It seems like I won't make contact with anyone.

"What's your name?"

I give him my name and ask for his.

"Gholam, they call me Gholam the Murderer."

"You got cigarettes?" he asks.

"No, I don't smoke."

He gets up, grumbling. "But you'll become a smoker in jail," he says, walking away.

I sit on the cement steps in front of the row of stalls. I am in Block 3. I should get used to the people and the walls and the doors around here. The sooner the better, as they say. I should find the kind of people I can have a conversation with. A tall, scrawny man walks by me. Lingering, he looks at me for a moment. My heart beats faster. He scratches his gray beard and walks away. I hear the door to the block open. It's Naser the Lifer. He pauses every now and then as he walks. The door closes behind him. He is short and stout. He catches my eye, smiles, and comes toward me.

"I see you've come to the block."

He sits beside me and lays his hand on my shoulder. His hand is heavy. "What's with this unfriendliness?"

"Why? I'm not unfriendly." I smile.

"What's your room number?"

"Four."

"That's good. I am in Room 10," he says.

The rooms are set in a row. In each room, there are at least ten people. There is a covered hallway in front of the rooms. The windows open to the courtyard.

"Let's take a walk."

I get up and start to walk with Naser the Lifer.

"In jail, if you don't walk for a couple of hours a day, your body will puff out," he says.

I count my footsteps. The courtyard is ninety-three steps long.

He goes on, "If you think too much about it, you'll rot away. You should be outright happy-go-lucky in jail."

The sunlight has slid over the edge of the roof. The cobalt blue gable over the security tower is changing color. I hear Naser the Lifer's voice: "Say something!"

"How long have you been here?" I ask.

"If you lay it out to a kid, he'll get sulky," he says indifferently.

I don't quite follow what exactly he means by this.

He smiles and continues, "It's been twelve years and three months."

"Twelve years?" I am shocked.

He bursts out laughing. Tears well up in his eyes. "I told you, if you lay it out to a kid, he'll get sulky," he says.

He seems to be a nice guy. Kindhearted too. His expression scares you away, but his smile is pleasant.

"How is it that you can go wherever you want to?" I ask him.

He deepens his voice, pounds on his chest with his fist, and says, "I am a free man. I am the jack-of-all-trades for the jail."

We walk to the end of the block and come back. Over and over again. I begin to like Naser the Lifer. Suddenly, I think of Rahim the Donkey Keeper. I ask him if he knows him. He looks straight into my eyes. "The one who killed his wife?" he asks.

I get excited. "Yes, that's the one," I say quickly.

"He's in Block 4," he says.

I grab his arm. Hard as a rock. I ask about Rahim.

"Do you know him?"

"We were neighbors."

He frowns. "Those bastards tease him a lot."

"They tease him? Who do you mean?" I say sadly.

"I mean the other prisoners . . . They finger him like an old crow."

Something moves in my heart. I hear Mash Rahim. His voice quivers. It has aged. "Do you see, Khaled, what's happened to me at the end of my life?"

He looks feeble. Tears have welled up in his old eyes. His mustache has turned yellow from smoking too many cigarettes. He barely has the strength to talk. His voice sounds as if it's coming from the bottom of a well: "Do you see, Khaled?"

I squeeze Naser the Lifer's arm. "But way?"

"In jail, the weak are the more miserable ones," he says.

It's getting dark. The tall walls of the jail weigh heavy on my heart. Naser the Lifer breaks away. "I am going to check out my room."

I sit down again on the cement steps.

A tall, bent, skinny old man is standing in front of one of the brick stalls. He is counting with a matchstick the lines drawn on the bricks. I look at him. He smiles. Two of his front teeth have fallen out. "Seventy-three days have passed," he says.

At the sound of the block's door opening, I take my eyes from the old man. A guard of medium height comes in. He is young, with a swarthy complexion. He takes over from the guard in charge of watching the block, lights a cigarette, and starts to walk inside the block. First he walks along the hallway and checks the rooms. Then he walks into the yard. He walks past a group of prisoners who are gathered together talking and drinking tea. Then he comes and stands in front of me, twirling the baton in his hand. The floodlights in the four corners of the block come on.

The guard takes a drag of his cigarette and plays with the smoke. "Are you new?" he asks.

"Yes," I answer indifferently.

"What's your name?"

I don't feel like answering him.

He stubs the cigarette butt out under his foot and again prods me for my name. "I asked for your name."

"Khaled," I say under my breath.

A passing smile that I don't care for brightens his face. He comes closer and stands right over my head. I stand up to walk away. He blocks my way and gets in my face. My mind is a torrent of stray thoughts. As I move to walk past him, I hear him say, "Your eyes tell me that you are not from the south . . . so does your complexion."

My heart is about to jump out of my chest. I feel my face flush. My voice quivers: "As a matter of fact, I am."

"Then you should like *hilsa* fish."

"But I prefer the *bon-e nay* fish of the Karun," I answer enthusiastically.

5

The lower court has sentenced me to three years in prison. Imagine, three years! That's a lifetime for a child. It's only been two months and nineteen days so far.

Naser the Lifer's treasure chest of goodies has become my private library. He calls it a *zabt-duni*, and it's where the opium addicts hide their smoking gadgets. Nobody dares to look at his box. His swiveling eyeballs will scare the hell out of you. I think he suspects that the guard with the swarthy complexion brings me the books. He has become interested in learning to read and write. I've asked him, "Why do you want to learn to read? What's the point when you're going to spend your entire life here—"

He cuts me short, "You never know how things will turn out in this world! Who knows? There might be an exemption, a suspension, or something . . . and besides, literacy serves you better in jail. This way you won't have to beg some bastard to read you a damn line."

I agree to teach him. "Good enough, Naser, but you have to promise me to do whatever it takes to get Rahim the Donkey Keeper transferred to Block 3."

"You got it!"

I have moved from Room 4 to Naser the Lifer's room. In prison language, we have become "food mates." Both Judge and Buyeh have joined us too. "Look here, lad, if you're gonna eat the jail's food, you'll kick the bucket before you know it."

"So what should I do, then?"

"Here is what we do," Naser elaborates. "We put our money together, buy stuff from Napoleon, and perk up our daily food ration."

Napoleon is sentenced to life too. He is the food hawker of Block 3. He sells sheets of paper, stamps, and envelopes too. If you know how to keep your lips sealed, you can sometimes secure some opium too.

So this is how I have become "food mates" with Naser the Lifer, Judge, and Buyeh. I do the dishes, Buyeh washes the clothes, Judge cooks, and Naser the Lifer comes and helps himself as soon as the meals are ready. He is not used to lifting a finger around the room.

"But, dear Naser, that's not how it should be. You should do something around here too."

He flexes his neck muscles, deepens his voice, and says, "Eh! Who would watch out for you guys, then?"

Not a living soul in the jail dares to mess with us. The chief of the jail, the officer on duty, the guards, and even the guards' supervisors all count on Naser the Lifer.

When he gets angry, or whenever he wills it, he can turn the block upside down, be it over a cigarette butt, an onion, a tomato, or any other trivial thing. In the blink of an eye, he draws a blade out from under the cord holding his pants up and creates a spectacle. The entire surface of his large shaved head is covered in cut marks that have become white, fleshy scar tissue.

Yep, Naser the Lifer looks after us real good.

It is the second month of fall. The weather is not scorching hot anymore. The heat no longer burns, though it is still hot during the day. Sometimes, rainless, lamb-shaped cumulus clouds pile up in the sky, making the air more humid, but around sunset it cools down, and a breeze comes in at nighttime.

Mother has come to visit me. Jamileh is with her; so is Aunt Ra'na. Bolur Khanom and Leila, Mullah Ahmad's eldest daughter, have come too. Leila's gaze is intrepid. I wonder why she has come to visit me. Thanks to the mighty muscles of Naser the Lifer, I can have a private visitation. The iron door opens before me. I leave the covered hallways between the blocks and walk into a large room next to the guards' office. Mother runs toward me, embracing me and covering my face in kisses. The scent of Mother's body fills me with sadness.

Leila's daring gaze fixes on me. Aunt Ra'na talks nonstop. Jamileh is choked up. I kiss her and stroke her hair. She's about to burst out crying. Her face looks so unhappy. Father hasn't returned from Kuwait yet.

"He's written that he'll be back for Nowruz," says Mother.

"Does he know that I am in jail?" I ask her.

Mother struggles to speak. "How can I write that to him, dear?"

Bolur Khanom does not say a word. She just keeps looking at me. I smile at her.

I hear Leila's excited tone: "Is your place all right in here?"

Bolur Khanom has brought me a large pack of Japanese watermelon seeds. Mother has brought me potato patties. Aunt Ra'na folds a five-toman bill and hands it to me. This reminds me of Gholam. I feel like I can hear his voice. His tone is flattering: "But, sir, I don't have that kind of money. I'd be surprised if I could even manage borrowing some money to get myself a can of boot polish."

Aunt Ra'na's voice takes my mind off Gholam. "It's not much, my son!" she says, squeezing my hand. "I feel embarrassed, my son. I wish I could afford more."

The guard on watch hovers over us, smoking and listening.

Mother asks about Rahim the Donkey Keeper.

"He is in Block 4," I tell her. "I don't get to see him."

Bolur Khanom says that Ebrahim has been knifed. "He is in the state hospital. It's been three days. They say his arm and chest are badly damaged." She adds, "May God have mercy on him. He has lost so much blood. As much as a cow loses when it's slaughtered."

Mother talks nonstop. She talks about everything. Aunt Ra'na asks about prison food and sleeping conditions. Mother asks how I spend the days in prison and what sort of people I have met. It feels like we haven't seen each other for ages, as if we haven't talked for years. The guard on duty reminds me of the short time left. "Khaled, make it quick, your time is about to be over."

How fast the time has passed! It's as if it's only been one minute, a second. Mother reaches her arms around my neck, showering me with kisses again. When I free myself from her embrace, I see that tears have welled up in her eyes.

I walk out of the room next to the guards' office. A large crowd, waiting for their visitations, has gathered in front of the iron bars. Men shove women aside. Women squeal. Kids get trampled under foot. A guard leans against the wall of the prison's main office. Right in front of the guards' office, a tall lieutenant is sitting at a large desk taking down the names and contact information of the visitors. Two male guards and two women search the visitors' bodies, not making any exceptions. The voices are muddled:

"Hey, Mother, come over here!" (They even search the crotch of her pants.)

"Hey, I mean you, what's that in your hand?"

"It's a pot of cooked rice."

They poke the cooked rice inside the pot with a spoon.

"How can you search everywhere in their bodies? They even hide opium in their buttocks," one of the guards complains.

"Where are you going?" the other guard yells out, blocking the way of a tall young man. "Come over here . . . let me see what you got in that box?"

The young man turns pale.

"It's nothing, just some snake cucumbers."

The guard opens the box and slices the snake cucumbers with a knife. A piece of opium as big as mouse droppings falls out of the belly of one of the cucumbers. The guard grabs the young man by the wrist.

. . . I have been sentenced to three years of imprisonment by the lower court.

Buyeh, squatting beside the Primus burner, makes tea. Through the vent in the ceiling, sunlight falls into the room. Today, Judge is excused from cooking. The prison food is lentils and rice. We have the potato patties Mother brought. Buyeh hums a song under his breath. He is tall and bony. He always wears an Arabic dishdasha. He wears an Arabic keffiyeh around his head too. He has a salt-and-pepper beard. Buyeh used to be a boatman. Now he is the prison dealer.

"Buyeh, can you find me a pair of secondhand pants?"

"You got it."

"Buyeh, can you sell this watch for me?"

"Man, who needs a watch in prison?"

Buyeh's humming is heart wrenching. It throbs with emotion. My heart takes flight. I long to see the Karun. The smell of fish fills my nose. The Karun is calm. Its water is as clear as tears. It looks indigo under the moonlight. Boats glide by quietly. It's as if they are on velvet clouds. Buyeh hums. The boatman's tune drifts through the air, carrying with it a sadness that fills my soul with grief, a grief that has been transmitted from heart to heart from the banks of the Karun down to me. The grief of all the fishermen and boatmen of the Karun. I cherish this grief. It makes my heart burst, but I cherish it. Buyeh continues to hum.

"Buyeh, what happened that caused you to strike Nasru on the head with a boat paddle?"

"Foolishness made me do it, my son . . . foolishness."

Buyeh has been sentenced to fifteen years in prison. He has done nine years and a few months already.

"What will you do when you get released?" I ask him.

His long teeth show as he smiles. The roots of his teeth are discolored. "Once I get out of here," he sighs, "same old same old."

"Again—"

"Yes, Son," he cuts me short, "again—boats, paddles, and oars."

"And I am sure another argument and another fifteen years in jail," I add, trying to crack a joke.

Buyeh's humming moves you. His eyes are always wandering. Buyeh is the prison's dealer.

"Buyeh, can you sell these shoes for me?"

Judge walks in. Loud and talkative, as always. The guys have given him this name, "Judge." He is the jail's walking law book.

"I have been dealing with the court and jail for seventeen years. Even if I just learn ten clauses of the law each year, that puts me way ahead of the prosecutor himself."

Judge is a small-framed man. He has grown a pencil-thin mustache above his lip. He is always in a hurry. Very clever. He is a petty thief. Even if you kick him out the door, he gets back in through the window.

"What am I supposed to do out there?" he says. "Who's going to take care of me? . . . There's no work for me, and even if there were, I am not the man for it. In jail, I can at least get by somehow." Narrowing his hurried eyes, he continues, "I can manage my cigarettes here, and there too, so . . . what else could you wish for?"

Judge teases everybody. "You killed someone? . . . Clause number 127 says you'll definitely be executed." Then he smiles, waves his finger before your eyes, and mocks, "A mullah's turban is considered religious property, so if you steal it and turn it into a pair of pants to cover your ass, you'll be subject to clause 127!"

Judge squats beside the Primus burner. "Pour me a cup of tea!" he says.

It's quiet in the hallway. The whirr of the Primus seems to intensify the silence. Naser comes and stretches his body out on the kilim rug. "The tea is still not ready?"

The sound of the lunch bell fills the block.

By now, I can close my eyes and count how many rows of bricks are in each wall of the latrines. A pair of sparrows has nested in a hole in the last stall. I know how far the sunlight will reach into the prison's yard, and I know that the gable on top of the security tower is cobalt blue; and the walls of the tower were built using sugar-colored bricks, and the gaps between the layers of bricks have been filled with plaster.

I have become friends with Gholam the Murderer. I have taken a liking to him.

"Didn't I tell you that you'd become a smoker in jail?" he says, sitting down next to me. The block floodlights come on. It's cold at night. We sleep inside our rooms.

"Give me a cigarette, man!"

He's gotten quite used to borrowing cigarettes from me. I give them to him. His striking eyes sparkle. I light the match for him, and he starts to talk nonstop. "You know, Khaled?" He takes a drag of his cigarette and goes on, his voice agreeable. "I just turned twenty," he says in a tender tone. "By the time I get out of here, I'll be thirty-five . . . By then, what good is my life?"

His tone is regretful. "You know what, Khaled?" He pauses for a few seconds, his eyes sparkling. "I have to get out of here . . . even if it means I'll get shot."

His arms are as hard as rocks. His skin is blotchy and pale. The striped jail clothes fit him tightly.

"Can you think of something for me?"

I look at him.

"Can you come up with an idea that could get me out of here?"

I smile at him.

"I'm serious."

My gaze drifts over the tall walls of the jail. The guard with the swarthy complexion walks into the block. "Let's talk about it later," I tell Gholam, and get up and walk toward the guard. He has brought me new books. With a mischievous glint in his eyes, he motions for me to follow, and walks into one of the stalls and then comes back out quickly. Anxiously, I walk into the latrines, pick up the books, and hide them under my shirt. From what the guard tells me, I gather there must be something going on outside. The bazaar has been closed down. The schools have been closed down. The offices are half closed.

"The prime minister has asked for complete authority," he tells me. "Some people are at a sit-in at the telegraph office. They are on a hunger strike," he adds.

Later, before the guard's shift is over, I have to take the books I have read and hidden in Naser the Lifer's box and give them to him to take away.

"This afternoon," he says hurriedly, "there was a rally at Statue Square in support of the government . . ."

I have a deep yearning to be out there, to see Black-Eyed. All the sadness in the world rushes into my heart.

I walk away from the guard with the dark complexion.

"Put the ones you've read somewhere I can easily find them!" he whispers.

I nod to him and walk back to my room. I lean on the pile of bedrolls, hug my knees, and drift away in thought. I feel Black-Eyed's presence next to me. "I love you," I hear her say. The Karun stretches out before me. The smell of freshly cut grass, the smell of the sweet juices of ripe dates, and the acrid smell of mimosa trees fill my nose. My body burns with a yearning to see her. I should somehow let her know that I am in jail. I should get in touch with her.

Buyeh's coarse voice shakes me out of my thoughts. "What's with that mournful face, Khaled?"

I let go of my knees and shift a bit, stretching my legs. I look at Buyeh. A lifeless smile splits my lips open. Manuch the Black comes in. As usual, he is intensely bothered by something. Abruptly, he starts to talk: "If you gave jail food to a dog, I'm sure it wouldn't eat it."

"Take it easy, man," Buyeh says with a smirk.

Manuch the Black frowns at him. "What do you mean, take it easy? I'm starving to death here, and I can't even touch this food. It smells of shit."

Buyeh bursts out laughing. He keels over he's laughing so hard.

Manuch the Black gets mad. The skin under his right eye twitches. His tone becomes coarse. "You can laugh your ass off. It's not like you eat jail food and know what kind of shit it is."

Manuch the Black's face is as black as charcoal. The whites of his eyes are really nauseating. The color of his lips has faded. His hair is as curly as lamb's wool. He is short and stout. Buyeh sits down and starts sewing and mending stuff. I give Manuch the Black a cigarette. Gholam the Murderer's singing reverberates under the arched ceiling of the hallway. His voice is bitter and moving: "My skull is a ship. My tears are the sea."

I take refuge in my thoughts again. My heart is heavy. I yearn to see Black-Eyed. I leave Manuch the Black and Buyeh alone together and walk out of the room into the prison yard, which is as bright as daylight, even though it's night. I pace up and down the yard. The security tower is empty. The guard, with his rifle slung over his shoulder, has left the tower and is pacing on the roof, tramping heavily, as if on my heart. I look at the sky. It's clear. The stars twinkle here and there. I wish I could fly beyond the four walls of the jail and go straight to Black-Eyed's house.

I hear Mother humming a bitter tune. Sitting beside the kerosene lamp, she hugs her knees and sings. Her voice reaches my ears from far away, fluttering toward me like a wounded pigeon:

"If only I could fly around your roof like a turtledove."

My heart overflows with grief.

"May falcons eat my flesh and dogs my bones."

Out of nowhere, Esi the Red Faced grabs my arm. I jump.

"Did I scare you?"

I smile at him.

"Why are you walking alone?"

"I'm homesick, Esi."

Esi the Red Faced sighs. His hair is amber-colored. His face is bloodred. He is small and swift, just like a wasp. He and Manuch the Black are partners in crime. We walk together.

"Manuch has become very bad-tempered," he says.

I listen.

"He hasn't eaten for two days. I tell him, if you wanna act like this, go ahead, but you won't get anywhere."

Esi the Red Faced and Manuch the Black are charged with stealing cars.

Esi goes on, "I tell him, your soul will part from your body through your ass in two days if you don't eat, but he doesn't listen."

"Manuch is right. The prison's food is not edible," I finally say.

His shrill voice bothers my ears. "I know it myself. But what choice do we have?"

There must be a way. Even a hungry dog would not eat the prison's food. Meals are usually two boiled rotten potatoes with a black date, or a bowl of watery soup, or a plate of lentils and rice dry enough to choke on, and two loaves of black bread full of bran, which makes barley bread sound a hundred times more appealing.

"You got a cigarette?" I hear Esi ask.

I give him a cigarette. We keep to ourselves. Both of us are lost in our own thoughts. We walk the length of the entire block and come back, then again and again, over and over. Esi stubs out the cigarette butt under his foot. The door to the block opens, and Naser the Lifer steps inside. He has a hold of Rahim the Donkey Keeper's wrist. I rush toward him. Mash Rahim carries his bedroll and other odds and ends under his arm. A wide smile has spread on Naser the Lifer's face.

"Just for your sake!" he says.

Mash Rahim lets go of his bedroll, dropping it to the ground. We hug each other. The smell of depilatory powder and Oshnu tobacco fills my nostrils.

It feels as if I have been granted all of the joys that are left in the world. My grief lets up and my heart opens up. I pick up Mash Rahim's bedroll, and together we walk into our room. We sit down beside each other. Judge makes tea. Mash Rahim has picked up some of the phrases used in court. His neck and the veins running through it look dark. His dry Adam's apple moves up and down. His voice trembles. He has gotten so much older.

"My lawyer was not compensated. And that means . . . practically no lawyer," he says.

The skin of his lips is dry and cracked. His mustache has turned yellow. His face is pale and his eyes wander. He lights a cigarette. Words get stuck before they make their way out of his mouth. "They sentenced me to death."

My heart trembles. I try to console him. "They could never execute you."

But deep down I am not so sure. Judge starts to crack jokes. "First-degree murder, clause number 170, execution without any question."

Mash Rahim's scared eyes freeze on Judge's subtle face. Buyeh bursts out laughing. Naser the Lifer grumbles. Buyeh stops laughing.

Mash Rahim squats down as if sitting under the sun with a pipe he has just stuffed, like he used to do. Looking at the donkeys' sun shelter, he talks with Amu Bandar. I listen to them as I feed millet to my pigeons.

"I doubt that this sun shelter will stand another rain."

"But winter is almost over."

Mash Rahim's voice quavers. He swallows his spit and says, "You talk for a good two hours, but nobody pays attention . . ."

Judge pours tea.

Mash Rahim continues, "And at the end they put a sheet of paper in front of you and order you to sign it with your thumbprint . . ." Sipping tea from his cup, he says, "But if they don't even bother to listen to you carefully, how can they know what's really happened? How would they know—"

Naser the Lifer's coarse voice cuts Mash Rahim short. "Look at me, old man!" he says, tapping on his own chest, "I killed someone, but they didn't execute me."

Naser the Lifer killed his own sister. One day, when he got home, he saw that his mother was worried. He found out that his sister had gone out early in the morning and hadn't come home yet. He searched through the entire city, street by street, looking for her. Then, he searched all the cities for her. Finally, his search ended in Zolmabad. He found out that his sister was serving at Akram the Black's house. He drew his knife out of his pocket, and without bothering to ask her a question, slit her stomach open. He then twisted the knife around in her bowels and pulled them all out at once. Before anyone could think what to do, Naser himself ran to the police station and informed them that he had killed his sister, that he had defended his own honor.

Naser the Lifer pours his tea in a saucer, blows at it, and says, "That's right, old man . . . don't worry about it . . . One should never lose hope!"

Mash Rahim's cracked lips move . . . He has grown very old. "I'm not afraid of being executed." His voice trembles. ". . . What has this life brought me except sorrow, anyway? . . . Besides, what am I going to do outside jail?" Fixing his eyes on mine, he says, "But you know, Khaled . . . this way, it's terrible."

Mash Rahim's lips close. He keeps quiet for a moment. Stubbing out his cigarette butt, he then goes on, "It's so horrible to hang in front of everybody in public just like a sheep at a butcher's . . . It's disgraceful."

He hugs his knees and sighs.

"Don't beat yourself up too much, old man," Judge says hastily.

Buyeh pours another cup of tea for Mash Rahim.

Resting his chin on his knees, Mash Rahim says, "It's such a shameful act, to take someone to a wasteland and bury him alive . . . A man has dignity."

"Old man, you're talking nonsense . . . You're just torturing yourself," Naser the Lifer says in a thick voice.

The guard with the swarthy complexion appears in the doorway. I need to give him the books. Naser the Lifer smiles at him and offers him tea. "Come and have some tea with us, Guard."

No doubt Naser the Lifer suspects something is going on with us. The guard drinks the tea and leaves. I go to Naser the Lifer's chest and take out the books. I hear Naser the Lifer say, "You should start teaching me tomorrow."

I fiddle with the odds and ends inside the chest, pick up the books—each the size of my hand—and hide them under my shirt.

It's gotten cold. The morning sunlight feels pleasant. Right after we're done eating breakfast, we head out of our rooms into the yard and sit around together against the towering wall of the prison yard, chatting and smoking in the sun. Naser the Lifer has started his lessons. It'll take him another month or so to read and write well. For now, he is able to recognize words. He's all wound up. It's amazing how much enthusiasm he has for learning. He has a sharp memory.

We lean back and stretch our legs out on the blanket we have spread next to the wall, taking pleasure in the sun, forcing the dampness of the night out of our bodies. Mash Rahim has become very quiet. He just sits, hugs his knees, fixes his eyes on a spot, and drifts away in his own thoughts. If you don't talk to him, he won't say a word; and then if you ask him something, he gives such a short and quiet answer that you'd rather have not asked him at all.

Mash Rahim's stomach is bloated. He believes it has absorbed too much water. His hands and feet are all puffy too. His neck is getting thinner every day. He doesn't walk at all.

"Mash Rahim, you should walk and move your body a bit."

With his hollow eyes, he looks at you in a way that makes your stomach churn.

Eskandar has chewed up the crusts of his bread, kneaded them, and is now making a statue with the dough. That's what he does all day long. He has started a business doing that. From dawn to the middle of the night, he sits, chews the crusts patiently, kneads the dough, then starts to make various statues. He then dyes them, glazes them, and sends them out of jail for sale. "If I don't do this," he says, "who'll provide for my wife and kids? . . . I have to stomach another eleven months in this pig sty. Somehow, I have to make some money to keep them going."

Hossein the Soup Maker and Esi the Red Faced are playing a game of *duz*. Buyeh heads to the prison yard, looking to make some deals. Manuch the Black and Mehdi the Wide Chest are sitting on the cement steps in front of the latrines, talking. Manuch the Black eats every other day. You wouldn't believe how skinny he's gotten. There's barely any life in his eyes. Sometimes he feels dizzy, his knees tremble, and his entire body begins to shiver.

The door to the block opens. They bring in the baskets of bread. Two hundred and eighteen loaves of bread for a hundred and nine people. This is our ration for twenty-four hours; two loaves of black bread for each of us.

Ali the Harelipped picks up his share and comes and sits next to me. He reaches over and takes the half-smoked cigarette from my hand. He takes a few drags, one after another, inhales the smoke, and, puckering his lips, says, "That Manuch is right." Holding the bread, blackened and hard as a brick, he hits it against his knee and says, "Look here, if you hit an elephant on the head with it, it would die on the spot. It's hard as stone."

Manuch the Black's words are working their effect. His complaints circulate from mouth to mouth. "The bastards are giving us dog meat."

Some have begun to purse their lips in discontent. "They give us garbage to eat."

Dumping out their bowls of watery stew into the dead flowerbeds, they grumble, "It's like the filthy water from a bath."

Leaning against the stone wall, the guard on duty in the block holds on tightly to the baton hanging from his belt, and smokes. A few black pigeons soar in the sky above the prison yard. In the sunlight, their wings shine like a piece of well-cut black mica. The sky is clear all over. Coming out of the room, Judge yawns noisily and pounds on his chest with his fist. Mash Rahim has stretched his legs out and looks ahead idly. A few inmates are walking around. Judge comes toward me. "Let's walk a bit!"

I get up and start to walk.

The old man sitting in front of the latrines counts the notches he has carved on the wall. I hear the door to the block open. I turn around and look. A small-framed young man comes in.

"Shove him in!" someone says in a loud voice.

The newcomer has a swarthy complexion. He has large eyes and a shaved head. He looks familiar. I walk toward him. Judge follows me, asking, "Where are you going?"

I point to the young man, who is now shaking hands with Mohammad the Brainless and kissing him on the cheeks.

"I think I know him."

Judge grabs my arm. "You know him?"

"Where do you know him from?" he asks in a surprised tone.

"I think I have seen him somewhere," I say.

"Well, that's Reza the Pickpocket," he says in a low voice.

I get an urge to talk to Reza the Pickpocket. He walks away from Mohammad the Brainless and goes into the hallway, carrying his bundle under his arm. I follow him quickly and call after him. He stops and looks me up and down, then fixes his incredulous eyes on mine. His eyes seem vaguely familiar. I step forward and stand in front of him. We look at each other for a few moments. Reza the Pickpocket says, "What do you want from me?"

I still can't put my finger on why it is he looks familiar. "I wonder where I've seen you?" I reply.

His eyes take on a surprised expression. In a muffled voice he says, "Where do you think?"

His voice shakes me. He's about to walk away. It's cold in the hallway. I grab his arm and stop him. "Wait a second . . . I must have seen you somewhere."

Shaking his arm free from my grasp, he raises his voice: "What do you want from me?"

Suddenly, everything comes back to me. The smell of arrack fills my nose. His voice rings in my ears: "I'll cut your veins with this razor."

Blood rushes to my face. Before I know it, I have clutched his arms violently and shoved him into my room. His bundle drops from his hands. I don't allow him to move and push him into the corner of the room. My voice quivers with rage: "Why did you want to cut me with your razor that night in the police station?"

Reza the Pickpocket's eyeballs bulge. My hand is tight around his throat. His mouth is open, but he cannot talk. He struggles to free himself from my grip.

"Why? . . . Huh? If you don't answer me, I'll strangle you right this minute."

He is shocked, stunned; in fact, his jaw has dropped. His face is darkening. His large eyeballs bulge.

"Talk!" I demand as I squeeze his throat harder.

He cannot talk.

Naser the Lifer's raspy voice hits my ears: "What're you doing, Khaled?"

I turn around. Naser's piercing eyes bring me back. I let go of Reza. Looking down, I say, "He's the guy who wanted to cut me with a razor in the police station."

Naser's eyes narrow. Reza moves to get away. Naser blocks his way. "Is that so, Rezi?"

Reza doesn't answer. Naser pinches his earlobe and squeezes it hard between his fingers. I step aside. Reza's face has turned the color of saffron.

"I said, is that so, Rezi? Was that you?"

Reza keeps quiet.

"Why did you want to cut Khaled with a razor?"

Reza mumbles and blubbers something.

From what he says, I see that Ali the Devil had put him up to it.

Naser hasn't let go of his earlobe.

"He told me to scare him," Reza tells Naser. "He said it would even be all right if I had to cut him."

Letting go of his ear, Naser asks him, "But why?"

Beside himself with fear, Reza has turned into a paralyzed mouse. He has shrunk and become even smaller.

"You didn't say why?"

"What do you mean, why? Isn't that obvious?" snaps Reza. "I need him . . . If I didn't do that for him, he would've given me a real hard time."

Naser strikes him softly on the ear with four fingers. "You are such a coward!"

He reaches for my arm, pulling me gently aside. "Let's go and take a walk!"

We have barely stepped into the yard when I hear a horse neigh. It's Gholam the Murderer, trotting and neighing. He kicks his legs as he comes from the end of the block. Everyone has stopped walking and is looking at him. Gholam is trotting, neighing, and kicking. The guard inside the block dashes toward him and blocks his way. "What the hell is wrong with you, Gholam?"

Gholam waits. Shifting from one foot to the other, he breathes heavily. Just like a horse that has run across the fields in full gallop.

"Go and sit your ass down!" the guard rasps.

Yet Gholam stamps and starts trotting and neighing again. Judge leaps into the yard and makes fun of Gholam. Gholam stops, beats his hooves against the ground for a few seconds, then turns around in a circle, and tosses his head like an unruly horse.

The guard steps forward and strikes Gholam's hips with his baton. Gholam jumps up and stands as straight as a pole in front of the guard, saying in a sincere tone, "I swear I am a horse, Guard."

His eyeballs roll back into his head. The guard steps back and waves the end of his baton before Gholam's face, barking, "If you don't stop fooling around, I'll send you to solitary."

Gholam bursts out laughing. He jumps at the guard and starts circling him and kissing his lips. The guard moves away and hits Gholam on the neck with his baton. Naser the Lifer runs toward them and grabs the guard's hand as he raises it to hit Gholam's face once again. He pulls the guard aside, takes hold of Gholam, and shoves him in our room. The guard on the rooftop has come out of the security tower and is looking inside the block. The prisoners follow Naser and Gholam. Gholam neighs again. Naser's voice explodes: "Shut up, Gholam!"

Manuch the Black, sitting on the cement steps in front of the latrines, does not budge at all. I peek my head in through the window. Gholam is utterly mute. No matter how Naser tries to talk to him, he does not respond. The sun is really hot. It looks as if it'll rain tonight. Esi the Red Faced puts his arm around my shoulders and nods at Manuch the Black. "Look at him . . . He's mourning."

Manuch the Black just stares at the two loaves of black bread placed in front of him.

"He'll die of hunger soon."

I push Esi the Red Faced's hand off my shoulder and stand in front of him. "Look, Esi," I say, "if we all refuse to eat the jail food, just like Manuch the Black, they'll have no choice but to make it more edible."

Esi the Red Faced is as nimble and delicate-looking as a wasp. His high-pitched voice irritates my ears. "I swear on your life," he says, "it won't make them budge, not even a bit. And if we stick to it, they'll surely kick our asses."

Pursing my lips, I look at him for a few moments. His cheeks are bloodred. His forehead is spotted with pimples. His pale lips look dry and flaky. I remember Shafaq and the strike at the textile factory. Esi the Red Faced disappears before my eyes. I find myself in the basement, sitting opposite the Doctor. The fan is turning. The basement is filled with smoke. The faint glow of a light struggles to penetrate the smoke. The Doctor's short beard moves as he talks. I stare at Esi the Red Faced and quietly say, "Do you think it's not the fear of starvation that makes everyone eat the damn jail food?"

Esi grumbles, but I rob him of the chance to speak. "Do you think that if they were not faced with hunger, they would ever eat this garbage?"

Esi the Red Faced growls. All his teeth are showing, like an enraged dog. "I know that too . . . but—"

"Esi, believe me," I cut him short, "we could do this. If we all want this, we could definitely improve the quality of the food."

Yet again I hear Gholam the Murderer's neighing echoing in the corridor. The guard, once again waving his baton, dashes toward him.

Esi the Red Faced releases his shoulder from my hand and goes after the guard.

The rain has stopped. There was a short-lived downpour early in the night. But thundering clouds still grumble in the sky. The sound has awakened me a few times so far. It must be around midnight. The ceiling light is on. I can't go back to sleep. Buyeh snores quietly. Naser has wrapped the blanket around himself and drawn his legs up to his stomach. I haven't been able to get any news of Black-Eyed. A few times the words have come up to my front teeth, but I simply couldn't say them to Bidar. I decide to tell him the next time he comes to visit me. I will ask him to go find news of Black-Eyed. Pendar's damn voice won't leave me alone. It claws at me whenever I think of Black-Eyed. "You should learn not to get carried away by emotions when you are engaged in combat."

I make faces at Pendar. "What about now?" I glare at him. "Now that I am trapped like a rat?"

The Doctor's melodious voice gives me confidence. "Now you have another duty . . ." His eyes are piercing. "A critical duty."

I close my eyes. I hear the Doctor say, "I mean the strike on jail food." I stare at his mouth.

"Everyone's unhappy with the situation. They just need someone to tell them what to do."

I hear Manuch the Black's voice. The pupils of his eyes move under his upper eyelids. He doesn't have the strength to talk. His voice is muffled.

Ali the Harelipped's bulky legs, like two clay pillars, come toward me. His neck has sunk into his chest. His muzzle is pointed. Shaking the loaves of black bread before my eyes, he says, "You can break an elephant's neck with it."

His short arm swings to the left and right along with the bread. "Look at it! It's just like stone."

I brace my arms, pull up my body, and lean against the wall. I hug my knees and then pull the blanket up to my chin and close my eyes.

"You have to work hard . . . ," I hear the Doctor's voice. "You should talk to them one at a time . . . You should prepare them all . . . You should change their living conditions . . . You should prove that you are smarter than they are . . . You should make them realize that they can do a lot of things if they want to . . ." His small goatee moves as he talks. "You should make them realize that everything can be changed . . . everything . . ."

I open my eyes. I don't know why Leila's daring gaze suddenly appears before me. Her eyes fill the room. I can't look at them. I close my eyes. I hear Black-Eyed's voice. It permeates like the sweet scents of all the fragrant flowers in the world.

Gholam's voice shakes me out of my thoughts. It's past midnight. Buyeh's snoring has died down. Gholam the Murderer has gone into the yard, reciting the call to prayer at the top of his lungs. I get out of my bedroll and open the window. A cold wind rushes in. Naser the Lifer rolls over and sits up. "For the love of God! That motherfucker won't let us sleep even at this time of night."

I stick my head out of the window. Gholam is standing on the cement steps in front of the latrines. Cupping his hands around his ears, he recites the call to prayer out loud: "God is great!"

The windows open one after another. Inside the yard it is as bright as day. Gholam is mixing up the verses now and reciting them in a strange way. "I bear witness that Ali is the Messenger of God."

The guard on the roof, wrapping himself in a dark jacket, walks out of the security tower and peers into the yard from behind the barbed wire.

Thunder explodes again. Gholam the Murderer keeps at it: "I bear witness that Mohammad is the Hossein of God."[5]

Stepping back, the guard on the roof blows a whistle. By now, everyone has woken up. Gholam has finished reciting the *azan*. Squatting there on the steps, in his thin striped prison shirt, he starts giving a sermon. Gholam's voice, despite the gibberish he's blabbering, stirs one's heart. "You, fortunate prisoners, lead God to the right path . . ."

As the prisoners stand in front of their rooms, their jumbled voices echo in the corridor. Some throw a blanket over their shoulders and walk into the yard. Some have peeked their heads out of their windows and are making fun of Gholam. Gholam, indifferent to all, carries on with his sermon. "I had a dream that God came with a forked beard and told me: 'Rise, Gholam, recite the call to prayer, and preach to these cowards . . .'"

Laughter and jokes mingle in the air.

Gholam's voice gains strength. "And you, lazy asshole prisoners, you, who snuffle like bald sheep . . ."

The clang of the iron door explodes like thunder in the yard as it is thrown open.

---

5. In his attempt to feign madness, Gholam is deliberately distorting the Muslim testimony of faith, which is "I bear witness that Mohammad is the messenger of God." Gholam, however, says, "Hossein of God."

Gholam continues his sermon: "And you, the good, wretched folks of God, come and kiss my hand and accept me as your prophet, or I will have the chief of the jail batter up your pretty asses with batons."

The prisoners' hooting and cackling has filled the rooms. A middle-aged guard hurriedly elbows his way through the crowd toward Gholam.

Gholam's soft hair has curled over his eyes. His well-shaped eyes wander around, and his warm voice rises over all the other voices. "You, the chicken stew prisoners—"

"What the hell is wrong with you?" the guard's old and sleepy voice cuts Gholam short.

Gholam keeps quiet for a second, then continues: "You, the chicken stew prisoners, worship Gholam the Murderer and curse the guard with henna-colored hair."

Words and laughter are jumbled.

"He's gone nuts."

"Come on, he's just faking it."

"What are you talking about?" another one says. "It's the blood he's shed that drives him mad like this."

"Nonsense, man, I know this son of a bitch. It's all a show."

"You think murdering someone is a trivial thing?"

The guard steps closer, grabs Gholam's arm, and drags him off the platform. Glaring at him, the guard warns him in a rasping voice, "Go and sit your ass down, or I'll . . ."

At this, Gholam wrestles his arm free from the guard's grip and yells, "You, prisoners, my people, my cowardly people, punish this guard who is more cowardly than you, or else—"

Gholam does not have a chance to finish his sentence before the guard's fisted hand punches his wide neck. Words get muffled in Gholam's throat, yet he won't budge. He just stands there firmly, like the beams that hold a roof up. Holding his head up, he pushes his chest out and smiles at the guard; then his voice blasts forth like firecrackers: "You cowards!" He turns around, stands facing the guard, and says in a low voice, "I was thinking of appointing you, bastard, as one of my imams, but now . . ."

The guard moves to grab Gholam's arm again, but he leaps over the guard's back and smacks his neck with his open palm so hard that the guard is thrown to the ground.

Again we hear the iron door being flung open. The sergeant major, along with two guards, rushes inside. Waving their batons, they weave their way through the dense crowd of prisoners.

Gholam bellows, "The war is defeated now." And as if in the pit of the Zurkhaneh gym, he starts whirling around, and before the sergeant major and the guards reach him, he jumps onto the steps and starts reciting a poem. "I pummel you so hard with my precious club, just like the blacksmith hammers iron flat."

At this, he starts drumming on his own belly.

The block descends into chaos.

The sergeant major and the guards, twirling their batons in their hands, shift from one foot to another as they stand before Gholam. One of the guards cusses everyone and everything. He cusses Gholam's relatives, dead or alive. "Come down, you motherfucker . . . Stop fooling around, or I'll shove a baton up your ass."

Gholam drums on his own belly, reciting more poetry. "Tomorrow, when the sun is up, there's the ring, me, the club, and this guard."

The sergeant major rushes toward the guards and yells, "Drag him down! Why are you circling around him like wounded dogs around a wolf?" Reaching for one of the guards, he pushes him forward, but Gholam the Murderer's kick drives him back at once.

The sleepy voice of the officer on duty rises from behind the crowd: "What's going on here?"

We let the officer through.

"Step aside, come on already . . . Let me see what the hell is wrong with him."

Clicking his heels together quickly, Gholam salutes the officer and shouts: "Attention all! Turn around!"

The officer is tall and well built. He has an air of confidence about him as he speaks. He stands facing Gholam. Quietly but firmly he says, "Step down, Gholam, and go get some sleep like a good boy."

Suddenly, the sky bursts with thunder.

Gholam says quietly, "Did you hear that, Officer? . . . That was God speaking . . . He said I am a prophet."

"Go to your rooms!" the officer snaps.

We back off a bit, but we don't go to our rooms.

The officer's eyes are puffy. His hair is rumpled. The sergeant major and the guards stand in a row behind the officer. The sergeant major is fuming with rage. Gholam squats down. He doesn't seem to feel the cold through his thin shirt. He gazes at the officer. Once again, the officer snaps at us. We back off a bit more.

Gholam's pleasant voice fills our ears again: "You are a very undisciplined officer . . . You don't have a religion, either . . . I am telling you that I am your pimp prophet . . . Come on and prostrate yourself before me!"

"All right, Gholam, but you come down and go to sleep," the officer reasons with him in a soft voice.

Gholam screeches like a panther, leaps, and embraces the officer, knocking both of them on the ground and sending them rolling.

It starts to rain again.

Aunt Ra'na and Mother have come to visit me. They are both clad in black. My heart sinks the moment I see them. Aunt Ra'na's gray hair peeks out from under her headscarf. Her eyes are puffy, her voice barely audible. Mother's eyes well up with tears. "Gholam has gotten shot."

I almost faint. My knees wobble. With a choked voice, I repeat, "Gholam has gotten shot?"

I imagine him standing in front of me, talking. His black mustache, curved up at the ends—like the tail of a scorpion—trembles as he talks. "But, Sergeant Major, take pity on me, please . . . Where can I get that kind of money from?"

Aunt Ra'na sobs. The tip of her nose has turned red. She wipes her runny nose with the hem of her headscarf, and in a broken voice, whimpers, "He died young . . . Now, my back is broken."

Aunt Ra'na's eyes are red. Her cheeks are hollow.

Gholam, his legs crossed, is sitting on the stool. Swaying, he says, "Dear Aunt, can you go to the colonel's house and do their laundry tomorrow?" Grief sweeps through me. I am angry with myself. I never realized I cared so much for Gholam.

Tears trickle down Aunt Ra'na's face. "May you be safe from any harm!" She sobs, and stammers, "On the rifle range . . . he got shot accidentally . . . My dear young boy . . . may you be safe from any harm, dear . . ."

Gholam's body was carried to Aunt Ra'na's house in a hearse. Aunt Ra'na threw the dust in the alley on her head in grief. She ripped her dress open, plucked her hair out strand by strand, scratched her cheeks, screamed her heart out in the alley, then clenched her teeth and fainted.

Mother's eyes weep tears of sorrow. "Stones always come down on closed doors!"[6]

Gholam's corpse lies before my eyes. His chest, wide and broad, bulges out of his uniform shirt. He seems to be smiling. His mustache quivers. His lips are half parted. "You dare breathe a word of protest, and you're detained . . . You talk back, and your military service time is increased . . . You stand up for your own rights, you'll end up in the barracks' jail . . ."

I can see Gholam sitting at the small courtyard pool. Bolur Khanom moves around the courtyard. Gholam's head turns and his eyes follow her. Having unbuttoned the collar of his shirt, Gholam displays his hairy chest.

"Khaled! Can you take a message to Bolur Khanom for me?"

I wish I had taken his message to Bolur Khanom that day. I wish I hadn't treated him so badly.

It's nighttime. The light in the courtyard is grayish. Khaj Tofiq is sitting beside the brazier. Banu is dozing beside the lamp. Aunt Ra'na walks in, whimpering, "May your mother die for you now that you are at the mercy of the oppressor."

Father is squatting next to the wall. He is not very fond of Aunt Ra'na. He smokes as he looks at her. Aunt Ra'na sits down and starts to slap her head and chest. Her son has been drafted.

"Sister, do you think that the orderly of His Excellency the Captain can do us a favor?"

"Of course he can, Sister," says Sanam, "but you should know, it won't happen without money."

The army uniform suits Gholam well. I move closer to him and strike a pose. Hasani and Ebrahim are burning with envy.

Time is up and my visit is over. I can't part with Aunt Ra'na. I can't part with Mother. I press Aunt Ra'na to my chest. A lump of grief is lodged in my throat. I circle my arms around Mother's neck. Time is up.

---

6. A proverb meant to convey that bad things always happen to good people.

I have to leave. If I don't get a hold of myself, tears will wash over my entire face. I kiss Aunt Ra'na, hurry out of the visiting room, and walk into the block.

I lean against the pile of bedrolls and hug my knees. Judge walks in hastily, takes a package out of his box, and hurries out. I rest my chin on my knees and close my eyes. Gholam is riding in a boat. His arms turn into two rocks as he paddles. Beads of sweat have formed on his forehead. It's humid. The splash of water echoes in my ears. Tiny fish bounce along the surface of the water. The boat jolts as its bow sinks in the sand. Gholam has painted his boat in the colors of the Iranian flag: green, white, and red.

"Hop out!" I hear Gholam say. He lets the paddle drop into the boat and jumps out onto the moist sand. Stretching his arms wide, he scoops me out of the boat, as if picking up a feather, and puts me down onto the sand. Gholam has planted the entire island with cucumber seeds, watermelon seeds too. The watermelons have yet to ripen. The cucumbers are incredibly green. I search around the cucumber vines and pick a couple of tender baby cucumbers. They are cool. Gholam draws a knife from under his belt, releases the catch, and peels the cucumbers with its blade. I rub the cool peels of the cucumbers onto my hot cheeks. I enjoy their coolness. The sun is aglow. The sun's rays reflect off the tall elephant-gray arches of the bridge. Tiny waves on the surface of the Karun reflect the sunshine. The sharp smell of fish, the scent of unripe dates, and the smell of twisting cucumber vines all mix together.

Naser the Lifer calls me. I come to myself. He stands facing me, his arms akimbo. "Boy, I've been hovering over you for an hour now."

I look at him.

He reads the grief on my face. "What's wrong?"

I tell him what has happened. Naser sits down next to me. He tries to console me. I tell him that I want to be left alone. He lights a cigarette, hands it to me, and leaves.

Gholam materializes through the rings of cigarette smoke. He is sitting on the stool. Mother has fixed him a glass of sherbet.

I hear Bolur Khanom's voice: "Gholam, is mandatory service tough?"

Bolur Khanom irritates me. I want to choke her. I want to clutch her throat and squeeze it hard, until it bruises, so that she won't tease my cousin like that.

Gholam, boasting, says, "The commander reaches a finger under everyone's puttees to see if they're tight enough. If they're not, you'll have to face the Angel of Death."

My eyes are filled with tears. The image of Aunt Ra'na's son is magnified through the prism of tears, then shudders away. I take a deep drag of my cigarette and exhale the dense smoke. I realize I'm talking to myself. "No, Cousin, no . . . I had no intention of annoying you . . ." Aunt Ra'na's son bursts out laughing, then falls silent. He puts his arm on my shoulder and starts to kiss my cheeks. "Don't worry, Cousin," he says gently, "sometimes, even brothers yell at each other."

I stub out the cigarette and lay my forehead down on my knees.

The image of a bullet piercing Gholam's neck stays before my eyes. Blood spurts out like water from a fountain. Aunt Ra'na's wailing makes the hair on my arms stand up. "My Gholam . . . Ah, what a misery . . . My precious son!"

Aunt Ra'na's husband is in complete shock. As he squats down on his heels, staring at Gholam's body, his eyes are about to pop out of their sockets. Cousin's face is smeared with blood. Aunt Ra'na's husband is a laborer. Aunt Ra'na's son was a boatman. Her daughter has been married and divorced twice. The lump in my throat is suffocating. Buyeh knew Gholam. Beating his wide palms against each other, he asks in a sorrowful tone, "Gholam?" Then, gathering his Arabic dishdasha around him, he sits down beside me. "May God bless his soul," he murmurs. "He was a nice boy."

But Gholam is not dead. He has grown even taller before my eyes. He has wrapped his puttees tight around his ankles. His chest bulges. The army uniform suits him well. A smile has parted his fleshy lips.

"God bless his soul," Buyeh says again.

I look at Buyeh, but I can't see him. Everything is blurry. I think it's sunset, the day that my uncle's body was brought home. I hear Mother singing as she cries softy:

> *If I knew that my fate would be like this,*
> *I would've drunk poison instead of my mother's milk.*

Reaching an arm out to me, Buyeh helps me to my feet. "Come, Khaled, let's walk!"

It's sunny. Sunny yet cold. Dragging my feet, I walk with Buyeh. He talks about Gholam. "May God bless his soul; he was a nice boy. Some nights, he'd buy a bottle of arrack, and right there on the boat, he'd grill a good southern *hilsa* fish and eat it, and drink arrack. Then he'd sing. He had a good voice, vibrant too. It would take away all your sadness."

Buyeh talks as if to himself. Clasping his hands behind his head, he keeps his head bowed and matches his pace with mine.

Rahim the Donkey Keeper is sitting on the steps in front of the latrines. His stomach looks like a big drum. His parched skin has a tinge of yellow to it. He doesn't interact with anyone. He has no interest in talking to anyone, not even to me. Buyeh keeps talking. I hear his voice, but I cannot make out any words. The words fill my ears as if they are the buzzing of bees. I am adrift in my own thoughts. Without saying a word, I leave him and walk toward Mash Rahim. I sit down next to him. He doesn't even bother to turn to me; just gazes off into the distance.

"Mash Rahim," I call out to him.

No response.

I call out to him again. He turns and looks at me. I don't dare look into his cheerless eyes. Lowering my head, I say under my breath, "Did you hear, Mash Rahim? . . . Gholam is dead."

He doesn't say anything. My heart feels heavy. All I want is to be free of all this sorrow. "Did you hear that . . . he was shot in the neck . . . on the rifle range? . . . I mean my cousin."

I doubt that he has heard anything I've told him. Engrossed in his own thoughts, he finally says, "It's better that way . . . It's better to be shot."

"But, Mash Rahim, Gholam didn't do anything wrong," I say.

His burnt eyelashes close. His dry, cracked lips part. "Imagine, before the eyes of all those people, those who know you and those who don't . . . No, my son . . . that's not a proper way to die."

His voice trembles. He opens his eyes. The sadness in his eyes causes my heart to shudder.

His teeth are stained. His mustache is yellow. His neck is as thin as a water pipe hose. The skin under his eyes is dark and puffy. His shaved head, uneven. His forehead, creased. Cigarette smoke gets entangled in his mustache. "You know, Khaled," Mash Rahim says, "it's been a long time since I last saw Ebrahim and Hasani . . . I miss them . . . What do you suppose has happened to them?"

He takes a deep drag of his cigarette as he looks at me with a stunned expression hanging over his face. As if coming back to himself, he asks abruptly, "What did you say?"

"I said, Aunt Ra'na's son is dead . . ."

He slaps the back of his hand hard and, in a dismal tone, recites, "There's no god but God."

"He got shot, Mash Rahim . . ."

"There's no god but God."

"On the rifle range . . . he was accidentally shot."

He stares straight ahead.

"Mash Rahim!"

No response.

"Mash Rahim, Gholam was a nice boy."

He is quiet.

"Mash Rahim!"

He gets up and walks toward the corridor. His *giveh* shoes crumple as he walks. Just as I get to my feet, two loaves of bread, one after the other, are suddenly thrown out of the window of Room 10, hitting the facing wall and bouncing back like two rocks. I look around carefully. Manuch the Black's curly hair peeks out of the window. The whites of his eyes have become much whiter, and the black of his pupils is fading each day.

I am about to go looking for Mash Rahim when Naser the Lifer calls me. "They're calling your name at the block's door."

As I walk away, he reaches for my arm. "What's with you?"

"I'll tell you."

I walk toward the iron door of the block. I can see the eyes and nose of the guard with the swarthy complexion. He tells me that he has been transferred to the police station. "Someone else will probably contact you soon," he says.

"What about the contact code?" I ask.

"If your father doesn't come back for Nowruz, will you miss him?" he states.

"I already miss him," I am supposed to answer.

"Then let me tell you that he'll be back for Nowruz!"

And I have to say, "I hope you're right!"

By word of mouth, we hear that Gholam the Murderer has been practically beaten to death under the guards' batons. We hear that he was tied up to the short palm tree in front of the jail's office and was lashed until he passed out. And when he fell silent and fainted, they untied him, put him in manacles, threw him like a piece of dead meat into solitary, and shut the iron door behind him.

At noon, on the way to get our lunch ration, we linger and try to see if we can hear his moaning or something, but there seems to be nobody in solitary at all.

At night, we hear from Buyeh that Gholam called out to the guard on duty in the corridor and told him that he is back to his senses: "Guard, may my mother's breasts be scorched if I lie . . . I'm back in my right mind."

Then he made the guard in the corridor promise to call the officer on duty. "Ask him to come, for the love of God! Aren't you a good Muslim?"

Now we all wait to hear any news of Gholam the Murderer.

As the sun's rays brighten everything, Naser the Lifer comes down the corridor and brings us news.

Apparently, after a new guard started his shift, the officer on duty went to see Gholam. Gholam, his hands bound, his back against the wall, pulled himself up and said, "Officer, I am regretful, I made a mistake . . . but I'm back in my right mind."

"Now you're talking," the officer said, smiling.

"You know what, Officer . . . I thought about it a lot," Gholam said. "I am not a prophet anymore . . . God wants me to be his imam . . . just an imam."

Hearing this, the officer pursed his lips, and without saying a word, walked down the corridor lined with cells and left solitary confinement.

At noon, we pick up our copper bowls, tuck them under our arms, and go get our lunch. Gholam the Murderer, his face stuck to the round hole in the iron door, calls out to us: "Hey, Khaled . . . tell Rostam that Bijan got drowned in the well."

His lips are swollen. Dried blood darkens the tip of his nose and his upper lip. "Hey, Buyeh . . . you Arab . . . tell Rostam that Bijan says if he doesn't come to save me, I'll have Esfandiar shove a two-headed club up his ass."

Gholam the Murderer's voice is hoarse. His eyeballs bulge. "Hey, Judge . . . I'm talking to you . . . Tell this guard that he is such a jackass

. . . Tell him to beat it before Rostam comes."

The guard in charge of watching the corridor comes and shoos us away from Gholam's cell.

It's been three days since Gholam was put in solitary. He has gone nuts, and is getting worse every day.

The officer on duty opens the cell and orders his manacles unlocked. He tells Gholam, "As long as you want to act nuts, this will be your place."

In response, Gholam squints his eyes, purrs like a cat, and then suddenly leaps at the officer. They put the manacles on his ankles again and leave him there.

Gholam the Murderer has not eaten in three days, and he doesn't even care. Passing through the corridor to get our food, we sometimes hear him singing, or reciting the call to prayer. Other times, he cusses out anyone related to the prison chief, dead or alive.

Ali the Barber brings us news. "They have given him food, but he shit in it, stirred it, and rubbed it all over his own face."

It's getting more dangerous than we thought. What plans he must have! I remember him saying, "I've got to escape . . . even if I get shot."

Now, it's the morning of the fourth day. We hear that the prison doctor, standing at a distance, has looked at him and tickled him with the end of a long stick. Gholam burst out laughing, and the doctor, shaking his head, said, "He's in bad shape . . . He must be taken to a lunatic asylum as soon as possible."

Around sunset, they call Naser the Lifer to pack up Gholam the Murderer's stuff and take it to the office.

"Two armed gendarmes came to take him," Naser tells us. "First, they searched his pockets, then handcuffed him, and then asked him to walk! Gholam, shifting from one foot to the other, stretched his neck and asked, 'Where?' The prison chief, holding his arm gently, said, 'You are free, Gholam . . . You're leaving the prison.'"

Gholam took a deep breath and yelled, "I won't go!"

One of the gendarmes tapped Gholam's shoulder with the stock of his rifle and ordered him in a violent tone: "Walk!"

Gholam, like a meek mouse, softened his voice and said quietly, "I'm not going anywhere . . . You're going to kill me . . . I saw God in my dream last night. He told me that two mountain-men gendarmes would come after me; one of them would be fat, with black eyes, the other

would be round and red-faced . . . God said they would take me to the
top of a yellow hill, and right there . . . bang, bang, bang . . . No, I am
not going."

And suddenly, Gholam hurled himself into the arms of the prison
chief and pleaded with him: "Please, Mr. Prison Chief, for the love of
your wife . . . for the sake of your shoulder straps . . . don't let them take
me . . ."

The prison chief tried to calm him down. Patting him on his face
and head, he held Gholam's arm and gently said, "No one will hurt you,
Gholam . . . You're getting released . . . Did you hear that, Gholam,
you're getting released."

Then, the gendarmes, having lost patience, frowned and forced him
out of the gate of the prison.

Mash Rahim has been summoned to court. He is walking out of the
block. He hardly has any strength left, so he shambles along, dragging
his *giveh* shoes on the floor.

In the revision court, my own sentence was reduced from three years
to one year. I have appealed to the supreme court, but I know it is useless.
I know that my attempts will just be in vain. No matter what, I have
to stomach a year. Not exactly a year, at least! I have already done five
months of it!

The public defender assigned to me didn't do a damn thing for
me. He came, sat his ass in a chair—just like a mountain of flesh—and
nodded like a dumb lamb. I doubt that he knows beans about the law, or
perhaps he knows but doesn't bother to put it to any use. He could have
had my sentence rescinded. There was nothing in my file to keep me in
jail. It was all the report of the fox and its tail.[7]

The prosecutor finished his speech; my lawyer shifted his bulky body,
shook off the chair, and rose to his feet. He panted a bit—his double
chin inflated and emptied like a toad's—and started to talk. "My poor,
miserable client—"

"I am not miserable," I cut him short.

---

7. The proverb is used to indicate that the trial is a sham.

Words froze in his mouth. His face turned bloodred. He paused for a few seconds, mumbled a bit, and then started again, rephrasing his words, "My client is young and inexperienced . . ."

I could tell where things were going. I let him blabber on. I looked around at the walls of the courtroom, which were completely discolored. I noticed that the judge's face was rectangular, and that the prosecutor's ears were so wide that Mirza Nasrollah could easily write the long prayer, Herz-e Kabir, on the back of each of them.

My name is called. I have visitors. I get up, and I am about to walk out when Naser the Lifer stops me, lays his hand on my shoulder, and says, "Have you heard the news?"

I am terrified by the word "news." Nothing I have heard lately has been pleasant. Aunt Ra'na's son getting shot; Aunt Ra'na in bed with an illness. "She is down with an illness," Mother said. "Her hair has turned gray in only a month. She whimpers day and night, scratching her cheeks. God only knows if she will survive this grief."

Yet the news that I await does not arrive. Bidar was supposed to keep me informed. I asked him to bring me news of Black-Eyed. He has since disappeared.

Naser the Lifer takes a cigarette out of my shirt pocket and says, "Gholam the Murderer has escaped."

My jaw drops. "No way!" I exclaim.

Naser, taking a drag of his cigarette, says, "Yeah, near Susa. He broke the window in a bathroom and jumped off the train."

I squeeze Naser the Lifer's arm. "You must be kidding."

"The bastard duped us all."

I know that Susa is not far from the Iraqi border city of Amarah. I know that if he passes through the forest near Susa and crosses the river, he'll be in Amarah before sunrise.

I envy Gholam's cleverness. He materializes before my eyes. A hint of yellow colors his face. His well-shaped eyes are full of sorrow. His tone is heartfelt. "You don't have any plans for me on how to get out of here?"

I hear my name being called again. I walk through the corridor, passing the row of cells in solitary, and then head into the room next to the guards' office. I see Mother standing there. Leila, Mullah Ahmad's eldest daughter, accompanies her. I suppose Bolur Khanom too will come soon; perhaps Aunt Ra'na, being so ill, couldn't make it. Mother folds a five-toman bill and hands it to the guard on duty. The guard steps aside and leaves us to ourselves. I sit next to Mother. The scent of her body brings back memories. Leila sits next to me. I ask how she's doing.

"I'm fine. How are you doing?" she says, blushing.

I face my mother and ask about Father.

Leila interrupts us hastily. "If your father couldn't come on Nowruz, would you miss him?"

I am taken aback. This is the last thing I was expecting. Leila's gaze is daring. She has full lips, an oval face. Her hair is henna-colored. Mother opens her mouth to speak, but I rob her of the chance and answer Leila: "I miss him already."

"Then let me tell you that he'll be back for Nowruz."

"I hope you're right."

Leila's releases her breath noisily. Mother, flabbergasted, does not understand what we are talking about. The guard on duty, keeping his distance, smokes. Mother tells me that Jamileh is sick again. She has got a sore throat and a fever. Every winter, Jamileh gets a bad sore throat. Mirza Nasrollah prescribes an herbal decoction. She takes the remedy, but soon she throws up and breaks out in a fever again.

Leila offers me cigarettes. I am surprised. I have never seen her smoke.

"Please, take one!"

I pick one and search for matches.

"I have matches."

As I reach to take the matchbox from her, she presses it into my palm, winking. There must be something going on, I think to myself. I light the cigarette and try to return the matches, but she winks again. "Keep it!" she says, "You'll need it in jail."

Whatever is going on must have to do with the matchbox. I put it in my pocket. Leila smiles. Her smile gives me such joy. Her pale, daring eyes make me feel proud. I want to kiss her hands. Mother's face tells me that she's completely taken aback. I hold her hand. "Everyone sends their regards," she says.

"How's Amu Bandar?" I ask.

"He's all right. He'll come to visit you one of these days. Khaj Tofiq and Aman Aqa too. Karam Ali might come as well."

Mother asks how Mash Rahim is doing. I let her know that he was summoned to court this morning. She hands me two packs of Oshnu cigarettes to give to him. I ask about Mohammad the Mechanic.

"His shoulder is sprained—," Mother says.

"He was hit with the stock of a rifle," Leila cuts Mother short.

"He's been in bed for three days now," Mother says.

There must be something going on out there.

Bolur Khanom arrives. She has brought me mixed nuts. The guard on duty shifts from foot to foot.

"He was at the demonstration—I mean Mohammad the Mechanic," Leila whispers in my ear.

The guard comes forward. He is impatient. "Make it quick, Khaled."

"Let us look at him for a minute," Bolur Khanom grumbles.

Mother lets go of my hand and kisses my cheeks and neck.

"Time's up!"

Mother kisses me again.

"You have enough bedding?" Bolur Khanom asks.

"Yes. I'll ask when it gets colder—"

"I'll bring you a blanket," Mother interrupts me.

The guard warns us again. Mother releases me. I say good-bye to them and walk out of the room next to the guards' office. Quickly, I go back to the block and run into the room. I pull the drawer of the matchbox out and take out the matchsticks. There is a piece of folded paper, thin as onionskin, stuck at the back of the matchbox. I open it. The script is not handwritten but typed: "All is well. Gather all your efforts for organizing the prisoners of Block 3. Their mutual call for better food guarantees your success. You should stand up firmly to the prison's authorities in demanding your rights. Inform us of anything you need. We'll arrange for you to receive books." I wonder who's conveying news of the conditions in the prison? I think of all the prisoners, the guards, and even the officers.

I tear the paper into pieces, chew them up, get up, and walk out of the room. In the latrines, I spit out the chewed-up paper into the toilet. It's almost noon. The sun has no warmth. It's cold. I lean against the stone wall and think. Some of the prisoners have spread out a blanket and are stretched on it in the sun. Others are walking. "Mutual call for better food" resonates in my mind. I close my eyes and think about how to start the mission. The door to the block opens. Rahim the Donkey Keeper comes in. I rush toward him. His back is completely bent. He stops and looks at me, his eyes bulging—just like those of a slaughtered calf.

"Mash Rahim, what did they want from you?"

Clasping his hands behind his back, he just walks on, without saying a word.

Walking along beside him, I say, "You didn't answer me."

He remains silent. Blocking his way, I stand in front of him, grab both his arms, and shake him. He starts to mumble. Chewed-up and broken words spring out of his mouth.

His execution sentence has been announced to him.

I fall apart. My head spins. I hear Chinuq's voice coming from miles away, from the bottom of a well: "Hey, Khaled, let's go to Prison Square."

"What's going on there?"

Chinuq's face is just one large mouth. "They have hung three people."

So we take off. Chinuq strides ahead of us. Khaleq and I, no matter how fast we run, can't catch up with him. It's a hot day. The alleys are full of sunshine. Dust has covered everything. We take a shortcut and jump over a short wall into an empty lot, where we find ourselves among a herd of sheep grazing under the shade of green-fringed palm trees.

The shepherd's dog leaps at us. The shepherd calls it off. We squeeze out through a crack in the wall. By the time we get to Prison Square, we are completely out of breath. Prison Square, which extends all the way up to the edge of a tamarix thicket along the Karun, is bright and sunny. We slow down. Three gallows have been erected in the middle of the square. Their posts are white, freshly cut and chiseled. They look like they were made just last night by a carpenter. A man is hung from each gallows. We step closer. Khaleq and Chinuq get so close that they are only ten steps away from the posts. I don't dare step any closer. My knees are paralyzed. I feel like throwing up. All three men have turned black and blue. One of them is fat. His tongue sticks out of his mouth. His hair is rumpled. His stomach is protruding. He is wearing soft Turkish boots. Another one is short, skinny, and dark-skinned. One of his *giveh* shoes has fallen off his foot, but the other one is still hanging on to his toes. The third one is tall. The rope around his neck is twisted. I can only see the profile of his face. A gentle breeze plays with his large mustache.

His head is shaved. There is not a living soul in the square. Only a short guard paces near the gallows, his rifle slung on one shoulder, his cap pushed off his forehead. He says something to Khaleq and Chinuq, but I can't hear his voice. I feel as if I'm about to faint. The world spins around me. The gallows spin around me. The bodies spin around me. They get entangled, break away, and get entangled again, making faces at me. My bowels churn. The breakfast I ate earlier comes up and spills out of my mouth. I feel Khaleq and Chinuq reaching under my arms, dragging me away from Prison Square. The sun is scorching. My entire body is drenched in sweat. I sit in the shade of a wall, shivering. I am being hanged. I turn black and blue. I feel suffocated. My tongue is swelling out of my mouth. I scramble to my feet and run, leaving Khaleq and Chinuq behind. I am out of breath. I sit down. Suddenly, I notice two kids from the prison neighborhood hanging a kitten. The kitten struggles in the noose. It thrashes about, gasping for air. I get up and walk over to them. The kitten's eyes are about to pop out of their sockets. I tackle the kids and pummel them with my fists and my feet. I grab the noose and bring it down. The kitten scurries away, dragging the rope behind it. Unexpectedly, one of the kids punches the back of my neck. Before I can make a move, another blow lands on my temple. Feeling dizzy, I sit down on the ground. Mash Rahim's voice echoes in my ears: "I'll be hung one of these days."

I open my eyes. Mash Rahim leans against the wall and then slides down to a sitting position. I grab him under his arms. He doesn't budge. His body has grown slack and heavy.

His mouth opens, and he throws up whatever he had left in his stomach.

Bidar has come to visit me. There is an unfamiliar coldness in his eyes and no sign of his usual pleasant expression. A dead smile is frozen on his anemic lips. I have a feeling that he doesn't have good news to convey.

"What news?" I ask him.

"From whom?" he replies in a cold tone.

"From Black-Eyed."

"I couldn't find her. I think they have moved."

My heart sinks. My face turns pale. "They've moved?"

"You shouldn't upset yourself, " he says in a matter-of-fact tone.

My head burns. My temples begin to throb.

"You should forget about Black-Eyed. I have told you this already."

I will die before I forget about her. The only reason I have been able to tolerate all the suffering in prison is because of my hope of seeing Black-Eyed again.

I think I'm dreaming.

I look at Bidar, the dead smile still on his lips.

"I tried my best, Khaled . . . I couldn't find her."

"I appreciate it."

"You're upset, right?"

I don't respond. He won't understand. However hard I try to explain it to him, he is not going to get it. Nobody can understand those joyous and wonderful moments I spend thinking about Black-Eyed. I look down and mumble, "Good-bye, Bidar. Thanks for everything."

He grabs my hand. "Wait a minute!"

I stop. My head is still lowered. "You should be realistic," he says.

I want to yell at him. Instead, I just look at him. His striking eyes are aglow again. "If you are realistic," he continues, "you won't fall prey to emotions and feelings like these so easily."

His tiny earlobes are slightly yellow. A line has appeared under each of his pale cheeks. His colorless lips move. "So, what do you say, Khaled? Now do you want to turn prison into hell for yourself?"

I shake my head. I can barely breathe. I can't talk. All I want is to walk away.

"Now that we're at it, I should also tell you that I'm not supposed to come see you anymore."

It doesn't matter to me. I just want to smash my head against the wall so hard that my brain squishes out.

The iron door to the block is shut behind me. The faint winter sunlight has spread inside the block.

Judge blocks my way. "There you go again with the face!"

"I'm not myself at all."

Stepping aside, Judge fixes his eyes on mine and says hastily (as always), "That's life. Take it easy!"

I walk on.

Judge follows me and stops me. His concerned face is filled with sympathy. "Something's the matter?" he asks softly.

I feel like pouring out my heart, so I tell him, "I'm heartbroken."

He steps out of my way.

I go to our room. It's cold. Lying down on the kilim, I draw a blanket over my head. Bidar's voice irritates me: "You should be realistic!"

I don't dare think about being "realistic." I fight the thought, wishing he hadn't come to visit me. That way, at least I could still hope I'd see Black-Eyed after I get out of here. No! I will search every corner of the world till I find her. I can't live without my Black-Eyed, even for a moment. I need to gaze into her eyes. I need to hear her laughter. I need to hear her voice. Her chipped front teeth are the most beautiful teeth I have ever seen. I'll find her, even if she has disappeared among the clouds in the sky. I can't forget the black color of her eyes, the color that makes all other colors fade away.

My head feels hot. I think I am breaking out in a fever. My thoughts are overflowing with the image of Black-Eyed's graceful body. She is wearing her school uniform, embroidered with red trim. Her skirt is very short. Her soft hair cascades over her shoulders. I am overwhelmed with joy. I hold my hand out for her. She holds out her hand for mine. Our fingers touch. Suddenly, the pointed leaves of a palm shoot spreading over the ground rise and sting the tips of our fingers. Black-Eyed steps back, fades away, and disappears from sight.

I want to cry. I want to cry for all those in love and in pain.

"You should be realistic."

"No, Bidar, no, I can't forget my love . . . I love Black-Eyed," I cry out in my heart.

I relive every moment I spent with Black-Eyed in my head. But every moment turns into pain. I want to get up and shout that I am a captive, a captive of those black eyes that invite and reproach me at the same time. I hear her scolding voice: "Where have you been, Khaled?"

Everything is happening in a dream.

"I am right here, my dearest darling."

She is wearing a long dress, a silver-colored dress made out of thousands of tiny scales that sparkle like a lit chandelier. She lets herself fall into my arms and rests her head on my shoulder. The scent of her body intoxicates me.

"I love you," she says.

I kiss her cheeks and neck.

She bursts out laughing. "Where have you not kissed on my body?"

I put my lips on hers. They smell of spring, of fresh field grass, of pennyroyal growing on the edges of brooks.

"You're biting my lips."

I am breathing heavily and utterly drenched in sweat. Suddenly, she disappears. I fall apart. I shatter. My entire body starts to shake.

"You should be realistic."

I yell and jump up.

Naser the Lifer is hovering over me. "What's up with you, Khaled?"

I feel as if a jug of icy cold water has been poured on my head. My entire body is soaked in a cold sweat. Naser the Lifer's piercing eyes, which burn like two balls of fire, are fixed on my face. His gravelly voice shoots through my ears. "Are you all right?"

"Yeah, I'm good," I say; I barely have the strength to talk.

Kneeling down, Naser says, "Tell me, what is it?"

My voice is muffled. Words break in my throat. "It's nothing. It's just . . . my heart feels heavy."

He lights a cigarette and hands it to me. "You should go and get your lunch!"

I get up, but I can't walk. I put the copper bowl under my arm and shuffle out of the room.

The smell of spring wafts through the air. Cold air no longer stings. The sun is already a bit hot, but still enjoyable. When it beats on my back, a pleasant tingle shoots under my skin.

What's missing is Rahim the Donkey Keeper sitting idle on the steps in front of the latrines. Last week, they came for him. It was dawn. The sun had yet to rise. The tramping sound of footsteps echoing in the corridor woke me up. It woke all of us up. Our eyes full of sleep, we leaned against the walls and the doorframes and just watched. They woke Mash Rahim. He had no strength to walk. His eyes popped out of their sockets. His eyes were open, but I doubt he saw anything or anyone. My knees were paralyzed. I couldn't stand, so I sat on my heels. Mash

Rahim passed me by. His feet dragging. His knees bent. He shambled on. Behind him, I saw the officer on duty's legs, rock hard and strong, passing by. Then, I saw the legs of the prisoners, all mixed up.

Mash Rahim's voice echoes in my ears: "You see, Khaled? . . . Do you see what's happened to me at the end of my life?"

The smell of Mash Rahim's body fills my nose. I smell his Oshnu tobacco and the depilatory powder. His voice resonates in my mind: "This is not the proper way to die . . ."

I can't see anything. His old, broken voice, with an ever-present tremor to it, sends a shiver through my entire body. "That's not a decent way to die, before the eyes of those who know you and those who don't."

The sun is already hot, but it's enjoyable. Mash Rahim is missed. I still haven't gotten used to his empty place. I imagine him still sitting on the steps in front of the latrines, leaning against the wall. His voice is always in my ears: "Khaled, it's been such a long time since I've heard from Ebram and Hasani."

The skin under his eyes is puffy. It's purplish-blue. His hands and feet are swollen. His stomach bulges out like a drum. I can hardly hear his voice: "See, Khaled? . . . Do you see what's happened at the end of my life?"

The smell of spring wafts through the air. The sky is clear. Talk of prison food is on everyone's lips. I have talked with many of the guys. "Can you put up with hunger until they improve the food?"

Manuch the Black's lifeless eyes roll upward under his eyelids. "Are you asking if I am ready?"

He glares at me, pounds on his chest with his fist, shakes his large head as the veins in his neck swell, and says in a throaty voice filled with rage, "I'm already disgusted with eating this garbage, but who's man enough to listen to me?"

Hossein the Soup Maker kneels down, places his long, bony arms on the floor, pushes his upper body forward, and says, "Yeah, why not?"

His right eye, which always looks as if it's about to pop out, stares ahead. His jutting Adam's apple shifts up and down in his long, thin throat. "If we could do something about it . . ."

Hossein the Soup Maker is taller than Buyeh. Pushing his chin forward, he says, "But do you think the others will agree on this?"

"If they want to eat better food," I say, "they have to agree."

He swallows his saliva, moves his swollen tongue over his dry, purplish lips, and says, "I, for one, am ready."

I move along to Esi the Red Faced. He has a shrill voice. His already red cheeks become redder. "But just know," he says, "that they'll shove their batons up our asses."

I try to make him understand that if we all unite on this matter, they won't be able to do a damn thing.

He pushes his amber-colored hair away from his forehead, trying to avoid the issue. I have no intention of letting him go.

He gets in my face and says, "You know what, Khaled? I have only a few more months on my sentence. And I have no intention of spending those last few months in solitary."

"But did you know that Manuch the Black is ready for anything?" I say, trying to encourage him.

"He's gone nuts," he cuts me off quickly.

I put my hands on his shoulders, look straight into his eyes, and say, "No, Esi, he is wiser than all of us . . . You are wrong."

He slips his shoulders out from under my hands and says, "Do whatever the hell you like; I want to stay out of it."

Nowruz is fast approaching. The smell of spring wafts through the air. The sky is clear. I argue with Mehdi the Wide Chest. "They won't give a damn about us," he says.

"But I think we can make a lot of changes here."

His short neck is barely visible. His long chin has sunk into his protruding chest. Leaning his broad shoulders against the stone wall, he says, "But, dear . . . they are armed." He inflates his lungs, breathes out, and then, in a calculating, soft voice, says, "They have batons . . . handcuffs and manacles . . . solitary . . ."

"All that being said, do you want to go on eating this garbage?"

He moves his large head away from the wall and says, "No!"

"So, now that you're eating it, you must be thinking that we are predestined to eat this garbage instead of food, huh?"

His round eyes widen. "Who said it's predestined?"

"Then there must be a reason for it."

Not mincing his words, he says, "Fear, fear, my dear! If not for fear, any stupid man would know that we're being rubbed off assigned budgets for proper food."

I grab his wrist. "In that case, you think we can afford to be so terrified that we die from eating this garbage?"

Buyeh shows up. He stands next to us and says, "You're talking about food again?"

Reza the Pickpocket shows up too.

Mehdi the Wide Chest nods. "Yeah, man, it's food talk again."

"Then let's do it!" says Buyeh. "Let's all go on a hunger strike tomorrow."

The guard on duty appears. We change the subject.

A gentle breeze comes over the tall wall of the jail, cooling the inside of the block. I imagine I hear the roaring of the Karun and smell the fragrance of wildflowers. Naser the Lifer warns me: "Look, Khaled, I agree with you too . . . but if the prison chief finds out, he'll make you regret you were ever born. They'll throw you in two months' solitary confinement as punishment, so that you won't ever be able to see any of us. Listen to me, I know these bastards."

If Naser the Lifer joins the club, things will be much easier. I have to do my best to convince him somehow. "Naser, you should know that if we all stick together, we can do a lot of things."

He shifts his eyes, those eyes that burn like two balls of fire, and says, "We, at least, have good food here—"

"What about the others?" I cut him short.

"To hell with them," he retorts.

"But, Naser, they're human too, our friends."

"Friends?" he says as he stretches his neck out like a fighting cock.

Vakil Karam walks past us. He is so gaunt that a breeze could carry him away.

Pointing at him, Naser says, "You see that lizard? Close your eyes for a second, and he'll cut your ear. If you let him, he wouldn't have any mercy on anyone, Persian or Arab, with that skeletal body of his." He deepens his voice and continues, "Now, is it wise for me to writhe under baton blows for such a motherfucker?"

It's useless. He is not convinced. I'll have to be very patient to get him on our side. I take his wrist and say to him, "Let's go to our room, and I'll tell you in detail why—"

"All right, man . . . Whatever the hell you wanna do, I'm in," he cuts me short.

He shakes his wrist free from my grasp and walks away, annoyed. He's not in the mood. I shouldn't push him. With him, I'll have to be more tactful, more patient.

The air smells of spring. The sun is hot. The steps in front of the latrines are empty without Rahim the Donkey Keeper to sit on them idly. I still haven't gotten used to not having him around. I walk toward the cement steps to sit for a moment. I hear the iron door of the block open. Turning my head, I see the medium-height warrant officer coming toward me. He calls out to me.

I walk up to him. "What is it?"

He grabs my wrist. "Come with me!"

The look on his face tells me that it must be bad news.

"What do you want from me?"

"You'll see," he says in a wicked tone.

We have barely reached the block's door when Naser the Lifer comes toward us quickly and blocks our way. "Where to?"

"The chief wants him," the warrant officer says impatiently.

From the expression on Naser's face, I realize that he grasps the import of the warrant officer's words. "What's he want him for?" he asks.

The warrant officer pays him no mind. The door shuts behind us. We pass through the covered corridor lined with solitary confinement cells. It's cold in the corridor; cold and humid. A chill runs through me. We enter the prison's courtyard, which is filled with sunlight. Sitting in a chair, the prison chief is smoking. His beard is neatly trimmed. His dark, fleshy cheeks glow. Reclining deep into the chair, he barely manages to cross his fat, stubby legs. As soon as he sees me, he gets to his feet and, like a pregnant pig, heavy and awkward, walks toward me.

I stand in the middle of the yard in the shade of a lotus tree. It is utterly quiet in the yard. A column of black smoke rises from the kitchen's chimney, darkening the blue sky above.

The prison chief stands opposite me. The officer releases my wrist and steps aside. The chief flings the cigarette butt on the ground and stubs it out under the tip of his boot. Swiftly, he slaps me across the face with his open palm, which is as hard as a brick, making me lose my balance and wobble. Before I can pull myself together, he bellows, "I slapped you so you would know firsthand who you're dealing with!"

I keep quiet. The officer takes up a position behind the prison chief. In front of the guards' office, a few guards are watching us.

"I hear you're causing trouble inside the jail. Is that so?" he says in a coarse voice.

I get the picture. I wonder who reported my activities to him?

The prison chief's raspy and gravelly voice doesn't match his wide, fat body. "Dare to make trouble inside the jail, huh?"

I think of everyone. Is it possible that Esi the Red Faced has informed him? What about Reza the Pickpocket? Then I think of Napoleon. What would happen to his business if we were to get good food?

Stepping closer, the chief squeezes my earlobe, twisting it hard. My lips are pressed together like melted lead. Glaring at me, he says, "I'll have you handcuffed and shackled in a solitary cell, so you'll learn to be grateful for what you have now."

Letting go of my ear, he punches my neck with a swiftness I never would have thought possible coming from such a heavy body.

"But I didn't do anything, sir," I finally force the words out of my mouth.

He growls—just like a pestered dog would—showing his small teeth. "You didn't do anything?! You're starting a riot, and you dare to say you haven't done anything?"

Still talking, he lifts his short leg and kicks me in the crotch so quickly that I am thrown into the trunk of the lotus tree headfirst.

"Throw him in solitary—"

"But, Mr. Chief . . . ," I interrupt him.

"Shut up!"

The warrant officer comes forward and grabs my arm. "Let's go!"

I move. My neck stings. My earlobe burns. My cheek twitches. I limp along with my bruised pelvis.

The door of the solitary cell shuts behind me.

My entire body feels as cold as ice. A damp, moldy cold numbs me to the bone. It's been two days since I've seen the sun. Around noontime, a patch of faint pale sunlight falls on the wall through the mesh vent in the ceiling. The Nowruz's festivities are approaching—in a week, I guess. I have lost track of the days.

The sun is about to set when the prison chief comes and opens the door of the cell. I rise to my feet and stand before him.

His cheeks are aglow. The irises of his eyes look like they are made of stone. A short switch is in his hand. He looks happy. He must have had a good lunch and a good afternoon nap. "So, what is it going to be?" he asks calmly. "Do you want to go on staying in solitary, or have you learned your lesson?"

My knees quiver. I am about to faint from hunger. The cold air is about to break me. During the past two days that I've been kept in solitary, I have not been able to bring myself to eat, not even a bite.

"Come on out!" orders the chief.

I move toward the door, limping rather than walking. Pain shoots through my backbone. The chief's loud voice comes from behind me: "Just remember that I have the ability to bring you back to your senses anytime I want."

Naser the Lifer embraces me. Buyeh puts a match to the Primus to make tea. Judge, Mehdi the Wide Chest, and Manuch the Black all come and sit around me.

"Didn't I tell you?" Naser says gently.

I am not in the mood to talk. Manuch the Black shakes his large head of curly hair and says, "Now that this has happened, I am ready to lay down my life for it."

Reza the Pickpocket comes and sits next to Buyeh. "Let me pump it!" he tells him.

Buyeh washes the cups instead. Reza the Pickpocket pumps the Primus.

"Let me tell you," says Judge, "that going on a strike is legal . . . It's not a crime." Lighting a cigarette, he continues, "If we demand our legal rights and they don't mind our requests, we have every right to go on strike."

Buyeh, stretching his long neck, looks into Judge's eyes and, measuring his words, says, "But what if they don't care about this sort of thing and cram us all into solitary?"

Manuch the Black holds out his hands, interlaces his fingers, and says, "If we all stick together, they can't do a thing to us."

Reza the Pickpocket hugs his knees and remains seated right next to the Primus.

The moldy, damp cold of the solitary cell, which infiltrated my entire body, gradually leaves my stiff backbone.

"I suggest," says Mehdi the Wide Chest, looking us each in the eye, "we should first do something else."

I prick up my ears. His words are measured. His voice blends in with the roar of the Primus. "We should first find out who the mole is who's spilling the beans to Mr. Chief."

Naser the Lifer blazes like fire. "If I find out who that motherfucker is, I'll rip him apart like a piece of canvas."

I thought a lot about it while I was in solitary, but I couldn't point my finger at anyone in particular. Naser the Lifer is more and more on our side now. He is convinced that we should go on a hunger strike. Looking at me, he says, "Who do you think the mole is?"

I shrug my shoulders. "I don't know."

The kettle comes to a boil. Buyeh adds the boiling water to the teapot. Lowering the flame, he puts the teapot on the Primus. "We have to find him," he says.

"We have to be on the lookout to see who goes out of the block at odd times."

It is sunset. The weather is nice. Only three days until Nowruz. The sky is clear. The sun is about to disappear over the edge of the towering wall of the prison. As usual, I have taken up my place on the steps in front of the latrines, and next to me is Naser the Lifer. The block's lights are on. Naser talks about his dreams. He talks about Tuba. "Her eyes, large as a cow's," he says in awe. "Her body, like marble. Her lips, as if you had mixed salt and blood together . . . Being in love is such a pain, Khaled . . . You don't know . . . I was crazy about her . . ."

My heart takes flight. Naser the Lifer goes on. I hardly hear him. I am filled with the thought of Black-Eyed. The way she blushed out of bashfulness, the way her eyes turned the color of black olives.

Naser grabs my arm. "Are you listening to me?"

"Yeah, Naser . . . tell me."

He starts again, "If my bitch sister hadn't caused me this trouble, I would've married my Tuba . . ."

I find myself lost in my own thoughts again. Naser is talking to himself really. I have a feeling that I'll see her as soon as I get free of this place. My heart tells me that Black-Eyed doesn't care about any other man; that she doesn't smile at anyone else; that she keeps all her sparkle, all her joy, only for me.

I am brimming with excitement. I feel as if I'm not in jail anymore. I feel as if Black-Eyed is sitting beside me. I feel the warmth of her body. I hear her voice. "You mean the world to me . . . You are my love."

Her lips blossom like a rosebud. Her chipped teeth have a hint of blue. A wide smile has brightened her face. Her innocent gaze makes me ecstatic. I brush her bangs aside and kiss her smooth forehead. Her long eyelashes close on each other. She breathes heavily. Her breath burns my cheeks. I place my lips on her cheeks and feel the softness of her arms around my neck. The scent of her cascading hair overwhelms me. I close my eyes. Her whispered words fill my ears. "I love you," she says.

Mehdi the Wide Chest's husky voice jolts me out of my daydream. "They called Napoleon. He went out of the block."

Naser the Lifer pounces on this bit of information. "Napoleon?" he says, jumping off the steps. "I'll close his business . . . I'll make him pack his stuff up and get out of this block."

Napoleon is the Block 3 hawker, selling a few items: stacks of paper, envelopes, and stamps. And if you know how to keep your mouth shut, you may manage to get yourself the occasional opium, or *shireh*, or hashish.

Naser the Lifer starts to walk away. "I'll have a baton shoved up his ass," he grumbles.

I grab his wrist. "Maybe it's not him."

Ignoring my comment, he keeps going, muttering, "I'll have them wheedle the opium out of his wife's ass."

I don't quite follow his threat. "Wait, Naser!" I tell him. "What're you talking about?"

He stops and darts his usual piercing look at me. "What am I saying?" Manuch the Black shows up.

Naser the Lifer's bushy eyebrows rise, making his forehead wrinkle. "I mean that that wife of his wraps opium in a plastic bag and shoves it up her ass like a cock, so she can smuggle it into jail."

The whites of Manuch the Black's eyes swivel in their sockets. "Do you mean Napoleon's wife?"

It looks like everyone knows about it. Again, I reach for Naser the Lifer's arm. It feels hard, like rock. "But what if it's not him . . . ?"

I haven't finished my sentence when the door to the block opens and Napoleon walks in, holding a cardboard box under his arm. His shaved head wobbles on his thin neck. Naser pulls his arm out of my grasp, rushes toward him, and grabs his wrist. Napoleon's face turns pale. The lines under his cheeks deepen. "Why did you go out?"

Napoleon's hazy eyes swivel in their sockets. His voice is muffled: "What do you mean, why did I go out?"

"Come into the corridor and I'll tell you what I mean," orders Naser, leading Napoleon behind him.

In the corridor, he takes the box from Napoleon, puts it down, grabs Napoleon's shoulder, and pushes him to the wall. "Will you tell us why you went out of the block, or do you want me to plant an eggplant under your eyes?"

Napoleon's body starts to tremble. He points to the box and says, "I just went to get my stuff."

Naser's rough hand clutches Napoleon's throat. "But you have never gone to pick up your stuff yourself before."

Napoleon's dry lips, like those of a netted fish that has fallen on the hot sands, scarcely open as he replies, "Well . . . this time I went myself . . . It's not like I've committed a sin!"

Naser lets go of Napoleon's throat, squeezes his creased cheek, twists it, and says, "I hope to God that you went out only to pick up your stuff."

"But what . . . else . . . do I . . . have out there?" Napoleon mumbles, his voice breaking.

Letting go of Napoleon's cheek, Naser says, "Do you swear that you're not Mr. Chief's mole?"

Napoleon's voice gets louder. "A mole?"

Naser the Lifer narrows his eyes. "I said, swear!"

Napoleon turns in the direction of the qiblah, the house of God in Mecca, raises both his hands to heaven, and says, "I swear to Imam Hossein's son, on Ali Akbar's split skull, that I have not taken any news to anyone."

Naser the Lifer looks at me. "Then, what motherfucker . . . ?"

He doesn't have a chance to finish before Buyeh comes striding into the corridor, saying, "Mr. Chief has asked for Judge."

Things are getting heated. Judge has told us a few times that going on strike is not against the law. He has said that if the authorities don't listen to our lawful requests, we can go on a hunger strike.

Raising his head, Naser the Lifer looks into Buyeh's eyes and asks, "Was that the warrant officer again coming after him?"

Buyeh nods.

We walk toward the yard.

"How is it that we cannot find out who is taking information out?" asks Manuch the Black.

This makes Naser the Lifer angrier. "I'll find him, even if he hides in his mother's belly," he says.

The weather is pleasant. Spring is in the air. The guys, gathered around in groups, are busy chatting away.

We usually walk late in the afternoon. At night, we spread out a carpet, make tea, and sit around with each other in groups. Sometimes we play soccer, sometimes *duz*, and occasionally we talk about our dreams, or our memories. These days, though, our talk mostly revolves around the prison food, and who might be taking word out to the prison chief.

Ali the Big Lipped comes over from the end of the block, dragging his fat body on his thick heels, and sits next to us.

Naser is lying there fuming with rage. Mehdi the Wide Chest leans his thick shoulders and short neck against the wall. Buyeh pours tea. Ali the Big Lipped's mouth moves as he says, "I have made up my mind!"

No one responds to him. His bald head shines like polished copper in the glow of the block's floodlights. He says, "I am with you . . ."

Again, no one responds to him.

Shifting his position, he sits on his heels, rests his stubby hands on his stomach, and says, "Whenever you're ready not to take food, let me know too."

We just look at him. No one is in the mood for talking.

Obviously pissed off, he says, "What's wrong with you? At least say something!"

I am about to spit out the words trapped behind my teeth when I hear the sound of the iron door opening. Judge is thrown into the yard, headfirst. All of us run toward him. The iron door shuts noisily. Judge's face is smeared with blood. There is a deep cut above his left eyebrow. The skin under his eyes is swollen. He has no strength to talk.

I no longer have the privilege of private visitations. Now, like the rest of the prisoners, I have to talk from behind bars. Between each rows of bars, a guard always monitors everything. You can barely hear each other. Your voice blends with everyone else's. You have to holler to get your visitor to understand a word. These days, Naser the Lifer's words don't win the guards over anymore. It looks like he will no longer be allowed to come and go between the blocks like he used to.

Naser the Lifer is pissed off. He grumbles, "I'll make such a racket in the block that even a hundred riflemen won't be able to regain control!"

It's the eve of Nowruz. My heart feels heavy. I lie facedown on the blanket I have spread in the sun. The sun makes me numb and lethargic. Leaning against a wall, Naser the Lifer smokes away. He's lost in thought. He stares at the sky. The sky is a beautiful color. Sitting on the edge of one of the towering walls of the prison, two turtledoves, their feathers fluffed, huddle together. Spreading its wings back until they touch, a bustard dives toward the ground from the middle of the sky. Just outside the prison walls stretch wide meadows; then there are the fenced fruit orchards with short hedges and brooks full of water. If I listen carefully, I can hear the roaring of the Karun. It's not far from the western wall of the prison to the banks of the Karun, with its crushing waves in the springtime. I am jolted by the sound of my name being called. The iron door opens.

Naser the Lifer starts to get to his feet. "What's going on?" he says, stubbing out his cigarette butt. He gets up and walks along with me to the door of the block. Ali the Barber tells me that I have a visitor. I am taken aback. It is not visitation day. It's neither Monday nor Friday.

"It's a trick," Naser the Lifer grumbles.

I have to go and see. I shrug my shoulders and head out through the door of the block. The damp chill of the corridor seeps into my hot body. Manuch the Black is in a solitary cell. He threw a bowl of food at the security tower, let his mouth run loose, and cussed everyone related to the prison chief, dead and alive. Manuch the Black's crossed eyes peer through the round hole in the door of the cell. I can't talk to him. The guard in the corridor is walking with me. I head around the corner of the kitchen hallway, past the bathroom, and walk into the visiting room.

All at once, I freeze. Father is standing behind the bars. His hair has turned completely gray. His eyes look lifeless, but a hint of pride resides in them, and makes my hair rise. A faint smile forms on his lips. I think his eyelashes are moist. A lump grows in my throat. I can't speak at all. He stretches his arm through the bars. I too stretch my arm. I wedge my shoulder between the bars. Our hands touch. The roughness of his calloused hand moves my heart. He swallows his saliva. His Adam's apple shifts up and down. His voice is husky. "How are you?" he asks.

We let go of each other's hands. He speaks in a gentle voice, making my entire body tremble, as if something has collapsed in my heart. I feel as if the four limbs of my body are numb. The tight lump in my throat suffocates me so badly that I cannot say a word. I hear his voice again: "You have become a man."

I see teardrops sparkle under his eyelashes. He talks so softly and his tone is so filled with grief that I want to throw myself at him, kissing his feet and hands a thousand times over. I never expected him to be so understanding, so kind.

Father's voice is raspy and heavy with grief. "Don't be troubled, my son."

There is a tumult in my heart. I am beside myself with joy. I am ablaze with compassion. I don't dare open my mouth, terrified that I might burst into tears. I swallow my saliva.

Father's voice shakes me: "Don't be troubled, my son! Imam Ja'far Sadeq too was jailed."

All this misery and still such a strong faith? I am about to fall apart. I feel embarrassed. I feel I am nothing. Nothing! Nothing! I take a deep breath and exhale noisily. Lowering my head, I say under my breath, "No, Father, I'm not troubled . . . not at all . . ."

Then, I lift my head up and look into Father's eyes, which are sparkling with pride. A faint smile has lifted his bony cheeks. I have never seen his face so bright. I have regained my confidence. I think I can speak clearly now. The way he looks at me gives me confidence. I am overwhelmed by his abundant compassion. I feel so ashamed of all the pain I have caused him. "If I am in jail, maybe . . ." I pause. I wanted to say, "Maybe it was for you, for Mother, for Jamileh . . . for Amu Bandar, and for people like Mash Rahim and Khaj Tofiq, and . . ." But I stop. I feel so small before Father's overflowing generosity that all these words sound ridiculous to me. Father's voice rings in my ears. I see Mother sitting in front of me as I am reading his letter: ". . . There's plenty of work here, but there is also humiliation. It seems like the Arabs are the servants of the Europeans, and we are the servants of the Arabs . . ." Father is quiet. He is looking at me, expecting me to say something. He has gotten skinnier. His jacket is too loose for him now. His cheeks are emaciated. I just look at him and keep quiet.

"It'll be over, my son . . ."

Father's voice is raspy. He is holding his head up. "Instead, you will grow to be a strong and brave man in life. Put it down to experience . . . You'll learn a lot."

I murmur, asking him why they have allowed him to come and visit me. From what he tells me, I gather that he has bribed his way in. I become furious. He smiles and says, "Don't worry about it, my son. It was worth it. Tomorrow is Nowruz. I arrived last night. I needed to see you."

He has brought me a basket of cabbage lettuce and a bottle of syrup made of boiled vinegar and sugar. The guard, who's leaning against the wall, turns a blind eye. I figure that Father has bribed him too. The guard keeps his distance and smokes a cigarette, leaving us to ourselves. We have been talking for over half an hour now. The guard moves and comes toward us. Father stretches his arm out. I feel the roughness of his palm again. I don't know how to say good-bye to him. I wish I could say something that would express all my love for him. I can barely open my mouth when he says, "Eid Mobarak, my son."

My heart shakes. Tears roll down my face. "Happy Nowruz to you too, Father."

6

The weather has become very hot. Spring is taking its last breaths. The summer humidity is on its way. At times, the air gets so suffocating within the four walls of the block—just like the air at the bottom of a well. The humidity is brutal here. The rainless, lamb-shaped cumulus clouds just hang idly in the sky above our heads. It feels as if the four walls of the block have been lidded with clouds and fire. Our skin burns. Our entire bodies, spotted with prickly heat, turn crimson, like the fresh meat of a deer. We fan ourselves, drink water, fan ourselves, and drink more water, till our stomachs swell. Yet our bodies never stop burning.

Everything has changed since the day Pendar showed up in the block. We have formed a "committee" to carry out a strike. I am a member. Now the talk is no longer only about food. It's also about the water cistern, about ice, and about the condition of the latrines.

"Ah, the water cistern?"

Word travels from mouth to mouth.

"The water tastes like rust."

"Why is it they don't give us ice?"

The voices get gruffer.

"The water is so boiling hot that we might as well make tea with it."

They throw away the loaves of bread and holler, "Even dogs won't eat this bread!"

"Leave it for half an hour, and you'll be able to slaughter a bull with it."

Pendar is restless. He moves in and out of all the rooms, talking to everyone, shedding light on all the talk that's circulating. If there is a disagreement, he patiently uses reason to go over everything until everyone comes to an agreement. The way things are going, the protest will be more of a collective effort. If you pay close attention, you can learn a lot from Pendar. He brings up a topic, gets our attention, and then lets us discuss it among ourselves. Now and then, when in a heated discussion, his own opinions come through. For instance, he says, "A guard doesn't have the right to insult us."

Then we too take up his opinion.

"Not even the officer on duty."

"Not even the prison chief."

Again he adds something to the jumble of opinions: "I'll give them that we have been convicted. But aren't we doing time? That does not give any lowly guard the right to insult us."

He pays close attention to the discussions. Whenever he finds it necessary, he raises his hand abruptly. We all fall silent. He starts to talk as if he's at the pulpit. His tone of voice charms everyone. The way he looks at people attracts everyone. More and more, fresh talk travels from mouth to mouth.

"They're stealing the money from our rations of clothes, shoes, and blankets."

"The entire year, all we got was a set of canvas clothes and a pair of slippers that ripped in a matter of a few days."

Pendar has made quite an impression on Naser the Lifer.

We finally caught the mole red-handed. Naser the Lifer scared the hell out of him. "Come over here, pretty boy!"

Reza the Pickpocket became as small as a trembling mouse. He huddled in a corner of the yard, his lips quivering.

Naser the Lifer grabbed Reza's wrist and dragged him to the end of the corridor. There, he pushed him against the wall, clutched his throat, and threatened him. "If you ever again take any information outside, you're dead meat."

Reza came clean. His face turned the color of saffron when Naser waved his blade in his face. Reza's eyes were popping out of their sockets. In a gruff voice, Naser repeated, "If I ever catch you doing that kind of shit again—reporting on us—I'll slaughter you like a sacrificial lamb."

Everything changed the day Pendar showed up.

The door to the block opens. Pendar walks in. I am filled with excitement. I rush forward, hugging him. His hair has been sheared off like the wool of a sheep. We embrace and kiss. He knows Naser the Lifer already, and he greets a few others he knows. We then leave the guys and go talk in private. He talks about Leila. "Both of us were arrested at the same time."

The tone of his voice gives me hope and encouragement.

"We were making copies of pamphlets when the house was surrounded," he explains. "There was no way out. Leila was like a lioness, attacking them; she bit the wrist of one of them, making the pistol fall from his hand. Before I could make a move to pick it up, I felt the butt of a gun striking the back of my head. I don't remember anything else."

It's as if I can hear Leila's voice and see her bold and daring gaze: "Would you miss your father if he couldn't make it for Nowruz?"

I wish I could see her now. I miss her bold gazes.

"She is amazing," says Pendar, "I mean, Leila . . . She is an amazing girl . . . She showed great bravery in the interrogations too."

It's been twenty-two days since Pendar was brought to the block. The block committee is meeting. Buyeh, blocking the entrance to the corridor with his tall frame, watches for the guard on duty. He is supposed to sing in Arabic if the guard shows up.

Pendar gives us strength. He believes we should start the strike.

Manuch the Black too is a member of the committee. He's been much bolder and more serious since he was released from solitary.

"If we put it off," Pendar says, "the guys will be discouraged. The time is right. Everyone is ready and excited. Everyone is on fire right now."

Manuch the Black squats down, stretches his neck, and says, "I agree with him . . . but what about those who are not ready? What should we do about them?"

"How many are there, anyway?" I ask.

Naser the Lifer counts up to nine and can't think of anyone else.

"There are three others," adds Mehdi the Wide Chest.

Pendar's genial gaze pauses on Mehdi the Wide Chest's face. "Who are they?" he asks.

"Fereydun the Blackmailer, Nasrollah the Roughneck, and Nasrollah Batul the Tattooed," Mehdi lists.

"These ten, twelve people are not significant enough to make us postpone the strike," says Pendar.

Hot, humid air seeps in through the window. The weather is muggy. The doors, the walls, and the floors are damp. Our bodies feel sticky and slimy. I gaze out the window at the edge of the towering prison wall. The sun, pale and weak, is disappearing behind the wall. We continue with our discussion. Buyeh sticks his head inside the room, then comes in, but leaves quickly. Putting our heads together, we finally decide to issue an ultimatum.

"Shouldn't we let the guys know about it?" Mehdi the Wide Chest asks.

"We'll tell them later," says Pendar.

"They might not agree," insists Mehdi.

"But they have left it up to us to decide what to do," Pendar says as he begins to write.

Everyone is silent. The floodlights inside the block come on.

"Listen, everyone!" Pendar says as he lights a cigarette. He reads the final draft of the petition:

> The twenty-fifth of Khordad, the year one thousand three hundred thirty-one[8]
> From: The Prisoners of Block 3
> To: The Respected Prison Chief
> The purpose of this document is to inform the prosecutor that the food distributed in the prison is poor in quality and inedible. Furthermore, the fact that most of the prisoners cannot afford to buy provisions with their personal budgets does not allow them to avoid eating the prison food. Therefore, we, the prisoners of Block 3, demand that:
> 1. Sufficient and edible food be provided to each prisoner at each mealtime;
> 2. The water reservoirs be replaced in all blocks or be repainted so that the taste and color of the water will remain in a healthy, drinkable condition;
> 3. If our requests are not met, we will, on the thirtieth of Khordad, refuse to receive food and refuse to visit our family members until the above-mentioned requests are granted.

When we're done reading, first we look at each other, then, without saying a word, we put our signatures at the bottom of the paper. We put the letter in an envelope, seal it, and give it to the guard on duty to be delivered to the prison chief. We then break away and go inform everyone of the plan.

---

8. May 1952

The sun has barely set when the door to the block bangs opens suddenly. The officer on duty, wearing no cap, steps inside. His collar is unbuttoned, and beads of sweat have formed on his forehead and cheeks. Standing behind the officer is the prison's old warrant officer, frowning and fidgeting. The officer on duty walks to the middle of the block and orders us to line up in single file. The old warrant officer goes and stands in front of the latrines and spits. We haven't even formed a line yet when the prison chief walks in the yard, dabbing his face and neck with a damp handkerchief. We stand in a line that stretches from one end of the yard to the other. The chief fans himself with the handkerchief. His brown, fleshy cheeks glow in the light of the setting sun. I look up and see guards standing behind the barbed wire, here and there. I count them. There are twelve of them. I have never seen so many armed guards on the rooftop. It's as if they have suddenly sprung up from the ground. They don't move at all. Clasping the barrels of their rifles, they plant the stocks of their weapons on the rooftop. Their eyes are fixed on the chief. The officer on duty goes and stands in front of the door of the block. It's bright inside the block, like daytime. We hold our breath. The humid air is stifling. The chief, standing right in the middle of the yard, keeps fanning himself. We have now made a circle around him. He starts to talk, saying that our petition is against the law. "But, because a prison guard regards a prisoner as his convict son, I'll pretend I have not seen the letter." He falls silent, shifting his short, thick legs. He thinks things over, weighing what he wants to say. He walks to the latrines and then walks back to us, and starts to talk again. He tries to make us understand that he genuinely wants to take advantage of this opportunity to share with us some of his own experiences. "A wise man," he begins gruffly, "is someone who first thinks . . . One cannot just act based on his whims . . . It's not feasible . . ."

He stops, and then starts to pace again. The sky is stifling. It's scorching hot. I look at the guards standing on the edge of the rooftop. They look impatient, shifting from foot to foot. White, barren clouds have covered the sky. Not a star can be seen. I hear the chief's voice again: "I know who's behind this, of course."

His eyes run over the faces of the prisoners. For a moment, our eyes meet. His head turns on his short, fleshy neck. His gaze pauses on Pendar, standing next to Naser the Lifer.

"The news reaches us. We are informed. Your files speak for themselves. Right now, I could point out those of you, one by one, who have caused this uproar . . . ," he says, trying to instill fear in us.

Still staring at Pendar and fanning himself, he continues, "But, my conscience tells me to show you the way, so that you do not fall into traps. This is my moral duty, to make you see what dire consequences this could have for you . . ." The prison chief's tone becomes somber. His eyes rest on me and freeze. His voice gets gruffer: "You know, if this issue goes further, who's going to lose?" He looks at Pendar again. "As you well know, we are not going to lose this game." He falls silent again and waddles on his short legs like a pregnant sow. He takes a few steps and turns back. Then he pauses again, as if he's done and everything is over, and says, "All right!"

He is quiet for a moment, then continues, "I believe we are all on the same page."

We all look at each other. It seems like something should be said. Someone should gather his courage and make the chief realize that things are not that easy and simple. Everyone holds their breath. The chief is walking away when, suddenly, Naser the Lifer steps forward. We listen intently. The prison chief asks, "Do you have something to say?"

Naser the Lifer mumbles, lowers his head, and then in a rough tone says, "No, it's not a big deal . . . but, you know, Mr. Chief . . ." He scratches the back of his neck, and continues, ". . . The jail food is really not edible at all . . . and besides that, the water tank looks really bad."

The prison chief walks toward him. His tone is serious. "Are you deaf? You didn't hear what I said?"

Now it's Pendar's voice that attracts the chief's attention. "No, Mr. Chief, we are not deaf . . . Your words, well, were precious, . . . but . . . they were not the answer to our requests."

The chief growls. His teeth show. He waddles like a crocodile toward Pendar.

"You mean to say, *It was not the answer to our ultimatum.*"

Pendar remains cool. But his face has turned pale, and his upper lip is puckered. "It's up to you, Mr. Chief," he says, "to call it whatever you like."

The chief glares at Pendar. His eyes look like those of a hungry snake as it is attacking its prey. His lips are tightly sealed. Lines have appeared around his fleshy mouth and his round chin. He steps back into the middle of the yard. "All right!" He falls silent, and then after a few seconds says, "All right, whatever I like . . ." His tone has lost its softness. Every word he speaks smells of danger and threat. They shake our hearts. "All right!" he huffs. He opens the letter and reads it. When done, he falls silent, looks at everyone, and says, "Those who don't agree with this letter, step forward."

Eleven people step forward, without hesitation, and all together.

"Nobody else?" he asks, and starts counting them. "There's no one else," he raises his voice again, "who disagrees with the content of this letter?" He waves the letter over his head and looks around the prison yard.

We keep our heads down for fear of losing our courage but step forward as if we are looking into the chief's menacing eyes. From somewhere close to the door of the block, I hear a whisper. I look out of the corner of my eye. Sha'ban the Iceman pulls his wrist free of the grasp of the person standing next to him, and steps forward. Naser the Lifer grumbles under his breath, "You bastard! . . . You fucking thief!"

"What's your name?" the chief asks him.

"Sha'ban."

The center of his head is bald. From the back of his head, his long, thin hair comes down to his shoulders. He is short and his chin looks like the muzzle of a jackal.

The chief asks the other eleven prisoners' names too. Then, puffing out his double chin, he says, "Just know that the moment I step out of this door, I will not pay attention to anyone's pleading."

His eyes run over our faces. He walks toward the block's door and stands beside the officer on duty. "Anyone else?" he asks.

Our lips are pressed together like melting lead. I look at the guys' faces, all of which have turned pale. The floodlights have lit the yard like daylight. The old warrant officer starts to walk away from the latrines, toward the block's door.

"Open up your ears real good!" comes the threatening voice of the prison chief again. "Once I walk out of this door, everything will be over. You'll have to face the consequences."

Judge, who's standing next to me, intertwines his fingers with mine. Everyone holds their breath. We hear the block door opening. The chief walks out. Behind him walks the officer on duty, then the old warrant officer. The door to the block shuts. I look up. The guards standing on the roof disappear. Suddenly, the line breaks and words get jumbled:

"We stand by our words."

"But may God help us in the end."

"Nothing will come of it."

"What're you talking about, Brother? It's true that we stood up to them and for our rights, but they can still do whatever they want to us."

Judge says, "I am not optimistic . . . I'm not hopeful, not of the guys' strength, nor—"

"Put that out of your mind," I cut him short. "We can make a lot of changes."

He lays his hands on my shoulders, bends down, and looks at me, saying, "But you can't imagine what a vicious murdering Shemr this chief is."

The guys have surrounded Sha'ban the Iceman. "If you were not the man for it, why did you agree to it in the first place?"

Sha'ban the Iceman's look is one of fear. His lips tremble. He mumbles, "I don't know what happened . . . The chief's fierce eyes crushed my self-confidence . . . Suddenly my heart sank . . . I got scared."

"Scared?"

Sha'ban the Iceman's voice is muffled, as if someone is squeezing his throat. "But, Naser Khan, you know well what handcuffs and shackles mean."

Sha'ban the Iceman has tasted that pain once and has had his fill of the prison chief. "You know exactly what a baton means . . . You, above all, should know the old warrant officer's braided whip."

Mehdi the Wide Chest, his arms akimbo, is standing behind Sha'ban the Iceman. His large head wobbles on his short neck. "Everything you say is true, Sha'ban, but that doesn't mean you shouldn't always take the side of the just."

The guard on duty is standing at a distance, leaning against the wall. He does not have his usual stern look, and just plays deaf, as if he isn't paying attention to anything.

The rooftop guard has walked out of the tower. Standing behind the barbed wire, he cranes his neck so he can see inside the yard better. Reza the Pickpocket, standing next to Buyeh, just listens to what the guys are saying. Sweat runs down the four pillars of our bodies. Rainless clouds have covered the block like a metal lid. Words are jumbled. Naser the Lifer has the final word. "We gave our word, and we'll stand by it. Any motherfucker who wants to get out of this, do it right now." Then he squeezes Reza the Pickpocket's earlobe and says, "That's for you, who didn't back away."

Reza the Pickpocket's face turns pale. "Naser Khan, I swear to God, I am with you," he pleads.

"But I know that you have an ax to grind," Naser the Lifer smirks. He lets go of Reza the Pickpocket's earlobe and breaks away from the crowd. He takes his shirt off and fans himself with it.

Pendar reaches for my arm, and we head off together.

Sunlight has spread inside the block. The weather has become even hotter. Sweat pours down the four pillars of our bodies. Having left our rooms, we sit in a group in the shade of the walls. No one talks. We are much different now than we used to be. No one raises his voice. We don't play *duz* anymore. No one is in the mood to make fun of anyone else. If they don't pay any attention to our requests, we will go on a hunger strike in four days. We look at each other in silence. Naser the Lifer and I are sitting on either side of Pendar. Hugging their knees, Mehdi and Manuch the Black are sitting across from us. We're thinking of a way to send a copy of the letter out to the prosecutor. Last night, after the chief walked out of the block, Pendar and I thought about it a lot, but we couldn't come up with a plan. Buyeh strides over and sits down beside us. He says, "Abbas the Butcher will be released the day after tomorrow."

But Abbas the Butcher is in Block 4. Naser the Lifer can no longer come and go between the blocks as he used to.

"Maybe we could have him take the letter to the prosecutor."

Buyeh can no longer make deals and move freely between the blocks either.

"Maybe at lunchtime we could pass it to him," Pendar says.

We know that the prisoners go to get their meals block by block, and we also know that after the last prisoner of a block gets his food and leaves, the door of the next block opens up.

Something occurs to me suddenly. "Maybe what I am going to say sounds stupid, but anyway—"

"What do you want to say?" Pendar cuts me short.

"Well, maybe one of us could do something to end up in solitary . . . ," I say.

Everyone listens carefully, looking at me.

". . . And then, we could give the letter to him at lunchtime, and he, somehow, could pass the letter on to Abbas the Butcher when it is his turn to get his ration."

Naser the Lifer's burning eyes fall on my face. I lower my head. "You think the guard in the corridor will give us the chance?" says Naser the Lifer.

I regret what I have just said.

"Especially now that they watch us like hawks?" adds Naser the Lifer.

"Do you think we could use the cooks?" Pendar asks.

It seems like an idea.

Mehdi the Wide Chest stretches his legs and says, "I might be able to make an arrangement with Musa the Cook . . . but I need some time to talk to him."

There is always a guard standing in front of the window through which we get our ration of food, so we can't make any trouble.

"If we could somehow distract him . . ."

"It wouldn't be all that easy, but . . . ," says Naser.

Once we reach the window, we could stand in a line, get our food, and quickly return.

"But, I might be able to get into a fight with the guard," continues Naser the Lifer, "and this way, drag him away from the window . . ."

"Do you think you can have Musa the Cook agree to it?" Pendar asks Mehdi.

Before Mehdi gets the chance to give an answer, the block's door opens noisily. We turn around and look to see a man of medium height being thrown inside by a punch to the neck from the old warrant officer. The man is a tad fat. His shirt is soaked in sweat and its buttons are undone, showing his white, hairless chest and bulging stomach. The door shuts. Our eyes are fixed on the man, who's down on his knees. As he struggles to get up, he looks back and grumbles, "Bastards, they know no dignity or any sense of humanity."

The air is so muggy and saturated that you can see droplets forming in midair in the sunlight. The man shakes the dust off his kneecaps and rubs his wrist as he comes toward us. He moves as if he has no energy left. His head has been shaved and bandaged. A few red spots have stained the white bandage. We continue to watch him. He limps over and sits in the middle of the block. His voice is muffled: "I am thirsty, guys. I haven't had a drop of water in two days."

His voice is soft and kind, but his moist lips belie his claim.

"Over there . . . next to the latrines." Manuch the Black gestures with his head.

The man of medium height looks at the sunshade over the water tank. Putting his hands on his waist, he limps in the direction of the water tank. He waits under the sunshade for a few seconds, then turns around and looks at us. Bending down, he turns the tap on, holds his cupped hands under the faucet, and then turns off the tap with the back of his hand; he lifts his hands up, smells the water, frowns, spills it, stands up, and hollers in a fierce and throaty voice, "How can one drink this water?"

We all hear him, and we all look at him, but everyone remains silent.

The man of medium height looks at the water tank, then walks out from under the sunshade. His voice is no longer muffled, but rather clear and vigorous, and his words are tinged with confidence. "Don't tell me you're drinking this water?"

"No, of course not," Mehdi the Wide Chest mocks, "there's a huge refrigerator in each of the rooms."

Buyeh bursts into laughter. Judge keeps staring at the man of medium height, who now fans himself with the bottom of his shirt. His voice has gotten even louder: "I am surprised by you guys; it's just like boiling water, and it smells like rust . . ."

"That's how it is—take it or leave it," answers someone from the other end of the block.

I look at the rooftop guard, who has come out of the tower, and out from behind the barbed wire, craning his neck to see. I hear the man of medium height's voice: "That's not a good answer."

"In that case, don't drink it!" says another man, squatting in a window.

The man of medium height walks back to the middle of the block, dabs the sweat off his cheeks and neck with his shirt, and says in a voice loud enough for everyone to hear, "There's no 'me' and no 'you.' What's the difference between me and you?"

Pendar rises to his feet beside the wall.

The man of medium height talks fearlessly, as if not familiar with a baton or solitary. "All these people, sitting together, not saying a word of complaint against what they feed you? And you people think you are wise and logical?"

Judge gets to his feet too, his gaze still fixed on the man of medium height. He doesn't even blink, just watches closely every move the man makes.

I get up and stand next to Pendar. I hear Judge whisper in Pendar's ear: "I have seen this guy somewhere . . . I don't know . . . maybe—"

"Do you think you know him?" Pendar cuts him short.

"Yeah, I think I have seen him somewhere." Judge nods his head.

"Then think harder to remember where you have seen him."

The man of medium height says, ". . . If I were you, I would've thrown out this tank of dirt a hundred times already."

Naser the Lifer, Manuch the Black, and Mehdi the Wide Chest are also getting to their feet. Our arms are folded across our chests as we all lean against the wall and look at the man of medium height.

"The way he looks . . . The way he talks . . . How he gestures with his head and moves his neck . . . ," Judge says.

Pendar stares at Judge. "I think it's a trick," he says; his tone holds a hint of doubt.

Pendar is no fool. I have learned a lot from him. I have learned how to do the right thing during interrogations, how to deal with the police, and how to sense a conspiracy. At times, I envy Pendar. I envy his experiences, and the predictions he makes and how they come true.

Again, it is Judge's voice: "I know those fleshy lips well . . . I must have seen him somewhere."

The man of medium height's voice strengthens by the second, as if it were his responsibility to talk to us, to provoke us.

The guard on duty has gone into the corridor alongside the rooms. I have no doubt the he can hear the man's voice, yet he plays deaf. His behavior has changed since last night. No matter what we do, he has no reaction. He just stands in a corner, smokes his cigarette, and doesn't say a word.

Pendar is pensive. Judge doesn't take his gaze off the newcomer. His eyes are narrowed. His forehead is creased with wrinkles.

By now, everyone has risen to their feet; they are standing in the shade of the walls, saying nothing, and looking at the man who speaks so boldly and fearlessly. "What are you afraid of?" he asks. "What are you waiting for, anyway? Why don't you throw this tank out? Why don't you ask the prison chief to come and take a gulp of this shit, to see what you're going through?"

We find ourselves surprised and silent. We wonder why the hell the guard has gone into the corridor and doesn't come out? How come this man is so daring?

His voice rises. "I volunteer to be the first person to kick the block's door hard until they'll listen to us . . . If you're afraid, I am ready to tumble the water tank down right now and throw it at the block's door. What do you think they can do to us? Where else other than jail can they put us?"

And as he talks in a loud voice, he walks toward the water tank. His gait is firm now, and he no longer limps at all. Before the man reaches the sunshade, Pendar rushes after him and grabs his shoulders from behind. "Why are you in such a hurry, Brother? Be a bit patient!"

Shaking himself, the man tries to release his shoulders from Pendar's grasp. He has turned red. He shouts, "Let me throw this junk tank out! . . . Let go. You guys may not be the men for it, but I'm not even afraid of God."

Still holding on to him, Pendar pulls him into the shade of the wall. Everyone gathers around Pendar and the man. The guard on duty still lingers in the corridor, acting as if nothing has happened. Craning his neck and holding his breath, the rooftop guard watches. Pendar turns the newcomer around, clutches his shirt collar with both hands, and asks him in a rough voice, "Tell me the truth! Why do you want to sabotage the block?"

The man of medium height takes his eyes from Pendar's penetrating gaze and looks around. "'Cause even animals wouldn't drink that water."

Naser the Lifer, planting his legs one in front of the other, stands behind the man of medium height.

Pendar's voice is very pleasing. "But who among us has agreed that you should knock down the water tank?"

The man's hand rises to wipe the sweat on his forehead. Judge, suddenly all fired up, stares at the big Aleppo boil mark on the back of his hand. "You bastard," he yells, "now I remember who you are . . . I was going out of my mind!" And with his usual hasty steps, he comes forward, clutches the man's wrist as it is coming down, and hurriedly says, "Hey, mister, aren't you that secretary in the third branch of the Criminal Investigation Department?"

The man's enraged face loses its color. His lips begin to quiver.

"For the sake of any decent man, don't try to fool me," Judge tells him hastily, and, tapping on his own cheek with his hand, he adds, "Come clean! Aren't you the one who wrote my confession with this very hand—this very big Aleppo boil on it—last year, when I lifted a bastard's watch?"

"Me? . . . No . . . What are you saying?" the man mumbles.

"Aha!" we all yell at once.

"He is lying. I am not at all . . . ," the man says, panicking.

"Boo!" we all yell out.

"I swear that I . . ."

"Aha!"

"So, you wanted to make trouble in the block to give them an excuse, huh?" Pendar's voice rises.

The man steps back. Naser the Lifer holds him.

"You're mistaken."

"Aha!" everyone shouts again.

Suddenly, the door to the block opens. Turning around, we see the prison chief scurrying inside on his short, fat legs like a wounded swine. "What the hell is wrong with you? What's all this fuss about?" his voice explodes.

The man of medium height shakes himself free from Naser the Lifer's arms, shrinks, and steps back.

We clear the way for the chief, who comes and stands in front of Pendar. We look at the door to the block and see a few guards standing on the threshold, clasping the handles of their batons in their hands. Behind them, in the corridor, stand a few more guards. The man of medium height has moved away from our group. We remain silent. The chief's voice shakes our hearts: "If you go on making trouble like this, I'll have you thrown in solitary."

Pendar's face has turned pale.

"But, Mr. Chief, if it wasn't for Pendar, this bastard would have made a big mess," Naser the Lifer says, his voice rising.

"You shut up," the chief growls through his clenched teeth. He then walks toward the secretary from the third branch, who's standing under the sunshade covering the water tank. "You, get out of here!" he commands.

The man of medium height lowers his head and walks toward the door to the block. The guards have stepped out of the doorway and into the corridor. The prison chief dabs the sweat off his cheeks and neck with a handkerchief and, in a loud voice, warns us, "I have enough room for all of you in solitary. I'll throw you all into a cell like a herd of sheep, on top of each other. So that you realize you can't do whatever the hell you wanna do."

With that, his head spins on his short, fat neck, looking at everyone. His light blue shirt, drenched in sweat, sticks to his shoulders. His potbelly is sticking out. His belt has slipped down onto his hips. His sharp gaze pauses on Reza the Pickpocket. "You, come with me!"

Naser the Lifer's eyes, burning like two balls of fire, pierce Reza's face. The chief starts to walk away. Naser the Lifer growls in Reza the Pickpocket's ear, "Dare say anything about us, make sure you don't come back to this block, or else . . ."

The prison chief stops, turns around, and glares at Naser the Lifer. It seems that he has heard what Naser the Lifer said, as if he has the hearing of a snake. Naser stands firmly, like a roof truss, planting his feet one in front of the other. Large droplets of sweat cover his hairy chest.

Reza the Pickpocket's face has turned pale. Pendar chews the corner of his mustache. This time, the chief comes and gets in Naser the Lifer's face. Pointing the end of his switch at Naser's shoulder, he says, his voice choked with rage, "There was a time that I thought you might be paroled. I always thought of doing something for you. Now you can only see it happening in your dreams."

Abbas the Butcher got released, but the letter to the prosecutor is still in our hands. We haven't come up with any ideas yet.

Pendar calls out to us. One after another, we walk into Room 10, and sit down for a meeting. Judge and Buyeh watch out for the guards in the corridor and the yard. Pendar tells us that we shouldn't be silent, not even for a second. We should constantly go from room to room, talking to the guys and encouraging them. "You should be alert," he says. "If anyone is about to give up, you should talk to him . . . and boost his courage. If it doesn't go well, let me know about it immediately."

We dispersed among the other prisoners. Everyone is sitting in groups, but saying very little. Once again, we notice a change in the guard's behavior. Once again, he eavesdrops as he walks around—all the while deepening his voice and warning us. We take turns distracting him so that he cannot listen in on us.

Pendar's words travel from mouth to mouth: "Going on a strike is very different from making trouble. We should be attentive. We should stay calm. We should avoid doing anything that they could use against us. The day we start the strike, we sit down quietly and refuse to get our ration of food . . . and if it coincides with a visit day, we refuse to see our families."

Naser the Lifer is more anxious about the letter to the prosecutor than the rest of us. "You see, if he doesn't get the letter, who will know that we are on a strike?"

"What if we can't do it—send the letter out to him?" wonders Ahmad the Tarantula.

"We will still go on the strike," Pendar assures him.

Mehdi the Wide Chest brings up Musa the Cook again. "Maybe we should give it some more thought . . . Maybe we could send it out this way."

At noon, when we go to get our lunch, Naser the Lifer reaches under the guard's arm and pulls him away from the window to the kitchen. Buyeh takes up his position behind Mehdi the Wide Chest. Manuch the Black and Pendar stand on either side of Buyeh. A bit further away from the window, I intentionally step on Ahmad the Curly's foot, pressing it hard.

"Ouch! Khaled, are you blind or something!" yells Ahmad the Curly.

"You're blind," I raise my voice. "Watch where you step."

"You trampled my foot, and now you're blaming me?" Ahmad the Curly's voice gets louder.

The guard walks toward us. "What the hell is going on here?"

Naser the Lifer follows him.

Ahmad the Curly's shrill voice gets tangled in his throat. "Look what he did to my toes . . ."

Suddenly, we hear Musa the Cook's loud and gruff voice. "Do you want to take the meager sum I earn away from me?"

The guard leaves us and goes toward the window to the kitchen. "What's wrong, Musa?"

Musa, frowning, empties the ladle into Mehdi the Wide Chest's bowl and says under his breath, "Nothing, man."

The guard pushes Pendar and Manuch the Black aside. "Get back in line!"

Musa the Cook won't go along. The letter to the prosecutor is still in our hands. The sun is disappearing behind the top of the towering wall of the prison. Pendar's words travel from mouth to mouth: "Let's keep in mind that once we start the strike, we can't react, even if they beat us. We should tolerate everything calmly and continue with our strike."

Everyone is anxious and doubtful. Sometimes we feel so determined that we're ready to give up our lives for it. Other times we become terrified that some of us might give up and go begging the chief to let us take back what we've said. Pendar is relentless. He astonishes me. How can a human being be so patient and talk so much?

It is the eve of the twenty-ninth. Pendar is restless. He tends to everyone, going from this group to that one, from this room to the next. He talks more than all of us put together, and more eagerly than anyone else. The weather has cooled down a bit, more or less. The floodlights inside the block have come on. Occasionally, a breeze drifts down from over the towering walls of the prison, drying the sweat on our foreheads. The guys have spread carpets here and there in the yard, and are sitting in groups. The sky is clear and full of stars. The heat of the day has dispersed. The roar of the Primus burners fuses with the voices. Sometimes a joke is cracked: "The Last Supper."

"Let's say the Supper of the Lonely Strangers."[9]

We no longer keep anything from the guard on duty inside the block. We talk openly about the strike. It seems like talking about the strike has

---

9. This is a reference to the family of Imam Hossein. After his death at the Battle of Karbala, they were taken to Syria as prisoners; thus, this group of mostly women and children were lonely strangers in a strange land.

become a common thing, and it seems like our fears are diminishing—or if they still linger, they are only momentary fears.

"I'll eat a dinner the size of a buffalo tonight," Mohammad the Bearded says.

We have come to believe that the strike will begin tomorrow after sunrise.

"If we drink water, we won't break the strike, right?" Taqqi the Machine Foot asks.

We burst into laughter. "Go on and fill your guts up with water!"

A tinge of doubt touches the wrinkles on Taqqi the Machine Foot's forehead. "I am serious," he says in a subdued tone. "What if they say, 'To hell with them.' I think to myself, how long can a person go without food, anyway?"

"Look, Taqqi," Pendar says, "if you take a good look at their attitude, you can tell how their minds are all shitty and mixed up already."

Mohammad the Bearded inches closer on his butt and says, "But that doesn't mean they will sympathize with us."

Mehdi the Wide Chest's round eyes roll in their sockets. "But, Mammad," he says, "you should also know that they're responsible for our lives."

Many are still uneasy about the whole thing. Pendar keeps moving around, trying to convince everyone. Mehdi the Wide Chest shifts from one foot to the other as he listens to the talk. Naser the Lifer tries to play the heavy and look menacing. "If they don't listen to us," he threatens, "I'll create such a ruckus that even five hundred guards won't be able to take us down . . . I'll cut—"

Pendar cuts him short, reminding him of our peaceful plans. "This is the hundredth time I've had to tell you, Naser, that we shouldn't give them anything to use against us."

"What do you think they are going to do to us? . . . Huh?" asks Manuch the Black. "I threw food over the roof and cussed them all. So what did they do to me, huh? Only put me in solitary for a few days. Besides, I was the only one then. What're they going to do with a hundred of us now?"

"Going on strike is not a crime," Judge reasons hastily. "If they don't listen to us, we have every right to strike. They're responsible. We can sue them. If the prosecutor finds out, he might even request the chief's resignation. I know the law. I know it all by heart."

Pendar talks of his experiences. "If we quit in the middle of things, conditions will get even worse than they are now. We have to be strong. I promise they will give up on the third day. We need only three days."

Heydar Mashti, scratching his black, bushy beard, asks, "What about those who get their rations?"

"To hell with their stomachs," grumbles Naser the Lifer. "I'll plant myself like a pillar right in front of the block's door and won't let anyone out."

Buyeh's gray beard moves. "They're not our business."

"So you say," Naser the Lifer mocks. "If so, what's the difference between us and them?"

Buyeh's Adam's apple bobs in his long, dry throat. "But we can't stop them."

"We can't? My dead body alone will stop a hundred—"

Pendar interrupts Naser the Lifer, "Listen, Naser. Of course, it would be better if they too wouldn't get their rations, because if they do, it means that the food is edible; yet—"

Naser the Lifer cuts Pendar short, "That's why I'm saying we shouldn't allow them to get their food."

"But if we force them, we're causing ourselves trouble," Buyeh reasons.

Ali the Barber's hoarse voice fills the corridor: "Naser the Lifer!"

Everyone falls silent.

Naser the Lifer scratches his wide chin and fixes his sharp gaze on Pendar.

The door to the block opens. Ali the Barber shouts Naser's name again. The old warrant officer stands in the doorway. Naser gets up. "Naser, come along!" says the officer. "Mr. Chief has asked for you."

Naser the Lifer moves toward the door and leaves the block.

We look at each other. We now know exactly what these sudden calls mean. Sometimes, it is to intimidate us; sometimes, we're up for lashings, or perhaps solitary confinement. It all depends on who's being called and what he has done.

"What was he called for?"

"It's clear they wanna terrorize us."

I lie down and look at the sky, which is full of stars, and marvel at how beautiful it is.

The voices are now jumbled: "Didn't he say he had enough room for all of us in the solitary cells? Didn't he?"

Buyeh pours tea.

I sit up and pick up a cup of tea.

"He won't do anything to him," says Pendar. "He'll just talk to him. He'll try to intimidate him, or try to buy him . . ."

"Pfff, you don't know him," says Mohammad the Bearded. "This chief is one of those motherfuckers who wouldn't even spare his own mother."

I have yet to drink a second cup of tea when Naser comes back, grinning. The old warrant officer is with him. Bending down, he grabs Pendar's wrist. "Get up and come with me!" he says.

Pendar turns around and whispers to me, "Get ready to be next."

Pouring some tea into a saucer, Naser the Lifer tells us about what the chief said to him. "Well, Naser! You're going on strike tomorrow, huh?"

Naser the Lifer answered under his breath, "With your permission, Mr. Chief."

The chief burst out laughing. "With *my* permission?"

And then Naser said, "Well, you know, sir . . . our food, as you can see . . ."

The chief offered him a chair and asked him to sit down. Naser sat. The chief put his hand on Naser's shoulder and promised him he'd have them give him two rations of good food every day. Then, with sympathy, he said, "You know what, Naser? You shouldn't mingle with these people. I can appeal for clemency for you. Or I can ask for a suspension of your sentence. I can—"

Naser the Lifer interrupted the chief and mumbled, "Mr. Chief, I didn't do anything wrong."

Again, the chief started to make more promises and to give fatherly advice, and eventually he asked Naser to make the guys stop protesting.

Naser the Lifer, gulping down his tea, tells us, "I told him, 'You know, sir, the guys don't even listen to me.' But he said, 'They do, Naser, they do listen to you. Go and put some sense into their heads. Promise me that you won't let anyone make trouble tomorrow. And I'll do whatever I can for you.'"

At this point, Naser the Lifer bursts out laughing and says, "The bastard thought I was a jackass. I kept telling him it's a bull; he kept saying milk it, it's a cow. I tell him, 'It's out of my hands, sir'; he says, 'I'll give you two rations of good food.'"

The block's door opens. Pendar comes in, his face lit up with a smile. This time, the old warrant officer calls me.

"Be strong!" Pendar says.

I walk out with the old warrant officer. The front of the prison's office has been sprinkled with water and swept clean. It feels cool. The prison chief sits in his chair, smoking. The officer on duty is right behind him. The chief is gentle. His tone of voice is infused with a smile. "I am amazed that literate people like you and Pendar mingle with a bunch of thieves and thugs!"

A smile has parted his moist lips. Suddenly, I hear the sound of his slap hitting my face. I hear his raging voice coming from deep in his throat: *I slapped you so you would know firsthand who you're dealing with.*

The smile has made lines appear around his mouth. In a gentle tone, he says, "You think these people are decent?" He dabs his double chin with a handkerchief. A smile has lit up his entire face. "You think this lot can be redeemed? You think they can be trusted? I feel really bad for you."

He keeps talking in a gentle manner, trying to butter me up.

"You are a nice boy," he goes on. "You know a lot more than these people . . . Why do you have to mingle with them at all?"

He talks about his own experiences. "I have been dealing with prisoners for fifteen years. I tried so hard, and finally decided that these people cannot be changed. Today they bond with you, and tomorrow they cut your throat for a penny. This is how they have been raised."

His loquaciousness bores me. I shift from foot to foot and look around.

"I think what I should do," he says, "is set up a couple of rooms in another corner for people like you and Pendar. I should separate you guys from these folks. It's not suitable for you to be roomed together with a bunch of good-for-nothings."

Rising from his chair, he walks toward me. "How about you two go to the prison health center for the time being? It's cleaner there, and they have good food too."

I keep my head down and remain silent.

"What do you say?"

"Thanks a lot," I say under my breath.

He tosses the cigarette butt down, steps on it, and says, "You're like my own son."

Again, I hear his voice coming from a distance. It sounds like he is yelling. *I'll have you handcuffed and shackled in solitary, so you'll learn to be grateful for what you have now!*

I can imagine his short leg coming down on me, striking my hip.

The prison chief comes closer. "What're you thinking about?"

I lift up my head and look at him. His lips are still bright with a smile. "Nothing," I say.

He lays his hand over my shoulder. "Then, will you promise me to settle the commotion inside the block?"

I look at him, surprised.

"Naser and Pendar will also help you. They have promised me."

"They might have promised you, but . . . ," I say softly.

"But what?"

"But I can't do anything about it," I say under my breath.

He steps back, puffs out his double chin, and changes the subject. "How old are you?"

"Eighteen."

His voice takes on a rough tone: "In that case, you should be going straight to the military barracks after you are out of here."

My heart sinks. I look at his cheeks, which are covered in sweat.

"If you'll be a smart boy, once your sentence is over, I'll let you go. Otherwise, I'll send you straight to the military."

He goes back and sits in the chair. "How's that?" he says, lighting a cigarette. "Hmm?"

I am still silent.

"Say something."

"Whatever your power permits, sir!"

Taking a drag at his cigarette, he says, "Go and show me that you are a smart boy. Go and help Naser and Pendar to settle the noise."

I am about to walk away when he says, "Just know that if you decide to betray me, you'll pay a hefty price for it."

I walk toward the block. He sees me off with a last piece of advice. "I hope you listened carefully to what I told you!"

∽

It is the morning of the thirtieth day of the month of Khordad. The sun has yet to rise. The air is humid and clammy. Everyone has already gotten up, rolled up their bedrolls, and piled them up in a corner of the room. On any other day we would have slept till noon, but today everyone is up as if someone has come and dragged us, one by one, out of our bedrolls. Anxiety has taken hold of us. Everyone is quiet. Now and then, someone whispers something, but soon he falls silent. Pendar is everywhere, a smile perking up his face. His expression offers us confidence. His words encourage us, forcing fear out of our hearts. "We must be strong," he says.

Yet, again anxiety, panic, and fear return, looming over the entire block. It is visitation day. It is also the first day of the strike. Some of the guys have not yet left their rooms, still sitting there, smoking. The rest, however, have squatted in the shade of the high walls.

The sun is spreading inside the block. The block's guard is not on duty today. Pulling my knees to my chest, I lean against the wall. My entire body is drenched in sweat. I keep my gaze fixed on the rolled barbed wire along the edge of the roof. The sun creeps along the ground, moving closer to us.

Suddenly, Ali the Barber's holler reverberates inside the block as he yells out Heydar Mashti's name. He has visitors. He doesn't budge. Squatting in the windowsill, with his arms wrapped around his shanks and his big square chin resting on his knees, he just steals looks at the door to the block.

Once again, Ali the Barber's holler echoes inside the yard through the round hole in the block's door. "Heydar Mashti . . . Mammad the Bearded . . . !"

Naser the Lifer, pushing back his shoulders, walks toward the block's door. Mohammad the Bearded remains seated on the steps in front of the latrines, clipping his nails. Naser the Lifer places his hands against the iron door, brings his large mouth close to the hole, and says, "Don't rip your throat for nothing, man, 'cause today, nobody will go visit nobody!"

Pendar comes and takes the half-smoked cigarette from my hand. His smile has become so much a part of his face that it seems like it will become permanent. Taking a drag of the cigarette, he says, "We have started off all right."

He is happy. He takes another drag, rolls the smoke around inside his mouth, and says, "But you know . . ." He sits down beside me. "I'll say this only to you, so you can keep a watch out."

He plays with the cigarette smoke. "We have started off well, but maintaining it . . ." He hesitates, looking at me.

"Maintaining it is what?" I ask.

"It's not easy . . ."

"If we fail to keep it up," he whispers near my ear. "If some of them chicken out in the middle of things, everything will be over . . . Then, you can't do anything anymore."

His words smell of hopelessness, but the smile doesn't leave his lips.

I am shocked by his words. So I ask, "If the timing was not right, why—"

"The timing is right," he interrupts me. "If we had put it off, it would have been a long time before we saw this level of anticipation again."

"Then why—"

Again, he robs me of the chance to speak. "I told you this so you'd stay focused. I will tell the others too. We need to be sharp, like eagles . . . We can't let it leak out. I tell you this so that you won't sit here idle. You should walk around and listen to the guys. I'll tell this to the others too."

Ali the Barber's holler reverberates through the block again: "Sha'ban the Iceman!"

Sha'ban moves away from the wall and starts walking. I leave Pendar and go and stand in his way. "Where you going, Sha'ban?"

His long, bony muzzle, like that of a jackal, shifts. "I told you from the beginning that I am not with you guys."

He looks a little embarrassed. His bald head shines under the intense sunlight.

"I know that, Sha'ban, but if you stick with us, it'll be for your own good."

For a few moments, he puckers his thin lips, then he parts them and says, "But if I don't go, my mother will die of grief."

"Your mother's blood is not any redder than our mothers' blood," I say.

"Let him go, man!" I hear Manuch the Black's voice from behind me.

Then, I hear Reza the Mudguard Maker's voice. "This bastard, with that bald head of his, is such a son of a bitch."

I step out of Sha'ban the Iceman's way. He goes out the block's door. I walk away. The weather is taking things too far, making the sky look like lead. A humid fog has swallowed the block. The rooftop guard keeps walking out of the tower, surveying the block each second through the rolled barbed wire. Only twelve people from Block 3 have gone for visitation. No one else budges. Pendar's voice echoes in my ears: "We have started off all right."

We hear that it is chaos in front of the prison. Our family members who have come to visit but could not see us—since we have refused visitation—have started yelling and cussing out the prison officials. In return, the guards have used their batons generously, forcing the visitors out of the prison.

Javad Borujerdi scratches his large nose and says, "You think they'll have mercy on anyone?"

"The women were screaming so loud, you'd think it's Ashura," reports Ahmad the Curly.

"Kids cried like orphans," adds Jaber the Finger.

"Don't you have anything else to say rather than to discourage the guys?" Pendar says, trying to stop them.

Sha'ban the Iceman, snuffling, retorts, "If you think I'm lying, go and see for yourself!"

"You bastard, you cannot discourage us with this talk!" Naser the Lifer's voice explodes.

"It's such a hullaballoo . . ." Suddenly, we hear a man's voice from Block 2; he's climbed onto someone's shoulders to reach the narrow, round vent in the wall that opens to Block 3.

Everyone gets up from the shade of the wall and walks toward the vent.

". . . We can hear their screams from Block 2 . . ."

The guys gather in front of the vent. Pendar's voice comes from deep in his throat: "Who are you?"

"Chellab."

I wish I could head out of the block and run straight to the visitation room.

"Who has asked you to tell us this nonsense?" Pendar's voice gets louder.

Yusuf the Spoiled raises his voice from behind others. "Let him talk, so you'll know we don't lie."

I wish I could see Mother. What if she has also complained? What if she has been beaten with a baton?

The voice keeps coming from the vent: ". . . They piled women and kids on each other, like a herd of sheep, and battered them with batons to force them out of the jail."

"Chellab," shouts Naser the Lifer, "I'll rip your mouth apart if you have lied to us!"

"I saw it with my own eyes," Chellab's voice comes through the vent, "when I went to visit . . . Ouch . . ."

His voice ceases. A baton must have hit his buttocks. The guys look at each other, then they start grumbling.

"Look, fellas!" Pendar begins. "You know that people always make mountains out of molehills . . . I promise you that it's not as big a deal as they are saying. Besides, if we just give in so easily . . ."

The block's door opens with a clatter. It is almost noon. The hot sun has evaporated the humidity. They have brought us two big baskets of bread. Two stale black loaves for each person. Pendar picks up his ration of the bread, walks to the middle of the block, bends down, and puts the loaves on the ground. I do the same. Then it is Naser the Lifer who comes and puts his loaves on mine and Pendar's. Behind him is Manuch the Black, then Mehdi the Wide Chest, and before we know it, there's a pile of bread loaves in the middle of the block.

Sunlight creeps through the prison. We go and sit in the narrow strip of shade beside the wall. It is barely midday when the prison chief walks in with the officer on duty. When he sees the pile of bread, he stops. His face loses its color. He looks at the officer. We rise to our feet, fold our arms across our chests, and lean against the wall. The chief runs his eyes over all of us, one by one, then goes and stands next to the pile of bread loaves. "I have been very patient with you," he says, his voice trembling.

A few of the guys still sitting in their rooms stick their heads out through the windows.

We remain silent. The chief's fidgety movements shout that he is angry. He struggles to be calm and cool, but rage blazes out with every word. "There comes a time when . . . you come to believe nobility is evil. There comes a time," he says, staring at us, ". . . when you come to believe that you need to be evil . . ."

He falls silent and dabs the sweat off his forehead. He puffs out his double chin and then empties it. The sun's hot rays strike his head. He starts to talk again. "I just feel sorry for you. Otherwise, it doesn't really matter to me whether you eat or not. You're like my children, like my brothers . . . If you have a problem with the quality of your food, there are other ways to show it. You will not gain anything by going on a strike and making trouble. I could easily put you in your place. I can easily . . ."

He tries to hold back, but he cannot stop himself. His voice gets louder by the second, losing its initial gentleness. Now, his shrill words make the veins on his neck swell. His voice takes on a hint of brutality. "Your families want to see you," he says. "Why should they suffer? If you say the food is bad, what's that have to do with your wives and children? Why would you make them go through such pain? Stop goofing around and go see your families, otherwise . . ."

He stops talking and shifts from foot to foot. He looks at the pile of black bread. His tone becomes softer. "Otherwise, don't expect friendly treatment from me. I mean . . . How should I say this? . . . I mean, you will force me to change my attitude."

The prison chief is soaked in sweat under the sun's gleaming rays. The officer maintains his position next to the doorway. The sun has crept up to our feet. The chief starts to pace. He looks tired. His light blue shirt is stuck to his shoulders. The bald spot on the top of his head shines. He stops in front of Pendar, puts his hands on his waist, and stares at him, narrowing his eyes. Wrinkles form on his forehead. Pendar keeps his gaze fixed on the gabled roof of the security tower.

"Look at me!"

Pendar keeps looking up.

The chief is short and wide. Pendar is tall and broad-shouldered.

"I said, look at me." The chief's voice gets louder.

Pendar lowers his head slowly. His pleasant eyes meet the chief's.

"Look, young man! Do you resent tranquility?"

Pendar's lips are pressed together like melted lead.

The veins on the chief's neck darken. "Don't you have a tongue?"

"Yes, Mr. Chief," Pendar says under his breath.

"Then why don't you answer?"

"A graveyard is also peaceful," Pendar whispers.

Suddenly, the prison chief starts shaking, blood rushes to his face, his voice dies in his throat, and then he shouts: "Very well!"

Quickly, he turns on his heels and darts toward the block's door.

The pile of bread has gotten higher. The first day of the strike is behind us. Chellab's words almost ruined everything for us, but that's past too. It is a bit before noon. The heat is suffocating. Cigarette smoke makes our stomachs turn. Hunger and fatigue have brought some to their knees. It feels like the door to hell has been left ajar. The loaves of bread gleam black in the sunshine. A new wave of complaints is brewing:

"Why should they get their ration of food?"

"It's not like their blood is redder than ours!"

"If no one's supposed to get food, then those ten or twelve guys shouldn't either."

Word travels from mouth to mouth that *no one* is allowed to get any food.

"If they're getting it, we should get some too."

"You mean we should starve now, so that they'll enjoy it later?"

The whispers are becoming widespread. We should come up with something. They must be stopped. Pendar believes that if these complaints gather more strength, they will break up the strike. He calls for a meeting to decide what to do. We meet in Room 10 and close the door. Buyeh stands guard. Without wasting any time, everyone agrees that nobody should get any food. Pendar believes that if we don't listen to them, the strike will be over. He says that sometimes you have to accept a collective decision even if it is wrong. We should just go along with those who want to end the strike and gradually show them that they have made a mistake. "If we refuse to do this," says Pendar, "they won't give a damn about us anymore. They are hungry and angry. Edgy too. All it will take is to tell them 'no,' and they will get in our faces and say 'no' to us in return."

The twelve have separated themselves from us and now sit in front of the latrines.

"I'll go and reason with them. If they refuse, then we'll use force," Pendar says. He gets up and leaves the room. We watch through the window. Our guys, sitting in the shade of the wall, look fed up and limp. Pendar walks toward the row of stalls. Some of the guys get up and walk with him. Pendar sits on the ground and faces the twelve, talking. We can't hear him. The guys hover over him.

Suddenly, Nasrollah the Roughneck's voice rises. "Take your ass with you and leave us alone!"

Pendar comes back. Everyone gathers in the corridor. Lunchtime is approaching. We have no choice but to use force against them. Ali the Mustache says, "If you're not up to it, I can take them down all on my own."

The hubbub of voices echoes under the ceiling:

"We won't let them get food."

"We shouldn't let them."

"There's no difference between them and us."

Sunlight has crept to the foot of the wall, devouring the shade.

Naser the Lifer, Judge, Buyeh, and Ali the Mustache leave the corridor for the door to the block, and they stand there in a row. Pendar asks me to go and stand by them too. Buyeh's bushy eyebrows are knitted. He has tied his keffiyeh tightly around his waist. His long hands hang loose on either side of his body. His wide palms and bony wrists look as if they are weighing him down. Judge, his arms akimbo, stands next to Buyeh. He does not even reach Buyeh's shoulder. The look in his eyes is unreadable. A smile has parted his lips, making his thin mustache seem weak. Ali the Mustache is taller than Naser the Lifer. Wider too. He has taken off his shirt and tied it around his waist. Drops of sweat trickle down his dark skin. Ali the Mustache's muscles look like rocks. His black, bushy mustache conceals his mouth entirely. Naser the Lifer, leaning against the support pillar of the block's door, keeps his eyes fixed on the latrines. Everyone is silent. The block is quiet.

A few of the guys are sitting on the windowsills. Under the heat of the sun, the loaves of bread have hardened like bricks. The lunch bell sounds in the corridor. Once Blocks 1 and 2 are finished getting their food, it will be our turn. Javad Borujerdi walks out from under the water tank's sunshade, shambles into the corridor, returns with his copper bowl, and waits for the block's door to open. Then the other eleven prisoners rise, one after another, fetch their copper bowls, and linger under the water tank's sunshade, waiting for the door to open.

The sky is clear and bright. The sun beats down so hot it makes vapor rise from the earth.

The rooftop guard comes out of the tower for a second, peeks into the yard, and quickly returns to his sanctuary in the shade of the gabled tower. Mastan, the guard on duty in the corridor, hollers through the round hole in the iron door. "Lunch!"

The block's door opens. Guard Mastan steps into the doorway, runs his eyes over us as we stand in a row in front of the door, and asks, "What're y'all standing there for?"

No one answers him. We don't even turn around to look at him.

Placing the copper bowl on top of his head like a turban, Rostam Effendi shambles toward the block's door. His long, thin gray beard bounces on his chest. He barely reaches the block's door before Naser the Lifer stops him. Rostam Effendi just stands there with his legs planted wide apart. He has no strength left to talk. His words are distorted by his swollen nose, and come out muffled. "What's wrong, Naser?"

Naser, fixing his burning eyes on Rostam Effendi's drooping face, says in a heavy tone, "Effendi, don't make me disrespect you!"

Lowering his head, Rostam Effendi mumbles, "I am not with you guys. I've told you this from the beginning."

Naser grabs his shoulders, turns him around, and gives him a shove. "But now you have no choice," he says.

Yusuf the Spoiled, Javad Borujerdi, and Nasrollah Batul the Tattooed come forward and stand facing us. Rostam Effendi too turns around and joins them. Nasrollah Batul the Tattooed's black, bushy eyebrows are knitted. "Why are you blocking our way?" he asks.

Naser stands with his arms akimbo. "Just for the hell of it," he retorts.

A line appears on the pale skin above Javad Borujerdi's large nose. "It's not like we asked you to come and get your ration!" he says.

Fereydun the Blackmailer, who has just joined them, backs up Javad. "Jesus got his religion, and Moses got his religion."

Buyeh, bending down toward Fereydun the Blackmailer, says in a gruff tone, "No to Jesus and no to Moses. All for the religion of Mohammad."

Fereydun the Blackmailer is half-naked. His entire body is covered in tattoos. On his chest, he has tattooed two flying angels holding hands.

A huge dragon is coiled on his stomach. The legendary Rostam has been tattooed on his right arm. On his left arm rests a fleshy, unibrowed woman with a large mole above her lip. Fereydun the Blackmailer's neck veins swell. "If this is about bullying, I will bully too to get my food," he says.

He steps forward to pass through our line, but Naser the Lifer blocks his way like a solid pillar. He orders, "Fereydun, step aside!"

Nasrollah the Roughneck's large figure shifts. Guard Mastan has gone into the corridor. I go and shut the block's door, but the guard comes and opens it again. Now the voices are getting louder.

Nasrollah the Roughneck's wide face has turned pale. His voice trembles. "You think you can stop us by force?"

"Go back and sit in your places like good boys," Ali the Mustache says in a guttural tone of voice.

A few of the guys are standing at the head of the corridor, watching. Some have craned their necks out of the windows. Pendar, leaning in the doorway to the corridor, smokes. His face has lost its color, but the smile doesn't leave his lips.

"Will you let us get our food or no?" Yusuf the Spoiled finally asks.

"Now, hear a few words from the bride's mother!" Naser mocks.

"The final word is," says Buyeh, "that we haven't eaten for two days. So, you don't eat for two days either . . . What's the big deal?"

Ahmad the Curly, with his small body and large head, attempts to squeeze his way through us. I grab his shirt collar from behind and shove him aside. "Where do you think you're going?"

Jaber the Finger suddenly blows up. His pointed muzzle moves as he yells, "I'll get my food even if I have to shed someone's blood!" And jutting his bony shoulder out, he tries to push his way through us toward the block's door. Buyeh grabs Jaber's wrist with his long, bony hand, and twists it till Jaber's arm folds behind him. "Get lost!" Buyeh warns him through clenched teeth.

"What's going on here?" shouts the old warrant officer as he comes in.

The old warrant officer's henna-colored hair is rumpled. His short body is drenched in sweat. His gray mustache trembles. Blood has rushed into his cheeks. His squashed nose looks white and broken blood vessels web his eyes. "Why don't you let these guys get their food?" he says hastily, obviously panicked.

"None of your business," retorts Ali the Mustache in an indifferent tone. He's in a bad mood. His throat is dry. His voice is raspy.

The old warrant officer becomes enraged. He lunges forward like a fighting cock and gets in Ali the Mustache's face. "So, is it your business then, smuggler?"

Ali the Mustache turns blue with rage.

"I think it's your business, Guard." The words suddenly slip out of my mouth. I say the word "guard" in such a way that it sounds more like a cussword, in the same fashion that he expressed the word "smuggler."

The old warrant officer quickly turns to me, gets in my face, and glares at me. Unexpectedly, he walks out of the door, yelling, "Shut the door!"

Guard Mastan shuts the door.

The heat is killing us. Sweat oozes down the four pillars of our bodies. Javad Borujerdi, cussing and grumbling, steps away from the block's door and walks toward the water tank's sunshade. Rostam Effendi follows him. Esi the Red Faced lingers, still trying to pester us. Buyeh tells him that lunchtime is over. "Esi, there's no reason for you to be standing here; go sit in front of the latrines like the rest."

Esi is fast and sharp, like a wasp. His face has turned red from the sun. Naser grabs his arm and pushes him away. "Go away, Esi. We're not letting you go through this door."

Words get tangled in Esi's throat. "But I told you from the beginning—"

"Today is different from other days," Ali the Mustache interrupts him.

Naser pulls Esi along with him, deposits him under the water tank's sunshade, and returns.

We too go and sit in the shade, near the door to the corridor. Everyone is quiet. I get up and pace the corridor. A few of the guys are squatting and hugging their knees. A few are lying around and smoking on empty stomachs. Others are dozing. The corridor is utterly still. So are the rooms. I can hear the buzzing of flies. I turn back toward the corridor's door. A commanding voice explodes through the hallway. "Pendar!"

This is not the voice of the old warrant officer, nor is it the voice of Ali the Barber.

"Pendar!"

Pendar gets up. With heavy steps, he walks toward the corridor's door and stands there on the threshold. His name is called again. He looks at us. "This time is not like the night before last," he says.

Hesitation has filled his eyes; so have uncertainty and disbelief. "The other night, they thought we were bluffing, but now, they realize it's serious."

His name is called again.

Pendar advises us not to leave the block at all. He walks out of the corridor and into the prison yard. We get up and follow him. Some of the other guys follow us into the yard too. A few stick their heads out of the windows. The sun has swallowed the yard in full and is creeping up to the wall. The block's door opens. The old warrant officer stands in the doorway. "Come on out! Mr. Chief wants to see you," he says. His old voice trembles with rage.

Pendar, his arms akimbo, does not move. "Whoever wants to see me," he says in a dry voice, "let him come here!"

The old warrant officer's voice takes on a menacing tone. "Now _you're_ summoning Mr. Chief?!" he says quickly, swallowing his saliva and waving his hand.

Bringing his arms down, Pendar steps back. "No, I didn't summon anyone," he says in a cool manner.

The old warrant officer steps closer, stands in front of Pendar, and in a scratchy voice says, "You're playing with your own life, young man."

"At least I'm not playing with your life," he says, smiling.

The old warrant officer, uttering not a word, turns around quickly, scurries out of the block, and slams the iron door behind him.

We have yet to go back into the corridor, and the other guys have yet to move away from the windows, when the old warrant officer comes back again. He walks straight toward Pendar and grabs his wrist. "All right! Don't come out of the block, just come into the yard . . . I need to talk to you."

Pendar doesn't budge. "Say whatever you want to say right here!"

"I have to talk to you in private," the old warrant officer says gently.

Pendar darts us a meaningful look as he walks away with the old warrant officer and steps into the yard. The old warrant officer, dabbing the sweat off his forehead and cheeks, talks to Pendar. We can't hear him. Slowly, he leads Pendar up to the door of the block.

We stand by the door to the corridor, watching them. Some of the guys continue to squat on the windowsills.

The old warrant officer and Pendar stop in front of the door to the block. It opens unexpectedly. Suddenly, some guards rush inside, grab hold of Pendar, and drag him out of the block; and before we can reach them, the door closes. The prisoners run out of their rooms and pour into the yard. There's a hubbub of voices. All of a sudden, armed guards appear from one end of the rooftop to the other, standing behind the rolled barbed wire. Blood rushes to my face. I shout with rage, "Kidnappers!"

I hear the officer on duty's enraged voice from where he stands next to the security tower: "Shut up, Khaled!"

I yell out again, "Kidnappers!"

All the shouts and hollers become confused. Naser the Lifer, clenching his hand into a fist, stands facing the officer on duty. In a voice above everyone else's, Naser shouts, "Even if you crush us limb by limb, we won't eat that food!"

I can clearly see that everyone is growing angrier. Fists rise in the air and shouts get mixed up:

"Kidnappers!"

"Bring Pendar back!"

"We won't eat that food even if you crucify us!"

"Go to your rooms, or I'll have them shoot you!" the officer's threatening voice booms.

"You don't have the balls to do it!" Naser the Lifer yells back.

The prison chief's short figure comes into view, entirely drenched in sweat. He is writhing like a wounded swine. Raising his hands, he starts to shout, but we can't hear him. You can only hear the guys' jumbled shouts. The chief's movements are jittery, and he's clearly alarmed. He gestures to the guards standing ready behind the barbed wire. The guards, holding on to the barrels of their rifles, back off out of sight. Again, the chief's hands rise and his mouth opens and closes. The guys' hollering diminishes until we can hear the chief's voice. "We won't do anything to Pendar—"

"Bring him back, right now!" someone's muffled shout interrupts him.

Everyone is drenched in sweat. Their faces are glowing with rage. They're practically foaming at the mouth. The chief's voice soars in the air in a broken stream like a wounded bird's. "If you . . . keep calm . . . we'll return Pendar . . . and take care of . . . the food problem."

"It's a lie!" someone shouts from the middle of the crowd.

"You're bluffing," another man says in a husky, more vigorous voice.

The chief's voice trembles with rage. "I will call a truce until tonight . . . If you'll get your dinner, Pendar will . . ."

The rest of the chief's words get stifled in a stream of shouts that comes from dozens of mouths at once:

"Right now!"

"He must be returned right now!"

"You're a liar!"

"Kidnappers!"

"Bring him back!"

"I said what I had to say. You got time till tonight . . . That's it!" the chief says. He steps back from the edge of the roof and disappears from sight.

The shouting and yelling start again. Fists are waved in the air once again.

I reach for Naser the Lifer's arm. His neck veins are swollen. His eyes are about to pop out of their sockets. "Naser, it's not gonna work this way. We should come up with something else."

"What's there to come up with when they'll just give us Pendar's dead body?" Naser says in a solemn tone.

If we could somehow calm the guys down, have a meeting, and consult with one another, we might be able to come up with an alternative. I tell Naser that this sort of unrest will give the chief enough of an excuse to do whatever he wants to.

Naser glares at me. "In that case, you want us to sit down and shut up?"

"No, Naser . . . that's not what I want . . . but we can't get anywhere with yelling, either."

"But what about Pendar?"

"That's what I'm saying."

"Then what?"

"I am not saying that we should give in. I say we should deal with it wisely. We should come up with a levelheaded solution to make them bring him back."

The yelling has not yet dropped off. Bodies are entirely soaked in sweat. Neck veins are swollen. Naser the Lifer goes around calling for Manuch the Black, Buyeh, Judge, and Mehdi the Wide Chest. "We gotta have a meeting," he tells them.

We gather in Room 10. The confused yelling, which has subsided a bit now, can still be heard through the window. Some of the other guys come and sit in Room 10. Ali the Mustache and Ahmad the Tarantula join us. As we talk, more guys come in, one by one or in pairs. Room 10 is now crammed with people, some squatting on the windowsill, others standing in the doorway.

Naser the Lifer, sitting on his heels, presses his fists into the floor, which makes his muscles bulge even more. His voice is muffled and somber. "Now that they've taken away Pendar with such trickery, I say we should pummel these twelve people in return, till they kick the bucket."

"Why should we be punished?" Rostam Effendi grumbles from the midst of the crowd.

"What're you doing here, Effendi?" Naser turns in the direction of his voice. "Get out!"

"Why should I leave?"

Ignoring him, Naser the Lifer gets up, lifts Rostam Effendi up, strides through the crowd, and throws him out of the room into the corridor. "If you ever set foot in this room again, I'll squeeze your throat so hard that your eyes pop out of their sockets."

Rostam Effendi keeps quiet as he stands behind the guys in the doorway. Naser comes and sits back down. Everyone watches quietly. Mehdi the Wide Chest, drawing his knees to his chest, leans his jutting shoulders against the heap of bedrolls and says, "I think if we beat the other guys, we'll give the guards an excuse."

"Then they could open fire on us, or beat the hell out of us," Judge adds.

"But I agree with Naser," Manuch the Black says.

"It's not a good move at all," Mehdi the Wide Chest says again.

The room is filled with cigarette smoke. I feel sick. I get up and walk to the window. Buyeh is quiet. His eyes look frightened. His keffiyeh has fallen around his shoulders. His shaved head is covered in sweat. Manuch the Black's crossed eyes swivel in their sockets. Shifting his position, he says, "If you guys don't agree with Naser, I have something else in mind."

We turn our hopeless eyes to him. Hunger and heat have made us weak and vulnerable. Manuch the Black goes on, "I say we should tumble down the latrines' walls, and pile up the bricks in the middle of—"

"But if we do that, can't they—," I cut him short.

"Let me finish!" he interrupts me quickly.

"Let him talk!" Naser says.

Manuch the Black continues, "Then, we divide into groups of ten, and take turns hurling the bricks at the block's door. Each brick that hits the iron door will explode like a cannon inside the corridor . . . If we run out of bricks, we'll collect more and start all over . . . We keep doing it until they get mad . . . and bring Pendar back . . . and listen to our requests."

No one says anything. We just look at each other. Judge and I start to talk at once:

"That . . ."

"But . . ."

I hold back and let Judge talk. "That's not a good move."

"Why not?" Naser the Lifer asks.

"The biggest problem with it is that they can claim we have tumbled the wall down to escape."

"I wanted to say the same thing," I say.

Judge continues, "Once they accuse us of this, they can do whatever they want to us. They can even open fire on us. Breaking a wall down is a punishable offense to begin with."

"That's all a bunch of baloney," Manuch the Black says.

"Judge knows about the law . . . If he says it's an offense, it is an offense," Mehdi the Wide Chest says.

"Let's suppose we have this one option," I say, "but we can still think of something else, something better, perhaps."

I feel a bit better. I go and sit down next to Naser the Lifer. Buyeh starts to talk in a low voice. His bushy eyebrows are knitted. His eyes are bloodshot. His short gray beard moves as he talks. "I have an idea." He pauses for a few seconds.

"Spit it out," Judge says hastily.

Buyeh talks quietly: "We could bang our copper bowls against each other all at once. We still refuse to get our ration of food, but we bang our bowls against each other from dusk to dawn. Their clatter will fill the entire town. It'll drive the prison authorities mad."

His idea is so fine that I feel at peace.

"It's not against the law, is it?" Mehdi the Wide Chest asks.

"I don't think it is . . . ," says Judge. "Well, at least I have never heard from any of the examiners that banging bowls would be considered a crime."

Everyone welcomes Buyeh's plan.

"Let's start now," Naser suggests.

"No, not now," Buyeh says.

We look at him. He explains, "We write to the prison chief again. We'll let him know that if Pendar is not brought back by tomorrow night, we'll start banging our bowls."

Naser the Lifer's voice rises. "But, what if they bring us his body by tomorrow night? We should start—"

"It's best we write to him first," Judge interrupts him.

A discussion ensues, but soon everyone agrees with Buyeh's plan. I start to write a letter to the prison chief.

Soon it will be noon. Hunger and fatigue are getting the better of us. No news of Pendar yet. If he is not returned by sunset, we will start banging our bowls. We will make ourselves heard throughout the entire town. A hundred pairs of bowls banged against each other, all at once, will surely produce a sound louder than the explosion of a cannonball.

Word travels from mouth to mouth that last night Pendar was handcuffed and driven to the harbor to be transferred to remote Khark Island. We heard from Ali the Barber, who heard from the guards, that this morning, Pendar's mother went to the prosecutor's house, and laid her body in front of his car and smeared dust on her face, creating a heartbreaking sight. If this one piece of news is true—despite how unrealistic it sounds for Pendar's mother to have been informed so soon of her son's transfer to Khark Island—then the prosecutor must have heard something about our strike.

The guys are sitting in the shade of the wall in groups. The twelve are next to the latrines, under the water tank's sunshade. It's been three days since they alienated themselves. We haven't allowed them to get their ration of food for two days now. We haven't even let them buy anything from Napoleon. Napoleon's business has been shut down. Today is hotter than other days. Some of the guys have taken off their clothes and are lying down in the corridor. You can see their hollow stomachs, and their ribs sticking out. Now they're driven by stubbornness rather than by the strike itself. Perhaps if they hadn't taken Pendar away, the guys wouldn't have made it into the third day. A few others pace along the corridor, but soon they too get tired. Their legs give way, and they sit down in a corner.

Again, rumor has it that Pendar's mother has made a scene on the street, cursing the prosecutor in the worst possible manner. Nobody knows who brought this piece of news into the prison. Mastan is the guard on duty in the corridor. I doubt that he would ever bring any outside news to the prisoners. He is one of those bastards who, if you let him, will make a prisoner wish he'd never been born. The chief's viciousness is nothing in comparison to Mastan's. His eyes are always bloodshot. His cheeks look as if made of stone. His neck has sunk into his chest. He is short and quick. Anyone who gets dragged out of the block and tied to the palm tree will receive his whipping courtesy of Guard Mastan.

I walk toward the block's door. Guard Mastan's bloodshot eyes and large nose are stuck to the round hole in the iron door as he peers inside the block. I am certain that Guard Mastan is not the one who passed on the news. I walk back to the corridor. I hear the buzzing of flies. Everyone is quiet. The roaring sound of Primus burners used to fill the corridor at noon. The pile of loaves of black bread is three times bigger now than the first day. Mehdi the Barefooted's complaining alarms me. He is old and small-framed. He is squatting at the end of the corridor. His wrinkled skin is brown. His voice is barely audible. I go and sit across from him. His eyes are lifeless. His face has become wan. "But I'm old," he complains under his breath. "I have no stamina . . . There's no way I can stand it till tomorrow."

I am taken aback. If his words should become widespread! "Father, you, above all, should have more strength than a hundred weak young men," I say, trying to cheer him up.

His burnt eyelashes close.

I keep at it. "We should all learn from you."

He lowers his head and says, "But these bastards don't give a damn about us."

"But they care about their own status . . . If they go on like this, they will cause trouble for themselves," I say gently.

Here and there, I overhear more complaining. I walk away from Mehdi the Barefooted.

I tell Judge, Manuch the Black, and Naser the Lifer to go and listen to the guys. Then I go to Buyeh and Mehdi the Wide Chest.

Pushing his chest out, Naser the Lifer clenches his fists, lifts his head, and says in a loud voice, "A man should have honor. A man should stand by his word . . ."

"Even if they have to take my dead body out of this place, I won't eat until they listen to our requests," I hear Manuch the Black say.

"I have been dealing with the law for seventeen years," Judge explains. "The law allows us to protest. According to the law, the prison chief is responsible for our well-being . . ."

"The way they act shows that they are panicked . . . ," Mehdi the Wide Chest says gently. "It's clear they want to end this somehow and settle the matter . . . If we can just stand it one more day, everything will be all right."

In the middle of the corridor, Buyeh, with that tall body of his and his arms akimbo, hovers over a few of the guys who have squatted down beside each other. In a hoarse voice he tells them, "We have come this far. So what's the big deal in not eating for just another day? Think of it as if you were fasting. It's not like we're gonna starve . . . but instead, if we stand firm today and tomorrow, as we have so far, the chief will give in. I promise you, he'll give in."

The murmurs of complaint cease for now. With their ears open, the guys roam around the block. Mehdi the Barefooted rests his forehead on his knees and dozes off. His hair has turned completely gray. The lunch bell resonates in the corridor. Ali the Mustache gets up and goes toward the block's door. Naser the Lifer follows him. Both men lean against the door, standing in the direct sun. No one dares to move from where they sit under the water tank's sunshade. Now they know who they're dealing with. They know that if they try again, they will just embarrass themselves. Rostam Effendi is peskier than the rest. Shifting in place, he grumbles and blasphemes. Nasrollah the Roughneck swears loudly, loud enough that everyone can hear him. But no one pays any attention to him.

Naser the Lifer wants to go and quiet him down. "Let me go and shut this motherfucker up, so he won't blow his horn like that."

I block his way, reminding him of what Pendar told us. "Carrying out a strike is not the same as making a racket, Naser. If we try to stop him, he'll go to the other extreme, and then everything we have done so far will be wasted."

I manage to convince Naser the Lifer, though he remains annoyed.

It is hardly past noon when a new wave of talk starts:

"We should get the bowls ready."

Before we can react, it spreads throughout the prison:

"We should get the bowls ready."

"But it's not time yet."

"It's not long before sunset."

"But we said in the letter tonight."

"What difference does it make?"

The lids to wooden and iron chests open, and the bowls are being taken out. It's useless. They won't listen at all. We can't convince them. Clearly, they are anxious to know as soon as possible what is going to happen to them. You can see it in their eyes that they are all worn-out. Suddenly, the sound of bowls being banged together comes from Room 10. Buyeh runs to Room 10. A metallic clink rattles through the corridor for a moment and then dies out quickly. Once again, the banging of bowls echoes in Room 10.

"Mansur, it's too early," I hear Buyeh say.

We run toward Room 10. Mehdi the Barefooted lifts his head up from his knees, stretches out his trembling arm, and takes a copper bowl and a plate out of the chest. Another clink comes from Room 4. I run toward it. Taqqi the Errand Runner is banging his bowls. He is lying down and has drawn his legs into his stomach. His loose underpants have slid down. His kneecaps look more like two knots on a rope. The skin of his thighs is a pale yellow. His hazel eyes are sunken. Holding his hands up, he bangs his bowls: clang . . . clang . . . clang.

"Taqqi, it's a long time before sunset!" I yell at him.

Ignoring me, he keeps banging his bowls. It's useless. Nothing works, not our struggle to calm them down, not our yelling, nor our pleading. The sound of the banging of bowls continues to rise in each room. Mehdi the Barefooted wriggles like a dying worm. Stabilizing himself with his hand, he pulls himself up. Still banging his bowl and plate against each other, he starts to walk around, his knees trembling.

I block his way. "Father, it's not time yet."

He doesn't listen to me. As he continues with his banging, he walks toward the block's door. A few of the guys follow him.

Naser the Lifer grabs my arm. "The bastards started already."

"There's no stopping them," Judge says.

The clinking of the bowls is deafening as it echoes under the corridor's ceiling with the resounding sound of clang . . . clang . . . clang . . .

"What should we do?" Judge asks.

I remember Pendar's words: "If we don't listen to them, everything will be over . . ." I see Mehdi the Wide Chest going to pick up his bowls. I am stunned.

"Why are you just standing there?" Naser the Lifer asks me.

Having picked up their bowls, everyone is leaving the corridor.

I go and take my bowls out of the iron chest.

The banging sound is synchronized: clang, clang, clang . . . clang, clang, clang . . . clang, clang, clang . . . The sun beats down directly on our heads. Everyone is soaked in sweat in the heat. The rooftop's guard has come out of the tower, gazing at us with eyes ready to pop out. The colliding clinks of the bowls are petrifying. I have no doubt that the entire town can hear it. Clang, clang, clang . . . clang, clang, clang . . . All of the sudden, the short figure of the prison chief comes into sight, writhing like a wounded snake. Shaking his hands, he opens and closes his mouth. His hollering is stifled amid the dreadful banging of the bowls, which explodes like a bunch of cannonballs. Our eyes are still fixed on the chief when we suddenly realize a number of armed guards have appeared at the edge of the rooftop, behind the rolled barbed wire. The guards look alarmed. The officer on duty walks hurriedly, taking up his position behind the chief. The guards hold their rifles upright. The chief, tearing up his throat, struggles to make himself heard, but we still can't hear him. Amidst the banging, we hear a few broken words:

"Listen to . . ."

. . . Da-dang . . .

". . . Crazy peo . . ."

. . . Bang, bang . . .

". . . Stupid . . ."

. . . Clang . . .

The prison chief is going mad. His face has turned blue. His mouth is foaming. He stamps his foot and shakes both his hands in the air angrily. His hands are fisted. His mouth opens and closes. Without a doubt, the sound of the banging bowls reaches the far corners of the town. The chief's words reach our ears in a broken stream:

". . . I am saying . . ."

. . . Clang, clang, clang . . .

"Motherfuckers . . ."

. . . Clang, clang, clang . . .

With a sudden jump, the chief lunges at a guard, snatching the rifle out of his hands. He pulls the breechblock, brings one leg forward, and plants the stock of the firearm against his chest. By the time I can determine who the chief is aiming at, all the guards have kneeled, pressed the stocks of their firearms to their chests, and aimed the barrels of their guns at us through the rolled barbed wire. Quickly, the clanging of the bowls falls out of sync. I panic. I can't believe my eyes. Some of the guys turn around in confusion and look at the gun barrels. Their hands loosen up and drop the bowls. Naser the Lifer's bare chest is drenched in sweat. His skin shines in the sunlight. Planting his legs wide apart, he holds his hands up over his head and bangs his bowls. I stand beside him. My arms have no strength, but I bang my bowls together anyway. Some prisoners have backed off and are now squatting down in the shade of the wall. Their bowls on the ground in front of them, their mouths agape, they keep their eyes on the gun barrels. The explosive sound of the clanging diminishes by the minute, reduced to the clinking of just a few bowls. Buyeh, Naser the Lifer, me, Ali the Mustache, Mehdi the Wide Chest, Manuch the Black, and a few other guys here and there in the crowd keep on banging our bowls. Everyone looks bewildered. Some stare at the prison chief. Some, completely captivated and stunned, gaze at the guards without blinking. I look under the water tank's sunshade. There's no one to be seen. Rostam Effendi cranes his neck from behind the wall of the latrines, his long gray beard trembling. Nasrollah the Roughneck's head peeks out from behind Rostam Effendi's head. His eyes are about to pop out of their sockets. Some of the men slowly step back and retreat into the corridor. The chief's body is entirely soaked in sweat. He puts the stock of the rifle down on the ground, stands upright, and opens his mouth. His voice shoots like a bullet. "Stop it, Naser!"

Naser is the only one still banging his bowls.

"I said, stop it!"

The guards continue to kneel. Guard Mastan has aimed the barrel of his gun at Naser the Lifer. Mastan's face looks as if it's made of stone. His neck sinks into his chest. His large eyes are wide open.

The chief's shrill holler soars over the entire block. "Naser, drop those bowls or I'll shoot . . . !"

The chief has yet to finish his sentence when Naser hurls the bowls onto the ground, turns to the guys, and bellows in their faces, "You cowards, you're even less than a woman!"

The guys, stepping back, huddle in the shade of the wall.

"Shut up, Naser!" the chief warns.

Naser stands facing the prison chief, balls his hand into a fist, and yells out, "You too are a coward . . . all the guards are cowards as well!"

"I said, be quiet, Naser!" the chief warns again in a gruff and snippy voice.

I don't have the courage to step forward and calm Naser down. No one else dares to either. Buyeh, Mehdi the Wide Chest, Manuch the Black, Judge, and Ali the Mustache are all standing beside each other, looking frightened.

Naser the Lifer turns around in the middle of the block and shouts, "You are all cowards . . . all of you!" Pounding on his bare, hairy chest, he yells, "Shoot me if you can! . . . Empty your bullets!"

At that moment, Naser the Lifer catches sight of Rostam Effendi's long beard sticking out from behind the wall of the latrines. He lunges toward him, and before Rostam Effendi gets a chance to turn away, grabs his long beard, shakes it, and drags him out from behind the wall.

"Naser, stop it . . . Don't be stupid!" the chief's offended voice shoots through the air.

Everyone is rooted to the ground. The prison yard is almost deserted. Many have snuck into the corridor.

Naser the Lifer has gone completely mad. His eyes are like two bowls of blood. His neck veins have swollen up. His shaved head gleams white where the old scars have healed over, the scars left from the blades he slashed himself with. Naser the Lifer, writhing like a wounded leopard, snatches up Rostam Effendi and dashes away from the shade of the water tank toward the middle of the block. He hurls Rostam Effendi to the ground like a sacrificial lamb, and before I can figure out what he's up to, draws a blade, plants his knee on Rostam Effendi's bony chest, pulls his beard toward him, and puts the blade to his jugular vein. Rostam Effendi has become mute. He doesn't even budge. It's as if his soul has already parted from his body.

"Naser!" the chief shouts.

Naser the Lifer's roar stifles the chief's voice: "I'll shed blood . . . You motherfuckers, I'll make a pool of blood . . . If you don't bring Pendar back, I'll cut the necks of all twelve of those people, from ear to ear!"

We all hold our breath. My knees wobble. I can hardly stay on my feet. I can hear my heart pounding. My temples thump. Buyeh, utterly shocked, stares at Naser the Lifer. Ali the Mustache's face has turned white as chalk. Judge's eyes can't stop rolling around in their sockets. Manuch the Black's jaw has dropped. Naser the Lifer's bloodshot eyes are fixed on the chief. The chief is silent; he looks terrified. Guard Mastan's rifle is pointed at Naser the Lifer. The sun beats down. The air is heavy, even though it is not humid.

"Naser, let him go . . . ," the chief's voice quavers.

Rostam Effendi looks as if he has fainted. He doesn't move at all.

"Let him go, Naser!"

"I'll slaughter him like a goat!" Naser the Lifer's voice explodes.

"Let him go, Naser, or I'll have them shoot your brains out!" the chief shouts in a voice trembling with rage.

"Cowards never shoot!" Naser yells back.

Naser the Lifer's mouth is foaming with spittle. I wish I could rush toward him, hold him down, and drag Rostam Effendi out from under his knee, but I have lost my nerve. I can't even move. I look around the yard, and I see only a few of the guys remaining. The others have slipped into their rooms and are looking out from their windows. The guards' firearms are all pointed at Naser the Lifer. The chief tosses the rifle to the officer on duty, steps back quickly, and disappears behind the security tower.

"Why did you run away, Mr. Chief?!" Naser the Lifer's voice soars.

The officer on duty steps back too. Naser's bloodshot eyes are fixed on Guard Mastan. His yelling shakes my heart.

"Where did those cowards go, Mastan? I am talking to you . . . You are not a coward, are you? . . . Your wife is not a whore, is she? Why don't you shoot, then?"

Guard Mastan shifts his position, and puts his cheek on his firearm's stock.

"Then shoot, you coward!"

Mastan runs his hand over the rifle. The dry, metallic sound of the breechblock makes my body shake.

"Shoot!"

The safety trigger is being pulled. My stomach churns. I feel dizzy. I am going to vomit. I hear Naser the Lifer's voice coming from the bottom of a deep valley, from a faraway distance. "Coward . . . you have even pulled the trigger . . . You motherfucker, shoot—"

The blast of the shot makes my heart sink. Naser gets lifted off the ground like a ball that has been kicked. I fall to my knees. The block's door opens with a clatter, and the chief dashes through it. Behind him the officer on duty runs in, panicked. Naser the Lifer rolls on the ground next to the pile of bread loaves. Blood spurts out from beneath his left shoulder.

Rostam Effendi lies next to him, utterly motionless.

I carve the one hundred and first notch on the wall and sit down. It has been a hundred and one days since I was thrown in solitary. If I have not miscounted the days, I should be released tomorrow.

After Naser the Lifer was shot, everything was turned upside down. The district attorney interrogated all of us. We thought the prison chief would be replaced, but that didn't happen. They put eleven of us in solitary. I was handcuffed and shackled for two weeks. Then they removed the handcuffs, but left the shackles on my feet for forty more days. The notches that I carved while I was handcuffed and shackled are much longer than the others and are set apart from them . . . There is another set of twenty-six notches that I carved for those days that the handcuffs were removed but the shackles, connected by a large chain, remained heavy around my ankles. Even now, days later, the marks around my ankles from the shackles look white.

I think that they released the other guys from solitary right after the interrogations were over. I have heard that Guard Mastan has been stripped of his position and pushed into Block 4 until he is tried. For one hundred and one days I have had no news from the outside world, or from anyone else, for that matter. My visitation rights have been taken away from me too. Even when the guys pass through solitary to get their lunch or dinner rations, I am ordered to sit down, so that I will not get the chance to see another living soul through the round hole in the iron door. For one hundred and one days the only sight I've seen is the four narrow walls of the solitary cell. For one hundred and one days I have only seen a mesh square of sky. The air smells of fall. At night, all I do is stay up late and smoke. I talk to myself. Sometimes, I tell stories to myself. The guards who take shifts guarding the corridors have been instructed not to talk to me at all. Now and then I throw caution to the wind and call out to them, yelling, "Guard!"

They just glare at me as if looking at someone with cholera or leprosy, and yell in a gruff voice: "Sit your ass down!"

The only one who has spoken a few words to me is the head guard, Nader.

"Can you come here for a second, Guard?"

He looks around and then comes close. I press my face to the hole in the door and say a few words to him.

Giving me a faint smile, Head Guard Nader lowers his voice to a whisper. "But they say talking to you is forbidden . . ."

For one hundred and one days I haven't talked to anyone. When I found out from Nader that they had been ordered not to talk to me, I turned stubborn too. I even refused to talk to Head Guard Nader. I am on the verge of insanity. I cannot sleep. If I haven't miscounted the days, I should be released tomorrow. It must be past midnight. My body feels very hot. I must have a fever. My knees ache. My spine throbs. If only I could sleep. A soft breeze wafts through the vent. The air is cool. I pull the blanket up to my neck. My eyelids burn. I draw my legs up to my stomach, circle my arms around my shins, and squeeze them. Pain shoots through my knees. I must've caught a cold. These past few days, it's been real cold come dawn. I let go of my legs and try to close my eyes. My head is growing large. Larger even than the solitary cell. I open my eyes. I am burning like a furnace. My breath burns the skin above my upper lip as it comes out my nose. I close my eyes again. I feel like I'm falling into darkness. The ground beneath my feet has split open. I can hear myself breathing. It sounds like wet logs are being sawed. Through the net of my eyelashes, I look at the light hanging from the ceiling. It sways, just like a pendulum . . . just like Ja'far the Brickmaker's long body. A voice echoes in my head: "Father, why did Ja'far kill himself?"

Father's Adam's apple shifts up and down. His neck is as long as the top of the minaret of the main mosque.

"Hunger, Son . . . hunger . . . How long can one stand hunger?"

Bolur Khanom's hot breath burns my cheeks. There are no bruises on her belly from the leather belt. Her stomach is amazingly smooth and firm, like the rising dough of baking bread. She has wrapped herself around me just like an ivy plant. I feel suffocated. I am falling into the Well of Veil, into the heart of darkness. Banu blocks my way. Her lifeless eyes are about to pop out of their sockets. Her skin is so yellow it's as if she has rubbed turmeric juice on her face. "I see you have become cozy with Bolur Khanom, huh?" she whimpers.

I push her. She steps back and sits beside the pool. She is naked. It is hot. Hot. Very hot. As if the door to hell has been left ajar. Banu begs me. I can barely hear her voice.

Suddenly, the shrill cry of Hajar's sickly child shoots through my head. It writhes like a whip, scratching the inner walls of my skull. Hajar, squatting at the small pool, holds her scrawny baby's bottom over her arms so that he can pee. Her large buttocks are hugged tightly by her flower-print calico dress. Naser Davani's radio is at full blast. A woman sings:

> *Your scorpion-like lock of hair is in position with the moon*
> *Such is our fate as long as the moon stays for a brief moment in*
> *the House of Scorpio*

Naser Davani's eyes are fixed on Hajar's large buttocks.

Father closes *Qasemi's Secrets*. Never before have I seen Father looking so distressed. "Oussa Naser, how's business in Kuwait?" he asks.

Naser Davani doesn't say anything. He listens to the radio. His eyes stay fixed on Hajar's buttocks. Khaj Tofiq is lost in the dense smoke of opium. Wrapped in her chador, Bolur Khanom moves gracefully as she walks past me. "What a bad boy you have become, Khaled," she says. My heart is on fire. The warmth of Black-Eyed's lips burn mine. I am filled with joy. Her voice caresses my ears.

I stir on my pallet. Pendar's rough voice echoes in my ears: "You must not let yourself be carried away by emotions when you are engaged in combat." I yell. I jump to my feet, and dart out of the house. I run to Shafaq's bookstore. The bookstore is crowded. Shafaq is standing in the back of the store. A smile has lit up his face. He raises his hand and warns me with his index finger. He smiles and warns. His arm stretches longer and longer, growing out of the bookstore. I am shocked. I look at the tip of his finger, wagging in my face. I think I hear him: "Now that you have chosen battle, then you should forget Black-Eyed." "No!" I yell from the bottom of my heart. I am shaken. The dusty lightbulb hangs above my head in the solitary cell.

"What's with you, Khaled?" I hear the guard on duty say.

I exhale my pent-up breath, trying to keep quiet. I push the blanket aside and sit up. The guard's footsteps fade away. I feel dizzy. My lips are dry. They are cracked. I lie down again. I am asleep and awake. My head grows large again. Amu Bandar's voice echoes in my skull: "You think if I go to the police station tomorrow, there will be any hope . . . the police station . . . the police station . . . ?" Gholam Ali Khan's raisin-green eyes glare at me, each the size of a green-glazed jug, with their corn-yellow eyelashes. The eyes laugh. Gholam Ali Khan's pencil-thin mustache moves. His thin lips glide on each other. "Sir, he'd disrespect people's honor . . ." I get furious. "You call whores 'people's honor'?" Gholam Ali Khan's green eyes turn pale. I feel good. I hear Amu Bandar reciting his prayers. His tone of voice makes me feel calm. "Oh, God! Bestow good upon us in this world . . ." Suddenly, Aunt Ra'na screams, "My son! . . . My precious son!" Gholam, Aunt Ra'na's son, stands upright. His mustache glistens. A smile has parted his lips. His tone is gentle: "Khaled, can you take a message to Bolur Khanom?" Everything is jumbled. The Doctor, lost in the dense smoke from cigarettes, talks about the strike at the textile factory. Manuch the Black tosses the bowl of watery beef stew at the rooftop guard, cussing in a shrill voice everyone related to the prison chief, both dead and alive. Naser the Lifer roars. He is thrown against the pile of loaves of black bread, and now blood begins to spurt out from beneath his shoulder. My entire body shudders violently. I open my eyes. I find myself drenched in sweat. I taste a poisonous bitterness at the back of my throat. My mouth is as dry as a matchstick. I sit down and look at the notches carved on the wall. Three clusters in three different spots. The long notches are from the days I was handcuffed and shackled. There are a hundred and one notches, altogether. I have been talking to myself for a hundred and one days. If I haven't miscounted the days, I should be released tomorrow. I light a cigarette. The smoke adds to the bitterness in my mouth. It makes me cough, so I stub it out. I lean against the wall and hug my knees. It is quiet in the corridor. The guard on duty must have gone to the end of the hallway, and is now sitting on a chair dozing. My head feels heavy. My temples start to pound. A breeze blows in through the vent in the ceiling. I shiver again, so I pull the blanket over myself. I light the cigarette again, take two drags, and put it out. I cannot sit up. My head feels too heavy for my weak body to hold it up. I lie down again. My head barely touches the pillow before I begin to fall again. My stomach cramps up. Suddenly, Rahim the Donkey Keeper's sloped forehead materializes before my eyes. His forehead is so big that it fills the entire cell. His lifeless eyes pop out of their sockets. I think he's hanging from the gallows. His face is bruised. His tongue got stuck between his teeth. His expression terrifies me. I start to run, but stumble and fall to the ground. I push myself up with my arms and stand up. Before my eyes, thousands and thousands of kittens struggle with nooses around their necks. Their eyes have the same look as Ali the Devil's. I rush to the gallows and kick them down. The kittens start to run, dragging the gallows behind them. All at once, the kids from the prison neighborhood tackle me, pounding me with their kicks and punches. A jolt of pain shoots through my hip, making me jump up. My back and pelvis ache mercilessly. I writhe in pain, and unconsciously, my hand extends toward the stubbed-out cigarette. I light it and take a drag. I try to get up and walk around in the cell. My knees are no good. I struggle, bracing my hand against the wall, to get to my feet. The entire cell is five paces long and three paces wide. I creep along the wall toward the door, and put my face to the round hole in the iron door. It is bright in the corridor. The floor is made of flagstones. The stones are smooth and shiny. My stomach churns. I think I am going to throw up. Stars twinkle before my eyes. I can't keep myself up. I lean my back against the wall, slide down with my shoulders, and squat on the ground. I take the cigarette butt from between my lips and put it out. I drag myself along on my butt and lay my cheek on the pillow. Everything starts again. My body starts to boil again. I am drenched in sweat. My hot breath burns my upper lip. The solitary cell spins around my head. I start to run. "There's no point in running away," I hear Ali the Devil's voice tell me. "What do you want from my child?! . . . What's that bracelet you've put around his wrists?!" Mother questions furiously. Leila's daring gaze gives me courage. "You're a man now," Father says, filling me with pride. Shafaq has opened his arms. "We're proud of you, Khaled." His entire face is bright with a smile. I rush toward him. We embrace each other. I find myself in Black-Eyed's embrace. I am beside myself with joy from her love for me. The warmth of her lips fills me with every sweet taste in the world. I am calm. I feel numb. I fall asleep on soft, velvety clouds. The wind carries me like a dandelion, slowly and gently.

The clatter of the iron door wakes me up. The fever has ceased. My head feels light. Sunlight has fallen on the wall through the mesh vent in the ceiling. Nader, the head guard, is standing in the doorway of the cell.

"Get up and pack up your stuff!"

A smile has parted his lips. His gold teeth show. The wrinkles under his eyes are in the shape of a bird's claw. "Come on, pack up your stuff . . . You're getting out of here," he says again.

My heart trembles. Head Guard Nader smokes as he hovers over me. He is tall and skinny. "What're you waiting for?"

The smile has wrinkled the skin below his bony cheeks. He scratches the tip of his pointy nose. "You don't believe it, huh?" he says.

I smile at him. I pack up the few things I have. I fold my father's small, threadbare rug, put the bundle under my arm, lay the rug and the blanket over my shoulder, and head out of the cell. I stop and look down the corridor.

Ali the Barber shuffles toward us from the end of the hallway and says, "Come on, get moving! It's like you don't wanna get outta here!"

It must be before noon. I walk along with Head Guard Nader. The door to the corridor shuts behind me. The prison yard is full of sunshine. Suddenly, the thought of Black-Eyed fills me with grief. I will find her, wherever she is, I think to myself. I walk in the shade of the old lotus tree in the middle of the yard and head into the prison office. The prison chief, his arms akimbo, stands in the middle of the room, smoking; perhaps he's expecting me. His clean-shaven cheeks glow. Even his double chin glow. He doesn't say anything, just puffs at his cigarette and stares at me with his tiny eyes that shake my heart. They are quick at taking care of my paperwork. When I step out of the prison office, I turn pale. The draft officers are waiting for me. The prison chief darts me a look, smiling. His tiny, even teeth, which look like a dog's, show.

I take a step backward when I hear the chief's voice from behind me. "I hope you have learned your lesson, and you won't think of making any trouble in the barracks."

I don't answer him. I don't even look at him. I walk away from the prison's office.

A stream of black smoke rises from the kitchen chimney and floats up like part of a disentangled fur ball, darkening the blue sky. A small door within the prison's large gate opens before me. I walk out of the prison, accompanied by the two draft officers. The street across from the prison winds about. Sunlight drenches the entire street. I look down the street. I feel a hint of relief in the depths of my heart. I see my mother at the corner.

All at once, a familiar voice fills my ears. "Khaled!"

I turn around and see Ebrahim pass by me. Two guards are walking with him. His forehead is bandaged. Red blood has left a few stains on the white strip. He is handcuffed. Before I get a chance to talk to him, he walks into the belly of the prison's large gate. The door shuts behind him.

GLOSSARY

Amu. Literally, "uncle"; an endearing and respectful term used when addressing elders.

Aqa. Literally, "sir" or "Mr."; a respectful form of address for a man, especially a man of status.

Ayatolkorsi. This is the 255th verse of the second chapter of the Koran and is also known as the Throne Verse. It is the most recited verse of the Koran, and is often evoked by Muslims during times of trouble or when seeking God's assistance.

Dadash. A term of endearment often used for an older brother.

Dajjal. The Imposter, a reference to the false messiah, who it is believed will appear before the advent of Mahdi, the twelfth Shia imam.

duz. Similar to tic-tac-toe, but played with pebbles on the ground.

Esfandiar. One of the legendary characters featured in the *Shahnameh*, an epic poem written by the Persian poet Ferdowsi (940–1020 CE). Esfandiar is tragically killed by Rostam.

Farangi. A term used to describe Westerners.

giveh. Sturdy, hand-woven cotton shoes, usually worn in rural areas of Iran.

Hamd Surah. These are prayers of thanksgiving to the Almighty that Muslims are required to recite in their daily prayers. A surah is a chapter of the Koran.

Ja'far Sadeq. He lived during the eighth century CE and is recognized as the sixth Shia imam. He was persecuted by the Abbasid caliph Mansour, who ordered the torture and execution of many Shia Muslims.

jahel. The term was originally used to indicate a chivalric man who protected the neighborhood; however, over time, the meaning of the term has changed and now is used to describe men who disturb the neighborhood with their idiocy and drinking.

Khaj. Short for Khajeh; an outdated title usually given to the head of a tribe or an important official.

Khanom. Literally, "madam," "Ms.," or "Mrs."; a respectful form of address for a woman, especially a woman of status.

maktabkhaneh. Prior to the advent of the modern school system in Iran, children were usually taught basic reading and writing in Arabic by a cleric.

man. An outdated unit of measurement equal to 3 kilograms.

Mash or Mashti. Short for Mashhadi; a title given to someone who has made a pilgrimage to the shrine of the eight imam of the Shia, Reza, which is located in Mashhad, Iran.

mesqal. An outdated unit of measurement equal to 5 grams.

Moharram. This is the first month of the Islamic lunar calendar. It is a sacred month for Muslims and especially significant for Shia Muslims, since the Battle of Karbala occurred during this month.

Murderers of Karbala. A reference to the Battle of Karbala (680 CE), where Imam Hossein, the third imam of the Shia and the grandson of the Prophet Mohammad, was killed by the head of the Umayyad caliphate's army. His oldest son, Ali Akbar, was also killed during the battle, purportedly by having his skull split.

The Nahjolbalagheh [Peak of Eloquence]. This is one of the most well-known books produced by Shia Muslims. It is a compilation of the sermons, letters, and narrations of Imam Ali, the first Shia imam. The book was originally collected by Sharif Razi in the tenth century CE.

Naneh. Literally, "mother"; it is commonly used in rural areas.

Naseroddin Shah designs. A reference to the style of art popular during the reign of Naseroddin Shah (1848–1896 CE), one of the most prominent rulers of the Qajar dynasty.

Nowruz. The Iranian New Year, which is celebrated by Iranians, Afghans, and Tajiks on the first day of spring. Nowruz is a Zoroastrian celebration and dates back six thousand years.

Oussa. A title commonly used for a skilled worker such as a mason, a carpenter, or a blacksmith.

papasi. An old form of currency equal to a penny.

Rostam. The hero of the epic *Shahnameh*; he is often depicted fighting dragons and other supernatural creatures.

Salavat. The term for the phrase "Peace be upon the Prophet Mohammad and his family"; it is used by Muslims after they say or hear the name of the Prophet Mohammad.

Shemr. This is a reference to the man believed responsible for beheading Imam Hossein, the grandson of the Prophet Mohammad, during the Battle of Karbala (680 CE).

Sizdehbedar. The thirteenth day of the month of Farvardin is considered an ill-omened day, so on that day people gather together to celebrate in the outdoors to ward off bad luck.

sormeh. A type of makeup made of crushed kohl and either hazelnut oil or animal fat used to define the eyebrows or used as eyeliner.

Tasu'a and Ashura. Tasu'a is the ninth day of the month of Moharram in the Islamic calendar and Ashura is the tenth day. The Battle of Karbala is believed to have taken place on the tenth day of the month of Moharram; thus these are days of mourning for Shia Muslims.

The Well of Veil. According to the Koran, this place is described as the deepest level of hell, reserved for those who have done great evil in their lives.

Yazdi handkerchief. A very colorful cotton and silk handkerchief made in the city of Yazd, Iran, that men traditionally carried in their pockets.

Zurkhaneh. Literally, "the house of strength"; a place where men practice traditional Iranian bodybuilding. The practice dates back hundreds of years and is meant to develop not only physical strength but spiritual power as well.

CPSIA information can be obtained at www.ICGtesting.com
Printed in the USA
LVOW10s1323230813

349355LV00001B/10/P